Ro

Rose poised herself on
The line from her belt tensed and held her. She felt her stomach lift, as if she was hitting the first big dip on a roller coaster. The metal sleeve above her head roared along the cable. Far beneath her feet, roads and pavements flashed past. The sound of the wind filled her head. Up in front, Robert's body turned and bounced on the cable like a rag doll as he struggled in panic.

She twisted her head back at the retreating building. The dark figures had now engulfed Simon and Jay in a black, writhing mass. Suddenly the edge of a grey concrete building loomed beneath her feet, slightly too far below for her to touch the flashing gravelled rooftop with her shoe. There was a clattering noise above, like points changing, and she felt the lift and drop of a cable-car crossing a pylon. A tall steel rod whistled by on her right side, then the cable was dropping downwards again, over half-lit backstreets. Her heart was in her mouth, all thought pushed from her mind as the city flashed by in a whirling diorama.

ROOFWORLD

Christopher Fowler

ARROW BOOKS

62–65 Chandos Place, London, WC2N 4NW

An imprint of Century Hutchinson Limited

London Melbourne Sydney Auckland
Johannesburg and agencies throughout
the world

First published in Great Britain in 1988
by Century Hutchinson Ltd

Arrow edition 1989

Copyright © Christopher Fowler 1988

This book is sold subject to the condition that it shall not, by way of trade or otherwise, be lent, resold, hired out, or otherwise circulated without the publisher's prior consent in any form of binding or cover other than that in which it is published and without a similar condition including this condition being imposed on the subsequent purchaser

Phototypeset by Input Typesetting Ltd, London

Printed and bound in Great Britain by
Courier International Limited, Tiptree, Essex

ISBN 0 09 9623404

For my brother Steven

Acknowledgements

I would like to thank my agent, Serafina Clarke, for her continuing good humour and encouragement, Ann Suster at Century Hutchinson for making it such plain sailing and Jim Sturgeon for his extraordinary patience and kindness.

Extract from *Up On The Roof*
by G. Goffin and C. King
© 1962 Screen Gems-EMI Music
Inc, USA
Reproduced by permission of
Screen Gems-EMI Music Ltd,
London WC2H 0LD

Contents

'An ever-muttering prisoned storm,
The heart of London beating warm.'

Davidson

Sunday 14 December

CHAPTER ONE

Primal Material

Getting him into the bell tower proved to be a laborious business. The door at the top of the narrow stone steps had been securely padlocked, so that they had to stand with the boy propped between them, waiting for Chymes to suggest some way of gaining entry.

'It will have to be broken open from the inside.' The passionless voice flattened within the curved brickwork of the corridor, as if the stones themselves had absorbed his words.

'Which of us will go?'

Inevitably, it was Dag who was sent to scale the outside of the church in the pouring rain. He was the most loyal, the most foolhardy – and the most expendable.

Gripping the slippery keel moulding above his head, he inched around the parapet at the top of the building and kicked the wire mesh from the nearest arched window. Then he carefully lowered himself into the small square bell tower. Beneath the incessant drumming of water on the roof and the purr of sheltering pigeons he could hear the others scuffling impatiently beyond the sealed door.

'Stand away,' Dag shouted, raising his right boot at the lock.

'For fuck's sake get a move on,' came a muffled reply. 'He's starting to wake up.'

Dag kicked at the lock once, then again. On his third

thrust the wood splintered and the door burst open, revealing Imperator Chymes, his two hierophants and the prisoner. Dragging their captive to the middle of the room, they loosened his bonds and forced him to kneel while Chymes dug into his cloak and produced a small leather pouch.

'Tear his shirt open.' Chymes unthreaded the draw-string of the pouch and tipped its contents over the boy's head. The black powder cascaded like a fall of soot, clinging wherever it touched.

'Thus we destroy the outward form of the Primal Material,' Chymes intoned as the boy at his feet spluttered and coughed, *'to remove from this base matter the impurities of the soul. First must come the sublimation, then the calcination of the outward form, to pulverize the matter by fire. Through powder the volatile spirit is fixed and made permanent. Only then can it flower and bear fruit.'*

Dag and the others shuffled uncomfortably and kept their eyes downcast, unsure of the etiquette required for such a moment. Chymes reached down and raised the boy's chin with almost loving concern, as if addressing his own son.

'It is time for the Rebirth. *Winged Mercurius sits guarded by the sun and moon.* You are in safe hands at last.' The boy was barely able to react. He swayed to one side, hardly conscious of his surroundings.

'Now take him over to the window,' Chymes gestured to the others. 'We must wait until the height of the storm.'

So they sat in the vaulted red-brick bell tower of St Peter's Roman Catholic Church (Cantonese and Spanish services on Sundays), watching the rain lash the slated rooftops of the buildings below, waiting for the appointed time of execution.

As the prisoner slowly came to his senses, he found that he had been perched on the very edge of the chamfered stone sill with his thin long legs dangling out over Soho Square. Firm hands clamped his shoulders to prevent him from falling. The knees of his jeans darkened as water poured from the eaves above his head and mixed with the powder covering his body. His mouth seemed full of the sour black mud, but the muscles of his face were beyond his control and he was unable to spit it out. The drugs he had been forced to ingest in a sheltered corner of the church half an hour earlier were beginning to bristle and knot his body.

Gingerly he leaned forward and looked down. The drop was a considerable one, some hundred and fifty feet he guessed. Of course, it was nothing compared to the height of the old Centrepoint run, which now stood abandoned and neglected after so many near fatal accidents. . . .

'I feel that it is very nearly time,' said the voice behind him.

The boy refused to turn about and confront his captors. His face, patched in black and white, loomed eerily from the darkness of the tower, like some half-glimpsed gothic spectre. His bony hands clutched the wet outward edge of the parapet as he prepared himself for his death. The storm was reaching its peak. It may have been the effect of the drugs, but he was no longer afraid. Still, he knew that if he hesitated, one of them would come forward and throw him into the square below. There was no longer any choice. If he failed to act bravely, Chymes and his men would refuse him any dignity in dying. For them, humiliation had become an essential element in any death ritual. Slowly he leaned his body out once more.

He could no longer feel the bitterness of the wind as it swept around the tower, flapping the cable which led from one of the piers off into the drizzling darkness beyond. The lights of the London streets seemed blurred and muted by the falling rain, all sound muffled beneath the angry rush of air and electrical static. He had never intended it to end like this, bound and drugged far above the city, unwilling and unable to go on with the others. The rain plastered his lank fair hair across his forehead, the wind corpsing his skin with cold, but all he felt was the tingling of his nerves and the heightened pulsing of his engorged heart.

He closed his eyes and listened below; a taxi cab's insistent horn, the throb of a bus engine, faint sounds which grew clearer as the thunder died down. He leaned forward and tested the nylon cable with his fist. It was taut but slippery, thrumming in the storm gale, flicking wavelets of water along its length each time it shook, like pegs being tossed from a washline. Behind him, Chymes released a sad sigh.

'It is time for you to leave us, brother.' He stepped forward from the darkness, watching his prisoner intently.

The boy peered out into the night and tried to see the far end of the cable, although he knew all too well where it led. This was a run constructed like no other, created for this moment alone. Now that the time had come to use it, he felt a growing elation uprooting his fear. It seemed that he had been seated in the tower for an age and, as he rose shakily to his feet on the parapet, the joints of his knees creaked in protest.

Tensing with excitement, the others moved forward. This was the storm they had been waiting for, one which would cleanse the city and bring with it a new beginning.

Carefully he grasped the cable with both hands and tightened the muscles in his arms, as he had done a million times before. Further along, huddling against the abutment of the arch, half a dozen bedraggled pigeons watched disinterestedly as he clipped himself to the metal sleeve and attached it to the line.

Counting to ten, he drew a deep, slow breath.

Perfectly timed thunder rolled deafeningly over the city. It appealed to his sense of drama. He released an angry bellow of a battle cry and, with a mighty push, his plimsolled feet pressing hard against the ledge, launched himself from the arch and out above the streets of London. The blast of icy wind around his body, carrying with it great slews of rain, smacked his senses into crystal-sharp alertness. He watched the greenery of the park square passing between his feet far below and felt that, had he been able to slow his speed, the microscopic markings of each branch and leaf would become indelibly clear to him.

Back in the bell tower, Chymes had run forward to the window in order to study the boy's descent across the city. He and his men stood watching until the figure on the line had vanished into the rain.

The soaked orange brick of the bank on the corner of Greek Street loomed close and slid past the boy on his right side. His speed slowed as the angle of the cable between his hands decreased and he approached a junction point, rather like a cable-car station, mounted on the roof of the Prince Edward Theatre in Old Compton Street. Below, smart couples alighted from taxis and made their way across neon-streaked pavements toward the steamed windows of Chinatown restaurants.

The cable hissed beneath the metal sleeve, the tiny inner rollers of the sleeve vibrating in his hands as he swung across Soho to the roof of a bank near the bottom of Regent Street. The muscles in his arms, unused to working without his brace, began to cramp and sting as he neared his final destination. Sweeping over the Air Street junction point mounted from the roof of the Regent Hotel, he noted with surprise that he was considerably further from the ground than when he started. It was a run he would have been proud to have built himself, for the drops and inclines had been carefully planned so that they would steadily increase his height and speed throughout the journey.

As he shot out from between the buildings over Piccadilly Circus he glimpsed people halting in mid-stride and looking up, aware of something moving above their heads. Ahead of him a vast wall of pulsing light grew until it filled his field of vision. He screamed his terror into the sky and prepared for impact, raising his legs as if this futile gesture would somehow help to lessen the force of the coming collision. Finally the gigantic red and white Coca-Cola sign which covered the north side of the Circus loomed large before him, blotting all else from his mind.

He hit it like a bug on a windshield, dead centre, at just over sixty miles an hour. For a moment, his form was imprinted in the flickering neon strips which made up the football-pitch-sized sign. Then, silhouetted against bursting light, his body pulled away from the wall as the tubes exploded and broke loose, cascading to the pavement like jagged drops of luminous rain. He fell like a burning comet, his body ablaze with electrical fire, to be extinguished with a hiss as he hit the rain-bloated gutter of the city street below.

If there had been a last dim thought in his charred and shattered brain, it would have been the happy realization that he had returned to the place which he had been so long forbidden. At last he could say he had both feet on the ground.

Monday 15 December

CHAPTER TWO

The Newgate Legacy

At precisely 3.15, Robert noticed the gargoyles. There were five of them sitting along the tops of the windows. Squat and broad, they failed to spout water or enhance the appearance of the building opposite, but merely crouched on the narrow ledge around its brow, their broad mouths grinning in grotesque mirth. Cast in deep-grey stone, smooth and shiny, they had stubby, clawed bodies – no wings – and punk haircuts. At least, that's how it seemed to Robert, with tufts of hair rising over the crowns of their heads. Their mouths were closed beaks, their eyes characterless but vaguely friendly, like those of a pig.

Robert was sure he had never seen them before and did not know why he should suddenly notice them now. He sat with his feet up on his desk watching the rain steadily falling as he cradled the telephone receiver in one hand, waiting for the engaged tone to clear. Sometimes when it rained in London he wondered if there was anyone out there working at all, or whether they all sat looking out of their office windows, dreaming of being somewhere else, biding their time and nursing the same vague feelings of dissatisfaction.

'The line's still busy. Will you hold?'

'Yes, I'll hold.' This was the sixth bookshop he had tried in the last hour. He seemed to spend his life on the end of a damned telephone receiver. He looked down at the dial panel. Memory Search. Memory

Recall. Guaranteed User Friendly. How he loathed the new technology. Thanks to this state-of-the-art telephone system he no longer needed to memorize his friends' numbers and was therefore unable to call them outside company hours.

The gargoyles appeared to be staring into his office, like small stone spies employed to keep a check on his efficiency. Not that he was being remotely efficient today. What had begun as such a simple task was turning into an irritating dead end. He tilted back the chair and stretched. His arms and shoulders still ached from his trip to the swimming baths earlier in the week. He was too young to be getting out of condition, he told himself. The telephone receiver crackled.

'You're through.'

'Thank you. Hello?' Robert swung his legs from the desk and sat upright. 'I wonder if you can help me. My name is Robert Linden. I'm trying to trace a copy of a book by . . .' He checked the notepad in front of him. ' . . . Charlotte Endsleigh. It's called *The Newgate Legacy*. Published about three years ago, I think. Thank you.'

Another wait, this time for nearly five minutes. Robert was away from the telephone lighting a cigarette when the woman came back on the line. She knew of the book, but was unable to supply him with a copy. Had he tried his local library? Robert admitted that it had not occurred to him to visit a public library. He made thanking noises and rang off. Behind him, Skinner, one of the company's directors, entered the office.

'No luck with the book yet?' he asked casually. It irritated Robert to realize that he must have been listening outside the door.

'No. I'm trying not to get people too interested in it in case they start asking questions.' He pretended to tidy some paperwork on his desk, anxious for Skinner to leave.

'Fine. If it's as good as you say it is and you manage to track a copy down, we can get back to them with an offer by the end of the week. Find out their minimum time option and take it.'

Skinner had the annoying habit of constantly reminding him how to do his job. Robert threw a glance at the crisply suited figure in the doorway and coughed on his cigarette.

'You should try to give up those things in the New Year,' said Skinner airily. 'Make it your resolution. What are you doing for Christmas? Going home?'

'No,' coughed Robert, thumping his chest.

'Too far to travel?'

'Something like that.' Robert saw no reason to explain the indifferent attitude he held towards his parents.

'Oh.' Skinner could see that he was not going to be questioned on his own plans. 'I'm going skiing with Trish,' he volunteered. 'She can't bear the thought of being in England over Christmas.'

'I know how she feels. All those poor people about on the streets make you feel guilty for enjoying yourself, don't they?'

Skinner gave him an uncertain look. She probably can't bear the thought of an event which revolves around someone else, thought Robert. A very attractive woman, though. Given Skinner's negative sexual allure, the chemistry which presumably existed between them was a complete mystery to everyone in the office.

'I hope you have a great time,' said Robert. 'Think of me and the cat on Christmas Day.' Preferably just before you attempt an erection, he thought, grinding out his cigarette in the ashtray.

'Yes, well, keep at it,' sniffed Skinner. 'Remember you're on commission.'

As Skinner closed the door, Robert lowered his head onto the desk. He hated Skinner almost as much as he hated telephones. The man approached the other people in his life as if he owned fifty-one per cent of their stock. His bluff, unimaginative, let's-play-golf-next-Tuesday attitude with clients made Robert feel hopelessly inferior. But then Skinner was a money man, while Robert had been employed for his creative ability. Which was just as well, as the practical side of his nature was virtually non-existent.

He really had to start getting some sleep at night. Just lately he had been waking in a cold sweat, the remnants of the damned dream still plucking at the edges of his consciousness. Lighting up another cigarette in deliberate defiance of Skinner's advice, he tapped out a file entry entitled *Newgate* on the computer and prepared to negotiate a deal for the book rights, based on the assumption that a) he could find a copy of it and b) it was still readable.

In their never-ceasing search for adaptable television material, the company regularly optioned the works of obscure authors, in the hope of raising production money for a TV series they could then sell to the networks. Once in a while they hit the jackpot, but the whole time-consuming process was a frustrating affair, with works proving untraceable, books subsequently revealing themselves as unscriptable and the enthusiasm of the money men waning as soon as they saw typed-up budget proposals.

Robert checked the address of the nearest public library, then wandered along to the coffee machine, filled a plastic cup and took it across to his window. It had just begun to rain once more, the first heavy drops spattering the gargoyles opposite, darkening their faces into scowls. He had made no plans for the evening ahead, or indeed for any part of the approaching holiday season. By the look of the sky, it wouldn't be a lot of fun going out tonight. Below, people began to move off the streets as the strength of the rain increased, water pouring from the rooftop gutters with the crackling sound of chips in fat. Merry Christmas everybody, thought Robert, draining his coffee with a grimace.

The library, a fussy little building of Victorian red brick, had made a half-hearted effort to drag its image into the eighties by setting up window displays designed by local schoolchildren. One of them depicted an Asian Santa Claus on a skateboard, while the other had the infant Jesus being visited by the Three Wise Women. Inside, a pale young woman with frizzy red hair and attractive green eyes consulted her electronic filing programme for him.

'It's listed,' she said finally, tapping the screen with the end of her pencil. 'But I'm not sure if we still have a copy. If the book isn't borrowed much after a certain time period, it sometimes gets pulled from the shelf to make room for new stock.'

'Does the author get something every time a copy is lent out?' asked Robert. The librarian turned to look at him. She removed the pencil from her mouth and smiled, pleased by what she saw.

'No, there's a minimal Public Lending Right payment made and that's about it. Nothing to get excited about.' Her voice had a soft Irish lilt. 'Why, thinking of writing a book?'

'Me? Oh, no.' Robert hoped that the book he was after hadn't been lent out too often. Demand for it would surely affect any negotiations for the film rights.

'Well, if it's not in the General Fiction section, it's either been stolen or retired.' She leaned across the counter and pointed with a slender, freckled hand. 'If you need any help, give a whistle. You know how to whistle, don't you?'

'Thanks.'

Robert walked to the back of the hall, past a room filled with elderly men rustling newspapers on wooden poles. It was typical that he failed to notice when people who found him attractive or interesting made their interest known. Emmett . . . Endover . . . Endsleigh. *The Newgate Legacy*. There it was. Tracing his finger along a low shelf he located the book and hefted the volume into the palm of his hand, its pages refusing to stay apart as he opened them, the spine cracking with disuse.

On the flyleaf was a small monochrome photograph of the author, a middle-aged woman, plump, hair slightly greying, somebody's mother. He straightened himself upright and began to read the jacket copy:

> 'A startling first novel from one of the most talented new writers to emerge this decade' – *The Guardian*
>
> 'Goes straight into the Evelyn Waugh class' – *Sunday Times*

Yes, but would it make a TV series? Robert turned the volume over in his hands. A social satire set in a decaying, overcrowded prison. It didn't really seem the stuff that ratings-smashing shows were made of. He remembered packing a copy away in his holiday suitcase a couple of years ago. The book had absorbed him for days, even with the distractions of the beach, but he had stupidly left it behind in the hotel room and had not thought of it again until Skinner had asked him to rack his brains for unoptioned properties.

'If you want to borrow it, you'll have to join the library first.' The green-eyed librarian grinned at him. 'Although there's been very little call for that book in the past. Tell you what, stick it under your jacket and it'll be our secret.'

'I couldn't do that, it's against the law,' said Robert, suddenly aware of how wimpish he sounded.

'I don't suppose you believe in living dangerously,' said the girl.

'Not really, no.'

'Pity. I guess looks can be deceiving.' She slid a library membership form across the desk and returned to her paperwork, dismissing him with a glance.

Standing outside afterwards, Robert felt his face burning. The girl had offered him more than just the book. Why did he behave like a complete dickhead around women? As he headed for the bus, he mentally kicked himself for throwing away such an opportunity.

His office was quiet, emptied out by the usual pre-Christmas absenteeism. Thunder rattled the panes at his back, making him start. The gargoyles lining the building opposite seemed to have turned to rainwashed ebony. They looked exotic, reminiscent of some mad gothic thriller. Yet he had only to lean down and peer at the base of the building to destroy the illusion. An estate agents', a betting shop, a building society, a variety of plastic signs announced the occupations of those within.

Robert looked up at his reflection. He saw the curly black hair, short and glued back in a fashionable toning down of what had first been punk and then yuppie, narrow brown eyes, ears that right-angled from his head, mouth that turned down. It was a face that seemed purpose built for frowning disapproval and he certainly seemed to be doing enough of that lately. He supposed it was partly because he resented the thought of being alone for Christmas. After all, the season was supposed to be a time for togetherness. For someone who had lived in London all his life, Robert could only feel cheated by the paucity of friendships and liaisons he had formed to date. People seemed to like him well enough, but remained passively attached in a way that made him feel as if the effort to stay in contact was entirely his. It seemed that few were prepared to commit themselves to love or even prolonged acquaintance.

He thumbed through the book, reading a passage here and there. Certain lines jumped out at him, every bit as funny as he had remembered them. Had she written anything else? Nothing mentioned in the thumbnail biography. First edition 1985. No mention of any reprints, either. Published by Gunner & Crowfield. Never heard of them. He crossed back to his desk and punched out a number on his telephone. It took a minute to get hold of the publishing house, then another to find someone who recalled the book.

'You don't remember offhand who her agent is, do you? Could you check? Yes, I'll hold.' He stared out at the gargoyles. One of them had a cable of some kind around its neck. Something to do with the phones, probably.

'Paul Ashcroft and Associates . . . thanks a lot.' He jotted down the telephone number.

More thunder rolled overhead. He punched out the seven figures, recognizing the area code as that of Bloomsbury. It was uncomfortably hot in the office. He tucked the receiver under his chin and loosened his collar. A dizziness formed in his head, just as it had the other night, before the dream began.

'Hello. Yes, I wonder if you can help me. I'd like to speak to someone about Charlotte Endsleigh.' There was a click of connections. The thunderous thudding continued beyond the windows of the office. He pushed himself down into his chair, his head pounding.

'What can I do for you?' The voice was elderly, cultured, a senior representative of the firm.

'My name is Robert Linden. I was told that you represent a writer named Charlotte Endsleigh.'

There was a pause on the other end of the line.

'Well, that is . . . true. We *did* represent her. . . .'

'Oh, has she moved to another agent?' There was another moment of hesitation.

'No, she hasn't done that. It's all rather . . . um. Do you mind my asking, that is – are you a friend of hers?'

'No, I work for a film production company. We have

a business proposition that we think she might be interested in hearing.'

'Oh dear. In the light of what's happened, that could be very awkward to arrange. . . .'

'Our offices are nearby. Perhaps I could come around and see you?'

'Yes, that *would* be preferable.' The voice sounded relieved.

'If you've a few minutes, I could get over to you right now.'

'All right, Mr . . . ?'

'Linden. Thanks.'

Robert replaced the receiver and rubbed at his eyes. Before the dizziness began to recede, he saw the face of the man again. The image was hazy and indistinct, the man stepping back into shadow as the memory faded, but his eyes remained sharply in focus, bright and grey and empty, like those of a corpse. Instantly he knew where he had seen them before. In the dream that recurred and had no ending, no meaning. . . . He stirred uneasily in the chair, anxious to pinpoint the anxiety he felt. Perhaps he had seen the face in an old movie, falling asleep in front of the television late one night. There could be any one of a dozen explanations. He brought his attention back to the book on his desk and, opening it, studied Charlotte Endsleigh's picture, simply to drive any other image from his mind. What disgraceful thing could the woman have done that couldn't be divulged over the telephone?

He looked up at the window, lost in thought. Outside something glinted through the rain, a blur of movement catching his eye for a brief second. He walked over to the window, but whatever it was had gone. The cable attached to the corner gargoyle thrummed and shook in the downpour, as if moments before someone had plucked it like a guitar string.

CHAPTER THREE

Icarus

LONDON STANDARD Monday 15 December

Mystery boy in bizarre death plunge

A TEENAGE BOY was killed early yesterday evening when a power overload shorted out a huge electric sign on the side of the Allied Assurance building in Piccadilly Circus.

Horrified onlookers watched helplessly as the boy, whose name is being withheld by the police until relatives have been notified, fell from a Coca-Cola sign after it seemingly erupted in a wall of flame. Electrical engineers in charge of the building where the mishap occurred today denied that there was any fault with the wiring of the sign.

'This was a freak mischance, a one-in-a-million accident,' said Mr Arthur Matheson of Triangle Displays, the company responsible for the construction of the sign. 'There is absolutely no possibility that such a disaster could occur again.'

Boy 'flew' into sign

Police are at a loss to explain how the boy managed to gain access to the outside of the building. It is not yet clear whether he was in the act of tampering with the electrical system when the explosion occurred.

A number of witnesses insisted that the boy 'flew overhead' into the wall of the building, apparently under his own power. Upon further investigation, police discovered fragments of nylon cable attached to the display mounting which may have been used by the victim to lower himself onto the sign.

In view of the body's condition, it has yet to be proven whether the victim was under the influence of drugs or medication.

'Vampire' detective takes charge

Currently heading the investigation is Detective Chief Inspector Ian Hargreave. 'At the moment we have no reason to suspect that this is anything other than a straightforward accident,' he told us. 'However we are not dismissing the possibility of suicide.'

Standard readers may remember Ian Hargreave as the officer in charge of last summer's notorious and controversial 'Leicester Square Vampire' case.

Meanwhile, the north side of Piccadilly Circus has been cordoned off until Westminster City Council contractors can clear the area of debris.

'They're never going to let me forget that bloody "vampire" business,' said Hargreave, tipping back in his chair. 'It gets dragged out every time they ask for a quote.'

He watched with interest as Sergeant Janice Longbright clambered onto a filing cabinet with a pencil in her mouth. Her glossy auburn hair was arranged in a long-forgotten style and uncurled across her broad face as she reached for an envelope box.

'You want me to get that for you, Janice?' he asked, leaning further back. The sergeant's reply was unintelligible. As she stretched, her brightly painted lips rose to reveal hard white teeth biting down on the pencil in concentration. Hargreave noticed that she was wearing seamed stockings again. She looked a real policewoman, big, solid and sexy, like a fifties caricature. Nothing about her seemed to belong in the present day. He liked that.

'Would it constitute sexual harassment in the workplace if I told you you've got lovely legs?'

Sergeant Longbright eased herself down from the cabinet and dropped a pile of manilla envelopes onto Hargreave's desk.

'Yes, it would,' she replied finally. 'I don't go around telling people you've got nice tits.'

'Hey, I don't talk to other people about you,' Hargreave complained.

'Oh no?' Janice leaned forward and lowered her voice. 'Then how is it that just about everyone around here knows that we're sleeping together?'

'They're just taking guesses. You know what this lot's like.'

Hargreave knew how sensitive Janice was on the subject. That was why he made sure that they came in to work by different routes in the morning. She was a bright, strong-willed woman, fast to pick up on the changes of atmosphere in the office. And she was ambitious enough to make sure that nothing jeopardized her chances of promotion. Looking at her, Hargreave could not imagine what she saw in him. He was at least twelve years her senior and much the worse for wear. Overweight and thinning on top, he appeared to be slipping into comfortable middle age, but his clear brown eyes revealed the deception, for they retained a dangerous youthfulness which was not otherwise readily apparent. Then again, a disastrously early marriage had left him with a suspicious nature when he encountered women as attractive as Janice. In his worst nightmares, he saw her using him as a means of getting on within the force, but one look at her eyes told him this could surely never be the case.

'Did you want anything else?' Janice sorted the files and pushed one forward for his attention.

'Hmmm?'

'You're staring.'

Hargreave snapped forward in his seat. There was so much to get through today that he was aware of consciously delaying the start of his work. He hardly knew where to begin. Christmas in the capital was bringing with it a record number of bag snatches, thefts and break-ins. Last night, several of his men had entered the Knightsbridge apartment of an Arab woman and discovered over thirty thousand pounds' worth of stolen goods, most of it from Harrods alone. And there were hundreds of similar, if less spectacular, shoplifting cases to deal with, though mercifully most of those were too minor to demand his attention.

'You could ask Finch to give me a call. He should have some kind of preliminary diagnosis on the boy by now.'

Janice nodded and turned to leave.

'One other thing. You may want to stay with me on this one.'

'The Piccadilly suicide?' she asked, puzzled. Hargreave rarely consulted her about his own cases.

'It's just a feeling, I don't know. I mean, we haven't even got a positive identification on him yet. But it couldn't have been an accident and it's a bloody odd way of committing suicide. Did you know they found over forty feet of fine nylon cord tied around his waist? So stick close, eh?'

As Janice smiled to herself and closed the door, he stared beyond the glass wall of the office, where a special operations room had been set up to deal with the increased Christmas workload. Fingers rattled at keyboards and faces glowed green in the reflections of report monitors. Someone had made a half-hearted attempt to bring the season's cheer into the operations room with a few sprigs of mistletoe taped to the tops of the monitor screens. Hargreave rubbed a forefinger over his peppery moustache and watched the printouts passing from desk to desk.

Suicides were traditionally an irrational lot, but this made no sense at all. He caught the telephone on its second buzz.

'Finch here. I've almost finished with the boy. There's something I think you'll be rather interested in. Have you got a few minutes?'

'Don't go away. I'll come down.'

As he left the office, Hargreave threw a plastic file card to one of the detective constables.

'Transfer this onto disk, will you? Give it a codename as well as a file number.' He found it easier to remember disk codes than strings of serial digits. 'Call it – I don't know, how many letters can I have?'

The constable broke off from his keyboard and looked up. 'Seven, sir.'

'Ok. . . .' He counted on nicotine-stained fingers. 'Call it *Icarus*.'

'Sir?'

'Look it up, lad,' said Hargreave with a smile. 'Didn't they teach you anything at school apart from computer technology?'

Finch always gave him the creeps. A pale, serious man with creaking knee joints, he appeared to have stepped from an engraving depicting the activities of Burke and Hare. His lab coat reeked sourly of chemicals and as he strode creakingly from his instruments to the sheeted body he left a bittersweet trail, like a woman wearing too much perfume. People tended to steer clear of him in the canteen.

Hargreave stood at the back of the stainless steel draining board while Finch rinsed his hands and removed his rubber gloves. He had always found the morgue a fascinating place, full of grotesque secrets hidden in steamed-up Easi-seal plastic bags. He looked over at the scales, where some interesting-looking red lumps awaited Finch's probing instruments.

'Still no positive I.D.?' asked Finch, crossing to the boy's body and pulling the plastic sheet down to his chest.

'Nothing so far. What about teeth?'

'A couple of fillings, nothing out of the ordinary. We'll run X-ray matches, of course. But we should have him narrowed down to an area by this evening, anyway. Stomach contents were pretty specific. Also his system was packed with drugs, mostly soporific – Valium-based, probably. That should lend support to the suicide theory.'

'Actually,' said Hargreave, 'there are a couple of things that bother me more than his identity.'

'I think I know what you're going to ask,' said Finch, his face splitting with a rare and unearthly grin. With a long face like he's got, he shouldn't smile too often, thought the inspector. He'll scare people to death.

'It wasn't an electric shock that killed him. He's full of broken glass, but it was he who hit the sign, not the other way around.'

'You mean it didn't explode over him.'

'No, look here.' The face and hands of the boy were blackened beyond recognizable form. The skull was fractured in several places and peppered with fragments of glass, the lower jaw resting flat against the boy's throat, torn wide at the joints. Finch pointed his pencil at the remains of the face.

'He must have hit the sign with incredible force. The nasion – the top of the nose – has been pushed back into the brain and several other points on the lower part of the body, notably the crushed state of the knee joints, indicate a pretty ferocious impact. The shattering of the glass particles beneath his skin are consistent with a collision.'

'So we're dealing with someone who threw himself –

say, he swung down from the cord found at the site – into the sign of his own volition.'

'Either that, or somebody gave him a shove,' said Finch thoughtfully.

'Why do you say that?'

'Well, I was saving the best for last,' said Finch, unleashing his grin at Hargreave once more. The inspector shifted uncomfortably.

'When the body was brought in, the upper part of the clothes, the head and the hands were covered in a fine black dust, like soot. At first that's what we thought it was, but we ran a scan and it didn't match with the grime taken from the wall of the building.' Finch removed a small plastic bag from a trolley beside the body and carefully opened it. He shook a small quantity out into the palm of his hand. 'You see, it's too refined. Spectral analysis showed that the grains were far too evenly graded, as if it had been through a pretty thorough reductive process.'

'You mean it's something produced in a factory?'

'No, not necessarily. It could be natural.' Finch tipped the powder back into the bag. The small amount he had poured into his palm had left an irregular black smudge, like a birthmark.

'Pebbles on a beach are part of the reductive process, subjected to an endlessly repetitive wearing down which brings them uniformity. Now with that in mind, I did some scans and rematched our "soot" with substances found in nature and here's what the computer came up with. I didn't believe it at first, so I ran a double check.' He removed a folded printout from his lab coat and passed it to Hargreave, who perused the columns of mineral contents uncomprehendingly.

'It's silt,' said Finch triumphantly. 'A rare kind of black silt that could only have come from one place.'

'The Thames?' the inspector asked doubtfully.

'The Nile, Mr Hargreave. The contents of this boy's mouth could only be found in an Egyptian riverbed.'

CHAPTER FOUR

Charlotte

The offices of Paul Ashcroft & Associates had that ancient, dingily respectable look that Robert had come to associate with the British literary establishment. A vague-looking secretary came down to meet him, then led the way along endless narrow corridors and up tightly twisted stairways lined with stacks of books.

Mr Ashcroft's room overlooked the homegoing Bloomsbury traffic. The windows were opaque with dirt, the walls studded with the garish jackets of Christmas bestsellers, the modern equivalent of Victorian penny dreadfuls. Ashcroft himself turned out to be a small sprightly old man with smiling eyes the colour of old pewter. He looked suspiciously like a character actor from a building society commercial. Perhaps because of this seeming familiarity, Robert immediately felt comfortable with him. They sat across from each other, drinking insipidly weak tea over a large green desk cluttered with contracts and manuscripts. Ashcroft replaced his cup and looked at Robert apologetically.

'I'd like to help you, Mr Linden,' he began. 'The problem is that Charlotte Endsleigh died recently.'

'I'm sorry,' said Robert, 'I didn't realize . . .'

'So you see, your call seemed rather, ah, unfortunately timed.'

'Does this mean that someone else now retains the rights to her novels?'

'Novel,' corrected Ashcroft. He hunted through the

papers on his desk for a minute. 'She only wrote the one. It received a marvellous critical reception . . . never made her a penny, sad to say.'

'But I thought it was successful.'

'In the eyes of the upmarket Sunday papers indeed it was. But the public didn't take to it. We never went into paperback.'

'And the rights?'

'Well, you see . . .' Ashcroft perched forward on his chair. 'Therein lies the problem. Mrs Endsleigh died at her home about two weeks ago. It seems she had the misfortune to surprise a burglar. Charlotte was long divorced and rather a game old stick. She tried to see the fellow off, but he got there first and knocked her head in. She never regained consciousness and died in hospital a couple of days after the attack. Naturally you will understand my reluctance to give out details on the telephone.'

Ashcroft switched his attention to the bottom drawer of his desk and at length pulled out a red cardboard file. 'There is a daughter, Sarah, and by rights all decisions concerning the disposal of Mrs Endsleigh's royalties – not that they amounted to anything much – would have gone to her, but I gather that the girl didn't get on very well with her mother.'

'You mean that she wouldn't be prepared to let Charlotte's book be filmed?'

'Well, I don't know about that.' He lowered his voice to a confidential tone. 'As far as I can gather, she's a bit of a radical, a punk, all that sort of thing. She got into some kind of trouble with the police . . . drugs, I think. She's supposed to be living in a squat somewhere, probably not even under her own name. The point is that so far we haven't been able to trace her. And as she now technically holds the rights to her mother's book, we're in rather a standoff position.'

'You really have no idea where I could find her?' asked Robert. 'What about her father?'

'He died some time ago, I'm afraid. How keen are you to acquire the rights to this?' He tapped the book on his desk with a forefinger.

'Let's just say that I'm expressing an interest.'

Robert knew that if the novel had failed with the general public, the rights, if they could only be traced, could probably be purchased for a song.

'Well, you might try visiting the flat,' suggested Ashcroft. 'I'll tell you why – there's a neighbour in there at the moment, sorting out her affairs. Charlotte died intestate, but they're hoping to turn up something amongst her papers. It could well be that she made provision for the book rights in the event of her death. Not much of a hope, but it's surely worth a try. . . .'

'It is. This has been a great help, thank you.'

'It's in my interest,' smiled Ashcroft, holding the book in front of him. 'I've always wondered when some sharp young person would come up with the idea of turning *The Newgate Legacy* into a film.'

The old man rose and showed him to the door. 'Do let me know if you have any success. It would be a pity to have to wait fifty years for the book to fall out of copyright before you could touch it. And with all these new satellite networks crying out for quality product, I believe . . .' He twinkled pale eyes, a caricature of a harmless old pensioner offering a farewell handshake. 'So nice to have met you, Mr Linden.'

The crafty old bastard, thought Robert, as he marched through the rain toward Tottenham Court Road tube station. He wants me to stay interested so that I'll do all the groundwork, then he can step in at the negotiation stage and cop a fee. But the old man was right about one thing. The book would make a damned good film and new technology meant that opportunities for selling such a series internationally were growing daily. It suddenly occurred to Robert that if he kept the project from Skinner he could even have a go at scripting it himself. He could estimate a rough budget breakdown and present a complete package.

In his raincoat pocket he had a folded piece of paper with Charlotte Endsleigh's Hampstead address on it. He uncovered his watch. Nearly six. He'd head home and make the call, catch the neighbour in with any luck and arrange to go up there first thing in the morning.

Robert joined the umbrella-rattling queue at the station ticket office, wondering what it would be like to live in a hot, dry country. His sneakers were soaked through and squelched when he walked. His radar-like ears, so cruelly exposed to the elements, had gone completely numb in the rain. London in December. A day passed in a dream, the hours largely spent flicking paper clips into a wastebin, and a night to be spent drying out and keeping warm. He resented the weather dictating the pattern of his evening. But then, there were a lot of things Robert Linden resented in his life.

Opening his apartment door was a moment Robert nightly dreaded. The three-room flat above the video rental shop in Kentish Town High Street was, in the landlord's own words, comfortably furnished. This meant that the huge old sofa in the middle of the lounge released a steel spring symphony when sat upon and the chairs and tables looked as if they'd been thrown away at least once before in their lives. Mercifully he did not have to share the place with anyone other than his ex-girlfriend's hateful, balding cat. Robert loathed the moulting creature which spent most of its days lurking beneath the sink. It was a remnant of the past, a constant painful reminder of the one girl he had truly loved and then stupidly lost.

After living with Anne for three years he had made the accidental discovery that she was seeing a DJ called Darren on the evenings she was supposed to be attending adult institute classes in Women's Studies. Back then, well over a year ago, he had been amazed at her duplicity and naively convinced of his own innocence in the inevitable break-up which followed. He was aware that the experience had increased his cynicism concerning relationships to the point of bitterness, but found himself powerless to change the way he felt. Consequently he seemed to have become a person best described by negative words – untrusting, unfriendly, impractical, disorganized.

'If you don't come out from under there, I'm going to kill you and bury your body in the litter tray.'

Robert knelt beside the sink waving a can of cat food at the hissing creature for a full five minutes before giving up and opening a tin of spaghetti hoops for himself. While waiting for the food to warm, he crossed to the kitchen window and pulled aside the curtain. Running slim fingers through black curly hair, he released a snort of annoyance. Ahead, swirls of street lights led down to the Telecom Tower, the river and beyond. He had a vague feeling that somewhere out there, behind an all-obscuring curtain of drizzle and darkness, people were having a wild time, but he could not imagine how to be a part of it.

CHAPTER FIVE

Rose

Two hundred years ago, when the areas around Pall Mall and the Haymarket were still rubbish-strewn sites where rogues and whores crowded the inns and houses of entertainment, it was deemed that a road should be built connecting the centre of the city with Marylebone Park, a 500-acre area of dense woodland now known as Regent's Park. Despite the original scheme of the architect being greatly altered as work on the road began and despite the dusty chaos under which it was constructed, John Nash was able to bring such unity to the great sweeping quadrant that it made his new street as grand and stylish as any of its European counterparts. As decade followed decade, Regent Street remained a centre of fashion, a street so dependent on the custom of society that out of season it was virtually deserted. Now, at the end of the nineteen eighties, at 11.30 on a wet Monday evening in December, the street was once more empty – and despite the modern shop facades, the computerized traffic systems, the buses and taxi cabs, the elegant simplicity of this hundred-and-seventy-year-old quadrant remained unchallenged by any of the modern architectural conceits surrounding it.

Which was exactly the reason why Rose could be found attempting to scale a padlocked fire escape door at the back of one of its buildings. The building in question was called Fordham House, a five-storey office block at the Piccadilly end of the street, and Rose had not expected to find the bottom of its stairway bolted and locked. She had intended to set her tripod up on the roof and take some photographs of the curving terrace in the moonlight, but two things were preventing her from doing so. First of all there didn't seem to be any moonlight at present and secondly there was the small matter of an eight-foot-high iron grille which surrounded the base of the escapeway steps. Rose lowered her camera bag to the pavement and began pacing back and forth along the length of the grille. There had to be a way of gaining access to the top of the building.

Last year she had briefly worked inside one of its offices as a secretary and while sunbathing on the roof in her lunch hour had been amazed by the panoramic view of London that it afforded. Now she found it offering the perfect location from which to commence her new-found hobby. She could see it now; *CITYSCAPE – An Exhibition Of Photographs Exploring Our Urban Environment, by Rose Leonard.* Swinging the camera bag onto her back, she placed one sneakered foot against the base of the grille and hoisted herself up.

She was sure that Rene Burri had never had this trouble when scouting locations for his magnificent city landscapes. He'd certainly never had to worry about finding the cash to get his pictures developed at Photomat, either. Rose was sure that she would graduate to developing her own photographs, providing she didn't lose interest in this particular project as she had with the weight training and the kinetic sculptures earlier in the year.

The top of the grille was covered in black grease to facilitate its opening and shutting. Her hand slipped, the weight of the bag shifted onto her shoulder and she tumbled back to the pavement. Nothing made Rose more determined to try harder than the placing of an obstacle in her path, although right now she knew that anyone passing by would be bound to think that she was a burglar. In addition, the police tended to accuse unaccompanied black girls of being hookers. Presumably they'd been watching too many cop shows.

The rain had finally stopped, but the street was still wet. As she brushed off her jeans she noticed a pair of drunken soldiers weaving their way towards her.

'You need a leg up, love?' The taller of them stepped forward. He had a cheeky gap-toothed smile and eyes which seemed more interested in exploring the denim-clad region of her thighs.

'I've locked meself out,' she said, laughing. Could they really be so drunk as to believe her? They could and did. After a few painful minutes of conversation peppered with sexual innuendo, she managed to convince them to give her an unsteady lift over the grille and onto the fire escape.

The main part of the roof was as she'd remembered, flat, tarred and gravelled, with grimy glass canopies rising at the front and back. Five floors below, the traffic stopped and started around the curving base of the street. With the exception of the connecting roads, the rooftops ahead lay unbroken for half a mile, unchanged since the terrace was first completed.

As she unpacked her tripod and extended it Rose noticed that the street sloped upwards toward the north, where the taller buildings of Oxford Street cut across its path. Below she could see the open area of Piccadilly Circus, a perpetual tangle of scaffolding and construction work, while further beyond the stately buildings of Pall Mall shielded the fountains of St James's Park. She turned around, threading a roll of film into her camera, the chill wind ruffling her hair. Behind Regent Street was the edge of Soho, a maze of jumbled chimneys, turrets and sheds, rooftops sloping and flat, gabled and angled in every direction, finished in every building material imaginable. But where she stood the rooftops were broad and stately and uniform, a multi-plane landscape waiting to be captured on film.

For the first half hour Rose moved from one end of the roof to the other, testing out different set-ups and shutter speeds; then she noticed the low stone ledge of the neighbouring building. In the centre of it an art deco moulding depicted what she took to be an interpretation of the three Graces, or possibly the Nereids, rising from a sea of stone. Why place such a beautiful sculpture here, where it could barely be seen from the ground, she wondered. Perhaps there were others further down.

The two buildings were gapped by a distance of approximately three feet, the intervening space serving no purpose other than that of detaching the properties. Leaning over and looking down into the five-storey brick canyon made Rose feel disoriented and faint. She believed in confronting each of her fears with a positive action and this seemed as good a time as any to remove any lingering doubts she had about heights. Telescoping the tripod shut she threw her bag over first, then jumped across the gap.

The exhilaration which followed her safe landing on the opposite roof beat any pleasure she had derived so far from photographing it. Dusting herself down, she stood and looked around. It seemed as if no one had been up here for years. Filthy piles of building materials lay strewn about everywhere. There were rotting slates, stacks of bricks and dried-up cans of paint, rusted wire bales and steel rods, as if construction work had long ago been planned and suddenly abandoned. There was even an old corrugated-iron workman's shed with a padlock on the door.

Rose looked down over the side of the building and noticed that the top floor windows were covered in dirt and gave into empty rooms. She started to take pictures of the moulding. Glancing at her watch she noted that it had just turned midnight.

The night was clear and cool and Rose was alone on the rooftops of London. It seemed peaceful to be above the city and yet still be a part of it. Carefully, she lined her camera up to the ledge along the building and looked through the viewfinder once more. But this time, instead of seeing an empty roofscape of the city, she saw the strangest thing. Running figures, some loping, some as if swinging on invisible ropes, bounding and leaping across the angled rooftops on the other side of the street. There were perhaps fifteen of them, young, old, men or women, it was difficult to tell. There was even a dog of some kind, darting silently between their feet.

Quickly she unclipped the camera lens and replaced it with a 100–300mm zoom lens. It proved difficult keeping them in the camera's line of vision. They would get to the edge of a building and suddenly they would be across to the next, as if they had just leapt or flown the entire distance. But on the other side of the road the buildings were much more widely spaced. It was impossible for them to have jumped. In a minute she had used up a 36-exposure roll of film, but there was no time to fit another. At first it seemed as if the group was coming nearer. Then she realized that they must be heading up towards Oxford Street, bouncing and hopping from roof to roof in a semi-human, almost simian manner.

When for a moment she thought that they were getting closer after all, she became scared of being seen and crouched down low behind the wall. There was a sound that carried on the breeze as they passed – a cadence of half-notes seemingly played on a woodwind instrument which formed a bizarre *pavane* to accompany their flight through the soft city darkness. As the sound faded, she arose from her hiding place to find that they had vanished as suddenly as they had appeared and once again there was just the noise of the traffic in the street below, a distant car alarm seesawing through the night air and the murmur of the wind slapping rain-soaked newspapers across the rooftops.

Rose threw her equipment back into her camera bag and leapt across the roof once more. As she clattered down the fire escape she prayed that the sale-priced film stock she had been using was not so out of date that her photographs would fail to print up. Scaling the fire escape door from the inside proved to be much easier than she imagined it would be, as she was able to gain a foothold from the stairs behind her. Back on the other side of the grille, she took a glance down at her sweater and jeans. Her clothes were covered in fine black grime. She dug into her bag and pulled out a small make-up mirror. Although her skin was like polished mahogany she could see the soot streaking her face and neck. She set off for the bus stop, suddenly feeling very tired, longing to be home and able to sink into a steaming hot bath.

On the grafitti-smothered upper deck of the night bus she began to wonder whether she had imagined the entire episode. It had frightened and intrigued her more than she cared to admit. She could not imagine what anyone else would be doing in such an alien and inhospitable place. The incident had driven from her mind the thought of taking any further pictures that night. Carefully unclipping the roll of film and pushing it deep into her jacket pocket, she wondered if the computer-controlled camera had been able to pick up any details of the extraordinary group that were not detectable to her own fallibly human eye. But finding that out could happily wait until the morning.

CHAPTER SIX

The Toad

Even in this day and age, London remains a city that tailors its behaviour to the hours of the day and the days of the week. The parliament of England lies in the shadow of a vast clock tower, as if to remind those within of the power of those ever-circling hands. For whatever you may be told, London is not a twenty-four-hour city. It rises at seven and sleeps after midnight. It stays up late on Saturday and sleeps in on Sunday. And by 1.00 a.m. on a cold Monday night in December, only strangers remain on its streets.

The starless night, hanging so thickly over the damp outer parklands of the city, was forced back here into a bluish-grey haze. Sodium-yellow ribbons of streetlight held the darkness at bay in the empty alleyways behind the Victoria Embankment. From the roof of the Playhouse theatre one could have watched the cars of the city's last revellers racing home from Blackfriars Bridge, past the Houses of Parliament to Chelsea and Battersea beyond. But no one was interested in ground-level activities up here, for there were events to consider of a far more serious nature. On this night, the second in a series that would herald the start of a terrible new era, the one they called the Toad was about to receive his sentence.

'You, the jury, have reached the verdict of Guilty and it is for me to decide what penance Brother Toad must make to redeem himself in the eyes of this court.'

The summing up, transmitted in a deep monotone, reached to the four corners of the theatre roof. The Toad sat cross-legged at the foot of a vast square chimneystack. His plump, soot-smeared body was tied tightly with baling wire. He had not looked up since the speeches commenced. Even when the jurors announced their verdict he failed to raise his head, but emitted instead a single stifled sob. Despite the chill of the night, sweat dripped steadily into his eyes.

Around and above him stood the rest of the court, familiar once-friendly faces now hidden by the shapeless black satin masks which were the symbols of judicial office. The voice now reaching the Toad's grubby ears belonged to the tallest figure of all, the only one to be clothed in a gown of flowing black linen. It stood unflanked and austere among the chimneypots of the Playhouse. Occasionally, a glittering steel hand appeared from within the folds of its cloak to gesture at the frightened boy.

Arms reached in and hoisted the Toad into a semi-standing position. He did not resist, but fell back against the rough brickwork of the stack as soon as the support was removed. The wire which bound his hands and feet prevented him from easily maintaining his balance. Finally, he raised his eyes listlessly in the direction of the judge's voice.

'Toad, you must realize that you have been found guilty of an extremely serious crime. You have acted with treacherous intent. The information you supplied could have curtailed our future plans and jeopardized our very existence. . . .' The voice grew cold. On the ledge above, a momentary breeze lifted the figure's linen cloak and slowly dropped it with a spectral sigh.

'Even now we are forced to live here, beyond our true territory, as a breed apart. And what is this but a direct result of the looseness of your sinful tongue.'

Toad fidgetted nervously as, somewhere in the distance, the forlorn bray of a barge horn sounded.

'But you are about to discover, Brother . . .' the voice softened slightly now, 'that even I can be forgiving.'

The eyes of all turned to the billowing figure on the ledge. Even the Toad tried, vainly, to hoist himself to attention.

'What you did was wrong, of course. But I believe that it was done in good faith, no matter how misguided your intent. It is for this reason that I find myself moving to leniency. You have been with us since the very beginning, rising through the ranks, helping to continue the task which was begun for us by the enemies Apollo and Diana.'

The Toad's face reflected a desperate, anxious thankfulness. Tears rolled down his chubby filth-streaked face. He raised his head still further as the hands which had helped him to his feet now loosened the bindings at his wrists and ankles.

'In the light of your crime you cannot, however, expect to retain your favoured position in our krewe. I am therefore granting your wish to return to the Insects this very night.'

Suspicion flicked across the Toad's face. He rubbed his chafed wrists as a broad-shouldered young man stepped alongside him and gently grasped his arm.

'Brother Samuel will put you back among the people to whom you so strongly desire to return. *Cast out the scorner, and contention shall go out; yea, strife and reproach shall cease*. We wish you happiness in your new life, Brother Toad, Now go in peace.'

The Toad released an involuntary sob. He was to be set free after all. He turned to the others. It was impossible to read the faces of those who remained about him.

'However . . .'

The single word cut the air. The Toad's heart missed a beat.

'You must take with you the symbol of this second night. *In the name of the Lord of the Universe and of the Fratres of the order of Isis go; for here the putrefaction of matter gives way to the soul.*'

Two shavenheaded men stepped forward from the gathered ranks. One of them was wearing a single black leather motorcycle gauntlet. Between them they carried a large brass cage. After setting it down on the roof they stood to attention once more. Within the cage a creature of black iridescence rustled and hopped. With this, the tall figure on the ledge spun on its heel and marched away across the angles of slate and stone, to be lost in an outline of dark chimneystacks.

'It's all right. Relax, Toad, for God's sake. I've just been instructed to see you as far as Trafalgar Square.'

Brother Samuel's words offered scant comfort when matched to the power of his grip upon the Toad's arm. The jurors had now broken their circle and were departing in their various directions. Behind Samuel and the Toad, the two men with shaved heads hoisted up the brass cage and, carrying it between them, followed on at a discreet distance. The Toad's nervous waddle was thrown into a hasty canter as Brother Samuel strode ahead across the roof. For a minute they moved on in silence, their footsteps accompanied only by the sound of the river breeze lifting gently over the copings of the embankment buildings.

'Do we have to go this way, Sammy?' asked the Toad. 'Can't you just let me go down at the railway station?'

'No, Toad. There are too many Insects beneath Charing Cross bridge. They might see you. You know better than that.'

If there was one thing the Toad knew, it was that the shelterers beneath the bridge were homeless tramps and alcoholics, camping down for the night in cardboard boxes, and that a colliery band could be marched before them without causing a disturbance. But he knew better than to draw attention to the point.

'Well, Toad, this is as far as I can take you.'

The two of them had reached the far upper edge of the roof to the back of the theatre. Standing side by side they made a ridiculous pair.

'But I thought you were taking me to Trafalgar Square, Sammy.' Barely controlled hysteria broke through in the Toad's voice.

'I'm afraid not, Brother Toad. His orders, you understand. If I had my way, things would be different. . . .'

A few yards away, the two shavenheaded men came to a stop. The one in the motorcycle gauntlet bent down and unclipped the door of the cage, then cautiously reached inside it. There was a chattering series of shrieks as he struggled to extract an enormous raven from within. Holding it at arm's length, he pulled the cord which bound its feet a little tighter. The bird flew at him, batting its broad muscular wings, but he managed to hold it off as the other untangled the length of cord around its legs and approached the Toad.

'No!' The Toad pulled and twisted desperately in Brother Samuel's grip.

'He's watching us from the next roof,' hissed Samuel. 'It *has* to end this way, don't you see? One look from him and we'll all be killed!'

The two shavenheaded men stepped quickly forward and tied the other end of the cord around the Toad's neck. Then they began to pull it tight, so that eventually the raven was tied directly in front of the Toad's horrified eyes. The bird screamed and clawed at the boy's plump cheeks in an effort to escape, tearing his face into crimson strips. He brought up his hands to fight the bird off, but with its wings wrapped tightly around the Toad's head it drove its beak forward again and again, pecking at his eyes until it penetrated to the back of each socket. Its claws dug into the Toad's neck as it turned its attention to his thick white throat. Falling to his knees the boy twisted madly, trying to escape the onslaught of the screaming creature, his voice a guttural rhythm of ragged screams and gasps. Finally Samuel could not bear to see the boy suffer any longer. In another moment he was behind the Toad, his muscular arms hoisting boy and bird high over the concrete lip of the roof.

'Farewell, Toad,' said Brother Samuel loudly, mainly for the benefit of the man he knew was listening just a short distance away. 'We're all sorry it had to end like this.' And with that he released his grip, stepping back from the roof after a moment with his arms still stretched apart.

In surprised silence the Toad and the attached raven fell four floors down, to be stopped by the tall enamelled railings of the Prudential Insurance offices below. High above, Brother Samuel's head appeared hesitantly over the building's edge and, briefly noting the shuddering red bundle which had been pierced through with crested spears like some grotesque biological specimen, vanished from view once again.

On a nearby rooftop, a billowing figure watched the end of the drama. He dipped his head in silent approval as the body ceased to twitch and the bird, tied even in death, flapped brokenly against its chest. Then in a low voice he began to intone:

' "*I am Mercury, the mighty flower,*
I am most worthy of honour,
I am the Mother of Mirror and maker of light,
I am the hot lion who devours the sun in the heavens,
Who witnesses the unfolding of the creation of the world!" '

Satisfied with the events of the night, Chymes smiled to himself and strode off into the deepening gloom.

Tuesday 16 December

CHAPTER SEVEN

Confluence

Charlotte Endsleigh's flat proved to be a further half-mile on from Hampstead tube station. At seven o'clock that morning the rain had recommenced and three hours later still rippled in slate sheets over the glistening green heathland above the village. By the time he managed to locate the apartment building, a Victorian mansion block built in the lower, less wealthy corner of the suburb, he looked like something that had just been fished out of the Thames. Standing in the shelter of the gloomy, steepled porch trying to decipher the names on the bells, he was surprised by the sound of the front door opening. A young West Indian woman in a bright sunsplash of a housecoat stood in the hallway. *Princess Ida* pattered out from a stereo in the background.

'Can I help you?' she asked, guardedly studying his sodden clothes. 'Can *anything* help you?' The flattened consonants of her speech betrayed South London origins.

'Can I come in?' asked Robert. His sneakers squished as he wiped them on the mat. 'I'm soaked,' he added unnecessarily.

'I can see that. No, you can't.'

'I was looking for Charlotte Endsleigh's apartment. You see . . .'

'You a reporter? One of Rupert Murdoch's lot?'

'No, not at all, I . . .'

''Cause I've had 'em all round here. "Got any nude

pictures of the deceased's daughter", that sort of thing. I told them to bugger off, the lot of them. "Dusky brunette refused our reporter admittance. Does she hold death clue? Shouldn't we be told?" That's what I half expected them to print the next day. As it was the story never even made the papers. So much for my sole chance of notoriety.'

Robert wondered if he would have the chance to get a word in edgeways.

''Course, it's going to be fun trying to let the place. Should I point out to prospective renters that the last tenant died in unnatural circumstances? Would you?' She looked at him mischievously.

'I don't know, I need to speak to the person sorting out Mrs Endsleigh's effects, if that's all right,' said Robert in a rush.

'Ah. Well, that's me.' She thoughtfully tapped a red false nail against brilliant white teeth, checking him over with a degree of unsubtlety that Robert would have found endearing had he been less uptight about meeting women.

'I'm trying to buy the rights to a book she wrote and I need to know if she left any instructions concerning the disposal of her work. You can call her agent if you want to check me out. I have his number here somewhere.' He began to search his raincoat pockets.

'Don't worry, you look ridiculously trustworthy. I suppose you'd better step inside.' She smiled generously and opened the door wide. 'After what happened here I usually make strangers take a two-hour exam before I let them in. But you remind me of that TV character, the one with the honest, hangdog kind of look. You know, the detective.' She clicked her fingers at him. Robert screwed up his face, puzzled.

'The one who wears the Armani suits?'

'Right, sure.' She looked innocently at Robert, as if dealing him a marked poker card. She had sexy and very possibly dangerous eyes, set in a round and pleasing face. Her tightly curled hair was cut into a man's flat-top, yet somehow added to her femininity. She slipped past him, leading the way to the back of the hall and a narrow, twisting staircase. As she passed close by, Robert could smell her perfume, an incongruously light and summery scent that seemed to defy the dismal weather outside.

'I can show you where all the paperwork is kept. Some wizened relative of Charlotte's appeared a few days ago and cleared the place of anything that could possibly be of any value.'

'Funny how relatives suddenly turn up when somebody dies,' said Robert, more to make conversation than for any other reason. They climbed the dimly lit stairs to the top of the house and stopped in front of a scuffed brown door. The young woman produced a set of keys from her voluminous housecoat.

'Rose Leonard,' she said, holding out her hand. 'I look after these luxuriously appointed shoeboxes. My place is on the ground floor. If you ever feel like renting an apartment here, see an analyst.'

'Robert Linden.' How do you do,' said Robert.

'I say, how formal. Come on in.'

What an unhappy-looking guy, she thought, he keeps looking at me as if he's just been told off for doing something wrong. She pushed open the door and they entered Charlotte Endsleigh's apartment. The rooms smelled strongly of damp and were devoid of all but the most basic pieces of furniture. Pale squares marked the oatmeal-coloured walls where paintings had hung.

'You probably want to know what happened to Charlotte,' Rose continued, not caring whether he wanted to know or not, but relishing the chance to discuss the subject anew. 'Well, it was horrible. Blood everywhere, screams in the night. I'm lying, I'm lying.' She laid a warm hand on his arm so suddenly that

Robert withdrew in surprise. 'In actual fact, nobody heard a thing. I wasn't even here when it happened. They never caught the guy who did it, either. I mean, he could come back, couldn't he? I managed to get our scumbag landlord to shell out for a decent alarm system, though. I mean, we could all have been murdered in our beds.'

Rose ushered him into what had obviously been Charlotte's study. On the far side of the room, beneath a sharply angled ceiling, a desk covered with boxes of paper stood below a small window. Rain pattered on a skylight somewhere. There was no typewriter, Robert noted.

'You wouldn't believe it. The woman who came by took everything, pictures, silverware, even the crockery. Thieving old bag. I hope no one does that when I die.'

'Typewriter?' Robert walked over to the desk and peered out of the window. The rain seemed to be easing a little.

'Yes, even that. I couldn't stop her. She *was* family, after all. Still, it seemed a bit much when you consider that in all the time Charlotte was here she only ever came around for a couple of quick visits. Those are all the remaining papers, over there.' She indicated the cardboard boxes on top of the desk.

'Did this lady take any of the paperwork, or any books?'

'No, I think she just stuck to things she could fence.' Rose stood by the door and watched fascinatedly as Robert pulled a stool out from under the desk and dusted it down. There's something uncertain about the way he moves, she thought. It's as if he expects something awful to happen at any second.

'You haven't seen anything resembling a will, by any chance? No written instructions to relatives?'

'From what I can gather, she never got around to having one drawn up,' said Rose. The subject of Charlotte Endsleigh's legal arrangements obviously bored her. 'You know, we've had a policeman on duty outside ever since it happened. He must be all of seventeen. Looks like a broomstick in a uniform.'

Robert began to turn out the contents of the nearest cardboard box. 'I feel a bit guilty, going through someone else's belongings,' he admitted.

'I wouldn't if I were you. It's not stuff that anyone's liable to come back and claim. Final demands, a load of weird old books and tons of magazines.'

'What kind of weird books?' Robert looked back at Rose. She was standing with one hand on her hip and the other on the door handle, watching and smiling.

'I dunno, the kind nobody reads any more. Obscure historical reference works, stuff like that.'

'Mind if I take a look through them?'

'They're not mine to mind.'

'I won't be very long.'

'I don't suppose you will. It's not exactly the Hermitage, is it?'

She's altogether too knowing, he thought, unnerved by her brazen stare. He turned back to the desk and started sifting through wads of unpaid bills, unfinished correspondence and illegibly scribbled notes. When he looked up again, Rose had gone. The cardboard cartons contained little of any help or interest. In the main, the old lady's letters were hastily jotted thoughts and observations, written for the benefit of friends but apparently never posted. He could find no mention at all of family affairs. Junk mail, circulars and ancient magazines comprised the remainder of the papers. After a while Robert neatly restacked the boxes and walked round the echoing apartment. The cool, damp air brought on a sudden sneeze and, pulling a handkerchief from his pocket, he sent most of his small change bouncing over the floor. It was while he was on his knees picking it up that he discovered the envelope.

At a quarter to eleven he came downstairs, knocked on the door of Rose's apartment and was invited to join her for coffee. The lounge he was ushered into was tiny, but cheerfully painted in eye-searing shades of red, yellow and blue. Beyond the windows the storm clouds were leaving the sky, but tall rustling hedges held back the ashen light.

'I'd like to take this with me and read it at home.' Robert sat down on the couch and placed his hand on the thin brown envelope beside him.

'It's not really up to me,' said Rose. 'But I'm sure it would be OK. What is it?'

'Nothing to do with the rights of Charlotte's book, but something which looks very much like the first draft of another novel,' said Robert. 'I found it under a table in the study.'

'I hope you find it useful. I'll have to put the boxes in storage.' Rose had changed into an enormous shapeless T-shirt and jeans. Her clothes looked as if they'd been dropped onto her from a great height, but displayed a certain bizarre style. She wore no shoes. Tiny painted toenails showed. She looked younger than she'd seemed earlier. Twenty-four or – five, he guessed. Probably had lots of loud friends, black and white. Probably spent her time going out and enjoying herself on the nights that he stayed in.

'I doubt very much if Sarah will be coming back to collect anything.' Rose dropped a disturbing number of sugar cubes into her coffee and began to stir.

'Sarah? You mean Charlotte's daughter?'

'That's right.'

'Did you ever meet her?' Robert picked up the envelope and thumbed casually through the handwritten pages of the torn school notebook within.

'Just a couple of times. That was enough.'

'Why, what was she like?'

'Black lipstick, purple hair, chalky face. King's Road

type, looked like she needed a bowl of chicken soup and a few nights in. Both times she visited, she had a shouting match with Charlotte. Fierce stuff, I could hear her from down here. She had a voice that could strip paint.'

'When was the last time she came here?'

'The day her mother was done in.'

'Wait a minute.' Robert turned his attention from the notebook. 'I was told that Sarah had vanished. Nobody mentioned her coming back to town.'

'That's 'cause I didn't tell anyone,' said Rose in a conspiratorial whisper.

'Why not?'

'Because she turned up with a couple of creepy-looking dudes who hung around outside waiting for her. Looked like they were on drugs. I caught one of them carving things on the front door.'

'Why didn't you mention it to the police?'

'I figured either she or the Brothers Grimm might come back and give me a hard time.' Rose looked down, picking a strand from her T-shirt. 'I have to manage this block alone. It's me who gets in trouble if we have vandals.'

'You seem a little young to be looking after the place by yourself.'

Rose looked away toward the window with studied disinterest. 'Yeah, well there used to be two of us, but he decided to move out. I manage just fine.' There was a coolness in her voice. Robert hastily moved from the subject.

'I don't suppose you'd know where I might find Sarah now?'

'Not really. She struck me as the kind of person who could turn up anywhere at any time, depending on who she was with.'

'OK, but supposing Charlotte was killed by one of her daughter's friends?' he said.

Rose wrinkled her nose at the suggestion. 'Seems a bit unlikely, getting your mates to knock your own mother off. I mean, what for? The old girl was broke. She could barely cover the rent.' Rose drew her knees up onto the sofa and hugged them. Her movements were slow and deliberate, almost feline. 'I used to get embarrassed having to ask for the money. She hardly ever went out, probably couldn't afford to. Besides, we all knew about the burglar.'

'How?'

'The guy broke in about six weeks earlier. He stole stuff from several of the apartments. Entered the same way both times, through Charlotte's skylight. And some other flats along the street were done over. But it wasn't until he got *here* that he did more than steal. Poor old soul. She'd probably still be here if she hadn't tried to put up a fight.'

'I've never been this close to a real murder before,' said Robert. He replaced his coffee mug and sat back. 'It's days like today that make my job so enthralling. I've got an untraceable book and a dead author and the only person who can help me has gone missing.'

'I always knew I was in the wrong job. What you need is a gorgeous pouting blonde to provide you with a lead.' Rose leaned forward with a crooked smile. 'I'll let you know if I hear of any.'

'Well, I was going to ask you if *you* had any bright ideas.'

'I don't know how you can get your book rights, if that's what you mean.' Rose stood up and smoothed out the front of her vast T-shirt. 'Maybe you should just go ahead with your plans and wait for Sarah to contact you when she hears about it.'

'It's too risky,' sighed Robert. 'We'd wind up with a lawsuit on our hands. I might as well forget the whole thing.'

'Now *that's* positive thinking.'

'It's not as if my boss would let me spend any money taking it further.'

'Doesn't personal satisfaction count for something?' asked Rose. 'Boy, you give up easily. Come on, I have to go down to the shops. You can buy me coffee. I forgot, you're a poor person, I'll buy *you* a coffee.' She pulled Robert out of his seat and together they left the apartment. In Hampstead High Street Rose deposited her rolls of film in a Photomat store and promised to collect them in an hour.

She discovered very little about Robert in the sixty minutes that followed. He seemed reluctant to discuss himself or his job on even the most superficial level, but at the same time he was obviously anxious to share her company. To keep the conversation flowing, Rose told him of her previous night's exploits on the Regent Street rooftops. The permanent furrow in Robert's brow deepened as he listened to what he obviously considered to be a total fantasy. Rose watched him fastidiously emptying 'Sweet 'n' Low' into his coffee and decided to give up. The guy was obviously a lost cause, a waste of space. When they finally agreed to leave the warmth of the coffee shop, he announced that he was going back to work and would consider contacting the police regarding the whereabouts of Sarah Endsleigh.

'Well, I'll call you if I hear anything,' she said half-heartedly, accepting his business card and slipping it into her purse. 'And you're welcome to get in touch if you need any help.'

They parted outside the station, convinced that they would never see each other again.

'*How* much?'

'Thirty-five pounds twenty pence.' The young woman behind the Photomat counter listlessly checked the receipt. 'There's a lot of film here. And you got them processed in an hour.'

'You shouldn't charge for my natural impatience. God, I'm surrounded by assassins. Look, I'll pay for one of the rolls now and collect the rest later.'

'You can't just pay for one roll.'

'Why on earth not?'

'Because they're all mixed up together.'

'Whose fault is that? Wait here.' Rose ran out of the shop and back up the street until she spotted the retreating figure of Robert, just about to enter the station. Her ensuing whistle, while lacking the timbre to set off all the car alarms in the neighbourhood, was shrill enough to bring every pedestrian in the area to a standstill. In the distance, Robert turned around. What he saw appeared to be a mad woman leaping up and down in a white T-shirt that was so huge that from this distance she looked like a cereal packet.

'Robert!' shouted the mad woman. 'I need your chequebook! I'll pay you back!'

'Are you always like this?'

'Like what?' Rose was barely listening as she thumbed through the photographs in her lap. They were sitting on a green wooden bench at the edge of the road while trucks and buses wheezed past them on their way up the hill, heading from the West End to the concrete wasteland of the North Circular. The air around them was blue with lead-laden fumes, but Rose had failed to notice in her anxiety to check through her precious photographs.

'They've come out really well. Look at that.' She passed over a picture of a roof. Then another picture of a roof. And another. She's completely demented, thought Robert, although at least they prove that she's been telling the truth.

'Now, where are the really interesting ones? Ah!' Triumphantly, Rose pulled out a set of photographs and spread them across her knees. Seen in slow progress from the middle of Regent Street to its upper reach were sixteen distinct tiny figures and, sure enough, something that could only be a dog. They looked inhuman, or rather, misshapen, but Rose was at a loss to explain why. The last few photographs were slightly blurred, but showed the stragglers of the group in startling proximity.

'I managed to get some close-ups just as they were heading off,' said Rose, turning over the final photograph. For a moment she stared at it in surprise, then held it closer. The picture showed a girl in her late teens, dark and attractive, laughing, frozen in mid-turn as she called to someone at her back. Her face was pale and free from make-up, her hair a blackish purple. Behind her in the distance glowed the Telecom tower.

'There, you kindly paid for the photos and now God has given you a reward.' She turned to Robert and held the picture in front of his nose. 'This is Sarah Endsleigh. I'd recognize her pasty face anywhere.'

'Is this some kind of practical joke . . . ?'

'I don't know.' She began checking through the other pictures. 'I wonder if her two charming friends were up there with her.'

'Sarah Endsleigh? I don't believe you.' Robert scratched his chin doubtfully. 'It's too much of a coincidence.'

'Listen, our building was burgled twice from the roof. One of those times, Charlotte was accidentally killed. Now her daughter's running with some kind of rooftop gang. Don't you see? It's all connected, it has to be.'

'You should go to the police with those pictures. They could check the whole thing out. I mean, if there are people running around up there the law's bound to hear about it.'

'You forget that I was trespassing when I took those shots. Anyway, it'd be more interesting to find out for ourselves. There's something weird going on around here. Don't you want to find out what it is?'

'Not particularly, no.' Robert rose to his feet. 'Look, I'll return the notebook as soon as I've finished with it.'

'Drop it in to her agent.' Rose was annoyed and disappointed at her failure to kindle a spark of interest in this skinny, worried-looking man.

'I'd rather leave it with you.'

'Whatever you want.' She shrugged disinterestedly and returned the photographs to their yellow evelope. 'I'll send the money you lent me back by post.' Rising, she thrust her hands beneath her T-shirt and strode off along the pavement. In taking him into her confidence she had misjudged him and he had failed her.

Suddenly Robert realized that she must have been freezing, sitting there all this time without a topcoat. He was tempted to call her back, to try and explain his reluctance to get involved, but instead he watched helplessly until she had disappeared around the corner. Then he tucked the notebook under his arm and disconsolately headed back in the direction of the underground station, his feelings of inadequacy redoubled.

CHAPTER EIGHT

Asleep

She slumbers on.

And while she sleeps, she dreams.

In her dream she is a maiden, young but far from innocent, lured to a skytop castle by foul brigands. She has been bound hand and foot. For committing an unforgivable crime, she is to be executed at dawn. Six hundred feet above the kingdom she hangs, her scarlet tresses raised and tangled by the wind which hurtles around her. Below her naked feet, kites wheel and scream in constant battle with the flowing air. Up here there is no hope of rescue. She is sure that the night will yield no thundering stallion, no gleaming saviour, for who even knows that she is here?

Now darkness has fallen upon the kingdom. Far below, the eerie cries of unnatural predators can be heard as they forage and fight. Her wrists and ankles ache from the tension of her bonds. Enervated, she starts to sob, her tears falling out into the night sky to be snatched away by the wilful winds.

She cannot reconcile herself to death, cannot face the knowledge that these hours of darkness are the last her senses will taste and touch. She tries to twist and turn, aware that she is imprisoned in a dream. But soon she will awake, to discover what she already dreads and knows to be the truth. That, far from being a dream, all this will prove to be so very real . . .

CHAPTER NINE

Anubis

Earlier that morning, as a faint silver mist still hung in the sloping streets which led from Charing Cross down to the embankment, Detective Chief Inspector Ian Hargreave gave his men the unenviable task of removing the Toad's body from atop the railings of the Prudential Insurance Company. Guided by a police surgeon, two constables manipulated the trunk from the spikes in an effort to prevent any further damage to its internal organs. Due to the grotesque state of the corpse, its head and shoulders had been wrapped in heavy opaque plastic. So far Hargreave had managed to keep the public away from the site by ordering the road to be sealed off at either end.

'What the hell is Cutts doing here?' The inspector aimed a thumb at the balding man in the brown raincoat who had climbed through the plastic tape of the police cordon and was now heading towards him. He rounded on one of the uniformed officers. 'I thought I made it quite clear that this was to be kept out of the papers until we've had a chance to programme the lab analysis.'

'I'd like to remind you,' began Stan Cutts, forcing his way to the front of the small group that had gathered around the operation site, 'that it's my duty to provide the public with information that may affect their rights and their personal safety. . . .'

'Come off it, Cutts. You're not a journalist, you're a

tabloid hack. You couldn't give a shit about personal rights.' He waved the little man back. 'Somebody get him out of here.'

A year earlier, Hargreave's reputation had suffered badly when Cutts' newspaper had publicly accused him of mishandling a case. Since then he had refused to tolerate the presence of reporters unless they were specifically requested to attend a press conference. At the same time, in deference to their power, he remained wary of alienating them too severely. One of the two constables who was diverting traffic away from the corner of Craven Street stepped forward and fixed a gloved hand over the reporter's arm.

'Answer me one thing, Hargreave,' called Cutts as the officer attempted to lead him away, 'is this connected with your "Vampire of Leicester Square" fiasco?'

Hargreave spun on his heel, his cheeks growing mottled in the chill morning air.

'You know damned well it isn't,' he said, his voice dropping to a menacing tone. 'You try to build a link with this and I'll suspend your access to all of the report channels.'

'Then it must be something serious,' Cutts reasoned. 'Anyway, these days you know we can access information from several other sources. But of course, I'd rather get it from the horse's mouth.' His grin suggested that he knew more than he was prepared to admit. The crumpled coat he always wore smelled of sweat and stale whisky. Cutts put Hargreave in mind of a shambling, amiable pornographer. 'Let me in on this and I'll guarantee to keep the past out of any reports that get filed.'

'You want in?' asked Hargreave, a sour smile playing on his face. 'C'mere. Let go of him, Duncan.' He beckoned the reporter over to the plastic sack which had been straightened out on the floor of the unmarked police ambulance. Carefully, he pulled back the top flap of the sack. 'We've got a male, early twenties, body impaled on railings which pierced clean through the neck, chest and right thigh.'

Cutts leaned over the corpse and blanched. 'What happened to his eyes and throat? You couldn't get scalp and facial lacerations like that from a fall. What is this?'

It was Hargreave's turn to play the innocent. He shrugged his shoulders in defeat. 'Well, Stanley, that's something we don't know yet.' He directed the reporter's attention away from the body of the huge bird which hung in its plastic sack at the back of the vehicle. That would have to remain a secret until he could figure out what the hell it had been doing tied to the body. 'Give me a couple of days before you print any conjectural copy on this and I'll make sure that you get an exclusive on any developments occurring in, say, the next twenty-four hours.'

'Come on, Hargreave, first the Piccadilly boy and now an impalement? Maybe there's a killer loose. "Rooftop Rambo Strikes Again". The city's full of Christmas shoppers. Could turn out to be a pretty big story.'

'Handled badly it could also start a pretty big panic. I have to tell you that if you print a single word linking the two deaths I'll bring you in for obstructing police procedure and – let's see now, how about falsifying information?'

'Who's falsifying? It's here for anyone to see.'

'You'll get an official denial.'

'Jesus, whatever happened to integrity?'

'It must have read your newspaper.'

'Thirty-six hours,' bargained Cutts, who knew enough to tread lightly when there was the possibility of an even better story further down the line. 'Give me information access for thirty-six hours and I'll delay filing the story until late Thursday.'

'You've got a deal. By the way, how'd you hear about this so quickly in the first place?'

'I can't give away my contacts, old man. You know that.'

Hargreave smiled to himself. He had been prepared to figure out another way of keeping the press off his back until Thursday. Now he would simply have Cutts arrested for witholding information if the reporter decided to step out of line. Meanwhile, he would keep two files on the case – one for himself, and another for the newspapers.

'They nearly lost it on the way over, did you know that?' Hargreave lit a cigarette from the end of another and looked up at the monument. The granite obelisk known as Cleopatra's Needle thrust upward into a sky that was the colour of old ice. Sergeant Janice Longbright stamped her boots on the pavement and followed Hargreave's gaze. 'The needle was being towed from Alexandria in an iron pontoon, like a huge cigar in a case. Halfway across the Bay of Biscay there was a terrible storm. Six men were swept overboard and drowned. But the needle was saved.' He turned to Janice and smiled. 'It's been around for nearly one and a half thousand years before Christ, a memorial to gods we can scarcely imagine, and what do the British do? We stick it on the embankment and bury a razor, a box of pins and a copy of Bradshaw's Railway Guide underneath it. That's one for the gods to puzzle out.' Janice watched the inspector's breath condense in the damp Thames air. She gently slipped her arm through his, mindful of breaking his train of thought.

She knew that there had to be a reason for his requesting to meet her at such an odd venue. Ian never did anything without a carefully reasoned purpose. Not that he was an unimaginative man – on the contrary, his thinking had an amiable perversity that pleased and surprised her. She brushed a curl of red-brown hair from her eyes with her free hand and looked back at the obelisk.

'What do you know about the ancient Egyptians?' He dropped his cigarette to the pavement and stepped on it, turning to face her. Janice thought for a minute.

'Well, they had an exaggerated reverence for the dead. Didn't they bury their servants alive with their masters? Anubis was something to do with that, I think. He had the head of a dog.' She shrugged. 'Guess I didn't pay much attention in history class.'

'Anubis was jackal-headed, the god of the dead. He was supposed to have invented embalming. OK, what about ravens?'

'Ravens?'

'The victim was attacked by one. A big bugger, over two feet long. It was tied to his face.'

'I think you can get them to talk. And they live a long time. Sorry, you're catching me on my weak subjects here.'

'Let's walk.' Hargreave gestured ahead to the broad curve of the roadway where it passed beneath Hungerford Bridge. 'There *has* to be a connection between the two deaths, but what has a boy with a mouthful of Egyptian silt got to do with ravens, for God's sake?'

'Why don't you wait for the lab analysis to come in before you try to find a link,' Janice suggested. 'You've presumably had a team up on the roof?'

'First thing we did. Nothing to be seen up there at all. The place looked as if it had been swept clean. Last night's rain didn't help much either.'

'The toxicology analysis on the Piccadilly boy showed elements of Methadone, Benzedrine and quite a few other drug traces, by the way. But there's still been no positive identification of the body.' They fell silent as they passed beneath the bridge.

'I have a very bad feeling about this,' said Hargreave finally. 'It's as if we're seeing the tip of a submerged mass. I used to think I understood this city. Now it seems like the old criminal loyalties have been chucked away. Something else has taken their place.'

'What do you think that is?'

'I only wish I knew.' He had already decided upon a course of action. Starting tonight he would spend a few hours in the computer room. The system was already capable of duplicating logical thought processes and Hargreave had found a way to make it dream, or at least to produce logic-jumps that seemed to operate with dreamlike associations. By calling up certain key words and phrases, then following their cross-indices, he could use the computer to freewheel through a series of random thoughts and ideas. He had considered trying to explain the system to others, but had decided instead to wait until the right occasion presented itself. In this case he felt himself growing increasingly disturbed by the thought of what might eventually surface in his investigations.

Watching the lovely Miss Longbright striding purposefully out from the shadow of the overhead bridge like a post-war pin-up marching to prosperity, he turned his mind to more cheerful things.

CHAPTER TEN

Notes

Members of the Order who have been designated certain official duties are entitled to wear a plain black tunic emblazoned with a sash of coloured cord. Head-dresses representing Phoebus exist for ceremonial purposes, but are rarely, if ever, worn. Ceremonies, once necessary in maintaining discipline, but now occurring purely as observances of past traditions, take place beneath twin lamps which represent the Brightness of Diana and the Purity of Apollo. The order remained unchanged until the New Age.

Robert carefully replaced the handwritten page in the notebook as the tube train lurched beneath his feet on its way into Belsize Park station. As soon as the seat in front of him was vacated, he sat down and gingerly opened the slim volume once more. This was no manuscript, rather a collage of scrawled notes and clippings which seemed to constitute the factual preparation of a first draft. As the train pulled out toward Chalk Farm Robert began at the first page of the book, which was blank but for Charlotte Endsleigh's address and signature, neatly inscribed in soft pencil. There was no date or description of the contents within. On the next page stood a vertically printed list of names. It read:

MAIN STATIONS:
Holford

Lombardo
Jones
Winde
Wren
Barry
Bedford

He stared at the list for a minute, searching for some kind of connection, unaware of any such stations, rail or tube, existing in London. Turning the page over he found scribbled across the back in Charlotte Endsleigh's now familiar hand: 'Many other stations exist throughout the city, but these seem to be the busiest.' Increasingly curious, Robert riffled through the next half dozen pages only to find them completely filled with cryptic names and ciphers. Occasionally he came across a dated remark, as if it had been designated for later inclusion into a diary.

The sudden change in air pressure made him look up just in time to see the end of the platform at Chalk Farm station vanishing into darkness. He would have to change at Camden Town and head into the centre to alight at Leicester Square. Skinner would be wondering what on earth had happened to him. He watched his reflection in the blackness of the window opposite. Further along, a pair of twelve-year-old skinheads were painstakingly inscribing obscenities with a black felt-tip pen on the glass partition. A tramp dozed in the corner seat, his head lolling with the rhythm of the train. The hanging straps throughout the carriage jiggled as the train crossed a set of junction points and came to a halt just outside Camden station.

Robert took out a pencil and attempted to decode one of the ciphers, but its cryptic message irritated him into casting it aside. He looked down once more. Another page, the seventh. Here the pencilled notes became tight paragraphs of black ink, as if the subject matter had suddenly changed. Another list was arranged, this one reading;

HERMES
APOLLO
DIANA
MERCURY
VENUS
MARS
JUPITER
SATURN

Robert was puzzled. Why should three such deities head a list of planets? He felt as if he were examining random footnotes to a main topic, the subject matter of which eluded him entirely. The book contained half-explained scraps of information that were possibly mere ramblings, a faintly delineated map charting the journeys of an increasingly senile and disoriented mind. Perhaps it took a sharper brain than his to bridge the distance between points. He needed someone to help him unravel the puzzling information held within the pages, someone with whom he could treat it as a kind of wintry parlour game.

The carriage began to move once more. Above the ground, fresh cold winds had long dried the previous night's rain from the streets and set furls of cloud twisting above the grey concrete office buildings. Far below, the occupants of the rattling tube train sweated in the unhealthy warm airstreams of soot-encrusted tunnels.

Robert's daily routine allowed him to beat a path from North London to the West End and back with little likelihood of detour. He was aware that he would have to learn to drive eventually, would have to go out and force himself to make some friends. That was what people did, after all, form a framework of acquaintanceship, of declared and undeclared lovers and enemies, people to be bumped into and greeted with affection or disinterest or feigned delight. But the thought of forced conversations with strangers at parties made him feel tongue-tied and dimwitted.

Maybe Sarah Endsleigh felt the same way. Ashcroft, the agent, had suggested that she was a drop-out. She argued with her mother, probably through the latter's disapproval of her lifestyle. It appeared she had got in with the wrong crowd, as signified by the pair of thugs who hung around with her and by the strange photographs Rose had taken. . . . What was it about Sarah's picture that had briefly touched a chord of unease in his mind?

He turned over another page of the notebook and read on: 'Notes on Nathaniel Zalian'. The surname rang a bell. Underneath was written: 'Practising physician at Hampstead's Royal Free Hospital until 1980. Resignation requested after allegations of malpractice. Case settled out of court. Divorced 1981. Subsequently joined alcoholic rehabilitation programme. Vanished after selling Hampstead apartment and closing bank account in 1982.' Stapled to the page was a newspaper clipping from the *Hampstead & Highgate Express* bearing the headline: 'Missing drugs case: Hampstead doctor suspended.' At the bottom of the sheet Charlotte had scribbled: 'Zalian – Ideals that soured'.

The next page was filled with circular diagrams drawn carefully in mapping ink. Across the top ran the heading 'METONIC CYCLE' and beneath, written in red biro: 'Lunisolar Year For 1989'.

A frown crept across Robert's face. It was at this moment, just as the train arrived at Camden station, that a vaguely formed idea began to grow in his mind. Shoving the notebook back into its folder he jumped up from the seat and swung out between the opening doors onto the platform. Taking the escalator stairs two at a time, he headed for the filthy telephone booths in the bottle-strewn foyer of the station.

'Wait a minute, wait a minute, slow down a little, I can't understand a word you're saying. First of all, tell me what brings about this sudden change of heart?' Rose's voice was cool with suspicion.

'I'll explain when I get there. I want to show you what's in the notebook I picked up from Charlotte's apartment.'

'You showed me already.'

'No, I thought it was a draft of a novel. Now I think it's much more than that. Hang on a sec.' Robert rested the receiver on a stack of destroyed directories and turned to the tramp who was blowing a harmonica in his ear. 'Here's twenty pence. Please fuck off.'

'Gor, bless you, guv'nor,' said the tramp, jigging off to the next booth along. Robert turned back to the telephone. 'I can get back to your place in about twenty minutes.'

'I thought you had to be at work.'

'I'll call in sick.'

There was a sigh at the other end of the line. 'If you want coffee you'll have to make it yourself.'

'That's OK. You haven't lived until you've had my coffee.'

'Believe me, honey, I've lived.' The line cut off.

Robert replaced the receiver and headed back down the escalator toward the Hampstead line platform. If nothing else, it would be a chance for him to make amends.

Robert looked at his watch. 2.15. Before him, spread out on the floor of Rose's apartment, were over forty sheets of typed and handwritten paper which he had carefully removed from the plastic spiral of the notebook. Kneeling in the corner, swathed in her vast shapeless T-shirt, Rose looked patiently on. The smell of fresh coffee enveloped the lounge. Robert padded across the typed sheets in his socks and pointed out a particular page covered in type and pencilled diagrams. 'It was this that started me thinking,' he said, holding up the sheet so that Rose could read it. 'A metonic cycle. It's Greek, to do with the phases of the moon recurring on the same days of the year. I checked my diary and, sure enough, there was a full moon when you took those pictures.'

'Uh-huh.'

'What do you mean?'

'There was supposed to be a full moon, but it was cloudy. So?'

'So, I'm looking through Charlotte's notes for her new book and – did you ever read *The Newgate Legacy*?'

'It's next on my list after the new Jackie Collins.'

'The book is strongly based on the present day prison system. The facts are very thoroughly researched. The style is almost documentary. Which made me think that these are factual notes for a new novel. But what was this book going to be about, I hear you ask?'

'Amaze me.'

'The study of a special group of people. A group that carries out its operations in accordance with the phases of the moon. There's a list here. It's headed by the deities Hermes, the messenger, Apollo, who's associated with the sun, and Diana, the goddess of the moon. Then there's a list of planets. Looks like Charlotte catalogued a full lunar schedule for the appearances of these people. . . .'

' . . . And they're the ones her daughter is running around with. The people I saw on the roof.'

'What do you think? Who could have put her onto such a subject in the first place?' Robert rocked back on his heels and waved his hand across the spread-out sheets. 'Now we have our scenario. Let's assume that

Sarah tells her mother about these people. Charlotte is more than just interested, she decides that it's a great subject for a book. The daughter supplies her with information. Then something happens, we don't know what. Maybe Sarah gets into trouble for revealing secrets to an outsider. She gets scared, argues with Charlotte. Tells her to give up the idea before they both get in trouble. And the next thing you know, mother's dead and the daughter has vanished, possibly abducted.'

Rose looked around at the door, then at Robert. 'Are you the same guy who came in here a few hours back?'

'I say "abducted" because if you look carefully at your picture of Sarah . . .' Rose passed the photograph over to Robert, who tapped the face with his forefinger. 'You'll see that she's not laughing at all. Couldn't you describe that as a look of fear? Now, the notes are full of similarities with your story. Imagine that these people always operate from the rooftops. They run in packs, just like you saw. Listen to this:

> Although it seems that some kind of initiation ceremony is necessary before a member may be ordained, a surprising number attempt to join in the course of a season. Most of the activities in which Sarah has participated seem to be of a fairly harmless nature, carried out purely for thrills. Indeed, there seems to be a rigid moral code among them which is constantly enforced by the group's leader.

'And this:

> Today Sarah revealed what happens to those who fail to gain the status of membership. I fear they operate under no such moral compunction. There would seem to be an underbelly of . . .' [this bit's illegible] . . . which Sarah seems unable to expose. See 'New Age'.

I think we have enough information here to take to the police.' Robert gave Rose a smug grin and began gathering the papers together.

'Except that you're not going to take it to them.'

'Why not?'

'In the first place if you presented them with this "evidence" we'd either be arrested as accomplices, or laughed out of the station. Secondly, why not find Sarah yourself? You've got everything you need to do it right here.' She tapped the stack of sheets Robert had bundled into her hands. 'Then when you've done it, *you* can write the book.'

Robert's eyebrows rose to the top of his head. 'I think there are some risks involved here.'

'Like what?'

'Like getting pushed from the top of a tall building.'

'Hey, fame doesn't come cheap.'

'If what I've read so far is anything to go by,' Robert said, reaching for his coffee mug and draining it, 'somebody may have already died just for knowing too much.'

Rose ignored him and waved her hands expansively around the room. 'Well Robert, I thought I'd give you the chance to come with me. I think I may go up there for a second look.'

He could see in her eyes that she was serious, and had already made up her mind to do it with or without him. 'I don't know,' Robert rubbed his chin thoughtfully. 'If I did come with you, we should really get started as soon as possible.' He rose, crossed to the window and pulled the curtains apart. Overhead a pale sun cast wan light across the bristling hedgerows. 'There may be a perfectly simple and rational explanation for what you saw. But if there's really some kind of cult in force above our heads, then there's no telling what they'll do to Sarah.'

Together they gazed out of the window, into the

misty coronae surrounding an already-risen moon in the darkening winter sky.

'I have a few questions for you, Robert.'

'Fire away.' They were striding down the quiet Hampstead back street side by side. A brief rainfall earlier had left a smell of fresh greenery in the air. The reassembled notebook was wedged firmly under Robert's arm. Chin up, he strode ahead whistling in a cheerful, tuneless fashion. His narrow eyes seemed to hold a soft, almost luminous glow. It was now nine o'clock in the evening. He had spent the rest of the afternoon with Rose, having first called the office and lied through his teeth to a disgruntled Skinner about suffering from a sudden throat infection. It was strange, but he felt comfortable with Rose. She seemed capable of adapting her energy and enthusiasm in any direction which seemed to her like a good idea at the time. Over a meal in the local Indian restaurant she questioned Robert about his work, his home life, his likes and his dislikes. She seemed to have an answer for everything, or if not, a question.

Robert, on the other hand, found it difficult to give an adequate account of himself simply because he was not used to being called upon to do so. Afternoon had slipped into evening and with it came a plan of action provided, appropriately enough, by Charlotte Endsleigh's notebook.

Rose, meanwhile, had changed into a navy blue sweater of indeterminate style and size and was ready for whatever the evening held in store. Her questioning remained indefatigable, but Robert was quickly learning how to deal with it.

'Where are we going first?'

'Tell you in a minute.'

'OK, here's a thought. If this gang is so rigidly moral and harmless – as Charlotte points out in her notes –

why would they murder an old lady just for jotting down their activities in a book?'

'Don't know yet. Next question.' They paused together at a zebra crossing.

'If they didn't get on with each other, why would Sarah confide in her mother in the first place?'

'Perhaps she felt she had to tell someone. She might have been in trouble. Then again, she might not have told Charlotte very much at all. The old lady was quite capable of making a few phone calls and finding out for herself.'

'How come this "burglar" didn't steal her notes, or destroy them?'

'Maybe he didn't know they existed. Or perhaps he couldn't find them. The envelope containing the notebook had dropped under a table. My guess is that it fell from one of the boxes that Charlotte's thieving relative was carrying out of the apartment.'

'Shouldn't we keep studying the notes before charging off like this?'

'Yes, we should, but there isn't time.'

'Suddenly we're in that much of a hurry?'

'Like I said, if these people *have* abducted Sarah Endsleigh in order to keep her mouth closed, they may already have decided to close it forever. Weird cult, full moons, sacrificial rites, who knows? You want to play detective, you're going to have to figure this stuff out for yourself.'

Rose slowed up for a second and watched Robert stride ahead. In his scuffed sneakers and scruffy jean jacket, with his long neck, unruly hair and soapdish-sized ears, he looked more than a little demented. 'Robert.' He halted in his tracks and looked back over his shoulder.

'Hmmm?'

'There's no history of madness in your family, is there?'

'No. Why?'

'Just that you seemed so different this morning. Scared of your shadow. A real wimp.'

'Thanks for the vote of confidence. I still *am* a wimp.'

Rose shot a glance at the undernourished body striding ahead of her. He seemed to move in an awkward swagger of bravado, as if anxious to impress upon her the fact that he knew exactly what he was doing. Which he obviously didn't. She smiled to herself.

'I guess you are.'

'So I'm relying on you to protect me if we get into trouble.'

They rounded the corner of the street and headed into the wind, falling silently in step as they set off on a journey which would take them further than they had ever intended to go.

CHAPTER ELEVEN

The Swan

Samuel felt terrible. For the past hour, cramps had been cutting through his intestines like white-hot wires. He clutched his stomach and sat down on the ledge overlooking the terminus platforms once more, waiting for the wave of nausea to subside. He was a large man who moved awkwardly, as if he was somehow ashamed of his size. He knew that his strength had been useful to Chymes. Now he wondered if he had outlived that usefulness. Below, the railway lines leading from Cannon Street station snaked out across the river, sweeping around to the left, where Southwark cathedral lay blackened and neglected within a noose of tracks. The sun had set behind an unbroken bank of heavy grey cloud, as if the effort of providing a little watery winter light had finally proven too much for it.

Despite the falling temperature and the fact that he was only wearing a thin cotton T-shirt, rivulets of sweat ran down Samuel's back and arms. For the first time in days his mind was unclouded by drugs. Now the mist was dissipating from his memory and he was free to face the terrible consequences of his actions. He had been a party to murder on two occasions. Yesterday he had participated in the death of someone whom he had once considered to be a friend. By the absence of his disapproval and his lack of ability to influence the horror taking place around him, he had implicitly condoned the atrocities committed on those he had once thought of as allies against a corrupt world. But this time something, some subconscious desire to reawaken himself, had made him refuse to take part in the nightly ritual of drug-taking. Earlier in the evening he had watched while the others shot themselves up into a conscience-numbing limbo and, as their minds submerged, his own had slowly returned and he had begun to recall events in the sharpest detail.

Later he had spoken up, had demanded an audience with Chymes himself. He was beginning to realize now that this had been a grave mistake, for how could he explain the burden of his guilt to a man who had no use for the very concept? Chymes had walked with him across the grey L-shaped section of the station roof, his arm around the waist of the shavenheaded giant like a teacher reassuring his favourite pupil. He suggested that if the latter felt so strongly about performing certain actions which would herald the start of the New Age, then perhaps he really should consider returning to the Insects below. Samuel immediately sensed the danger in agreeing to this. He had seen what had happened to others who had expressed a desire to leave the order and Chymes knew that he had seen.

Another wave of pain enclosed his gut like the tightening of a hot metal band. He leaned forward, dropping one hand to the ledge, and retched. To his horror, dark blood poured from his contracting throat onto the tracks far below. He had eaten nothing today, had only drunk a single can of beer with Chymes. Could his agony be put down simply to his body's withdrawal from poisonous chemicals? Perhaps it had caused an ulcer, or torn vital blood vessels. For a brief moment, the turmoil inside him subsided.

From behind him sounded the tread of heavy boots. Wiping his chin with the back of his hand, he turned to see Chymes approaching from the shadowed concrete canyon formed by the rear of the roof and the adjoining offices. As he stepped out into the centre of the station canopy there was a new sound – the slow, rhythmic wingbeat of a large bird. Grimacing, Samuel looked up in time to see a huge swan of almost ghostly whiteness swoop over the head of his master and land heavily on the rooftop before him. Uncoiling its long neck, it hissed and grunted like an old man snoring in his sleep.

'Why, Brother Samuel, I thought you would have returned to the earth by now,' said Chymes, his voice a stentorian bass.

Samuel did not care for his choice of words, but was in too much pain to say so. He breathed uneasily, his lungs labouring as they began to secrete blood. 'What have you done to me?' he managed to gasp, the wave of pain slowly building once again in the pit of his stomach.

'I am afraid that it's what you have done to yourself, Brother.' Chymes drew closer, towering above the wheezing man who could now barely manage to sit upright. His long, sallow face was framed by a mass of black hair, greasily pomaded behind his ears in a style which gave him the appearance of a Victorian dandy. He reached forward with his metal hand, the polished steel fingers uncurling in a gesture of supplication. 'You must realize that you have only yourself to blame for this turn of events, brother.'

'You put something in the drink, didn't you. You opened . . . the beer and . . . passed it to me, you fucker.' He broke off, racked with a spasm of coughing which filled his mouth once more with the hot, metallic taste of his own blood. He spat the liquid in Chymes' direction, but it fell far short.

'It occurred to me,' said Chymes, airily now, as if Samuel was sitting before him in the peak of health, 'that returning you to the Insects would gain us nothing. And after all I've done to improve your lot in life, it hardly seemed fair that you should leave us without performing some useful act in return.'

Samuel was barely listening. He began to cry when he looked down and saw the blood pooling heavily in the base of his trousers, only to release itself in a widening puddle around his useless legs. It was as if his body had suddenly become porous, springing leaks from every orifice. He wiped his eyes and was shocked to see when he lowered his hands that they were now streaked crimson.

'I then realized that your life could be made useful through the release of your blood, for just as the pelican allowed her offspring to gorge on the blood from her own breast, so your most precious body fluid could continue to nourish and increase our strength. I'm sure even you will appreciate that we are going to need all the strength we can possibly get.'

The swan waddled over and lowered itself into the considerable pool of gore which now surrounded Samuel. Unconcerned, it turned its head away from the dying giant and buried a long yellow beak in its feathers. As it settled into the pool, the underside of its body slowly stained a bloody vermilion.

'What . . . have you done to me?' was all that Samuel managed to gasp before toppling onto his side. His legs began to thrash as his nervous system ceased to follow rational instruction.

'It's nothing compared to what we're going to do, sunshine. . . .'

The two skinheads who invariably accompanied Chymes appeared on either side of him. They were armed with thin-bladed steel knives. Chymes leaned over Samuel's shaking body, his eyes glittering blackly as they reflected in the crimson pool below. 'I saw betrayal in your eyes long ago, Brother Samuel. But now I am sure that you will pledge me your unending loyalty one final time, even as you die.'

Samuel was helpless. His limbs refused to obey all but the violent flinching of his nerves. As the turmoil inside his arteries increased he knew that he would remain alive through whatever torture they had planned for him. In desperation he forced his mouth wide and spoke in a hissing exhalation. 'You . . . are . . . mad. . . .' were his final words.

'And you are dead,' said Chymes, as the skinheads closed in around Samuel's heaving body. Raising its noble head, the swan watched impassively on.

CHAPTER TWELVE

Contact

Although the rainclouds had now fled the city, there were no stars to be seen above Leicester Square. But then there never were. The spotlit streets and flickering neon signs of record stores, night clubs, cinemas and burger bars cast a sickly luminosity into the sky which forced such natural phenomena to take second place to earthly pleasures. The litter-strewn pedestrianized roadways were filled with noisy crowds. Even this far into the winter, coaches were depositing crocodiles of bemused theatre-bound tourists at one end of the square. Over by the Empire Ballroom buskers entertained, urging their audiences to press forward and so form a human wall against the suspicious eyes of passing police. The raucous combination of amplified music, drunken shouts and snatches of song drove the few remaining birds further into the tops of the trees, to add their shrill voices to the cacophony below.

Robert and Rose guided themselves through the crowds moving across the top of the square. On the corner up ahead stood a large brightly lit amusement arcade filled with bleating video machines.

'I think we have to see someone here,' said Robert, looking somewhat uncertain. 'One of Sarah's friends. He gets a mention on several of the pages in the notebook.'

'I'd feel a lot happier if you'd let me read that thing through with you,' called Rose, pushing through the oncoming tourists like a breaker splitting pack ice. 'What if this "friend" isn't here?'

'I don't know. It says he can always be found at the arcade. We should really find a Xerox machine and take a copy of this.'

'Why?'

'It's our bargaining power.'

They passed through tall glass doors into a building hung with dirty purple drapes and costume-jewellery chandeliers, a travesty of a casino. The few people who weren't hammering the sides of one-armed bandits and space war machines were standing around carefully watching events in a manner which suggested that they were either beyond the law or employed by it. Empty milk-shake cups and beer cans littered the floor. There was a stale, unwashed smell in the air.

'You don't even know what this guy looks like.'

'You start reading, I'm going to do a three-sixty.' Robert shoved the notebook into Rose's hands. She backed against a dustdraped wall to read, while Robert walked casually around the games room. The large sweating man in the perspex change booth in the corner looked like everyone's idea of a child molester. He paused in his money counting, slowly sliding the match in his mouth from one side to the other as Robert passed.

'Excuse me.' Robert knocked warily on the window of the booth. 'I'm looking for a guy who hangs around here every night. Short and fat, name of Mickey, or Michael. Would you know him, or know where I could find him?'

The child molester peered out at Robert from hooded eyes. This close up, he appeared to have engine grease in the lines of his jowled face. 'I don' know nobody aroun' here.'

'Is there anyone who does?'

‘Ask ’im. The skinny guy.’ The molester stubbed his finger against the booth wall.

‘Thank you.’

Across the room, a beanpole-thin punk with waxy olive skin was concentrating on trying to steer a starbike between two planets. His black corduroy trousers were so tight that his kneecaps were discernible through them. Tied around his left thigh was a red bandana, which presumably signified something to his friends – or his enemies. He looked like the sort of kid who carried a knife and wore a long-sleeved T-shirt to cover the track marks. Robert decided not to disturb him until his game was over. He was not very adept at making conversation with dangerous strangers, particularly in a place like this, where it could look as if he was someone who solicited waifs in arcades and put them into social work in the hotels surrounding Piccadilly. The machine next to him emitted a series of deafening electronic explosions. Finally the boy’s game ended in a shower of threats as he rained several blows upon the machine and shouted at it in what sounded like Turkish. As he became aware that someone was watching him, he slowly turned and raked his eyes over Robert.

‘You want somethin’, mate?’ His words had the clipped roundness of a cockney Cypriot. Robert stepped nervously forward and tried to look as nonchalant as possible.

‘I’m looking for a guy who hangs out around here in the evenings. His name’s Mickey. Short, fat. . . .’ Already, the skinny boy was shaking his head. ‘Nah, don’t know anyone called Mickey.’

‘His friends used to call him the Toad,’ said Rose, appearing by the side of Robert. ‘That’s what it says in here.’ She turned to him and touched the notebook. The skinny punk’s face suddenly lit up. ‘Oh, the *Toad*,’ he said, grinning. ‘He’s the only one who can beat me on this machine, the bastard. Yeah, everybody knows him.' He slapped the top of the machine hard with his open palm. 'He ain't been around for a couple of days.'

'That's too bad. We really needed to speak to him. It's very important.'

'Lissen, you see that guy over there?' Robert and Rose looked back across the seething arcade and nodded.

'That's Nick from the 7N Krewe, y'know? Nick's 'is mate. Go and talk to 'im.'

Robert thanked the Turkish boy, who had already turned back to his machine, and headed across the arcade with Rose.

'I don't know about you,' she said, 'but I'm starting to feel an age gap between me and the kind of guys who hang about on the streets these days.'

'How do you think I feel?' said Robert. 'I came from the kind of suburb where the only time you ever saw ethnic kids was when you visited a fun fair. Then I came to London and moved into a flatshare with a deranged West Indian cab driver, a Chinese student who never said a word to anyone in two years and a white rastafarian with dreadlocks and a major identity problem.'

'So you shouldn't have too much to worry about now.'

'Come on, these guys know I'm an outsider. It's in everything I do. I wear my lack of street credibility like a badge.'

Standing peering out of the glass corner wall onto the street was the boy who had been identified as Nick from the 7N Krewe. Robert assumed, quite rightly, that the affiliation had something to do with spray-painting slogans on buildings.

'Hi, Nick, have you seen the Toad?' called Robert, realizing instantly that the familiarity was a mistake.

'Who the fuck are you?' Nick turned to face Robert. He sported a leather jacket covered in swirling painted designs from the sixties, a spiderweb tattoo over one eye and some do-it-yourself hair colouring which badly needed a touch-up.

'I'm just a friend. Do you know where he is?'

'You're not a friend. The Toad doesn't know anyone who's going bald. Did 'e tell you to come over 'ere?' He pointed in the direction of the Turkish punk.

'Yes.'

'You got any money on you?'

'Er, a bit.' Robert rummaged about in his back pockets.

'Give us some then.'

Reluctantly, Robert looked in his hand and emptied some coins into Nick's outstretched palm.

'I haven't seen him for two days,' said Nick, suddenly friendlier. 'I'm a bit pissed off, 'cause 'e owes me money.'

'Do you think he's gone up tonight?'

It was a phrase which seemed to recur in Charlotte's notes. Robert figured he had nothing to lose by throwing it into the conversation. Nick stared hard at him for several long seconds. At his side, Rose tensed. Finally Nick relaxed his gaze.

'I was wonderin' about that, but 'e told me 'e was havin' nothin' more to do with them. I said to 'im, you're not like them lot. They don' like anyone except each other. All fuckin' stuck up. Think nobody else is as good as them.'

'Nick I know you don't know me. I'm not a cop . . .'

'That's fuckin' obvious. Yer too short for a start.'

' . . . But it's really important that I get to talk to him or another of the roof people tonight.' At this mention, Nick's already cool gaze suddenly iced over.

'Hey, you don't say that around 'ere. Not with what's going on. An' the Toad's not with 'em any more, he's got nothin' to do with it, you got that straight?'

'Yes, I understand. But the Toad is a friend of someone we urgently need to get in touch with. A girl called Sarah. Have you got the photograph, Rose?'

'Here.' Rose passed over the snapshot she had taken on the roof. Nick looked at it for just a moment before nodding and handing it back.

'Yeah, I seen 'er around, before she went up. Real trouble, that one.' Nick spoke with nervous speed, his eyes flitting past them to the tall doors beyond, as if he was expecting someone to come bursting in at any moment. Beneath the red and blue striplights of the arcade his skin shone with sweat.

'Is there some way we can get in touch with her? Is there some kind of headquarters for this . . .' Robert was cut short as Nick shoved him hard in the chest.

'Shut up, man, shut up! You wanna get me excoriated?' Nick made as if to push his way out through the glass doors, but Robert held him back. Behind the perspex of his change booth, the child molester stopped counting out coins and looked over.

'No one's going to hurt you and I don't care who Sarah's hanging out with. I just need to see her, or anyone else who can tell me where she is, OK?' Robert pulled two ten-pound notes from his wallet and showed them to Nick. The fear which had earlier flickered in Nick's eyes was replaced by greed.

'OK, man, this is what you do. Go down to the park by the embankment, the one at the bottom of Villiers Street, where the Player's Theatre used to be. You know that?'

'Sure.'

'You be there by the bandstand tomorrow night an' there should be someone who can help you.'

'Who, Nick?' Robert held the notes against Nick's jacket. He could feel the boy's heart pounding through it.

'His name's Simon. He dresses really weird, you can't miss 'im.'

'And when's the best time to catch this Simon?'

'Between eight and nine. 'E's always there by then.'

'You've got a deal.'

'But listen, lately people 'ave bin gettin' cut out. I can't vouch for whatever 'appens to you. It's nothin' to do with me if you don't come back in a single piece.' Nick held out his hand to take the money.

'Have it your way.' Robert tore the bills down the middle and handed him half. Nick's face fell.

'You get the rest later – *when* I return in one piece.'

Before he could reply, Robert had grabbed Rose's hand and ushered her through the arcade doorway back into the churning sea of pedestrians. He looked back to see Nick watching them leave with a look of puzzlement on his face.

'See?' said Robert, high on the success of his first positive action. 'It's just a matter of asking the right questions.'

'Yes, all right, you're a big macho stud,' grumbled Rose. 'It seemed too easy to me. You think he knows what he's talking about, or was he just saying anything to get money out of you? I mean, he's probably an expert at spotting a complete mug.'

Robert gave her a careful look. They left Leicester Square and darted between the stalled traffic in Charing Cross Road, Robert steering Rose between the hooting cars, pleased with himself. He had set up a deal with a punk in an arcade. This was street credibility in the making.

'Are you kidding me?' he called to Rose. 'He knew what he was talking about, all right. "Excoriated"? How does a sixteen-year-old badly spoken street kid come up with an obscure Latin word meaning "To flay"?'

'Maybe he's going to night school. I wonder what sort of crew he belongs to. Wrecking crew? Rowing crew? Or a krewe with a "k"?'

'What's a krewe with a "k"?'

'Oh, you know.' Rose waved her hands airily. 'Mardi Gras.'

'No, I don't know.' Robert was irritated. Rose always seemed to assume that you understood what she was talking about.

'Krewes are the orders who organize Mardi Gras for Comus, the Roman god of festivities. They're very old and very secret. And they've all got different names, like Iris and Osiris and the Caliphs of Cairo. It's to celebrate the day before the start of Lent. The day the devil walks the earth.'

Robert stopped dead and stared back at Rose. 'Where on earth do you get your information, for Chrissakes?'

'I'll tell you all about it some time.'

'Why not now? I don't know what more we can do tonight. You wanna go for a drink?'

'Sure. I can look over the notes.'

'I was going to tell you my life story, too.'

'Oh yeah?' said Rose, pushing open the door of the *Three Tuns Inn*, 'I think I can guess your life story.'

'In that case, can you tell me how it ends?'

'If you want to know that, I think you'd better ask me again in a couple of days.'

Chuckling uneasily, Robert let the door close behind him. He couldn't help feeling that Rose liked him better when he wasn't trying so hard to impress. He made his way through the crowded saloon towards the bar. Behind his back, peering steadily through the mock leadlight windows, sickly pale eyes watched his every move.

CHAPTER THIRTEEN

St Katherine's Dock

On the horizon of the rooftop she stood alone like a dark goddess, her shining legs spread wide apart, her jaw jutting defiantly at him across the intervening water. Her blackish-purple hair lifted and fell like burnt grass in the wind. She wore a tight-fitting suit made of black leather. Strips were cut away below her breasts and at either side of her crotch, either to ease her movement, or for some more erotic purpose. Tall patent-leather heels raised her to a statuesque pose, at once both defiant and inviting. Slowly she raised a gloved hand and beckoned to him.

'Sarah!'

Nathaniel Zalian took a step forward towards the edge of the roof. There was no mistaking that it was her – and yet how could it be? Had she managed to make good her escape from Chymes? He pulled the walkie-talkie out of his jacket and snapped it on. 'Zalian to Lombardo, come in.'

On the opposite building, Sarah Endsleigh continued to stand and wait, her eyes fixed on him, her pelvis thrust forward in unmistakable invitation. Zalian could just make out a smile on her broad, pale face.

'Nathaniel, where the hell are you? You've had your receiver turned off. We've been trying to find you ever since it got dark.'

'I'm in St Katherine's Dock.'

'That's no man's land. What are you doing there? Who else is in your group?'

'No one. I'm by myself.'

'Christ, Nat, you know that you're not supposed to travel alone any more.' Many of his men felt that Zalian was clearly starting to lose his grip as a leader. On a number of occasions in the past few days, his indecisiveness had nearly caused several of his own men to be killed. 'You're in no condition to look after yourself right now. What would happen if you ran into Chymes, or some of his men?'

'I got a call from Sarah. I can see her right now. She's standing in front of me.'

'Sarah? That's not possible. You know as well as I do . . .'

'She's here. It's her.'

'But we know that she's been captured. It's a trap, it has to be. Nat, you'd better get out of there while you still have a . . .'

Zalian snapped off the power switch and returned the walkie-talkie to his pocket. He looked back up at the leather-clad figure, his ice-blue eyes narrowing. In the distance, Sarah shifted her weight from one foot to the other and slid her gloved hands slowly inwards to the top of her thighs. Zalian was mesmerized. Suddenly she spun on her heel and walked away, striding over the angled roof in the direction of the city marina's main body of water.

Zalian unclipped the line-gun which was strapped to the top of his thigh, aimed it at the wall of the opposite building and carefully squeezed the trigger. With a sharp snap of steel the line connected and the cable pulled taut. He clipped himself on and swung out over the buildings in a single highly-practised movement, travelling far above the motionless yachts docked neatly along one side of the marina. The fire-engine-red paintwork of a lightship flashed by beneath his feet as he approached the broad sloping roof of the renovated warehouse which now lay directly ahead of him.

Sarah had vanished over the peak of the roof by the time he landed. Unclipping the line from his belt, he nimbly ran across the sheets of grey metal to the summit of the warehouse. From the corner of his eye he could see a security patrolman walking his Alsation around the corner of the naval museum which lay to one side of the marina. He slid quietly across the peak and moved unsteadily down the other side of the roof. Ahead at the far edge, Sarah stood with her back to him. He rose then and ran to her, seizing her shoulders and roughly pulling her around to face him.

Sarah kept her eyes lowered and stared at his broad chest, her hair falling forward. Her black-painted lips parted suddenly, glistening in the hard darkness of the winter night. He fell on her with a gasp, crushing her leather-cased body against his chest, sliding his hands around to the top of her buttocks as he searched for her open mouth with his. As his lips pressed over hers he raised his hands to touch her hair, but she gently moved his arms down. He closed his eyes gratefully and felt his sense of balance shift as she leaned into him, the warmth of her body radiating to his skin through creaking leather.

'Sarah, you made it back. I always knew you would. . . .'

Equilibrium shifted again as she pushed harder into him with her pelvis, then suddenly he was losing his balance as he opened his eyes to find himself falling towards the edge of the roof and the distant ground. He reached for her hair once more, the purple-black wig slipping off in his hands to reveal a shaved head as he saw now that the girl before him was nothing like Sarah, a painted doll in pantomine make-up designed to recall the face of the woman he loved. She threw her hands around his back and pushed hard, sending him to his knees and then onto his side as he rolled to the guttering and lodged there. Zalian looked up. The shavenheaded girl withdrew a hypodermic syringe from her breast pocket and uncapped it, spraying a thin jet of liquid crystal into the air as she advanced.

'A man in love is an easy target, Zalian,' she said, stepping forward and leaning over him. Behind her, three other figures appeared on the crest of the roof. Could they be his own men, or did they belong to Chymes? He couldn't see. There was a metallic crack as the guttering started to bend beneath his weight. Below, he could hear running footsteps, followed by the barking of the security patrolman's Alsatian.

'Get away from him, or you're dead meat.'

The voice belonged to Lee, one of Zalian's finest men. Zalian clung to the gutter as it slowly sagged. His body was too long and heavy for its weight to be sustained for much longer. The girl rose and turned, tossing aside the syringe and withdrawing her razor-gun. She fired at the approaching men. Suddenly Lee threw himself forward and brought her down with a crash, headbutting her in the stomach as the two of them landed flat on the roof and rolled toward the edge.

Other figures approached and in the next moment strong hands were lifting Zalian to safety, pulling him away from the fighting couple.

'Don't hurt her – we'll take her with us,' someone shouted as Lee flipped the girl over onto her back and stripped off her gloves, tying a length of cable around her crossed wrists.

'Let's get out of here quick,' warned Lee. 'The place is crawling with security.'

As soon as she recovered her breath the girl tried to scream, but was prevented by Lee. Supported on either side, Zalian was led away to the far end of the warehouse roof. Behind, Lee pulled his captive along by the cable linking her hands.

'Stay with us, lady,' he grinned into her sullen face. 'You're going to lead us to Chymes.'

The group prepared to disembark in the direction of the Tower Hotel, an ugly stack of brown boxes standing along the north side of Tower Bridge. Zalian seemed dazed and unable to talk as the other two helped him into his line-belt. For the first time, even he had begun to realize how much his actions were leading the others into danger. Lee was clipping a similar belt around the girl's leather-clad waist when there was a distant burst of air and the sound of something heavy thudded against her back. She fell forward, her eyes wide in shock, a small gasp escaping from her lips. The tip of a rusty iron spear, a makeshift weapon from part of a broken weathervane, protruded from between her shoulder blades. Lee let the body fall to the roof, waving to the others with the flat of his hand in a gesture which told them to keep low.

'I guess someone doesn't want us questioning the opposition,' he said, turning to Zalian's supporters. 'Might as well leave her here. She's no good to us now.' He stepped over the lifeless girl and attached his own line-belt. If he felt any emotion at all he failed to show it.

'Let's see if we can get back without attracting any more attention. You were bloody lucky we had some men in the area, Nat.' Lee wondered how on earth the former leader of the Roofworld could ever have fallen for such an obvious ploy. Apparently, things were worse than even he had realized.

The group headed away from the marina amid a confusion of barking and bellowed orders from below as the marina's guards ran first in one direction, then another. On top of the warehouse the leather-clad limbs of Chymes' dupe lay sprawled in death, her purple-black wig rolling across the roof like nylon tumbleweed.

CHAPTER FOURTEEN

Assailant

'OK, give me the book.' Rose waggled her fingers at Robert until he passed the small blue exercise book across to her. She opened it at a page she had noticed Robert studying earlier on in the day and began to read. The saloon bar of the *Three Tuns* was crowded for a Tuesday evening. Cigarette smoke hung heavily in the air above the ticket touts who stood at the narrow bar deafening each other with conversation. Robert slid a whisky and soda across the small circular table to Rose and sat down beside her as she read.

'This list headed "Main Stations" . . .'

'I have no idea about those.' Robert shrugged and took a swig of his pint. 'They're certainly not railway or coach stations.'

'You're right, they're not. No, the names are the easy part.'

'You mean you see a connection?'

'Well, of course. Holford, Lombardo, Wren, they're all architects.'

'What?'

'The stations, they're named after architects. Barry designed the Houses of Parliament. Christopher Wren, everyone knows about. Jones, we can assume is Inigo. Winde built Buckingham House . . .'

'Wait a minute, I thought that Nash built . . .'

'No, Nash designed Buckingham *Palace*. He replaced Winde's building in the early 1800s.'

'What are you, some kind of trivia mastermind?' asked Robert, dumbfounded. Rose ignored him. 'The odd one out is Lombardo. He was Venetian. Presumably the names give a clue to the actual location of the stations.'

'Perhaps they're not geographical locations. They could be like stations of the cross or something.'

'Don't complicate things by bringing religion into it, Robert. Think. Venetian. Water. "Lombardo" station could be by the river. . . .'

'Or Islington Canal. Or Little Venice. It still doesn't get us anywhere. Your health.' Robert drank a toast to her and replaced his glass. 'How come you know your architects so well?'

'It's not just architecture, it's everything. All the fault of my parents.'

'Your parents?'

'Warren and Shirley.'

'Come on, those can't be their real names.' Robert sat back on his stool and snorted derisively.

'They can and are. Second generation West Indian. The kind of names you expect to hear in old sitcoms, very white. Just like my parents were trying to be. White was a popular status to attain back then. They're living apart now. I don't see them any more.' Rose paused to take a slug of her whisky.

'Why, what happened?'

'Oh, it goes back a long way. They christened me Rose Hildegarde Leonard, which shows you how much my mother must have hated having stretchmarks. I went to a lot of schools. Each time I got settled, Dad decided it was time to move on, so we followed the work around until he decided to throw in the towel nerves-wise and have his breakdown here in London.'

'And you stayed here.'

'Yeah, but by that time I'd been streamed with the deadbeats and dim kids in school. I spent my days watching a twenty-one-year-old relief teacher trying to explain the intricacies of the Tudor monarchy to a bunch of no-hopers whose sole interests were heavy metal and streetfighting. As for me, I just wanted to understand the bloody Tudors.'

'Did you eventually get to figure them out?' asked Robert. 'I don't think I ever really cracked history.'

'I did, but not until I left school. While my girlfriends spent their evenings in the backs of vans learning how to fit condoms I came home each night and went straight to bed with the Tudors. Then it was the turn of the Victorians. Then Cromwell. The Industrial Revolution. The Tolpuddle Martyrs. And after history a little art, then English novels. Architecture. Economics. Mythology. I have a virtually perfect photographic memory and I'm a walking bloody encyclopedia on the dissolution of the monasteries, but could I get a decent job?'

She sighed and stared down into the remains of her drink. 'Believe me, there's not a great demand for supermarket checkout girls with a working knowledge of British constitutional history. So I became a superintendent up at Misery Mansions. Moved in with a guy who told me that he wanted to be the father of my children. Turned out that, owing to a slight inaccuracy in semantics, what he really meant was that he wouldn't be too concerned if I got pregnant. I still miss him on cold nights. And at least by staying on as caretaker I don't have to worry about paying the rent.' She raised her eyes to meet his. 'Now what about you?'

'Me? Oh, there's nothing much to tell.' Robert shifted uncomfortably in his seat. 'I started out as a journalist.'

'So you know how to hold your alcohol.'

'Well, it wasn't really journalism. I worked for a fantasy film magazine.'

'Don't tell me, while other writers were out interviewing Madonna at the Ritz you were covering comic conventions filled with weird kids in anoraks.'

'That was pretty much it. We had a small, dedicated and deeply disturbed following, the kind of readers who spent their spare time buying horror movie stills of girls with their faces ripped off.' Robert traced a finger through the spilt beer on the table. 'And the pay was rotten, so I left and found work in a film production company. That was three years ago and I'm still there on the same pay.'

'Are your parents still around?'

'Like yours. They split the photo albums a couple of years back. Pa went off to live on a Kent commuter estate with an Estée Lauder sales representative and my mother decided to investigate the wide world of alcohol for a while. Dad came back when my sister got knocked up and for a brief period we were a regular suburban family, heavily into noncommunication. Now I just go home at Christmas. We sit around and talk about decorating.'

'Sounds familiar.'

'When you spend time with people who don't care much about anything it starts to rub off on you.' Robert looked at his watch.

'You keep doing that. Are you rushing off anywhere?'

'That's a laugh. My life is nowhere right now. If there's one thing I have plenty of, it's time.'

'If you want my advice, you shouldn't feel so sorry for yourself,' said Rose sharply. In the uneasy silence that followed, she picked up the notebook once more and opened it. Robert could see that she felt guilty about speaking out and tried to repair the damage. He leaned forward and tapped a page of the notebook.

'Anything else in there catch your eagle eye then?'

'The lunar cycle chart is interesting, although it raises as many questions as it answers. And this is very odd.' Rose held the book closer to her face and read aloud.

' "The moon has two sides, that which basks in the reflection of earth's light and the side which is shunned, forever turning from view. How easy it will be for the dark to swallow light." Do you think they could be a bunch of mystics? Satanists, stuff like that?'

'With any luck we'll find out tomorrow,' said Robert, rising and draining his glass. 'Listen, if I get to write this book, can I dedicate it to you?'

'I'd be very flattered.' Rose cocked an eyebrow and smiled. 'Let's hope we don't find out so much that it winds up getting published posthumously. Can I borrow this tonight?' She held up the notebook.

'Sure,' said Robert. 'I have to go into work in the morning, but I'll call you. Come on, I'll walk you to the station.'

Together they rose and left the pub. Outside, the streets were still crowded as the cinemas and theatres discharged their audiences.

'I'll go from Leicester Square,' called Rose, divorcing herself from a gang of drunken secretaries who were just leaving a wine bar. On the corner of the square a Salvation Army band were gamely leading an unsteady crowd in a rendition of 'God rest ye merry, gentlemen'. Rose turned into a side alley which connected the square to Charing Cross Road. Behind, Robert fought to keep pace with her. The alleyway stank of urine and stale hamburgers as he followed the tic-tac of Rose's shoes into darkness.

'Couldn't we just have stayed on the main road?' he asked.

'Quicker this way.'

Rose was a black shape between the high walls, the flat-top of her haircut standing in relief against the lamplight ahead at the end of the alley. Suddenly there was a rush of wind and a thump, as if a heavy object had just flown over Robert's head into the shadows beyond. Seconds later, a shape appeared by Rose's side.

Robert could make out the unmistakable form of a man. Rose screamed as the figure dropped over her. There was a scuffling sound and a dustbin lid clattered against the far wall of the alley.

Robert ran ahead and blundered over a kneeling form. He tried to grab at Rose's attacker and received a brutal kick in the stomach. Falling back against the wall he watched helplessly as the assailant turned once more to Rose. There was a sudden hissing sound and the air was filled with an acrid smell of pear-drops. Shouting in pain, the figure loped off to the end of the alley and vanished around the corner. Robert tried to part his stinging eyelids, but was unable to make out anything beyond a blurred outline. He tried to catch his breath.

'Rose, are you all right?'

'I think so. Are you?' She rose from the ground with a grunt and started to dust herself down.

'Yeah. What on earth did you do to him?'

'I finally got to use my trusty can of Mace is what I did,' she said, coughing. 'Whoever he was, he won't be able to see straight for the next few hours.'

Robert felt for Rose's arm and steered her from the alleyway into the brightly lit street ahead.

'Did he manage to get anything from you?' he asked, wiping his watering eyes with a paper handkerchief. 'Where's your purse?'

'He wasn't after my purse, Robert.' She slipped her hand into her jacket and withdrew a fistful of torn pages from her inside pocket. 'He was after the book.'

CHAPTER FIFTEEN

Awake

She awoke and looked down.

This had indeed been no dream. She was bound hand and foot with rough nylon cord. She knew that she would be executed soon, at the dawning of the New Age, and that she would not be alone when she died. Six hundred and twenty feet above London she hung, her scarlet-black hair whipping across her tear-streaked face. She still wore a jacket, shirt and jeans, but somehow must have kicked off her shoes in the struggle earlier. How long had she been up here? Recent events had blurred together in her memory. Someone had come to feed her yesterday, or had that been the day before? She felt no cold now. She had been given drugs to counteract her pain, she was sure of that. There could surely be no hope of rescue. Darkness had fallen, but on either side of her lights buzzed, tall and yellow. Pigeons warbled beneath her bare feet, scrabbling for sheltered perches beyond the reach of the wailing wind.

Further below, she could hear the irate horns of snarled traffic. Her wrists and ankles were numb and bleeding from the tightness of the cord binding them. Exhausted, she cried again, unable to believe that soon she would no longer be alive. She was tied upright, in the position of the cross, on show for all to see, yet no one could see her. Above, a handful of stars cast a cold, lonely light. Up here the bitter night air seemed cleaner, fresher. Sarah breathed deep and prayed for sleep to come once more as the icy darkness slowly crawled into her heart.

Wednesday 17 December

CHAPTER SIXTEEN

New Blood

'You're late, Mr Nahree. And on a sale day, too. What happened this time?' The little man raised himself up on tiptoe and adjusted his tie in the huge gilt mirror behind the counter.

'I'm frightfully sorry, sir,' said the young Indian clerk, wringing his hands apologetically. 'The trains. A body on the line, I think.'

'Well, you had better open up. You should know by now that our pre-Christmas sale is our most successful event. There's already a queue forming outside.'

Mr Buckley, chief of staff at the little Regent Street jewellery shop, was a fastidious man who prided himself on punctuality. It simply would not do to leave customers waiting outside the store. As always, Mr Buckley had arrived at exactly nine o'clock but refused to check the display cases and open the doors himself. After all, that was a job for a menial, not an executive staff member.

'Mr Buckley, I wonder if I could have a word.' Mr Nahree held one pinstriped arm aloft, as if asking for permission to leave the room.

'Very well, but be quick.'

'As you know, sir, I locked up last night . . .'

'Yes, yes,' Mr Buckley made a display of staring impatiently at his watch. Outside, a woman cupped her hands across her forehead and peeped in through the window.

'You see, I heard a noise on the floor above. I went upstairs to investigate, but found nobody there. When I went to the window, I saw two people on the ledge of the shop next door. They saw me and vanished.'

'Good Lord! Did you check the vault?'

'Oh yes, sir. There was nothing missing and no sign of entry anywhere. I just wondered if we should tell the police.'

Mr Buckley rubbed his chins thoughtfully. 'No, Mr Nahree, I think not. Unless they've actually been burgled next door. You might check. . . .' Mr Nahree obediently made as if to check and was called back. 'Not now, lad! Lock the doors back first and, while you're at it, pull down the awning. They say it's going to rain later.'

Mr Nahree locked the doors back in position and moved aside to usher through a handful of well-heeled bargain-hunters. Beyond, the street was still free of casual passersby. Commuters were hurrying past the store on the way to their offices and they rarely stopped to look in the windows for special offers.

Mr Nahree looked up at the sky. Already, the unbroken early blue of the morning had been spoiled by a handful of thundery-looking clouds. He hurried inside and picked up the hooked pole with which to pull down the store's striped awning. Hooking it carefully into the brass ring in the middle of the blind, he leaned his weight onto one foot and pulled. Nothing happened. He tried again, pulling harder this time, but the awning refused to break free of its cover and unfold.

'Mr Buckley, sir, I cannot manage to do this by myself,' called Mr Nahree. 'It is jammed tight!'

His plea fell on deaf ears, for Mr Buckley was already in the process of making his first sale of the day. Mr Nahree tried again. This time, he arched his body backwards and pulled with all of his might. There was a sharp cracking noise and the blind pulled free. As it unfolded it gathered speed, for something long and heavy weighed it down in the middle. The underside of the blind was stained a deep crimson. Mr Nahree looked up in horror as the awning extended fully and a wet red body rolled out and fell to the pavement with a splattery thud.

At first he thought that it had been coated in glossy black-red paint. The body was bald, naked and of the male gender. Only its eyes and fingernails showed white.

When Mr Nahree realized that the man had been completely skinned, he fell to the pavement beside the corpse, much to the surprise and annoyance of his employer, who consequently failed to complete the sale of a handsome gold ladies' watch.

'What I'm saying is, I don't have to come down there and look at it again for you to give me some idea of the cause of death, do I?' Hargreave tilted his chair forward and cradled the telephone receiver under his ear as he flicked on the computer terminal. 'Well, you've had it for four hours. I would have thought you'd be in a position to make an intelligent guess by now.' Behind him, Sergeant Janice Longbright entered quietly and took a seat. Her solid, ample bosom seemed to be in danger of bursting from the smart blue linen jacket in which it was encased. Hargreave eyed her appreciatively before returning his attention to the forensic man on the other end of the line.

'Fine, here's what you do. Send me up your list of main possible causes of death, with the technical jargon from your blood and tissue analysis weeded out so that a complete idiot can understand it. Add it to the update on the other two bodies which I assume you were just about to let me have. How long do I have to wait for that? Wonderful, you'll make me a very happy man.'

He replaced the receiver and turned his full attention to the big, beautiful sergeant who sat patiently waiting to talk to him. 'I thought you were going to be tied up with the Arabs all day, Janice.'

In the last twenty-four hours the case of the Harrods shoplifter had begun to pay off. The addresses she provided had pointed to a complex network of companies specializing in the receiving and processing of stolen goods, all of which were based in Arab states.

'I will be. We've got a room full of very irate embassy officials downstairs. I have a familiar feeling that the subject of Diplomatic Immunity is about to get an airing.' Sergeant Janice Longbright crossed her heavy long legs in a slither of stocking and smiled at him. Hargreave self-consciously placed his hands behind his head and over his bald patch.

'I came up when I heard that they'd brought in another body,' she said. 'Where did they find it?'

'It appears to have fallen from the sky in the vicinity of Regent Street,' said Hargreave with a grimace. 'Virtually no intact or recognizable features and as usual we haven't a hope in hell of getting any positive I.D. within a couple of days. Finch started work on the body using data culled from the first two corpses some hours ago, but two of his technicians are on some kind of a go-slow over the Christmas duty roster.'

'Have you been down there yet?'

'First thing. Finch was gleefully prancing around the body sticking needles in it. Probably used to pull the wings off insects when he was a child.'

'Why haven't you called a departmental meeting on this, Ian? I mean, three deaths . . . it's getting a little too serious for you to contain for much longer, isn't it?'

'I know, but I want to maintain control for a while, just until we get some more data and at least one confirmed I.D. We'll get press speculation soon enough, not to mention Upstairs breathing down our necks pressing for a result. Hang on, looks like we've got something coming in.'

Hargreave swivelled his monitor around to reveal rows of luminous green letters unscrolling across the screen. 'I'm keeping direct access to Finch's report channel. He appears to have made a match.'

Janice pulled her chair forward so that she could watch the screen more easily. Dental records had confirmed the identity of the first boy, but there was still only marginal information on the second and the third corpse appeared to present an entirely new problem.

'He'd been rather ineptly skinned. Stripped of flesh. But Finch doesn't seem to think that was the cause of death.'

'Look at this, Ian. A massive quantity of Warfarin in the body,' Janice tapped an area of the screen with her pencil. 'God, what a nasty way to die.'

'Why? What does that signify?' He held up his hand, then punched out the number of the forensic laboratory. 'Finch, pick up your phone.' After a moment, the call connected. Hargreave switched it onto the office intercom. 'Finch, if I've got Warfarin in my blood, what does that signify?'

Down in the lab, Finch used his lightpen to highlight a number of chemical values for Hargreave to study on the screen. 'Take a look at your monitor. Those areas I've just marked indicate a system imbalance in the man's body. . . .'

'How old would you say he was?'

'Oh, I'd say about thirty, thirty-two. There's a link with the other two bodies only insofar as there's a heavy presence of illegal chemical substances again. Heroin, in this case.'

'The fact that they all dropped out of the sky could be seen as a link, I would have thought,' muttered Janice.

'But this time death was caused by the oral ingestion

of a large amount of Warfarin, or at least a substance with the same properties.'

'Which brings me back to my question – what does it do?'

'It prevents haemostasis in the body,' said Finch, cheerfully. 'It's an anti-coagulant.' The silence on the other end of the line indicated that he would have to elucidate. 'It stops your blood from clotting. The chap haemorrhaged to death. Any tiny internal tears he had wouldn't heal in the normal fashion. He literally drowned in his own blood.' Finch paused for dramatic effect before continuing. 'Normally Warfarin is almost totally metabolized by the liver, but we managed to find traces in urine and faecal matter. It's not a very normal way to die.'

'Time of death?'

'Well, the chemical would have taken at least a couple of hours to have an effect and we can add another six hours for the digestive system to process the toxin. I should think he expired at about seven o'clock last night and was then skinned – to what purpose I really can't begin to imagine.'

'Thanks, Finch. I'll call you when I've printed this lot out and had a chance to go through it.' He replaced the receiver and turned back to Janice, tapping his front teeth with a fingernail. 'I want to put somebody young and fresh on this before anyone else gets a crack at it. Someone who doesn't think in straight lines. I'm too old, my ideas filter through a regimented training pattern. . . .' Janice began to protest, but Hargreave silenced her. 'No, it's true. This needs new blood.'

'We've got Detective Constable Martin Butterworth in the department at the moment.'

'What, the Commissioner's son? Bit dodgy if there's a cock-up. Think of the comebacks.'

'He seems quite bright, though. He's helping me out

with the Arabs. I'm sure the change of pace would spark his creative juices.'

'All right, get him to come and see me.'

Hargreave tapped the keyboard before him and started a printout procedure for Finch's report. Computers were a necessary evil, but bloody useful all the same, particularly if you didn't stick to the regular programs. It was a pity that there were so many unimaginative people in the department who followed the letter of the law. Whatever had happened to the great characters of the force, the ideas-men of old, the people with a little flair?

'How do you mean?' Janice asked of a shocked Hargreave, who was unaware that he had been speaking aloud.

'Nothing. I've got a list of questions piling up that's as long as one of your exceedingly lovely legs.' The naturally healthy bloom of Janice's cheeks deepened slightly.

'You're assuming that the deaths are connected?'

'Come on, Janice, how could they not be? It just doesn't make sense. Why tie a raven to somebody before tossing them off a roof? Why poison someone's blood when it's *easier* just to toss 'em off a roof? And as for filling somebody's mouth with Egyptian silt before killing them. . . .' 'They knew the police would examine the bodies. Maybe they're doing it just to throw us off the scent.'

'We've been over that roof with a fine toothcomb. There's nothing but a couple of blurred footprints. But there has to be more than one person involved, someone to help with the killing. This last one was a big bloke, six two, six three. . . .'

'Why don't you have some coffee and relax for a while?' suggested Janice. Ian had not stayed over at her apartment last night. He had worked late and it showed in his face.

'I'm not going to relax until we get a decent lead.'

There was a knock on the glass panel of the office door and a secretary poked her head around the corner apologetically. 'Sorry to interrupt you, sir, but this just came in. . . .' She held up a folded copy of the evening paper's noon edition and then passed it to Janice, who eyed the banner headline with a glacial expression and passed it quickly on to Hargreave as if she had just been handling a letter bomb.

'Bloody hell!'

Police hunt rooftop madman

LONDON METROPOLITAN POLICE have been warned to be on the lookout for a maniac gunman terrorizing the crowded streets of the capital, writes crime correspondent Stan Cutts. After Monday's report of a boy found murdered in Piccadilly Circus, two more bodies have been discovered in the immediate vicinity, both showing signs of wounding which suggest foul play. Police fear that a gangland war may have erupted between London's underworld crimelords.

Official cover-up?

At a time when their resources are being stretched to the limit by the seasonal influx of Christmas shoppers, police are unable to spare men to investigate the possibility of a gangland link between the three victims. Detective Chief Inspector Ian 'Leicester Square Vampire' Hargreave, ['Bloody *Hell!*' groaned Hargreave] currently heading the investigation, has denied that there may be a link between the horrific murders (see centre page photo spread) and has actively discouraged the press from reporting the case in any detail. Today he could not be reached for comment.

'It's strange,' said one anonymous spokesperson, 'but there seems to be a cover-up going on. None of us knows what is happening.'

The violence every mother fears

Today, as bright-eyed mothers and toddlers, their arms filled with gaily-wrapped Christmas gifts, stroll unconcerned through bustling streets, the city waits in fear for a new wave of gang violence which could strike down innocent and unsuspecting bystanders anywhere, at any time. Bystanders who are unfortunate enough to be standing in the way of a crazed maniac sniper.

(See editorial)

'You've got to be pretty talented to get so many inaccuracies into one column,' said Hargreave with surprising calm as he opened the newspaper out. 'Good editorial, too. "Why, Oh Why, Is Nothing Being Done?" it says. Photo spread's a bit murky, though. Couple of grey smudges and an arrow pointing to some railings and the top of a building. But this bit's good. – "Horoscopes Can Tell If Your Man Is A Maniac." ' He angrily threw the newspaper across the room.

'Who is this "spokesperson" giving him a quote?' asked Janice. 'It can't be anyone from here.'

'Oh, he makes them up; they all do when they suspect something to be true but can't find anyone to confirm it. "Sniper", he says, ignoring the fact that there hasn't been a single shot fired into any of the victims. He's going to have the whole of London looking up in the air for rooftop assassins. You wait, by the evening edition he'll have come up with a nickname for the killer. The bastard. Late Thursday, he said he wouldn't file the story until late Thursday. Well, he's just lost his file access. I want him and everyone else completely frozen out until we get more information.' He indicated the chaotic offices beyond the window. 'You'd better make sure that they're all briefed properly about taking phone calls.'

'Ian, how could he possibly have known about the

latest victim? Where is he getting his information from so quickly?'

Hargreave pinched the top of his broad nose with a thumb and forefinger. He looked up at Janice and gave her a puzzled frown. 'That's what I'd bloody like to know,' he said.

CHAPTER SEVENTEEN

Simon

Skinner's suits were a constant source of fascination to Robert. They seemed to be made from an alien synthetic fibre that never creased or got dirty. Indeed, it seemed possible that Skinner himself was constructed of the same material. At any given moment, the man's fingernails were clean. It irritated Robert as he sat at his desk clearing away the remains of his workload before the offical Christmas break began.

Skinner eyed the untidy stacks of books and magazines piled in the corners of the office with distaste. 'Had any luck with your blockbuster yet?' he asked from his usual position in the doorway.

'There are a few obstacles in the way at the moment, but I'll get there eventually,' said Robert, pausing to light a cigarette which he knew would annoy his colleague. 'Hopefully this side of Christmas. I thought you and Trish were going skiing.'

'We're leaving this afternoon. Though there's likely to be less emphasis on the *ski* and more on the *aprés*, if I know Trish.' His laughter came out as a series of horrible mucus-inducing snorts. 'The office closes tomorrow, you know. I'm surprised to find you still hard at it. Why not wait until the New Year? Nobody else is working.'

'No, it'll be too late by then.'

'What do you mean, too late?'

'Nothing. There's a complication with the deal, that's

all. Nothing for you to concern yourself over on the *piste*.'

Robert resented having to tell Skinner anything more than the barest minimum about his search for Sarah Endsleigh. The man was bound to find some reason for him to not follow it through. Skinner could sense an air of hostility in the office, as if he was secretly being made fun of. The boy had a major attitude problem. He wouldn't survive the approaching staff changes. At least not if Skinner had anything to do with it.

'Well, I'll be off then,' he said awkwardly as Robert continued to remain hunched over his desk. 'Merry Christmas.'

'Same to you and Trish.'

The door clicked gently shut as Robert decided that it was time to call Rose and arrange a meeting. Outside, early evening darkness closed over the row of vigilant gargoyles, who remained at their posts as immobile and impassive as Chinese soldiers.

At eight o'clock Robert and Rose left the pub in Sutton Row and turned off into Charing Cross Road, the crowds quickly thinning out as they moved away from the main tourist thoroughfares. The tiny embankment park they arrived at was little more than a collection of drooped, dying elms standing in a damp and trampled strip of green. In the middle was a space reserved for deckchairs which was used in summer when the band played. Now it was deserted and litter-strewn. Along the top of the park, wooden benches rested beneath tall battered bushes, sticky with the deposits of ancient limes. Most of the benches were taken up by tramps who spent their time dejectedly passing wine bottles to one another and involving themselves in inane arguments. Others lay sprawled on the grass in uneasy sleep, seemingly oblivious to the cold night air.

'I couldn't see anyone over there.' Rose had returned

from the far side of the bandstand, where she had been searching for Simon, their contact.

'I guess he could turn up at any time between eight and nine.'

'If he appears at all.'

Just then, the clicking of boots on concrete made them both look up across the park toward the river. Silhouetted against the lamps lighting the embankment was a gangling figure festooned in rags and chains.

'My God, it's Marley's ghost!' whispered Rose, drawing in closer to Robert as he approached. The figure came to a stop in front of them. He was tall and thin, with an eggshell-pale face that had seen about seventeen summers, apparently from indoors. His hair alternated with shaved and tattooed patches, thrusting out in dirty blue spikes. His eyebrows, if he had ever had any, had been shaved off. A circular anarchy symbol was tattooed on his throat. The ragged remains of an old black denim jacket clung precariously to his shoulders.

'Hello. I'm Simon. I was asked to look out for you.' Simon held out his hand. His speech was so refined that he could have freelanced as a speaking clock. Robert and Rose stared in amazement. 'You're surprised by the accent.' Simon looked apologetic. 'People always find that funny. Goes against the preconceptions, doesn't it? Upsets the balance. Funny thing, fixed beliefs. Everyone has them. Like, you know, always imagining that lesbians only drink pints, or that stockbrokers give a fuck about poor people. Which of course they don't. But then these days who does. Anyway.'

Robert and Rose looked at each other, then back at Simon.

'Can't be helped. I had a good education, I just rejected it.' He seemed affable, but in a dangerous way, speaking too fast, offering friendship too quickly.

'It must be a bit of a stigma,' ventured Rose, 'what with you being a punk and all.'

'Who said I'm a punk? Another fixed belief, see? It's bad enough being called Simon without sounding like a public school fuck-up.'

'Perhaps you should use your middle name.'

'Nigel. Don't really think so.'

As Simon and Rose talked, Robert looked around at the damp, malignant trees in annoyance. He was beginning to wonder what on earth he was doing hanging around in this miserable little park holding a meeting with a potential psychopath.

'He's Robert and I'm Rose.' She held out her hand and Simon shook it.

'Rose. That's a very middle class name.' There was mistrust in his voice.

'Yeah, but I had really common parents. They always put the milk bottle on the table.'

'My parents never put the milk bottle on the table. I don't think they know what a milk bottle looks like. Only ever see milk in a jug. They don't give a fuck about anything but collecting shares. That's what people on the ground do now, isn't it, spend their time stockpiling share certificates, designer fucking Filofaxes and electronic gadgets, as if they could get it into the boat with them when the time comes to cross the Styx.'

An uncomfortable silence descended over the trio as Robert and Rose tried to decide who should speak. Behind them, a tramp belched and threw a bottle at a wall. Finally, Simon turned to them. 'I've been standing here for five minutes now and you haven't even tried to convince me to take you up.'

'Well, it's difficult for us. We don't know what's involved.' Rose looked cautiously at Robert, who remained silent.

'Well, don't worry. I was going to anyway. I've got instructions from above.' He pointed mysteriously at the sky. 'Normally, you wouldn't be allowed to meet with us just because you need to locate someone. But things aren't normal any more. Given the present situation, they'd probably even waive initiation for you.'

'Initiation?'

'It's necessary for you to pass some kind of test as a gesture of good faith. Give me a cigarette, would you?'

Rose handed him one. In the flare of her match, Simon's face seemed almost translucent.

'Would we be required to do anything that breaks the law?' asked Rose.

'Maybe.' Simon slowly blew smoke into the air. 'I've been told to warn you that it can be an upsetting experience, which is why you'll be asked to take an oath of silence after. The one thing you won't be able to do is go back once you've started.'

Rose turned to Robert, whose continuing non-verbal communication was becoming noticeable. His confidence of the previous evening seemed to have dissipated.

'You still want to do this, Robert? You don't seem to be too sure.'

Simon looked over at Robert suspiciously. 'If he's got any doubts, he shouldn't have come here in the first place, should he?'

'Hey listen, I'd just like to know what we're getting into,' said Robert. 'Is going along with you likely to help us find our friend?'

'I don't know anything about that.'

'Then maybe we can talk to someone who does.' Robert kicked irritably at the asphalt path.

'That's exactly what you're going to do. Have some patience. Christ, no wonder ground people are so fucked up if they're all like you.'

'Don't talk to me like that,' said Robert angrily.

'Listen, it's getting cold,' said Rose. 'Shouldn't we be thinking about leaving? I mean, if you're going to take us with you.'

Simon shrugged, then turned and headed off through

the park. As Rose ran and caught him up, Robert trailed further behind.

'Where to now?' he called out.

Simon turned with a sickly grin on his skull-like face and slowly pointed one bony finger to the sky. 'Up in the air,' he said. 'But first we'll go north, towards Euston. You have to meet some people.' His smile faded. His eyes, wide and browless, became disturbingly difficult for Robert to look into.

'I don't know what you're expecting to happen,' he said in a theatrical whisper, 'but whether you like it or not you are going to be taken into a different world. You might find it exciting. You might get killed. I don't know.'

Simon whirled about, his head tilting back, his eyes to the sky. He spun on the heel of his boot, a flailing scarecrow. 'There's another side to this city, see, a side that people like you know *nothing* about.' He reached out and placed a spidery arm around Rose's shoulders. 'And soon it may be gone forever. Along with you and me and just about everybody else worth saving.'

With his puzzled recruits at either side, Simon led the way north.

CHAPTER EIGHTEEN

Heights

From the rising glass elevator, the busy London streets slowly revealed themselves in perspective. To the right stood the glass-faceted column of the British Telecom tower, its summit adorned with radar dishes like clusters of mushrooms. Beyond it, the rows of busy restaurants centred around the lower part of Charlotte Street were filled with Christmas partygoers.

Rose moved to the front of the glass elevator. Just in front of them, traffic rushed and divided at the brightly lit head of Tottenham Court Road. To the left lay the gloomy Georgian terraces of Bloomsbury and directly below they could see the filthy, windswept no man's land that was Euston. The three of them stood shoulder to shouider facing out in the tiny lift as it rose in its glass shaft. They had entered the mirrored office block facing Euston Tower simply by unlocking one of the small glass side doors and passing by the deserted reception desk.

'Isn't it a bit risky, just walking into a private building like this?' asked Rose. Before she left home that evening, she had slipped Charlotte's notebook into a small shoulderbag, mindful of what Robert had said about it being their 'bargaining power'. 'I mean, it's not that late. There could still be people working in their offices.'

'Nothing for you to worry about,' answered Simon. 'Most of the nightwatchmen are ours. There's one guy who's a pain in the ass, but he misses this section of the building during the early part of the evening because he's watching TV on the third floor. We keep files on all the main gates.'

'Gates?'

'Buildings which provide access to the Roofworld. We're here.' The elevator slowed and came to a stop. Ahead was a short flight of stairs leading up to the roof exit. Simon pushed on the steel bar across the door and swung it open. The top of the building was smooth, clean and flat. The breezes which crossed it were hardly fresh, carrying traffic fumes from the crossroads below, but they were strong enough to have dried away all signs of the day's earlier rainfall.

Two young men, both dressed in grey sweatshirts and black jeans, stood waiting for them. One had cropped blonde hair which swept out from beneath a black woollen cap in a rockabilly quiff. Simon informed them that his name was Jay. The other was shorter, swarthy and serious, vaguely oriental-looking. He was called Lee and seemed to be the more high-ranking of the two. On either side of them, tall metal hoists stood at the edges of the roof. Jay motioned that Robert and Rose should sit at the foot of one of these. He remained standing as the small group gathered around.

'What have you told them?' he asked Simon.

'Not my job to tell them anything,' said the punk who hated to be called a punk, as he folded his long legs beneath him and squatted down on the edge of the roof.

'Better to show them than tell them, I would have thought,' he muttered. 'Not that anyone listens to me.' Jay ignored him, turning back to the newcomers.

'You're up here tonight on the condition that certain codes of honour and secrecy are respected,' he began. It was obviously not the first time that he had delivered this speech. 'What is happening up here is not a game. It's very real and it's now become very dangerous. I don't know what you've heard about us from the outside, but it's more than likely wrong. The only ones with enough knowledge to discuss our activities with strangers are people we turned away in the first place.'

Robert turned and looked at Rose. His backside was freezing on the concrete roof. He felt more than a little silly, sitting here being lectured to by some screwed-up kid. Rose seemed to be taking it all in though, her attention focused solely on the boy in front of her.

'Let me tell you something about us. For years this has been a closed world.'

'Won't be for much longer,' said Simon under his breath.

Jay leaned back and rested his head against one of the hoist's metal columns. Behind him, six floors below, came the distant sound of cars revving and braking.

'This is a working alternative to your ground system. We have our own laws and our own justice, a network which extends across the city in every direction . . . except downwards. Your paths and ours need never have crossed until now.'

He pointed out over the roof in the direction of Tottenham Court Road, where miniature figures paused before brilliant store windows and milled from the pubs to the cafes like insects caught in endless courting rituals. 'It's important that you understand our priorities are different to the ones they drum into you at ground level. We live by the rules *we* have created – no one else's.'

Cold and unconvinced, Robert felt as if he was about to be duped into buying a lifestyle-improving doctrine by members of an oblique arm of the Krishna-ites. He raised his hand to ask a question. 'How many of you are there up here?'

'These days we have people from all walks of life, university graduates, punks, rastafarians. . . .'

'Yes, but how many?'

Jay sighed and leaned back against the metal post again. He looked up into the sky.

'You're going to have to tell them, Jay,' said Simon.

'There were hundreds of us. Back in the twenties there were very nearly a thousand. . . .'

'The twenties?'

'A lot of people below the poverty line were willing to give up what little they had and start over.'

'But you can't keep something like this secret for long,' protested Robert. 'Didn't anyone ask questions?'

'You got any idea how many people go missing in this country every year?' asked Jay. 'They didn't keep tabs on you back then. There were no computers to check your address or the name of your bank. In those days the Roofworld wasn't just a way out, it was a sanctuary for anyone who needed to drop out of sight.'

'You still haven't told me how many of you there are now.'

Another hesitation followed. Robert shot a puzzled glance at Rose, who seemed not to notice. Jay seemed reluctant to reveal any further information. Perhaps he had already said more than he had intended to say. Robert decided that it would not be advisable for him to reveal what he and Rose already knew of the Roofworld themselves, in case it proved that they too had transgressed some secret law, like Sarah Endsleigh may have done.

'I guess there are about thirty of us left. Maybe fewer. And by dawn on Sunday most of us will be gone.'

'How? Why?'

'I've said enough. You may be told more after your initiation. It's up to Zalian.'

'But what do you do up here?' asked Rose. 'How do you travel around?'

'One thing at a time. Lee will have to teach you to cross the rooftops. It's easy once you know how, thanks to the architecture of this city. I hope you don't have trouble with heights.'

'Me, I'd have made a great cat burglar', said Rose, with an uneasy laugh. She looked across at Robert and something began to bother her. He appeared uncomfortable, his face slick with sweat. Rose frowned. He couldn't be scared, could he? These guys were strange, but they hardly seemed to be dangerous.

'OK, let's get the travelling sorted out now. Then you can do your initiation. After that, we'll take you to one of the stations and somebody will explain what we can do to help each other. Lee, take over.'

Jay sat down next to Simon as his partner took over. Lee rose and gave a broad white smile to Rose.

'Sometimes they call me Mr Fix, 'cause I come up with a lot of the equipment which keeps us movin' around up here. It's basically the same as they used to use back in the old days, 'cept that a lot of the old stuff was really dangerous. The only way to find out if a cable would take your weight back then was to hang on it. I've updated as much as I can using modern lightweight materials, throwing in a few safety devices along the way. First off, everyone gets to wear one of these. Ya never take it off unless ya have to, like if you're having a bath or somethin'.'

He pulled up his sweatshirt and pointed at his waist. Around it was a thin black leather belt, fitted along its length with small metal hoops. Above and below it, cut into the leather, ran a fine nylon cable.

'Stan' up a second, honey.' Lee unclipped his belt and passed it around Rose's waist, buckling it at the front. 'After initiation, you'll be issued with one of your own. Now come with me.'

They followed Lee to the far corner of the roof. The edge of the next building, a grimy Victorian office block which faced out onto the Euston Road, lay about fifteen feet away. Rose looked down and saw a narrow alley separating the two blocks.

'Some gaps are wide enough to jump. This one obviously is not. Look across to the next wall and you'll see a small steel bar. You have to look real hard.'

Rose leaned forward and squinted through the gloom at the opposite wall, where a shiny metal bar about three inches long, rather like a miniature towel-rail, stood out from the brickwork.

'The more you look, the more you'll see of our handiwork across the city,' said Jay, picking up a slim black nylon bag and opening it. He produced a device which looked like a modified hand-gun with an extra-wide barrel and aimed it at the bar.

'It works on air pressure,' he said, squeezing the trigger. 'The ones they used to have were fired by a mixture of potassium nitrate, charcoal and sulphur. Apparently used to blow your tits off if you got the ratio wrong.' There was a pop and something shot out of the nozzle, clattering against the wall opposite.

'Nice shot,' said Rose.

'Comes with practice, like everything else.'

Locked firmly over the bar was a small steel ring, attached to which was an almost transparently thin nylon cord. The other end of the cord extended back into the barrel of the gun. Lee detached this end and clipped it to a second metal ring.

'The way it works is simple. The bar you see on that wall over there has a spring-hinge in the middle. The ring that's fired from this gun is top-heavy, so that the weighted side always hits the bar, kicks open the hinge and locks in place.'

'Don't you have to be an incredible shot to hit a bar that small?'

'You probably would if the bars weren't magnetic,' Lee agreed. 'Normally it takes a while to teach this stuff, but we're going to have to crash you through the basics tonight.' He reached over the edge of the building and clipped his end of the cord to a matching bar set about a foot down the wall. He then tightened the line with a tiny steel ratchet, the slack vanishing inside the steel ring until the line was taut.

'There are all kinds of ways to do this. One is to hook the line onto the opposite wall and connect the other end to a reeler.' He held up a shiny steel disc about five inches in diameter and just over an inch thick. 'It fixes to your belt. You drop to the other wall, landing with your feet against it, and the disc reels in the line and pulls you up. It's really just for short distances and you can only use it when there aren't many people about, 'cause it's kind of noisy.'

'Not to mention ostentatious,' said Simon.

'I can imagine,' said Rose. 'A bit like Errol Flynn.'

'A lot of buildings are hard to cross even when they're terraced, because you'll suddenly come to one with an extra floor, or a steeply sloping roof. That's when the disc comes in useful. In some areas nearly all of the buildings have been fitted with these special bars. The older ones have a tendency to rust up, which stops their hinges from working. We try to replace them whenever we can, but there's not many of us left who still know how to. Other areas have specific "runs", fast travel routes mapped out through the town. These runs have permanent lines strung up and pass through a number of junction points called "stations". There's at least one station in every part of the city.'

'Right,' said Rose. 'We know about the stations. They're named after the people who built the buildings below them, right?'

'Right. How do you know that?'

'We'll trade secrets later. Go on.'

'Over the years, the field of operation has been extended as far down as Hammersmith. But nobody's ever found a way to get across the river.' As he talked,

Lee produced a loop of cord joined to a small metal sleeve. This he clicked from Rose's belt to the line. She was now sitting with her legs dangling over the parapet. Robert was beginning to feel sick.

'This is what we call a beginner's strap. It's a little slower than the ones Jay and I use. You can't fall. The cord will take fifteen times your weight. The metal sleeve is locked over the line and just makes it easier for you to pull yourself across.'

Rose looked uncertainly at Robert, but surprised him the next moment by pushing herself out into the air with calm ease. In seconds, she was halfway across the space between the two buildings. Then she came to a stop, rocking gently backwards and forwards in mid-air.

'What's wrong?' called Lee.

'Nothing, I just shouldn't have looked down.' Rose continued across, half by using her hands on the line, half by simply sliding under her own weight. Reaching the other side, she tried to haul herself up over the brick parapet. She had one leg over the wall and was panting with the exertion, but the cord running from her belt to the main line would allow her to go no further.

'The belt-line won't reach,' she called back. 'How do I get free?'

'The sleeve joining you to the line has a hinge which opens inwards,' called Lee. 'Push on it.'

Rose squeezed the sleeve and it suddenly popped free of the line. For a second she lost her balance and Robert thought she was going to fall out over the roof and down into the street. Then she had uprighted herself and clambered to safety, dropping behind the wall with a thud and a grunt.

'It's OK,' Lee called to her. 'The first time is always the worst.' 'How are you going to get over?' shouted Rose, peering over the low wall. 'Do you want me to throw the belt back to you?'

'Won't be necessary,' called Lee, who hefted the nylon bag onto his back and climbed over the edge of the roof onto the line. With a few quick steps across the gap he was by Rose's side.

'Now *that's* impressive,' said Rose. 'Does everyone know how to do that, or just you?'

'Most of us were taught how to ropewalk, but not many actually like doing it, because as you probably noticed, the lines are slightly greased. Me, I love a chance to show off.'

'The Astaire of the air,' Jay shouted gleefully. They were like children, thought Robert, as nausea assailed him once more, eager to show off their party tricks.

Lee looked around the roof upon which he and Rose now stood. Like the last one, it was wide and flat. It led to another building, one with a steeply raked roof covered in ancient slate tiles. 'The trouble with this area,' he said, 'is the guttering. It's old and can come away quite easily. But they're doing up a lot of these places and that means good roof conditions – as well as everyone's best friend, scaffolding. There's not a street in the city without some scaffolding in it and that's perfect for hooking onto.'

'I can't believe nobody knows we're up here,' said Rose, watching the banks of traffic lights running the length of Gower Street as they flicked to green in perfect synchronization. The air from the street was now dry and chill, sweeping between her legs and around the back of her neck.

'Nobody ever even looks up here during the day, let alone at night,' said Lee.

'The Roofworld has a lot of secrets,' called Simon, tapping the side of his nose conspiratorially. 'You'll see.'

Rose was exhilarated by her successful crossing. 'I feel a bit like one of the kids in *Mary Poppins*,' she admitted, 'going up to the roof for a view of London.'

'Oh, you'll get a view of London all right, when you do your initiation,' chuckled Lee. 'Let's get your friend over. I think we're going to have trouble with him.'

'How do you mean?' Rose looked back over at Robert, who was still sitting on the edge of the next building, staring down at the pavement far below.

'I'd say the poor bastard just found out he's scared of heights.'

'Look, much as I hate to interrupt,' called the unmistakable voice of Simon from the other side, 'but we're too exposed to stay out up here for long. Let's get these two through the Skelter Run and back to Wren.'

'Christ, Simon, you're such a worrier,' Lee called back. He turned to Rose, who was studying Lee's line-gun, fascinated. 'Think you're OK to go back again?'

'Just watch me. How do you get rid of the lines after they've been strung up?'

'We always used to unhook them and throw the things away, but now we roll up the line and repack it when we get back. It's time-consuming, but cheaper than losing the equipment. Come on.' Lee slipped back out onto the line and crossed in a few nimble steps. Behind him, Rose attached her belt-line once more and swung out from the building. As Robert silently watched, Simon and Jay gave her a hand climbing over the low wall on their side. They were obviously pleased that she had done so well on her first short journey out above the streets.

'We'll go straight to your initiation,' said Jay, swinging a small nylon pack similar to Lee's onto his back. 'Let's get this over with.'

'What do we have to do?' asked Rose, as Simon also picked up one of the backpacks and hefted it onto his shoulder.

'There's always been a symbolic ceremony for those who want to become part of the Roofworld. These days we've set aside most of the ritual bullshit, but the initiation still serves a practical purpose.'

'And what is that?' asked Rose.

'To find out if you've a head for heights,' said Simon. Together, they turned and looked at Robert, who remained squatting sickly on the edge of the parapet.

CHAPTER NINETEEN

Butterworth

'Well it seems pretty bloody obvious to me, Butterworth. Think, boy.' Ian Hargreave leaned as far back in his chair as it would go and thoughtfully scratched the top of his head. Before him stood Detective Constable Butterworth, desperate to please. With his baby-blue eyes and unkempt sandy hair, Butterworth looked scarcely old enough to be on the force. His face was smothered in freckles, rather like a Disney character.

'Well, sir. They've all occurred within the space of a week.'

'You and your grandmother could both be knocked down by a bus in the space of a week, but it wouldn't have to have been the same driver.'

Butterworth was silent. He stayed well beyond reach of Hargreave's arms, which he heard had a tendency to lash out and attack people and objects.

Butterworth had entered the force in order to keep the peace with his father, the commissioner. He figured that if he minded his own business and managed not to annoy anyone, he would be left alone until such time as he could quietly leave. However, he had not counted on meeting Sergeant Janice Longbright, who insisted that she saw great unrealized potential in the gawky youth and had talked him into being singled out by Hargreave for some kind of special assignment.

'Modus operandi, Butterworth?' Hargreave suddenly

creaked forward in his chair, causing Butterworth nervously to step back a foot.

'Well, uh, no discernible pattern emerging yet, sir.'

Hargreave dropped his head into his hands. 'Out of respect for your father and the good faith of Sergeant Longbright I will continue to try and make you understand the value of sound criminal analysis, Butterworth, though I realize I might as well be talking to that hat-rack over there. You have studied these cases on the computer file, have you not?'

'Yes, sir. Very carefully.'

'And is there nothing that strikes you about all three deaths?'

'Not immediately, sir.'

'What do you mean, "not immediately", you hopeless nit?' He thumped the top of the console before him, causing the screen to roll. 'A young man gets electrocuted on a neon sign. Witnesses say he "flew into it". A boy is found speared on the railings of an insurance office. Another is found skinned, for Christ's sake, inside a shop awning!' Having attacked the console, Hargreave thought it only fair to thump the desktop with his fist as well, spilling tea in his saucer and making Butterworth wince.

'To me it seems rather obvious that all three deaths occurred from somewhere above the ground. The only bloodstains found at pavement level were where the bodies had landed. Victim number two was the only one to be killed by the fall and even that we're not sure about as he may have had his skull damaged initially by a powerful bird. The other two were well and truly dead before they kissed the concrete. Now, how many dozen reports have we had in the last six months concerning rooftop prowlers in this area?'

'Which area, sir?'

Eyes closed, Hargreave pinched the top of his nose between thumb and forefinger. Why had he listened to

Janice and allowed the boy to have access to the files? Because he loved her? Reluctantly he agreed that this was very likely the reason.

'As the deaths took place in Piccadilly, Charing Cross and Regent Street respectively, Butterworth, I think we can risk defining the area, don't you?'

'Yes, sir. I'll find out right away, sir.'

'There's no need. I already have a report here.' Hargreave flicked through several sheets of computer print-out paper. 'There have been nearly sixty miscellaneous sightings, with the frequency of sighting increasing to a high over the last month. Sixty sightings! Why hasn't this been picked up by anyone? Because until now nobody has needed to collect such statistics. That's the way it is with a lot of crimes. The answers are there in front of you in the form of statistical analysis, but the right connections have to be made before you can think of pulling out the relevant facts.'

Butterworth looked thoughtfully at the carpet, in a manner which suggested that he was carefully weighing and digesting Hargreave's comments. In reality he was wondering how he could contrive to leave the office and return to his desk in the shortest possible time.

'Now what do we have to add to our sightings? Three deaths! The fact that people are dying at a rate of one a day implies that there may be more than one faction involved, wouldn't you say? So could it be gang warfare of some kind? One of the victims was a registered Methadone user, all three bodies showed traces of drugs. Is this a drug war, or does it merely indicate a pack of no-hopers slugging it out between themselves?' Hargreave glumly stared down at his desktop, as if hoping to find the killer there. 'It's a little difficult to find anything out about the third victim. It would have helped if he'd still had his skin on.'

'I can't imagine why he didn't have any, sir.'

'That's just it, Butterworth, you can't *imagine*. Maybe

he had an identifying birthmark, or was covered with telltale tattoos. Maybe he just took it off 'cause he was hot.'

'Sorry, sir?' Butterworth shuffled uneasily on the carpet.

'You will be if we don't get to work on this pretty damned quick. Your father was a great detective. If he could see you now he'd be revolving in his grave.'

'Er . . .' Butterworth coughed into his fist. 'He's not dead, sir.'

'No, but you'll kill him. The first victim had a record, just minor offences. He was officially registered as a Missing Person about a year ago. Interesting, wouldn't you say? Chase up the I.D. checks on the other two and find out if either of them was also registered missing. Here, take the files and make a copy for yourself.' Hargreave slid a box of hard disks across his desktop. 'Then start asking some discreet questions. You know the press status on this. When you've come up with some answers, we'll compare notes, shall we?'

After Butterworth had thankfully retreated from the office, Hargreave turned to the remaining printout folded across his desk. Like it or not, there was something big and nasty coming down on the city. Hargreave found himself wondering how many more bodies would have to turn up before they managed to find out exactly what it was.

CHAPTER TWENTY

The Skelter Run

'Try to get used to looking down. It's better if you learn to judge the distance beneath you.' Simon finished locking Robert's belt in place and stood up.

'I cannot do this,' whispered Robert, finally. 'I've got vertigo.' He was standing on the edge of the roof with Rose and Lee, waiting to be clipped onto the cable which passed above their heads. He could feel the wind buffeting his back and plucking at his jacket sleeves, trying to suck him over the edge into the concrete chasm below.

'You can and you will,' promised Simon. 'You haven't got vertigo. That only happens when you lose all your points of reference and can't orient your direction up or down. You only have to look at the rooftops below to figure out which way up you are.'

'That's a great comfort.'

'It's all in the mind. I don't think you're going to have a problem with heights once you've done the run.'

'Sure I won't, because by that time I'll be pasted to the pavement.' Robert's face had drained of colour. 'The embarrassment of dying in Euston,' he muttered, looking up at the cable. It was attached to the top of a disused hoist. They were now standing in the most southerly corner of the building, preparing to leave the roof.

'Most buildings have half a dozen bar-hooks on them for connecting lines, but this is a permanent run,' Simon was saying as he clipped the lines from their belts into metal sleeves which he produced from his bag.

'We used to have races down this, didn't we, Lee? We called it the Skelter Run, because it's one of the steepest runs in the city. It passes through a number of connecting stations before finishing on the roof of the Savoy in the Strand. And don't worry, Groundies, it's quite safe.'

'Yeah, we've never had a death on this one.' Jay swung himself up on the hoist and began joining the metal sleeves to the cable overhead.

'It's a fast run,' continued Simon, talking to keep their minds from the trip ahead. 'But you won't go down at full speed, because you each have the beginner's strap. It's really just a rough piece of leather that fits inside the sleeve your line is attached to, to slow your descent. We'll be following behind at regular . . .'

Suddenly, there was a strange hissing sound in the air above them, like an arrow being fired. Then another and another. Robert looked around in time to see Jay fall from the hoist, clutching his neck. His face was spattered with blood. Rose let out a terrified yelp.

'Fuck it! I knew we were taking too long!' Simon ran back to where the body had fallen. Further hissing sounds filled the air.

'For Chrissakes get down!' Simon crouched low over Jay, trying to staunch the blood which was pumping fiercely from his friend's slashed throat.

'Bastards! It's gone right in. Lee, give me a hand!'

Lee ran to Jay's side and examined the wound. Around them, the sound of tiny metallic objects rained down onto the rooftop. 'He's gonna die before we get him back to Zalian,' said Lee. 'Look at him.'

Simon held Jay down by the shoulders as his body began to convulse violently. Rose and Robert had fallen to the ground behind the low wall running along the edge of the roof. Lee jumped up and ran for the hoist, where the lines to their belts hung half-connected. Robert raised his head enough to see half a dozen dark figures running toward them on the next roof. He heard the clatter of steel on brick as they fired their line-guns. There was a hiss and something fell close by. It was a familiar glistening disc of metal. Robert reached out his hand.

'Don't touch it!' shouted Simon. 'The edges are razor-sharp and they're usually poisoned.' Robert looked closer. It was an old penny, polished and honed so that light glinted from its edge, a piece of deadly ammunition.

'You're connected!' Lee bellowed at Robert from the top of the hoist. 'Get going!'

He leapt down just as Simon stood. Blood had darkly spattered his chest and arms. Lee started toward Jay's twitching body.

'He's dead, Lee; that's his nervous system reacting to the poison. We have to leave.'

Behind them, the figures were now crossing the gap between the two roofs. Another hail of razor-sharp coins rang against the hoist. Rose pulled Robert to his feet and looked at the overhead cable.

'You have to do it now, Robert!' she screamed.

'Can't!' he shouted back, looking over the edge of the roof at the six-floor drop to the road.

'For Christ's sake go!' Lee ran to the edge and pushed against Robert's back. Robert thrust out his arms in resistance, but one foot slid from beneath him and he lost his balance. As he fell out beyond the edge, the line connecting his belt to the cable sprang taut and he swung around backwards, his other foot still hooked over the low wall. The first of the figures was only twenty yards away now. Lee kicked him hard in the shin and as Robert lifted his leg in surprise he found himself shooting out down the cable and away into darkness.

Rose poised herself on the wall and leapt out into space. The line from her belt tensed and held her. She felt her stomach lift, as if she was hitting the first big dip on a roller coaster. The metal sleeve above her head roared along the cable. Far beneath her feet, roads and pavements flashed past. The sound of the wind filled her head. Up in front, Robert's body turned and bounced on the cable like a rag doll as he struggled in panic.

She twisted her head back at the retreating building. The dark figures had now engulfed Simon and Jay in a black, writhing mass. Suddenly the edge of a grey concrete building loomed beneath her feet, slightly too far below for her to touch the flashing gravelled rooftop with her shoe. There was a clattering noise above, like points changing, and she felt the lift and drop of a cable-car crossing a pylon. A tall steel rod whistled by on her right side, then the cable was dropping downwards again, over half-lit backstreets. Her heart was in her mouth, all thought pushed from her mind as the city flashed by in a whirling diorama.

A steep tiled roof howled by on the left, then another. Ahead, the cable swung over another station and turned sharply to the right. She could see Robert hit the turn at tremendous speed. His body was flung out almost sideways before being whipped away into the darkness once more. Although she felt sure that she was safe, Rose clung onto her nylon belt-line with both hands.

A dark Victorian building adorned with peeling white balustrades was fast approaching dead ahead. The cable passed over a rusting pylon set in the middle of the roof. She raised her legs instinctively, but found that the line stayed at least eight feet from the surface of the building and she was buffeted over another station, to drop sharply away toward the brightly lit streets which glistened like pulsing arteries through the city's West End.

At first Robert could not bring himself to open his

eyes. He yelled, his stomach somersaulting as his feet struck out and found nothing but the air which screamed and wailed around him, punching at his body, blasting his mind into a half-conscious limbo. When he juddered over the first cable station his immediate thought was that the line was about to come loose. Wrenching open his eyes he forced himself to look up and watched as the sleeve passed smoothly across the cable junction and back out over the city streets.

He looked down again as the line swung him between two tall buildings somewhere behind Tottenham Court Road and realized with astonishment that he was no longer scared. The beauty of the passing streets below, seen as if he were buzzing the city in a low-flying helicopter, surprised and delighted him.

Ahead, the cable turned sharply away towards the city centre. He was able to swing himself around just enough to see Rose behind. Her body twisted with a slow sensual elegance as it strained against the line, the wind contouring her sweatshirt over her breasts. She had lost her jacket somewhere. Robert prayed that she had managed to hang onto the notebook. Her long legs thrust out to the left, then the right, as she rode the cable with what seemed like complete assurance.

Robert's nervousness briefly returned when he was suddenly wrenched sideways and downward, more violently than ever. He swung around and managed to face front just in time to see the Shaftesbury Theatre pass by at great speed just a few feet below. Experimentally, he held his arms out from his sides and found that by doing this he could control his body more easily.

The overhead cable was actually rising now, the velocity he had gained during his journey being enough to lift and throw him along the next section of the run, picking up speed like a roller coaster car. Behind, he caught a glimpse of Rose raising her arms as she copied his movements. He laughed hard and loud, the sound competing with the noise of the wind as the cable curved away over Covent Garden, skirting the edge of the Piazza, where diners sat behind the steamed windows of expensive restaurants, or strolled across the cobbled streets, the momentum rocketing him from one perfect miniature tableau to the next like scenes in a gigantic funfair ride.

His feet had begun to grow numb and his back muscles were starting to cramp as he shot over the Strand towards the Savoy Hotel. He could feel his jacket tearing at the armpits with each successive lift and fall. How was it, he wondered, that people on the ground did not raise their arms and point to the sky in alarm? Up here he felt visible and vulnerable, cutting a swathe across the night sky as if he were a comic-book superhero.

And then he was sweeping in over the back of the Savoy Hotel, the tarred metal roof looming fast beneath his feet. This was the end of the run, the cable terminating here on top of a short metal rod. Robert braced his legs for the impact as the ground rushed up, but was still knocked from his feet by the force of his sudden full-stop. He lay on his back, panting and clutching his side as Rose soared in behind him. She collided hard with the roof, but managed to stay on her feet. Her mouth and eyes were wide with the surprise and exhilaration of the trip.

'About time!' exclaimed a voice behind them. 'Where are the others?' Robert rolled over and raised himself on one elbow. Before him stood a tall man dressed in a heavy black rollneck sweater and jeans. His creased, tanned face was framed with short blonde hair. Cobalt eyes were separated by a long, sharp nose. He was in his early thirties, handsome in a weatherbeaten way. A broad hand reached out and pulled Robert to his feet.

'Somebody attacked us. One of them is dead, Jay I

think,' gasped Robert, still trying to catch his breath. 'We didn't see what happened to Simon or Lee.'

Behind the blonde man, several others appeared from within a jumble of enormous aluminium ducts.

'I knew this would happen. I *knew* it!' The blonde man smashed his fist into the side of a large metal pipe jutting from the floor of the roof, causing it to reverberate with a hollow boom. A slim, pale woman appeared at his side and clutched at his arm.

'How come you managed to make the run and they didn't?' Anger cracked his voice.

'They had already hooked us up,' said Rose defensively. 'There was nothing we could do.'

'So they'll be dropped like the Toad?' asked the pale girl.

'Who knows?' answered the blonde man. 'It's no longer possible to predict their movements.' He turned back to Rose and Robert. 'You two, I suppose you know why you were attacked?'

'No, nobody's explained anything,' said Robert. 'Who are you?'

'Walk with me a while. I think a little exchange of information would be useful.'

The three of them headed off across the roof, while all around people resumed their work, talking in low, urgent voices.

There seemed to be a vast amount of weaponry and equipment spread out on the rooftop. The blonde man reached the far side of the Savoy's roof and sat down on the low concrete lip running around the edge, inviting Robert and Rose to do the same. He seemed to search the night sky, his pale eyes flicking across the hemisphere. As they sat, a bleak yellow moon finally broke the cover of cloud. The blonde man turned to them. 'My name is Doctor Nathaniel Zalian,' he began, 'and you seem to have something I need.'

CHAPTER TWENTY-ONE

Keelhauled

At 11 p.m. the Leicester Square Video Casino was still packed with punters. Drugpushers and pickpockets roamed the lanes between the thundering electronic machines searching for fresh marks, ever vigilant for any sign of the police. Their careless-casual appearance masked heightened senses which were finely attuned to every change of pace within the dingy game room. Beyond the glass doors, the haunted eyes of the waiting addicts betrayed them to the world as their nightly need grew ever more desperate.

Nick still held the halves of Robert's ten-pound notes in the pocket of his filthy jeans. He was wearing dark glasses over his spiderweb tattoo. His eyes were still swollen from fighting, from crying. The Toad was dead and nothing could bring him back, but something could have been done to save him and the others. He presumed that his own life was now in danger, but somehow he could not bring himself to break his routine and stay out of the arcade.

He was still hammering hell out of the Starbiker machine when they came for him. The two skinheads spotted his 7 N Krewe jacket from the other side of the room and began to make their way between the players.

'Hey, what the . . . ?'

The skinny Turkish punk slapped Nick on the back a second time, causing him to misfire on the video machine. Nick turned and saw the consternation in the boy's face.

'You'd better get out of 'ere, man, double quick. They're lookin' for you.'

Nick ducked down behind the machine, then peered over the top to see the skinheads threading their way towards him. Squeezing the Turk's arm in silent thanks he took off, slipping around the back of the change booth and out through the doors at the side of the arcade. The alley beyond was deserted. Nick flicked the dark glasses from his face. He decided to head up into Chinatown, where he knew that he could lose himself in the crazy jumble of vegetable boxes and rubbish cans which stood in front of the restaurants there. Behind him the side door slammed back and the two skinheads emerged. He recognized one of them as Dag, a skinhead with a streak of voyeuristic sadism that allowed him to enjoy officiating at murder ceremonies for Chymes. Nick set off along the alley, trying to stay in the shadows, running lightly on the balls of his feet.

Moments later he looked back to see that the other skinhead had vanished, leaving Dag in solitary pursuit. Confused, he ran on, out of the alley and into the light of Lisle Street, past the back of the cinema complex and up into Gerrard Street, the heart of Chinatown. Here, surrounded by people who were hovering before restaurants comparing menu prices, he was able to slow to a trot. A hundred yards behind him Dag also slowed, waiting for Nick to make a move. This far along Gerrard Street there was only one way out. He would have to exit into the lower half of Wardour Street, which was always crowded with the clubbers who patiently queued for entry into the latest night spots. That suited Nick just fine. He would have no problem losing himself among the punks, rockers, skins and rastas who filled the street at this time of night. He was home free.

Quickly he walked towards the road junction where light and people flooded the pavements.

A sudden pain flared in his thigh. He looked behind and saw nothing, then looked down and saw the ribboned end of the thin steel dart which protruded from the top of his leg. Ahead, the other skinhead stepped out from behind a stack of wooden crates with a dart-gun in his hand. Dag had manœuvred him into a trap. Dag and his accomplice closed in as consciousness swirled away and Nick fell heavily to the pavement.

The billowing figure pulled its cloak a little tighter and stepped easily between the parapets of the two warehouse buildings. Far below, drunken laughter mixed with the muffled pounding of engines as pleasure cruisers chugged down the Thames against the tide. Dag coughed uncomfortably and caught up with his master, nervously jumping the three-foot gap which separated the two roofs.

'It's a fine night, the first of many such nights.' The velvet voice spoke without cadence or strength, yet managed to convey a wealth of power. 'These will be nights of cleansing for us all. They mark the end of weakness, the birth of victory over light. I wanted to thank you for your help in removing the treacherous ones from our midst, Brother. Your loyalty will not go unrewarded.'

Dag swallowed noisily, remembering how Brother Samuel's loyalty had been 'rewarded'. 'What do you want done with the bloke we picked up?' he asked.

'He will be treated most severely for his crimes. I will need your help in carrying out his punishment.'

Dag stole a look at the black, wrathful figure next to him. The face was hidden within the cowl of the dark linen cloak. In the middle of their preparations for the assault on Zalian he had been called away from cleaning and checking the armoury by his leader, the one who went by the name of Chymes, and sent to fetch the boy with the spiderweb tattoo on his face. Now, as they walked along the south wall of the empty dockside warehouse, Chymes began to speak to his acolyte in a low monotone.

'You know that we could not allow the Toad to venture back among the Insects, for he had betrayed and renounced our cause. You assisted admirably in dealing with Brother Samuel, but do you realize why *he* had to die?'

Even a brain the size of Dag's recognized the fact that it was wise not to interrupt when Chymes was employing rhetoric.

'Brother Samuel thought that he had allayed my suspicions by helping to deal with the Toad. But I could see into his heart. I could see the falseness which lay there.' Chymes reached down and prodded Dag in the chest with a bony finger.

'The meddling bitch Sarah Endsleigh,' he said suddenly, as if her name had just occurred to him for the first time. 'When she came to me with promises of undying loyalty, it was Brother Samuel who vouched for her. He knew that the Toad fed her with information, yet he kept his mouth shut and remained her friend. He was the last link in a chain of treachery.

'But now, before the week is out, all those of doubting faith will be gone, for even now there are still traitors among us. Only after the purging will we be pure enough to carry on our task.' The hooded figure stopped and turned. 'Now we must go and deal with Nick.'

Two young men with shaved scarred heads and tattooed faces stepped from behind a smashed chimney stack and grabbed Nick by the arms. Minutes before, the effect of the drugged dart had worn off and he had awoken, stiff with cold and sick with the realization that he had been brought up into the heart of Chymes' dark kingdom.

Chymes stood before him with his arms folded. Metal glinted from one of his hands. His face was shrouded by the black linen hood. At his feet, a disinterested peacock pulled at its feathers.

'You were never good enough to join the Roofworld, were you, Nick?' Chymes gave a dry, mirthless chuckle. 'It must have hurt seeing your friends go up and leave you behind. You couldn't be a part of it, so what did you do? You decided to sell its secret to the newspapers. What a good job we caught you before you told this reporter friend of yours anything too damaging. Refresh my memory . . . who was he?'

'Go fuck yourself. You killed my mate, you can burn in hell.'

'It's of no consequence. I have his name written down somewhere. He was foolish enough to print his byline on the piece, I recall. Journalists crave credibility. They want to be loved so badly that they'll put their names to anything.' The peacock raised its head and gave a sudden startled cry.

'Well, Nick,' sighed Chymes, 'it is time for the disintegration of solution:

' "*The hot lion devours the sun in the heavens,*
And the fiery man will sweat to resolve his body,
To carry it afar through moisture, so that
Happily and beautifully Mercurius may issue forth." '

He reached down and seized the peacock by the neck, selecting a single long plume which he plucked and passed to Dag. The skinhead approached Chymes' new victim and forced his mouth open, then pushed the peacock feather down his throat as if helping out in a sword-swallowing act. Nick began to retch and choke as the feather passed deeper into his trachea. On either side, men held him steady. He tried to throw off his assailants as he staggered back against the chimneystack, but they clung on tight, their stocky muscular bodies slowly pulling him down toward the tarmac floor. Chymes unfolded his arms and gave a signal.

Each time Nick rose and tried to fling the men from him, one of them pierced his hand, then his arm, then his stomach with a long steel needle until he screamed and dropped once more to the ground. In moments, the two muscular brothers had stripped him naked and tied him tight with nylon cord, leaving several hundred yards spare from a knot at his waist.

'You think they ain't got a chance against you,' Nick bellowed, knowing that his death was now just minutes away. 'And you're probably right, but you'll be stopped somehow. You call yourself a lord, you with all your fancy talk and mystic bullshit! Lord over what? A bunch of fucked-up psychopaths, junkies and crazies who'll break into buildings, wound and maim and kill, do whatever you tell them because they need their next fix? Some fucking kingdom!'

'Keelhaul him!' The dark figure spun on its heel, cloak flaring outwards, and strode away.

One of the young thugs pinched Nick's face, pulling it around until it was close to his. 'You ever been keel-hauled, Nicky boy? It's a barbaric practice. Don't half muck you up, looks-wise.'

Nick spat into the grinning face as hard as he could. The other thug kicked him viciously in the chest. He heard, rather than felt, a rib crack.

Together, they knotted a rag across his mouth, then dragged him to the side of the building and lowered him over the low concrete lip. Wrapping the cord tightly around their arms, they allowed the kicking figure to descend, naked and now firmly gagged, down seven floors until his feet were almost touching the ground. Then, laughing, they ran back from the building's edge, hauling Nick's body up the concrete wall, floor by floor.

The stippled roughness of the brick grazed away his

skin, welling first with tiny pinprick drops of blood which fast turned into trickles, then rivers. Foot by agonizing foot he was raised, the flesh from his back and shoulders, face and legs tearing over the piercing, stinging brickwork. Each time he tried to kick away from the passing wall he swung back harder into it, catching and dragging, higher and higher. Soon the pain removed any strength he had left in his legs and he fell back against the wall, the soles of his feet audibly ripping as they caught on tiny spikes of stone.

As he was hoisted over a narrow concrete ledge he swung against a window, which cracked and shattered as he struggled and butted into it. As he rose further up, the jagged glass in the top of the frame found flesh and stuck, bending and snapping off in his skin as the brothers above continued to haul in the cord.

By the fifth floor he had bitten clean through the gag and his tongue, as he left a bloody track up the building and the bricks rasped over areas already scoured clean of skin. When he finally reached the top and they had laid him out on the surface of the roof, he had mercifully lost consciousness. He lay, a bloody skinless puppet of raked meat, barely breathing, nose shattered, face unrecognizable.

'He's no fun, is he?' said one of the brothers, peering over the inert figure with interest. 'Where shall we put him?'

'How about in the window at Harrods?'

'Nah, you don't wanna start a fashion.'

'Could be another shop-awning job.'

'Been done before. I've got a better idea.'

Half an hour later, anyone walking home through the city would, if they had taken the trouble to look up at the buildings surrounding them, have seen an extraordinarily grotesque sight. Jammed over the ornate metal clock which jutted from the wall of the Midland Bank near the Royal Exchange was a blackened red figure in the shape of a crouching man. High above the pavement it hung, growing from the spattered bloodiness of the surrounding wall, its glistening white jaw gaping wide to the sky like the foul figurehead of a ship crewed by the dying and the damned.

CHAPTER TWENTY-TWO

Zalian

'Take a look down there.' Dr Nathaniel Zalian pointed over the side of the building. Taxis were pulling up in front of the Savoy to release their ballgowned and tuxedoed occupants as porters and doormen fussed around them. 'Christmas in London. A time for revelry. The forecourt below is the only street in Britain where you have to drive on the right. Rather fits with the unreal atmosphere that surrounds the Savoy, don't you think? As if you slip into a past world when you come within sight of the building. Over there now.' The pointing finger moved in the direction of Charing Cross Station. 'You know what that is?'

Robert looked over to the tall stone spire which stood in front of the station. 'No, what?'

'It's a replica of the Eleanor Cross. The resting place of Edward the First's Queen, before she was moved to Westminster Abbey. But nowadays the taxi drivers tell tourists that it's the spire of a sunken cathedral, almost as if by fabricating the history of the area they're in some way adding to it. And just along, you have the Strand.' Zalian righted himself and dusted powdery concrete from his hands. 'Of course, there were houses on this road as early as the twelfth century. Boswell used to have his shilling dinners at the chophouse here and paid sixpence to the whores who hung around Tom's. In the 1890s there were more theatres in this street than anywhere else in London. Places like the

Tivoli and the Gaiety . . . now there are just three. "Burlington Bertie walked up the Strand with his gloves in his hand . . . " '

He tilted his head back at the sky. 'Now look at it. Smirking glass banks have replaced the timber-framed houses. For centuries, this was a residential street. Now it's the same as everywhere else – an avenue of faceless multinationals, a concrete shrine to the power of the yen and the pound and the dollar.'

He turned back to face them, ice eyes glittering in the shadowed gloom. Thoughtfully rubbing the blonde stubble on his chin, he drew closer. Rose could see now that the doctor was older than he first appeared to be. The blueness of his eyes seemed to be blurred with the disconsolate fatigue of a battle which had been fought hard and finally, irretrievably lost. Robert wanted to question him as to the whereabouts of Sarah Endsleigh, but sensed that the time was not yet right to ask and elected instead to wait until the doctor had finished speaking.

'Down there wealthy banks exist side by side with rundown rented apartments. Scurrying stockbrokers brush past out-of-work punks. Don't you think it strange that two worlds can exist side by side, knowing nothing of each other, never touching?' He flicked his head away, looking out at the glittering vista below. 'Now to that picture add a third world, the Roofworld, up above the heads of rich and poor alike. That's when you start to get an idea of the dreams we all had. . . .'

Zalian drifted off, as if forgetting that he was actually addressing someone. Away across the roof, his workers were clearing spaces by packing equipment into holdalls and stacking them. He silently studied them for a moment, then looked back at Robert.

'After you've been up here for a while, you begin to gain some kind of perspective to your life. It comes from constantly imagining people on the ground as insects. You just have to watch them at night, wandering around in the filth of the streets, filling in the hours until work begins again. But for most of those with jobs, life is a dead end, like living in a room with a single window that looks out onto a brick wall.' Rose wanted to interrupt, but one look at the almost fanatical gleam in Zalian's eyes convinced her to stay silent.

'And what about those who can't find work? They still want all the things they've been taught to need. Most people's fantasies extend no further than winning a vacation on a quiz show. Hardly their fault. Asked what they really want from life, few will be able to tell you, not because they don't know but because they can't find the words for it. The system doesn't teach articulation.' Anger coloured Zalian's voice. 'It shows them how they should want to live, but not how to be alive. Well, that's not our world. It remains below, forsaken by us. Up here we share one thing in common – a hatred of their dehumanized existence on the ground. A hope that somewhere, life could offer something more than a gruelling fight to keep a job and make ends meet.'

Robert threw Rose a cynical look, but she pointedly ignored it as Zalian concluded his speech.

'This was a secret army which grew across the decades,' he said, 'developing its own rites and rituals.' He paused, choosing his words carefully. 'And eventually it created the seeds of its own destruction.' Robert looked up as a flotilla of clouds swept the edges of the moon. Zalian continued to talk in a soft monotone, half to himself. 'But kids still turn to drugs and adults still lose their hope and, as the remaining lines of human communication break down, some of those people still come up here to us.'

'I don't understand,' said Rose. 'If that's the case, why are there so few of you now?'

Zalian broke from his reverie and towered over the

puzzled girl standing by him at the parapet. His disconcertingly blue eyes were difficult to look at for more than a few seconds at a time.

'It doesn't concern you,' he said at length. 'The less you know, the safer you'll be. You're here for one reason – to provide us with the information we need. I was expecting you, but I didn't forsee that your arrival would be so late in the game.'

'You were waiting for us?' said Robert, disturbed. 'I don't get it. What could we do?'

'Exactly what you did.' Zalian shrugged his wide shoulders. 'You brought us Charlotte Endsleigh's notebook.'

'You knew it was in our possession?'

'Of course.'

'I still don't get it,' said Robert. 'I mean, how did you know about it in the first place? And what made you think we would actually deliver it here?'

'We don't have time to go into this,' said Zalian with a sudden urgency in his voice. Behind Rose, one of his men was making a series of bizarre hand signals which the others watched and began to obey.

'Follow me back to headquarters and your questions will be answered later.'

'No, you explain, or we'll go back to the ground right now,' said Rose firmly. 'And we're taking the secret of the book with us.' She could see that Zalian was not a man of violence. There was an open honesty in his creased face which inspired trust. Still, for a brief moment, she thought that he was going to attack her. Then the tall blonde man seemed to reach a decision.

'You already knew that Sarah Endsleigh was one of us.' Zalian looked from one face to the other. 'When she first joined, she told me that her mother was a novelist. One day I found out that Sarah had been telling her about the Roofworld. . . .'

'And you killed her mother just to stop her from publishing?' asked Robert.

'Don't be stupid, boy. None of us laid a finger on her. We figured she was harmless, that even if she did manage to write a book about our life up here nobody would take it seriously. After all, she only knew a fraction of what really goes on.' Zalian ran long, tanned fingers through his pale hair. 'Then I discovered that Sarah had done a stupid, dangerous thing. She had told Charlotte about the New Age.'

'What's the "New Age"?'

'The one subject she was sworn never to mention to outsiders. Sarah knew more about it than any of us. But she gave the information she had amassed to her mother instead of delivering it to me.'

'Why would she do that?'

'I'm not sure. We knew that the notes had to be somewhere inside the old woman's apartment because she hardly ever went out, so we decided to keep a watch on the building day and night. Suddenly we desperately needed the notebook for reasons of our own.'

'Reasons you'd care to divulge?' asked Robert.

'No.'

'Why didn't you just break in and turn the joint over?'

'We attempted to, shortly after Charlotte was murdered, but *she* – ' Zalian pointed at Rose, 'she made sure that the place was wired to the sky with alarms.'

'So you kept watch . . .'

'Hoping that someone would search the apartment again and turn up the book. We scared the hell out of some old woman who left with a pile of Charlotte's belongings.'

'The aunt,' said Robert. 'Then I conveniently came along and ransacked the place. But as soon as you saw that we had the notebook why didn't you just take it from us?'

'It was one of our men who attacked you in the alleyway behind Leicester Square,' admitted Zalian. 'I trust he didn't hurt you.'

'You could have saved yourself a lot of time and trouble simply by asking for the bloody thing,' said Robert indignantly.

'And would you have handed it over?'

'No, I suppose not.'

'It was too risky staging a kidnap. You've been surrounded by people all the time you've had it in your possession.'

Rose quickly felt inside her sweatshirt for the book. Locating the edge of its pages she gripped it tightly to her. 'I don't get it,' she said. 'We've read through the damned thing and it makes no sense. There's no clue to the identity of Charlotte's killer. What are you hoping to find out from it?'

'If you want to stay alive for much longer, it's better that neither of you know that,' said Zalian, looking at his watch. 'It's time to leave. I'm afraid that you're going to have to come with us whether you want to or not.'

CHAPTER TWENTY-THREE

Attack

'I can't breathe.'

'Well, loosen it a little. Come here.' Rose unbuckled Robert's line-belt and refastened it. All around them, people were dragging boxes across the roof and transferring their contents to small nylon bags. They were preparing to leave the roof of the Savoy and return to headquarters somewhere in the city. Zalian had left them in order to supervise the repacking of a small armoury.

'It's not the belt. It's the thought of going out on one of those lines again.'

'You did it once without any problem, you can do it again. There.' Rose stood up and stretched. She and Robert were both now wearing shapeless black jumpsuits, rather like one-size factory overalls, although hers seemed to fit a lot better than his. They had been fitted with belts by the sullen young girl who had appeared earlier at Zalian's side. Her name was Spice and she seemed to resent their ready acceptance into the group. Robert glanced at his watch. It was almost 11.30. 'This isn't right. It's past my bedtime. I should be at home, decorating the tree.'

'You bought a tree?' asked Rose. 'You go to church at Christmas, all that stuff?'

'No, the tree's one of those folding plastic ones.'

'Yes, I figured it would be,' she said, glancing down as she adjusted the clips of her jumpsuit.

'What's that supposed to mean?'

'Just that we're different people, Robert.'

He released a low growl of irritation. Looking at Rose now, he recognized the type all too well. She was one of those women who saw themselves as romantic and free spirited, while all the time putting men down as emotional cripples. Well, he thought, we'll see who comes running to whom before this thing is through.

At the edge of the roof, seven or eight men and women were stacking bags. Altogether there were more than fifteen people working up here, yet virtually no sound came from them as they carried out their designated tasks. There was a light clatter of metal as someone fired a line to another building.

'I wouldn't trust Zalian as far as I could throw him,' said Robert as he slipped a line-gun into his back pocket. 'He has a disconcerting habit of walking away just when you want him to explain something.' He twisted the line-gun around until it fitted snugly. 'I hope this bloody thing doesn't go off by itself when I bend over.'

'It's got a safety catch, remember?' said Rose. 'If you don't stop worrying so much you'll give yourself an ulcer.'

'Worrying?' muttered Robert. 'What have I got to worry about, apart from staying alive. Christ, it's freezing.'

'You're supposed to clip up the top of the jacket like this.' She pointed to her own suit. Behind Robert, there was a whisper of cable as the first group left the roof of the Savoy. Rose turned to watch as they vanished over the side of the building.

'That's why they moved strangely when I saw them that night in Regent Street. They were transporting equipment. Don't see any dog, though.'

The young woman called Spice climbed onto the parapet in preparation for launching herself off on one of the newly established lines. She reached down and scooped up a huge sack of equipment in her free arm, looking back at Zalian as she did so. One of the men was carrying what looked like a tripod.

'I wonder what that's for?' said Robert. 'I guess if they've been living up here for so many years they must have developed a special tool for just about everything.'

'. . . Except for fighting,' said a voice behind them. They turned to find Zalian standing alongside watching the departure of the others. 'We never had need of weapons until now. We're too exposed here and there are too few of us to risk losing any more. It's common knowledge that we use the Savoy roof in times of emergency. We must return to headquarters.'

The last of Zalian's crew swung away from the roof. The pile of equipment had been divided up and removed. Only the three of them now remained. Zalian scooped up two small boxes and handed them to Robert and Rose. 'Keep these in your supply bags. They contain medical aids. Up here you never know when you'll need them. We should be going.' Zalian's eyes fell to Robert's jumpsuit. 'You have the notebook on you?'

If he tries to snatch it from me, thought Rose, he's in for a fight. Robert seemed to read her mind and was careful not to let Zalian see which of them was in possession of it. 'Wait a minute, Zalian. This "exchange of information" seems to be a little one-sided. You get the book after you tell us where Sarah Endsleigh is.'

'You're a fool, boy,' said Zalian tiredly. 'I could have it taken from you in a second and have had both of you tossed over the side.' Despite the threat, he made no move forward. He's bluffing, thought Rose. Maybe he doesn't know where Sarah is either. Slipping her hand back into the top of her jumpsuit she laid her palm across the dark-blue cover.

'Tell us where we can find the girl and the notes are yours,' said Robert rashly. His newly acquired street credibility had obviously gone to his head. At this precise moment he no longer cared about securing his book rights, for he had been granted a glimpse of a genuine mystery, and now he wanted to see more.

'I can't tell you that,' said Zalian finally. 'I need the book to discover Sarah's exact whereabouts. We have reason to believe that it contains information which will lead us to her, as well as others who are being held captive.'

'Then we'll work together on it.'

'No! There's an evil around us, something far too dangerous for you to know about. From the moment they know of your involvement, I can no longer keep you alive.'

'You mean you're protecting us right now?' asked Rose.

'You have no comprehension of the forces at work here. I was a fool to even let them bring you up.' Zalian cocked his head to one side. He turned, slowly searching the nearby roof top for something, a scuffle of sound, a blur of movement in the encroaching darkness.

'They're coming,' he hissed. 'We've left it too long. Hand me the book, then get out of here quickly.'

Behind them the ping of a cable sounded, then the clatter of metal on brick. Robert held his position as Rose moved closer to his side.

'You must give the book to me, then forget all of this ever happened. Knowledge of us can only bring you harm!' Zalian reached out his hand to take the book.

Robert reached into his jumpsuit, then suddenly withdrew his hand and pushed him as hard in the chest as he could before breaking away into a run. Zalian was caught off balance and slipped on the gravelled asphalt. Rose screamed, but caught up at Robert's side.

'You're fools!' shouted Zalian. 'I'm trying to save your lives!'

'Robert, what the hell do you think you're doing?' shouted Rose. 'He's trying to help us!'

'You ready for this?' asked Robert breathlessly. 'It's a long drop.' Together they ran to the side of the building and fastened their lines to the already strung cables leading away up the Strand. Against her better judgement, Rose pushed Robert out first so that she could keep an eye on him, then released herself on the line a few yards behind. As she pushed out, she turned to see Zalian closing fast behind them as a number of shadowy figures appeared beyond.

'Dr Zalian!' she shouted hoarsely. 'Behind you! Look out!' Zalian turned and faced the racing figures as the first of their poisoned missiles whistled past his ears. He reached the side of the building further along, leapt over the edge and dropped onto a line.

Rose reached the wall of the next building. As she detached the line and jumped onto the roof one of the razor-sharp projectiles bounced over the sole of her left boot, neatly slicing the leather. Behind her, Robert slammed into the wall, misjudging the distance. She helped him to clamber over the parapet, praying as she did so that the coin had failed to cut her skin.

'How's your shoulder?' Robert was clutching the top of his left arm.

'All right. You get hit?' He bent down to examine Rose's foot. They had dropped behind a chimneystack and were now out of firing range. 'It hasn't gone right through the leather.'

On the far side of the roof Zalian pulled himself up, unfastening the line as he did so. He ran on ahead across the wide sloping grey tiles to the connecting building which was a full floor higher. Reaching its base, he fired a line from the metal disc in his pocket, hooked it and allowed the device to haul him up the twenty-foot-high concrete wall. 'Come with me,' he called. 'They'll try to follow. We've got to outdistance them until it's safe to get you back to the ground.' He threw the disc down to Robert, leaving it attached at the top of the wall.

'He knows the territory, Robert. Without him we're dead,' said Rose, looking around anxiously. 'Let's do as he says.'

Robert hooked the disc to his belt and flicked the button which recalled the line, using his legs to keep him from being dragged against the wall as he rose. Two men, dressed in dark shapeless clothes and hoods, appeared at the edge of the roof. Robert threw the line down to Rose just as the poisoned coins began to pock the wall. In her panic to get to the top, Rose pushed her disc switch hard to allow the fastest rewind possible and shot straight up the brickface as if fired from a slingshot, very nearly flying straight over, to be caught instead by Zalian's powerful arms.

Ahead of them was a vast expanse of black and grey rooftop where several buildings were connected in a sprawling terrace. In seconds they were running as fast as they could to the far side.

'They'll just keep coming after us!' shouted Rose. 'I'm getting a stitch.'

'I have something for this,' Zalian called back. 'Stay close.' He withdrew from his supply bag a larger version of his pocket line-gun and loaded a cartridge into it. Carefully aiming at the broad face of a glass-pillared office block situated further along on the north side of the Strand, he lined up the magnifying sight on the gun barrel until he had located a connecting bar on the opposite wall and fired. Incredibly, the line connected with a thud, across a distance of three hundred yards.

'How?' was all Robert could say, his mouth falling open in amazement.

'Laser light,' said Zalian, pointing to a tube the thickness of a pencil soldered along the top of the gun. 'You fire when the light hits your target. We've got a couple of these, stole 'em from the Oxford Street Christmas light show last year.' He grinned. 'Come on.'

Zalian clipped the line from the gun to the parapet of the building with practised speed, then attached Robert's line and pushed him off. He had no time to take up the slack in the cable and Robert dipped alarmingly over the road.

'Don't ever get your belt-line twisted, or it'll stop you dead,' he said, checking Rose's belt. He paused for a second and looked at her, screwing up one eye. 'Under any other circumstances I'd take you on a night tour of the city,' he said with a sour smile. 'You're a born natural.'

Rose smiled nervously back and lowered herself over the edge of the building. 'Thanks,' she said. 'I may take you up on it, if we live to see the dawn.'

She kicked away from the wall with her feet and dipped out between the buildings. Ahead, Robert had crossed the Strand and was nearing the office block. Zalian was just about to attach his own line when one of the hooded men came at him from across the roof. Whirling, he pulled his pocket line-gun free and fired it at the running figure, hitting him square in the chest. The impact threw the man from his feet, knocking the breath from his lungs. Two more hooded figures appeared, one of them a woman. Both stopped to take aim and fire their coin-guns. Zalian felt one pass by an inch beyond his face as he launched himself free and flew across the broad city street.

'My God, they're going to cut the line,' screamed Rose, pointing back at the roof they had just left. Robert had just hauled her up over the side and detached her line. Two dark figures were bent over the chevroned moulding along the top of the far building as they tried to free the cord from its mooring, but Zalian's weight on it prevented them from doing so. One of them produced a knife and began to saw at the line. Zalian was still only two-thirds of the way across.

'Get ready to grab him as he comes in,' called Robert. On the other side, the dark figures hacked at the cable frantically, while on the line below them, Zalian was beginning to slow down. Rose outstretched her arms and leaned as far as she dared over the edge of the roof. They succeeded in cutting through the cable moments too late. The cord whipped free with a sharp snap just as Robert and Rose grabbed Zalian's arms and hauled him up to safety.

'They've cut themselves off,' said Zalian, laughing hoarsely. 'Only we have the laser guns, thanks to Lee. Keep moving, though. There could be others around and we've still a way to go.'

Shaking with nervous excitement, Robert reached out to Rose and Zalian, who supported him as they half ran, half walked, moving swiftly across the tiles and away from danger.

'All right, slow down. We're safe now.' Zalian turned to face them, walking backwards. 'This is where I have to leave you. There's a fire escape over there.' He pointed across to a set of grey metal railings. 'It'll take you down into Covent Garden. Don't let anyone see you descend.'

Rose was still trying to catch her breath. It was Robert who spoke. 'The book. What if we give it to you for safekeeping?'

'That may not guarantee your own safety now. But it could save the lives of others.'

'Shall I give him it, Robert?' Rose leaned forward with her hands on her knees. Robert nodded reluctantly and passed the notebook from Rose to Zalian, who immediately began to flick through it. For two or three minutes all that could be heard was the rasping of breath and the traffic below as the doctor shone a pencil torch on the rumpled pages. Then he slowly closed the book and looked up with a scowl on his face. 'It's not here.'

'What's not there?'

'The plans to the New Age. This is just full of minor details about us.'

'That's the right book though, isn't it?' asked Robert.

'It's *one* of them all right,' said Zalian. 'Somewhere there's a second volume to this.' He held the notebook up and turned it over. On the back, they could see something that neither of them had noticed before. A large number '1', drawn in faint green pencil.

'Oh, Jesus. I think I know where the other one went.' Robert turned to look at Rose. She suddenly looked very uncomfortable.

'What do you mean?' he asked.

'You remember I told you about the elderly relative taking Charlotte's belongings away?' Rose's look of discomfort had turned to guilt. 'I gave her a hand with the boxes. She couldn't manage. One of them was overloaded. Some stuff fell out . . .'

'Including the notes I found.'

'It's possible. I just remember picking up an exercise book and putting it on top of the box.'

'I thought you said she didn't take any books with her?'

'This wasn't a *real* book, just a notebook.'

'Wait,' said Zalian. 'How can you remember so clearly?'

'I noticed it at the time because it had a big number "2" on the front.'

Zalian and Robert groaned simultaneously. 'You're going to have to get it back,' said Zalian. 'Tomorrow morning. Now I must go and make sure that the others have reached headquarters safely.'

'Wait!' Robert shouted after him. 'Are you ever going to tell either of us what this is all about?'

'Let's hope you never have to know,' called Zalian,

striding away across the roof. 'If we fail, you'll be reading about it in the papers. Get me the other notebook, then we'll talk.'

'Come on, let's get down from here, Robert. I'm exhausted.' Despite the cold December night Rose's face was running with sweat. Streaks of soot contoured her shining cheeks. By the time Robert had turned back, Zalian had vanished from sight, hidden among the turrets and escarpments of the city.

Together they stood looking out across the roofscape as their heartbeats slowed and their breath finally subsided to a natural rhythm once more. In the distance, the misty lights of the Trafalgar Square Christmas tree twinkled. The strains of a carol could be faintly heard – 'Silent Night'.

'Listen to that. It's as if the whole thing never happened,' whispered Rose. Aching and enervated, they levered themselves onto the fire escape and began the slow climb down to street level, as the ochre moon bore silent witness to their secret journey.

CHAPTER TWENTY-FOUR

Morgue

Nobody patronized the *Capricciosa* for the food, which mainly consisted of soggy pastas, leaking Chicken Kievs and indifferently prepared veal cutlets. They came for the ambience, which was created by day-glo murals depicting street scenes of Palermo, and flamboyant singing waiters, who made sexually suggestive advances with their peppermills and who were able to make many of their female patrons dismiss the poor cuisine and even tip heavily by handing them a carnation and a cheeky line about their sexy eyes.

Ian Hargreave and Janice Longbright ate at the *Capricciosa* for neither reason. They came there because the chef was still prepared to cook a meal after midnight and because it was close to the morgue. Janice loved eating with Ian, who would fill these mealtimes with anecdotes and questions on all manner of subjects. She found his restless, enquiring nature extremely appealing. She only wished he would take their relationship more seriously, by asking her to move in with him.

Tonight, Hargreave was quieter than usual. He stared in fascination as Janice tucked away the last of her profiteroles. Her appetite was prodigious, which befitted a woman who looked as if she still might have a ration-book tucked about her voluptuous person. For weeks now he had wanted to ask her if she would consider becoming engaged to him, but so far he had been unable to find the right time and place to attempt this momentous request. Consequently the pair of them kept the conversation circling around every subject but the one they most wanted to talk about.

'I always like a heavy meal before a visit to the morgue,' said Hargreave finally. 'It pays to line your stomach.' He watched as Janice creased her napkin to a point and wiped flecks of cream from her perfectly formed upper lip. 'This makes corpse number four. One a day.' He signalled for a waiter. 'Young male of mixed descent, found over in the city's financial district. That's why it's better that we see what we're dealing with tonight, before the papers start speculating. One more story from Cutts suggesting a rooftop sniper and we'll have a panic on our hands.'

'The BBC covered it on the national news tonight, did you see?'

'No, I was downstairs running through the Missing Person computer checks.'

'Have you spoken to Cutts?' asked Janice, pushing her plate away. 'He seems to know more about what's going on than the police. I'd like to know who he's talking to.'

'I was thinking of pulling him in, but you know he'll never reveal his information source. As it is, there's evidence falling out of the sky all over the bloody city. It's just that none of it seems to lead anywhere.'

Earlier that evening, identification of the remaining victims had finally come through. As Hargreave had suspected, each one had been officially registered as a Missing Person some while before his death.

'It seems as if the more you find out, the less you're sure of,' said Janice. 'You know that our beloved assistant commissioner has already suggested posting teams on the rooftops at strategic points around the West End, don't you?'

'So he told me. We've been randomly pulling in every kid with a criminal record that we can lay our hands on and what do I keep hearing? "Oh, yeah, there's something big going down, but I dunno who's involved." "What sort of something big?" "Dunno, just something I heard." "Who did you hear it from?" "Can't remember." Well, we'll have to see if we can make some progress tonight.' Hargreave threw his napkin onto the table and rose. 'Let's get out of here before they bring the sweet trolley within grabbing distance of you again.'

*

'Ah, Butterworth, how very nice of you to join us, lad,' said Hargreave in a somewhat disrespectfully jolly tone, considering that he was leaning against a drawer containing a dead body. 'I thought perhaps you were prancing about in some disco, where you couldn't hear your bleeper.'

'No, sir,' said Butterworth sleepily. 'I was in bed.' He pulled the waistband of his pyjamas above the belt of his police trousers as an offer of proof.

'Well, early nights make a man healthy, but in this job you'll never be wealthy and as for wise, Butterworth . . .' Hargreave chuckled. The garlicky dinner and Janice's company had put him in high spirits. He wondered if he should be a little more wary of teasing the young detective constable, even though the boy's father would soon retire as commissioner. But Butterworth seemed like a good egg. He could take it. And Lord knows, he needed his ideas bucking up if he was to amount to anything.

'Well, who knows, you may surprise us all yet. What we have here . . .' He paused to prod Butterworth's podgy stomach with a nicotine-stained finger, 'is a singularly gruesome sight. What did you have for dinner?'

'Pork curry, sir.'

'Just the thing. Cop a look at this. Mr Finch, if you would be so kind.'

Finch, the forensic man, pulled out the drawer Hargreave had been leaning against and unzipped the plastic body bag within to reveal the remains of Nick, late of the 7 N Krewe. Peeping out from inside the rumpled grey plastic shroud, the corpse, its red-black skin hanging from it in shreds, was contorted out of all recognition of humanity. Behind them, Janice leaned forward and studied the body with purely professional interest.

'You'll never guess where they found this beauty, my boy. Less than two hours ago he was discovered gracing the top of the clock outside the Midland Bank near the Royal Exchange. Finch, you've had a chance to look him over, I believe. Anything of interest to tell us?'

Finch walked around to the head of the drawer and bent down, his long nose almost touching the face of the corpse, his knees cracking as he did so. He was wearing the most appalling aftershave in an effort to cover up the smell of the chemicals he had accidentally spilled on his lab coat earlier in the day.

'Well, despite the cold night air, the body's still a little warm, pretty much in the early stages of rigor mortis.' He circled around it, prodding the flesh occasionally with the end of his biro. 'His rectal temperature . . .'

'Is that entirely necessary?' asked Hargreave, pulling a face.

'It is if you wish to ascertain the time of death,' Finch cut in, irritated. He liked Hargreave, but found his flippant attitude infuriating. 'We subtract the rectal temperature from the normal body temperature and divide by 1.5. Now, you'll see that the gravitational staining – the sinking of the blood – is around the legs and buttocks, here and here,' he prodded with his biro, 'suggesting that he was wedged on top of the clock just minutes after death occurred.'

Butterworth tucked his pyjamas back in and stared

at the twisted body, his curry slowly ebbing in the pit of his stomach.

'There's an incredible amount of external damage to the body,' Finch continued. 'The clavicle is broken, as are the shins and a number of ribs. Many of the main muscles, in particular the transverse abdominal muscle and the obliquus externus, are badly torn. The skin has suffered so many lesions that it's almost impossible to catalogue them. Many of the wounds have occurred on top of each other, so that we have this muscle damage below skin lacerations and in some cases damage right down to the scapulae.'

'Which leads Mr Finch here to conclude the cause of death . . .' began Hargreave with an unpleasant grin, aimed quite deliberately at making Detective Constable Butterworth feel ill. The boy's ashen face had thrown his freckles into such relief that he looked like a measles patient.

'Well, I wouldn't say that his experience necessarily killed him, so we could assume that he eventually died through loss of blood.'

'Poor devil,' murmured Janice, the only person in the glaring green and white room to show any sympathy for the deceased.

'Mr Finch, be so good as to explain what you imagine his "experience" might have been.'

Finch leaned on the top of the drawer, warming – as it were – to his subject.

'He's been dragged over something like cobbles or bricks. There are fragments of stonework lodged under the remaining fingernails and beneath the skin. There are even splinters of wood and glass buried as deep as the ventriculus . . .'

'What?'

'Tummy,' said Finch, pointing to his own stomach, 'and there are brick fragments scraping the femur and tibia. As you can see, several shards of glass have pierced the vitreous humour of the right eye, and possibly the back of the socket, and they've even gone through the roof of the mouth. He's bitten his tongue clean through. There's no evidence of the missing piece. I thought he had swallowed it until I realized that there was something blocking the throat. I haven't removed it because it's a little too early to start an autopsy, but I wouldn't mind ligating the neck and removing a portion of the trachea from below. I think it's a peacock feather.'

'I beg your pardon?'

Finch leaned forward and grinned horribly. 'You know, feather from a peacock, *Pavo cristatus*. Badtempered creatures, used to have one in my garden.'

'But what the hell is it doing down his throat?' asked Hargreave, staggered. 'Can you get it out?'

Finch rubbed his chin thoughtfully. 'I don't know about keeping it in one piece.'

'I'm not worried about that. I don't want it as a bloody souvenir.'

'I'll have a go. I'll slash the base of the trachea and have a root about.'

Hargreave smiled cheerfully at Butterworth, who looked up just in time to see Finch absently put the end of his biro in his mouth. He suddenly felt terribly sick.

'Thank you, Mr Finch. In other words, you couldn't find a more thoroughly pulped piece of meat if you bought it from McDonald's in a bun. So, my good friends Longbright and Butterworth, thoughts and conclusions. . . .'

'Were there any signs to indicate that he'd been murdered on the ground?'

'Good point, Janice. No, we can assume that the blood on the pavement fell from the body after it had been placed on top of the clock. Large splatters, dropping from a considerable height.'

'So it's the same as the others. Killed from above?'

'It would seem so.' Hargreave rounded on Butterworth with a smile that had now assumed grisly proportions. 'Which brings me to the reason for dragging you away from your bunny-rabbit nightlight, Butterworth, and out into the unkind neon of the morgue.'

Butterworth gave Hargreave an odd look. He could sense that the game was afoot and that the chief was starting to ride high on the adrenalin of the hunt. Suddenly he had a horrible feeling that he would be asked to do something challenging and possibly injurious to his health. He looked first at Janice, then eyed his boss with nervous suspicion. They walked out in the corridor to the coffee machine and Butterworth swallowed mouthfuls of the scalding liquid in an effort to remove the sickly chemical smell of the morgue from his head.

'The word is out in the West End,' said Hargreave, peering over the top of his plastic cup at the now yellow-faced detective constable. 'Our men are picking up a buzz from the pubs and the arcades and the snooker halls. Everybody and his dog seems to know that something bad is going to happen before the end of the week, but nobody – *nobody* – is willing to say what that event is, or how many deaths it might entail. So what have we got on our hands here? An approaching massacre? Torching a dodgy drinking club, or having a knife fight in a Chinese restaurant, that's gang warfare. But what do you call torturing people to death and mounting them on public buildings? What are we supposed to conclude from this, eh?'

He drained his cup and tossed it into a nearby fire-bucket. 'Perhaps we have a gang of renegade architects on our hands. To hell with post-modernism, let's give the city a medieval look. Or it might be,' he wagged his finger at Butterworth, 'It *might* be tied up with our mysterious rooftop sightings. Come on, my son.' He threw a paternal arm around Butterworth, who tried hard not to flinch. 'We're going to be up all night. That way, we won't be accused of napping on the job if something does start to happen. If we start to fall asleep we'll take some of Janice's diet pills. They work wonders. Let's start with a visit to the computer room.'

As they trotted up the steps of the morgue and out into the bleak night air, Hargreave winked at Janice before turning nimbly to Butterworth and clapping him on the shoulders. 'You have been chosen to help me in this adventure for two very good reasons,' he said. 'Firstly, so that you may get a chancc to prove to your father what an excellent detective you will make one day.' And here he stopped, becoming lost in thought as he walked.

'And the second?' prompted Butterworth.

Hargreave looked up, distracted. 'Oh, it's the baby face.' He circled a finger in the air. 'For some reason it looks as if you missed puberty. If we get any leads, we'll be able to send you up there with 'em. Don't worry, you'll have Janice here and me to protect you. Learn to think of us as your extra mummy and daddy.'

Beyond the black rooftops of the sleeping city, stars glimmered faintly in the crystalline night air. Below in the morgue, Nick's earthly remains were sealed back in their drawer to await the heartless ravages of Finch's scalpel.

And Butterworth's face turned an interesting shade of kipper once more as he obediently followed his boss back to headquarters.

CHAPTER TWENTY-FIVE

Trash

The empty grey eyes stared straight ahead, interested in nothing and no one. Slowly the lips parted to reveal neat ivory teeth and the mouth curved up in a broad mirthless grin. The face was bland and bloodless and conscience-free, the features set in a square and even fashion which prevented even the slightest sensation from showing through. It was the face of a man who would watch you die without feeling a flicker of emotion. . . .

Suddenly Robert was awake. He sat up and looked at the clock on the bedside table. Unsurprisingly, he had overslept. Beyond the confines of the duvet, the flat was bitterly cold. Presumably the boiler was misbehaving again. He climbed out of bed and into his dressing-gown just as the telephone began to ring.

'Robert, are you awake?' The voice was one which had grown all too familiar in the past forty-eight hours.

'Christ, Rose, don't you ever sleep? Leave me alone for a few hours. The boiler's on the blink. It's like Alaska in here. I'm going back to bed before I get hypothermia.' Robert pulled open a curtain. The sky beyond the pane was heavy with low cloud, the colour of dead ash.

'You can't go back to bed. I've found her address. The woman who took away Charlotte's belongings.'

'Well, why don't you go around there? Let me know

how you get on. I'll just be here chipping the cat out of his basket.'

'Hey, I thought you were the one who wanted to write the screenplay.'

'And wind up dead like Charlotte. Yeah, I did say that, didn't I? But you can't write with frostbite. So I'm going back to bed now. 'Bye.' Robert replaced the receiver and crawled back beneath the quilt.

Twenty minutes later there was a knock at the door. He stumbled into the hall, unlocked the burglar bolts and before he had time to focus his eyes Rose was inside. She was wearing a black denim jumpsuit which had deep pockets full of spanners and screwdrivers.

'You see, in order to manage my apartment block properly,' she said, as if there had been no interruption in their conversation, 'I have to know all there is to know about the workings of the central heating system, including the boilers. You go and make coffee – I'll do the rest.'

Too exhausted to argue, Robert bumbled off into the kitchen.

Rose had a habit of making him feel so damned inadequate. Robert's lack of practicality had always bothered him. His father, the most empirical of men, had always mocked his efforts when he had tried to win a little admiration and affection. He had eventually given up attempting to emulate the old man and had been forced to face up to the fact that pragmatism was not in his nature.

As he was setting the steaming cups down on the kitchen table, Rose came through and washed her hands at the sink.

'Heat's on,' she said with a smile. 'Your diverter switch was jammed. You need to get the whole system drained down and descaled. They haven't been making boilers like that since Rod Stewart was popular.'

'I'd like to know who Zalian's at war with,' said Robert, launching an extreme change of subject.

'Presumably we'll find that out from the other notebook. You realize that he's using us to find it?'

'True, but you stand a better chance of recovering it than he does. You've already met the woman. Where does she live?'

'Other side of the river. Greenwich. You think they're watching us?'

'Who?'

'Zalian's men.'

'I don't know. I'm more concerned about his enemies.' Robert watched Rose as she drank her coffee. There was a surprisingly delicate grace in her movements. Yesterday she had travelled among the rooftops like a high-wire artist, cat-like and confident. He couldn't have said the same for himself. . . .

'They only seem to move about at night. It's probably too risky during the day. They'd be seen from the ground. Besides, we're safe over in Greenwich. It's not like the centre of town – the roads are wider and the buildings are lower. There's nowhere for them to hide.'

'Even so,' said Robert, 'Let's try to avoid alleyways this time.'

They alighted from the bus outside the east entrance to the National Maritime Museum and consulted the slip of paper Rose had in her purse. The soft grey mist from the parklands beyond had moved down into the surrounding streets and hung hazily about them.

'She must have money, living here,' said Robert. 'Look at these houses.' The terraced Georgian properties lining the street were immaculately maintained. Reproduction Victorian interiors glistened behind each window. Every house was fitted with a burglar alarm.

'I bet there's not a single chip shop around here,' said Rose. 'I know what these yuppie areas are like. They're all right if you need a fluted Edwardian grate in a hurry, but try to buy a decent flip-top bin . . .'

The doorbell of number forty-three chimed melodiously as Rose stepped back from the front door and hastily smoothed out her jumpsuit, as if it would make the slightest bit of difference to her appearance. Robert glanced at her and smiled. She looked like a sexy car mechanic.

The elderly man who came to open the door looked at them with all the mistrust that the old have for the young.

'I hope we're not disturbing you,' said Robert, stepping forward. 'We're looking for Mrs Russell.'

'I am her husband.'

'She's related to a friend of ours,' said Rose. Robert noted that she was making an attempt to refine her cockney accent. The resulting manner of speech was odd, but rather endearing, rather like Dick Van Dyke in *Mary Poppins*. 'We wondered if it would be possible to speak to her for a few minutes.'

'I'm afraid it wouldn't,' said the old man wearily. 'Mrs Russell is in St Peter's hospital.'

'I'm very sorry to hear that,' said Rose. 'What's wrong with her?'

'She was attacked two nights ago. We don't know by whom.'

'I hope it's not serious.'

'Who knows, at her age? She had concussion, a broken arm, some cracked ribs. You're not safe anywhere these days.'

'Perhaps we could . . .' began Robert, but Rose stamped on his foot. 'Thank you for telling us, Mr Russell,' she said. 'I hope your wife is feeling better soon. Please let her know that Rose Leonard sends her best wishes.'

'I'm going to see her later. I'll tell her.' The door closed.

As they walked away from the house Robert hobbled, massaging his foot. 'What did you have to do that for?'

'You were about to ask if we could visit her, yes?'

'So?'

'What if he had said no? You could see how suspicious he was of us. It'll be better if we find out the visiting times and go along there by ourselves.'

'And what if we run into her husband?'

'We'll get there early and be gone before he arrives.'

The hospital ward was just about as inhospitable as such a place could be. The distant clip-clop of sensible shoes echoed between rows of great iron beds and bounced from the murky green wall tiles, stirring forgotten schoolday fears. In fact, the vast room was so spartan, so lacking in anything which could be defined in modern terms as comfortable that Florence Nightingale herself might have looked on and wished for a little more luxury.

At first it surprised Robert that Mrs Russell had not opted for a private room. Then he remembered the haste with which she had stripped Charlotte Endsleigh's belongings from her home and realized that they were not dealing with a generous woman.

'Mrs Russell, do you remember me?' Rose leaned forward over the bed. Visiting hours had just started and as yet few people had entered the ward. The old lady peered up at her from a valley of white linen and forced a smile. One eye was covered with a gauze patch. She looked in a bad way.

'Rose.'

'That's right.'

'Is Teddy with you?' Rose presumed Teddy to be her husband. She shook her head. 'No, but I'm sure he'll be along any minute now. Who did this to you?'

'I've already talked to the police,' she said in a voice

that was little more than a croak. 'It was skinheads, two of these skinheads. Like him.' She pointed at Robert.

'Oh, great,' muttered Robert, ruffling his hair until it stood up. She was the second person this week to make a reference to his receding hairline.

'Do you have any idea why you were attacked, Mrs Russell?'

'I came out to empty the dustbin. They were outside, waiting. One of them hit me in the stomach.'

'What about the other one? What did he do?'

'Kept shouting.'

'Do you remember what he was shouting about?'

'I couldn't understand him. He kept shouting in my face. Over and over. . . .'

'Then what happened?'

'I hit him across the nose with my poker.' Robert was forced to stifle a laugh. One up to the old broad. 'I keep it just inside the door.'

'That's the way, Mrs Russell. We think we know what they were after. You remember collecting Charlotte's belongings? Do you recall seeing a blue notebook?'

The old lady turned her head aside. Rose could not tell whether she was thinking, or if she no longer wished to be reminded of the event. She persisted.

'It looked like a school exercise book. It's very important that you try to remember.'

'That was it. I think that was what they were asking me about,' she said softly. 'There were a few things of Charlotte's I didn't keep. Bits of paper, nothing important.'

'But a notebook. Think hard.'

'I don't know. . . . If there was one, it's gone now.'

'What do you mean?'

'When I opened the door. I was putting the rubbish out when they came at me. Throwing out the last of Charlotte's papers. I had no use for them.' The old lady appeared to be drifting off to sleep. Rose shot Robert a glance.

'Mrs Russell, when does your rubbish get collected?'

'What day is it?' Her voice was faint and frail.

'Thursday.'

'Today. Gets collected today.'

Rose and Robert nearly collided with a bewildered Teddy as they slid on the polished tiles at the end of the ward.

As they reached the corner of the old woman's street, their worst fears were confirmed. They could hear the whine of the garbage truck and the hissing of pistons as its steel jaws closed over the contents of the neighbourhood's bins and digested them. On the back step of the truck, the dustman shook a bin free of black plastic bags, newspapers and potato peelings and stepped back from the edge of the lowering teeth. It took a few seconds for them to realize that they were too late. Another dustman was just replacing two empty bins on the doorstep of number forty-three.

'Wait!' shouted Robert suddenly, launching himself after the truck as it began to move off down the road. 'Don't go yet!'

The dustmen failed to hear him over the grinding of the compressor. A moment later, Rose looked on in horror as Robert vaulted the low barrier at the back of the truck and vanished into the garbage that was about to be pulped. Shouting, she ran after him as the truck continued on its way. The low whine of the compressor rose as the curved steel jaw started to descend. One dustman was leaning into the pulping area shouting obscenities while the other ran around to the front cabin.

Robert was on his hands and knees, shovelling aside bundles of old magazines and squashy piles of rotten fruit. In the reeking mess below he could see what appeared to be a blue cover. He pulled at it, but the slime on his hands prevented him from getting a good grip. There were only seconds left. The whining sound above him reached a new pitch as the steel jaws suddenly began to descend much more quickly than he had anticipated.

With one final desperate pull the book came free and he stumbled back towards the fresh air and the waiting arms of an irate dustman. His foot was caught. The jaws of the compressor had closed over his heel and were tightening. Kicking wildly, he decided that the sacrifice of his shoe was better than losing his foot at the ankle.

As they helped him out, the dustmen expressed their extreme annoyance. One of them uttered a phrase that was so colourful and original in its use of sexual imagery that Rose later wrote it down in her diary.

'I've got the book!' he said, running down the street ahead of Rose, which, considering what he had been wading about in, was the way she preferred it.

'I thought I was going to die when you jumped into the trash,' she called. 'Don't ever do anything like that again.'

'Why, would you miss me?'

Rose waved a hand in front of her face. 'Right now, nobody could miss you,' she said.

They were walking across the broad stone piazza where the tea-clipper *Cutty Sark* sat in dry dock when they became aware that someone was following them. Two dark shapes had separated from the shadow of the ship and were closing in at a brisk pace.

'Keep looking straight ahead,' said Rose. 'It's probably nothing.'

'They could be Zalian's men,' suggested Robert hopefully as he quickened his step.

'No,' said Rose. 'Skinheads, two of them.'

'Why didn't *they* think of looking in her trash?'

'Are you kidding? They're skinheads. Come on.' They rounded the vast black bow of the ship in the direction of the river's edge. Behind them came the abrupt sound of running footsteps. Rose glanced over her shoulder.

'Shit – Robert!' she shouted, as he turned around and saw one of them drawing a razor-gun from the inside of his sweatshirt.

'Down into the foot tunnel!'

The curved glass dome housing the lift which descended to the foot tunnel beneath the river lay less than thirty yards ahead on their left. Rose reached it first. She did not wait for the enormous creaking lift to arrive, but galloped down the wide spiral staircase as fast as she could. Robert reached the entrance and slid over, the sole of his remaining shoe still slippery from the trash compressor. Picking himself up, he kicked it free and headed down the staircase as Dag and another of Chymes' men, known as Reese, reached the top step.

As they descended they lost much of the light, until they were faced at the base with the low gloomy dip of the tiled passage which would lead them under the river to the Isle Of Dogs.

The hundred-year-old tunnel had originally been built to take workers across to the West India Docks. Now, with the resurgence of London's docklands, it was once again in full use. As Rose ran between children and pushchairs her breath formed in clouds before her. She knew that they could not fire at her down here for fear of hitting too many other pedestrians. In the straight narrow tunnel there was nowhere to go but forward. She looked behind her as she ran. Robert seemed to be falling back. Dag and Reese were slowly gaining, their pounding boots filling the tunnel with echoes.

Ahead lay the circular shaft of the north tunnel entrance. Rose reached it just as the liftman was closing the steel gate of the elevator. Alarmed, he watched on his wall monitor as the skinheads approached, allowed

Rose and Robert to slip inside, then firmly sealed the door. 'Bloody hooligans,' he said, nodding at the screen. 'We get 'em down here all the time. Got no respect for decent people.'

'They'll be waiting for us at the top,' gasped Rose. 'They tried to mug my friend and me.'

'Oh, did they indeed?' He eyed Robert carefully, wrinkling his nose. 'Well, we'll soon settle their game.'

The liftman removed a telephone receiver from a box on the wall and spoke into it. Moments later, two policemen appeared on the monitor, waiting at the top of the shaft.

'Looks like it's going to be our lucky day after all,' said Rose, resting her head against the vibrating wooden wall of the lift. Robert glared glumly back, looking as if he'd just been fished out of the Sargasso Sea.

'You must forgive my friend,' she said to the liftman. 'He works down the drains.'

'Reckon you may have to bring his bath night forward,' said the little man as he brought the elevator to a gentle halt.

CHAPTER TWENTY-SIX

Freewheeling

Robert sat at his desk and finished tapping as many details as he could remember from the first notebook out onto the screen of his computer. He then loaded the information into the file marked *Newgate* on his disk. The office was silent and empty. Skinner had presumably packed his skis the day before and headed off for the pleasures of the *piste*. Robert sat back in his chair and lit his last cigarette.

His eerie, sleepless night, compounded by the dash beneath the river, had removed the reality from the day, lending a bizarre quality to the smallest details. God, how he regretted having handed Zalian the book without first taking photocopies. He walked over to the window. Today the gargoyles seemed so much more commonplace, squatting against the cold bright sky. He peered down. The street was filled with Christmas shoppers laden with carrier bags, briskly tacking from store to store. With surprise he realized that the wire he had spotted attached to the neck of one of the gargoyles was not a telephone cable at all, but part of a run. He turned hastily from the window. It was no use. He knew now that his curiosity would not allow him to drop the subject. He punched out Rose's number. She answered on the second ring.

'Did I disturb you?'

'No, I was just going out for something to eat. There's

a doner kebab out there somewhere with my name on it. You all freshened up?'

'Yeah. How do you feel about what's happening to us?' Robert tried to make the question sound casual.

'I'm having a little trouble with it, if that's what you mean. Either we go the whole way, or we pull out right here and now.'

'That's exactly how I feel. I mean, we could be dealing with a bunch of psychos.' He drew deeply on the cigarette, filling his lungs with cool smoke. 'But somehow I don't think so.'

There was a brief moment of hesitation on the other end of the line. 'In that case I vote we laugh in the face of danger and go back up. The question is – how? Zalian didn't go out of his way to arrange another meeting.'

Robert ground out the stub of his cigarette and peered gloomily into the empty Marlboro' packet. 'If he wants the book badly enough, he'll engineer a meeting. Besides, we can work it out for ourselves.' He glanced at his watch. 1.15. 'You want to discuss this somewhere?'

'I'll skip the Greek delicacies and meet you for coffee.'

'Deal.'

They arranged to meet at Patisserie Valerie in Soho's Old Compton Street in an hour's time. Robert rang off. He fingered the empty cigarette box with a sigh and rose to his feet.

As he headed for the tobacconist, he found himself staring up at the tops of the buildings on either side of the road. It seemed hard to believe that so many people had been thundering and swinging and leaping across them just a few hours earlier. He watched the faces of the men and women who passed him. Not one of them ever looked higher than face level. Most people preferred to stare at the pavement as they hurried by, lost in a mental vacuum created by their haste. Yet because of the varied eras of their construction there remained a hundred different types of rooftop, no matter how drably similar the buildings then became at street level. Gambrel and mansard, pitched and hipped, they created a mountainous landscape of stone and slate that remained undetected by the city's own unwary inhabitants.

It was strange, but even when he stopped and stared hard at the buildings around him he failed to pick out the cables running between them which constituted permanent runs. He knew they were there, constructed of transparent nylon that simply reflected the colour of the sky.

Later, he would suggest heading towards the Strand with Rose, and together they could look for the cables that he knew must crisscross the broad street like spiderwebbing all the way down to the Aldwych.

He was slipping between the poles of a scaffolding construction in St Anne's Court, lost in thought, when a shout attracted his attention. Then an old woman screamed, a high-pitched shriek like a startled bird. He turned his head to see her plastic shopping bag fall to one side, tins and packets tumbling into the road as she pointed upwards. Following her raised arm, he found himself looking directly overhead through the metal maze of scaffolding as it suddenly parted with a deafening clanging and ringing, clamps and rivets bouncing in all directions, and a huge steel wheelbarrow cartwheeled towards him on its way down to earth. He threw himself forward, miraculously staying on his feet long enough for several leaping strides as the sounds behind him turned into a continuous roar.

When the noise had stopped and the dust had settled, he could see that the wheelbarrow, loaded with cement, had fallen several storeys, smashing its way through planks and pipework to land exactly where he had been standing. As a crowd began to gather, he pulled himself to his feet and pushed away behind their backs, darting into a nearby record store just as people began to gather in doorways.

Leaning against a record rack, he fought to keep his body from shaking, focusing his eyes instead on the cover of the nearest album. Slowly he released a grim chuckle. It was a BBC Radiophonic Workshop effects record – *Sounds of Death and Disaster*.

'I told you smoking was bad for your health.'

'If you'd been there you'd know that it was no accident.' Robert stirred his tea irritably and looked up at Rose, who had selected a huge cream slice from the plate before her and was now biting into it, smearing her face.

'Was anybody hurt?'

'I don't know. I don't think so. I didn't stick around. The thing fell four floors and landed right where I'd been standing.'

'I guess they drew a bead on you by aiming for the ears.'

'Isn't it kind of disgusting to top off a kebab with a cream slice?'

'I was going to have the strawberry flan. You know, I think we should find Zalian before somebody else takes a pot shot at you. Or me.'

'How are we going to do that?' Robert lit a cigarette from the stub of his old one.

'Do you have to do that while I'm eating?'

'I was nearly killed a few minutes ago; I think I'm entitled to a cigarette.'

'It shouldn't be too hard to find him. I have the list of stations.'

'Where?'

Rose tapped the side of her head and smiled. 'We still have our line-belts. Plus, we might be able to work out the location of their headquarters.'

'If we can stay alive until tonight. Perhaps we should go up right away.'

'And risk running into whoever it was that wanted to play Bounce The Wheelbarrow Off Robert's Head? Zalian's enemies must be desperate to get you if they're attacking in daylight.'

'Listen, my office is just around the corner. We can load all the details you can still remember from the first notebook into my computer file. At least then we'll have a hard copy.'

'Have you had a chance to look in the second yet? Has it got the information Zalian's after?'

'I'm not sure. It's the same as the first, full of cryptic symbols and codes. It's also been immersed in coffee grounds, which hasn't helped the legibility much. You know, if your memory is half as good as you say it is, you may have retained enough information to get us back up to Zalian in one piece.'

Rose considered for a moment, wiping the last flakes of pastry from her lips.

'I may not be word perfect, but I'll try to recall as much as I can.' She rose from the table and threw down some money for the bill. 'Let's go.'

Before them, the screen glowed green in the gloomy third-floor office.

'Wait, wait,' Rose grabbed Robert's arm. 'There was another list as well as the stations. Let me see . . . there was Lud and New, Cripple, Moor and Alders. . . . No, forget it. They're of no use.'

'Why not? What is it?' Robert swung his chair away from the screen.

'They're the names of the seven gates of London which were built into the wall surrounding the city. Trouble is, I don't know where they were located. Anyway, they were all demolished over a couple of hundred years ago. There was also something about "No. 1, London".'

'And what might that be?'

Rose gave him the airy look she reserved for casually imparting extraordinary pieces of information. 'It used to be that if you posted a letter to "No. 1, London", it reached the Duke of Wellington. He used to live in Apsley House, at Hyde Park Corner, which was the first large house you came to entering London from the west. It's a museum now. I guess Zalian must have built a station on the roof. Although I have a feeling that some of the information in the notebook was just historical research that Charlotte was planning to use as background material.'

'Great, that makes our job even harder.'

'Let me type the information in as I remember it. If only you hadn't hogged the damned book the whole time I'd have had a chance to memorize more than just the first few pages.'

'How was I supposed to know about your brilliant memory?' complained Robert. 'You should have told me earlier.'

'Just try to be a little more constructive. Where would Zalian be most likely to build his headquarters?'

Robert sat in silence for a minute, then leaned forward and tapped the screen.

'Well, the Roofworld has strong associations with mythology and the planets, especially the sun and moon.'

'Horses.'

'What?'

'They could be on the roof of a stable, or any place which has horse-brasses hanging on the wall.'

Robert stared at Rose. 'How do you figure that out?'

'Horse-brasses usually represent the sun and the moon,' said Rose airily. 'They were always worn on the martingales of London cart-horses to represent the gods of the two planets.'

'Fucking hell, Rose, it's got to be something simpler than that.' Robert shook his head. 'No, you're definitely coming out of left field there. How about the roof of the Planetarium?' Rose looked at him and sighed loudly. 'You disappoint me, Robbo. So obvious. Besides, the Planetarium is just a steep dome. It's too exposed. It would be unthinkable that they'd manage to hide out anywhere up there.'

'All the more reason for them to do so. It's worth checking out. Grab your coat and hat.'

'OK, but I promise you, I'm not going to leave my worries on the doorstep.'

Together they headed for Baker Street.

Meanwhile, Ian Hargreave was going through an identical exercise at his computer terminal, 'freewheeling' his information in random word strings, hoping to complete a logic-jump that would set his thinking in a new direction. He had added onto his earlier *Icarus* file, rechristening it *Anubis* for reasons that he himself did not fully understand. There was something Egyptian about the style of each execution – that's right, he felt sure that they were executions rather than murders, but to what practical purpose?

Pausing to light yet another cigarette, he loaded the names and functions of a variety of Roman, Greek and Egyptian deities onto the disk. Then he added anything he could think of that might open a new avenue of thought: zodiac signs, secret societies, Missing Persons statistics, even zoological descriptions of wildfowl. Finally he booted the file into his privately secured and coded *Freewheel* program and sat back in his chair to watch the results unscroll.

UNLOCKING *FREEWHEEL*

There was a pause while the computer analyzed the information before adding to it. Then the familiar green lettering began to tack across the screen.

YOUR REF/ SECRET SOCIETIES
SEE/ RELIGIOUS ORDERS
CHIVALRIC BROTHERHOODS
FREEMASONS
SHRINERS
ORDER OF THE EASTERN STAR
ORDER OF THE GOLDEN DAWN
ORDER OF BUILDERS
ORDER OF JOB'S DAUGHTERS
MYSTIC ORDER OF VEILED PROPHETS
OF THE ENCHANTED REALM

With a snort, Hargreave reached forward and stopped the screen before it continued to run through the endless number of secret societies that existed around the country. He positioned the cursor beside 'FREEMASONS' and pressed 'Return'. Instantly the screen scrolled down new information.

YOUR REF/ FREEMASONS
NON-CHRISTIAN ORGANIZATION
WORLD'S LARGEST SECRET SOCIETY
BELIEFS
*THE EXISTENCE OF A SUPREME
BEING
*THE IMMORTALITY OF THE SOUL
THREE MAJOR DEGREES
*ENTERED APPRENTICE
*FELLOW OF THE CRAFT
*MASTER MASON
GENERALLY REGARDED AS A SYSTEM
OF UNFAIR PRIVILEGE,
FREEMASONRY HAS FREQUENTLY
ADOPTED AN ANTI-CLERIC
STANCE AND IS BANNED IN THE
FOLLOWING COUNTRIES:

*EGYPT/USSR/HUNGARY/SPAIN/
POLAND/CHINA/PORTUGAL/
INDONESIA (More to follow)

Great. The computer was now making value judgements. It would be telling him to quit smoking next. Hargreave halted the readout and suggested that it should search amongst similar groups which held ritual practices. The screen rolled blank, the memory banks sorting through an unimaginable network of information. Beyond the door of his office the occasional face peered through at him, concerned. Sod them, thought Hargreave. At least he was applying his imagination to the problem. They weren't coming up with anything at all. His attention was drawn back to the screen. Type began to appear once more.

YOUR REF/ SIMILAR SOCIAL STRUCTURES
*MARDI GRAS KREWES
RITUAL SECRET ORDERS
CELEBRATING CARNIVAL
DERIV/ CARNEM LEVARE = LATER,
CARNELEVARE = 'FAREWELL TO
FLESH'
*MARDI GRAS DERIV/ 'MARDI GROS' =
'FAT TUESDAY'
ORIG/ ROMAN CUSTOM OF
ATONEMENT CORRUPTED INTO
LEWDNESS, VIOLENCE, MURDER
CURRENT STATUS/ HARMLESS
RITUAL CELEBRATION
MYTHOLOGY/ RITE INITIATED BY
EVANDER, SON OF HERMES
HERMES = *ANUBIS*

Hargreave swore beneath his breath and slapped his hand against the monitor in frustration. It was there, all of it, right in front of his eyes. Why the hell could he not make a connection with the violence it was causing in the modern world? He drew hard on the stub of his cigarette and ground it out. There was a secret society afoot, all right, something that ran parallel to the Masons and the Mardi Gras krewes, something that shared a common root with societies all over the country, perhaps all over the world. But it wasn't Christian. He looked back at the screen.

Mardi Gras celebrated the pleasures of the flesh before the commencement of Lent. Likewise, the doctrine of the Freemasons had often angered the church. But the rituals connected with both had grown harmless in recent years, had become too well-known. So, what else was left? Satanic societies? Covens? Their mumbo-jumbo rituals seemed to pale into harmlessness compared with what he was facing here.

Hargreave looked back at the flickering emerald ciphers on the screen. The dark side of the city was slowly revealing itself. Perhaps it had been there for many years, perhaps it was only forming now. One thing was certain. It was far deadlier than any of them had imagined. Deadlier, perhaps, than they *could* imagine.

CHAPTER TWENTY-SEVEN

Planetarium

Rose stamped her boots on the pavement. Her toes were freezing. She reached into her padded jacket and pulled her rainbow scarf tighter. 'See anything yet?'

'No, the roof looks completely sealed and seamless. It's just a dome. There's a ledge running around it, but it's barely wide enough to stand on. Here, your turn.' Robert climbed down from the upturned wooden fruit box. The hectic Marylebone Road traffic charged and slowed all around them. Vast coaches, their engines idling, sat by the side of the road waiting to discharge strings of tourists for Madame Tussauds. Above them, visited only by pigeons, the bright green dome of the London Planetarium rose, a model planet perched at its apex.

'There don't seem to be any openings, or added structures to the roof,' Rose called down. 'I think we're barking up the wrong . . .' Just then, a slim oblong segment of the dome rose from its base a few inches and out from beneath it slipped the sullen-faced girl they had seen with Zalian the previous night. She was dressed in a grey jumpsuit and seemed unaware that anyone was watching her as she strapped on a small backpack, pushed the rectangular metal sheet closed and reached into the suit for her belt-line.

'Well, I'll be . . . hey, you up there!' called Robert. The girl looked down, her large eyes growing in astonishment.

'Really subtle, Robert,' said Rose from the side of her mouth.

'Your name's Spice, isn't it? Listen, we have to speak to Zalian,' he continued to bellow. 'Somebody's tried to kill us twice so far today!' Behind them in the street a pair of elderly American tourists turned around and looked up. The man unsnapped the lens cap of his camera. Horrified, the girl ran around the dome to its back and dropped flat to the narrow ledge. Robert ran after her, following around the curve of the building.

'For Christ's sake, do you want to get us all killed?' she hissed furiously, gripping the ledge in her hands and pulling herself forward to talk with him. 'Bloody amateurs.'

'I'm sorry,' called Robert, 'but we've got to see Zalian.' She could run off right now, he thought, she could dash away across the rooftops and maybe we'll never find any of them again.

Above, Spice remained hesitant, eyeing them with suspicion. 'I can't take you to Nathaniel,' she said. 'It's too dangerous. Besides, you don't know how to travel in daylight without being seen.'

'Oh, is that a separate skill?' asked Robert, cocking an eyebrow. 'I like the day uniform, by the way. Very spiffy.'

'We can help him if you'll let us,' said Rose. 'We're prepared to search the entire city until we find Sarah.'

Spice pulled herself back from the ledge, remaining silent.

'We gave Zalian the notebook as a sign of good faith, didn't we?' said Robert. 'And we've managed to secure the second half of it. We just want to deliver it to him in person. Come on, we've done his dirty work, the least he can do is see us.'

Spice hesitated, considering this, then rose to a crouching position.

'All right, if you want to meet up with Nathaniel, be here at nine tonight.' She turned to go.

'Wonderful,' muttered Rose. 'We have to find a way of staying alive for another six hours.'

'By the way,' called Robert, 'that was a neat trick with the roof door. You can't see it from down here. How does it work?' Spice stopped in her tracks, nonplussed.

'False panel,' she shrugged. 'Same as all the other buildings.' She turned and darted off around the other side of the dome.

'Great, thank you. I'll remember to give you guys a ring when I need cupboards put up.' He turned to Rose.

Rose grabbed his collar and pulled him around to face her. 'Robert, I think you'd better try closing your mouth now, before you blow the whole deal.' Her eyes widened as he grabbed the padded shoulders of her jacket, pulled her forward and kissed her hard on the lips. Rose's response to this, after a brief moment of shock, was to fetch him a resounding smack on the side of the head. Robert fell back against a poster advertising the Laserium light show. 'I think you've loosened a filling,' he moaned, clutching his face in pain.

'Don't you ever try something like that again. You're lucky these jeans are too tight for me to get my knee up as far as your groin.' She spun on her heel and headed off along the Marylebone Road in the direction of the tube station. Thirty yards on, she stopped and waited.

Gratefully Robert ran and caught up with her and together they plunged into the sluggish river of traffic.

'Look, I'm sorry,' he said. 'I wouldn't have done that but . . . I thought maybe you wanted me to.'

'Well, you misread your signals, Robert.' Rose turned to him. 'I like you, but like is as far as it goes and if you can't keep it on that level, then we go separate ways, understood?'

'Understood,' he reluctantly agreed. What a dumb thing to have done. At least she seemed willing to continue with him. Maybe he had just picked his time badly.

'I was thinking,' he said, hastily initiating a change of subject, 'you don't suppose it's all a game, do you? Like one of those role-playing games where everyone takes an identity and follows a planned scenario.' He jumped back on the curb to avoid a taxi. 'I mean, they spend their time charging around above the city at night having some kind of a war. You've got to admit it's pretty unstable behaviour for a group of adults.'

The main Baker Street intersection was gorged with cars and buses. Pedestrians dashed between them, climbing over chugging exhausts to reach the comparative safety of the traffic islands.

'There are other lifestyles apart from your own, Robert,' said Rose, watching for a break in the traffic. 'I'm assuming, of course, that you have one. Anyway, it would have to be a pretty serious kind of a game that involved killing people for real.'

'Yes, but *has* anyone been killed for real?' Robert persisted. 'We only have Zalian's word that those razor-coin things are poisoned. Perhaps Charlotte Endsleigh's death really was accidental.'

'What are you saying? That somehow they're staging this just for us? This is real life, Robert, not a Zen parable. We saw someone *die* up there. That was no fake, kiddo.'

'Well, I'm not entirely convinced.'

'I bet you believe what you read in the Sunday papers and yet you don't accept the evidence of your own eyes.' Rose grabbed his hand and steered him between two shuddering trucks. 'Tell me something.'

'What?'

'Did you believe the story about the Hitler diaries?'

'Yes,' Robert admitted sheepishly.

'Then you're in no position to talk.' Her bronze eyes narrowed and mocked him. 'Perhaps we'll see something that will convince you tonight,' she said. 'Although I really hope we don't.'

'Where do you want to spend the rest of the day?' he shouted back over the noise of revving engines.

'I don't mind so long as it's somewhere peaceful and clean and, above all, safe.'

'How about the underground?' Robert suggested. 'One out of three ain't bad.'

Together they ran down the litter-strewn steps into the comparative safety of Baker Street station.

CHAPTER TWENTY-EIGHT

Night Sight

Stan Cutts may have filed some pretty dumb stories in his time, but he was no fool. When his informant, Nick, failed to reappear in the arcade the previous night, he had begun to sense that something was seriously wrong.

Stan had long suspected that something strange was going on above the heads of the populace. At first he had just been able to pick out the odd word or phrase from the groundswell of arcade conversation. Within the swaggering machismo, the wheeling of drug deals and the sexual hustling was a new topic of conversation, one filled with whispered threats and hidden meanings. Hargreave may have called him a 'gutter journo', but Stan could still smell a powerful story in the making. It had taken time and money – and even a couple of drug purchases – to ingratiate himself with the arcade's residents, but the ploy had paid off. He had been introduced to the sometime members of the 7 N Krewe and in particular to Nick, who had the body of a sickly child and the mind of a forty-year-old cardsharp.

Nick was greedy for money. You could see it in his eyes. And he'd been getting enough of it, every time he had offered Stan with information. He had provided tip-offs about the murders, but remained reluctant to discuss their perpetrators. The last time Stan had seen the boy there had been a new look in his eyes, a look of fear that had outstripped even his desire for money. And now Nick had vanished, possibly to join the growing number of corpses that appeared to be raining from the night skies.

As he walked home along a deserted Fleet Street, Stan wondered if he was also in danger. After all, his face had become well known in what were rapidly turning out to be the wrong circles. He would have to stay away from the arcade for a while, change his tactics by attacking the case from another angle. Perhaps he could run a profile on Hargreave, highlighting his past incompetence, or even submit a story suggesting that his mystery informant had now been placed in a life-threatening situation.

Stan looked back along the empty pavements at the newspaper building beyond. It was virtually the only one remaining in the street now that the others had shifted to areas which were better suited for housing their new technology. He sighed and pulled his scarf tighter to his throat. Here it was, almost Christmas and the once-great street was dead. How he would love to have seen it in the time of Queen Anne, filled with freaks and fire-eaters, elephants and dancing dwarves. He had no doubt that it would survive in some new incarnation, but things would not be the same without the newspapers. . . .

As he made his slow and pensive way towards Holborn, Stan failed to see the huge loop of nylon cord dropping down behind him from the rooftop of the now-abandoned *Daily Express*. Sweeping forward, it lowered beneath his arms and suddenly rose again, scooping him from the ground and up past the glistening windows to the roof where he landed before even having a chance to struggle free from its grip. Wiping the grit from grazed palms and untangling the cord from beneath his burning armpits, the shocked journalist looked around him. Arranged on the flat roof ahead was a strange sight indeed, but before he had a chance to take it in, hands were on him, gagging his mouth and tying his wrists together behind his back. Helpless, he looked on at the people who had just reeled him so effortlessly from his own safe, familiar world.

The skinhead's name was Reese. It was tattooed on his neck and he was reading aloud from a tattered library book in a thin, halting voice:

> ' "*Quod est inferius, est sicutid quod est superius,*
> *et quod est superius, est sicutid quod est inferius,*
> *ad perpetranda miracula rei unius.*" '

He briefly ceased reciting to step back and create an opening from the broad rooftop the next, much narrower and older one. Here, at the end of a filthy, steeply slated valley sat the one they called Chymes, his cloak spread loosely across the brickwork around him. He was listening intently to the recital, his steel hand resting lightly on one knee. In addition to his two shavenheaded helpers and the gasping, dyspeptic hack there was another person on the roof, a girl – young, and terrified.

'Bring her forward, Dag.'

The other skinhead obeyed, pulling the rope which bound his victim a little tighter, encouraging her to move forward along the slim lead gutter. Stan brought his hands to his head, unable to make sense of the scene unfolding before him.

Pale eyes glittered from within the shadow of Chymes' hood. His metal hand whipped up and caught the struggling girl by a bony arm. Dag continued to hold her by the other, as Reese stumbled on through the recital for the pleasure of his master:

> ' "*Pater ejus est Sol, mater ejus Luna:*
> *portavit illud ventus in ventre suo:*
> *nutrix ejus terra est.*" '

As the girl bucked and heaved in their grasp, Dag and Reese tore at her clothes until she was naked. Her mascara had smeared in broad streaks over her terrified face like some ancient tribal marking. Just an hour earlier, she had been walking home through the empty backstreets of the West End. Then two men had dropped like shadows out of the sky and snatched her back up into the clouded night. Chymes sighed and rose, his hands sliding over her shivering breasts. 'Tie her hands, then leave us.'

The skinheads quickly obeyed, ignoring the journalist as he rose unsteadily to his feet ahead of them, and turned to their master expectantly, as if awaiting a tip. Casually, Dag gave the girl a malicious push with his elbow, watching as she toppled and fell to the ground.

'Here, you've done well.' Chymes threw them a small packet, twisted in foil. 'Don't use too much. I need you to be alert tonight.'

They knew better than to stay around any longer. Silently, the skinheads padded off across the roof, to be lost in the maze of chimneys crowning the slender, ancient dwellings which still backed onto the ancient thoroughfare.

Stan looked on, horrified, as the girl rolled over on her stomach, trying to hide her naked body from view, ashamed and disgusted that the tall hooded figure before her should be able to see her like this.

'Come, come, my love, I think it's a little late for modesty,' said Chymes. For the first time, he acknowledged the presence of the journalist. 'You should feel honoured, Mr Cutts. Tonight we prepare for our greatest battle and it is from this young lady that I will draw my strength. I am about to baptize her in the name of darkness.'

He reached out his hands and caught her shoulders, slowly forcing them down to the ground so that she was exposed to him once more. Above her gag, her eyes searched frantically for a clue to her attacker's identity, but his face was lost within the darkened folds of the hood.

'It is time for the fourth step, the Conjunction,' murmured Chymes, his voice heavy with desire. 'So it is that sulphur and mercury are now joined together, for what has been separated must once more unite completely.'

As he released one hand to reach into his cloak, fumbling with sexual excitement, the girl suddenly swung her leg and caught him squarely in the groin, causing him to fall back with a shout against the angled roof. She pulled herself upright and, with her hands still tied behind her back, ran as fast as she could down the narrow gulley formed by the rooftops of the two terraced buildings.

Ahead, the gulley dropped down a series of tarred steps into a bricked-in area of total darkness. Crawling far into one of the corners formed by so many crazy angles of brick and slate she waited, heart thudding agonizingly within her chest.

Stan looked on at the bizarre tableau, a forgotten presence in the unfolding game between Chymes and his victim, whom he could no longer pick out among the blackened chimneystacks.

The girl attempted to gauge the passing of a minute, then another. Her eyes adjusted slightly, but all she could make out was a wall of darkness against the tough leather-black edges of the winter sky. Far below, a car hooted, an echo from a distant world. Up here all was silence as the wind moaned softly over aerials and through cables, stirring whorls of soot on the terraces of slate.

Her senses, heightened with fear, could detect nothing in the all-surrounding velvet pitch. Oblivious to the cold and the cramp setting in at the backs of her legs, she prayed for only one thing, that this obscene madman would not be able to find her. Hardly daring to exhale, she leaned against the wall at her back and released a low breath. Perhaps he had gone. There was only the sighing softness of the night breeze to be heard, a lonely sound more suited to the country than a metropolis.

With a guttural scream he plucked her into the sky, icy hands suddenly slipping beneath her sweating armpits to haul her back into the scouring wind. The gag slipped from her mouth and now, knowing her fate, she screamed too. He waited, waited until there was no voice left to scream before he addressed her.

'You can't hide from me,' he said, his voice a gentle hiss, dangling the doll-like figure before him, 'didn't they tell you? That's how I knew I was chosen to lead. My eyes can pierce the vale of darkness. Satan has given me the power of night sight.' He stared at the girl with interest, still refusing to let her feet touch the ground.

'And so we must begin,' he said, setting her down at last, but still holding tightly on to her arms. 'The time has come for us to merge, you and I, and create the power that is needed for absolute victory.' As he descended upon the screaming girl, his cloak blotted her pale skin, enfolding them within the bonded brickwork of the city horizon. Withdrawing a slim pearl-handled blade, he gently pushed it into flesh and slit her open from throat to groin. As he pressed his body into hers, hot blood cascaded like a geyser, enveloping him in wave after spraying wave of ecstatic release.

Stan screamed into the gag until it was hot with spittle, until he had no voice. When next he dared to raise his eyes, he saw Chymes still towering above the spent steaming body, his bare head turned to the sky, the hood having fallen back on his shoulders. His opened hands, fingers of steel and flesh spread wide apart, dripped crimson. An age seemed to pass before he returned his attention to the terrified journalist. At length he approached and began to speak. 'I suppose I should thank you for giving us our first taste of publicity,' he said evenly. 'Unfortunately your timing was wrong. We are not yet ready to be seen by the world below.'

Stan struggled to release his hands from their binding,

knowing now that Nick was dead and that his death was sure to follow suit.

'It's a shame that you won't live to see tomorrow's newspapers. They're bound to run the story of your informant's grisly end. With colour pictures, probably.' Chymes pulled his cloak across his chest, covering the torrent of blood which had drenched him.

'Sadly, you are not the only hindrance to my victory and to the progression of the New Age,' he continued. 'The fool Nathaniel Zalian persists in holding on to what little territory remains his and it seems he will continue to plague us until we discover his whereabouts. And then there are a pair of Insects, the little nigger girl and her friend, making trouble for us on the ground, carrying our secrets around with them as if it were all some game. I'd like to be able to send you down and let them see just how much of a game it is.'

Stan fervently hoped that he'd be safely released back to the ground as well, but having witnessed the atrocity which had just occurred before him, he held out little hope. Even in his darkest moment, he could not help thinking what a great story he would get to file if Chymes decided to set him free after all.

'Unfortunately you must die without knowing my plans,' said Chymes with a chuckle. 'I've seen too many films wherein the villain embarks on a full explanation before dispatching his prey. I also know that you must never turn away from your victim's impending death, or they will attempt to escape until the last. No, you must stand over them and watch until the final breath escapes from their lips.' He drew closer to Stan, who began to back away towards the edge of the roof.

'And make no mistake, Mr Cutts,' laughed Chymes, 'I *am* the villain. No eye-rolling madman I, but an intelligent, selfish, cunning leader of men. All black, no white, no shades of grey. I know what I want, and I know how to get it. Why, I could have been a *poli-*

tician.' Stan Cutts' world was reduced to the view of a single approaching black-cloaked figure.

CHAPTER TWENTY-NINE

Spice

'What is this place?' asked Robert, slowly turning around on the vast flat roof. Only a handful of office blocks stood taller, the highest of them being the National Westminster building, over a quarter of a mile away. The wind moaned forlornly across the concrete plane on which they stood, plucking at their clothes before sweeping away through the granite canyons of the city's financial institutions and down toward the deserted reaches of the sluggishly ebbing river.

'We're on top of the new Stock Exchange, our temporary home,' said Spice. 'We've had to move half a dozen times in the last few weeks.' True to her word, she had collected Robert and Rose from the Planetarium, even if she had arrived over half an hour late. Supplying them with fresh climbing equipment from the hidden panel in the building's copper dome, she had led the way across the city, expecting them – unfairly, thought Robert – to keep pace with her during the journey.

Rose looked at her watch. It was almost 11.30. She was starting to feel tired. The rarely used muscles in her arms felt torn and stretched and even in the cold night air she was once more aware of her body sweating. Her face and hands were covered in grease from repeatedly grasping the overhead lines.

Far below, the traffic was thinning as cars roared around the one way system leading toward Tower

Bridge, their drivers anxious to return home after a night filled with parties and Christmas celebrations. Rose failed to feel much seasonal spirit as she rubbed the backs of her arms briskly, watching Spice's nimble fingers at work as she reloaded her line-gun for her.

'This is probably a stupid question, but is there somewhere where I can take a wash?' she asked. Spice pointed across the roof to what looked like a large cream-coloured conduit.

'In there. It ain't exactly the Ritz, but it's OK for makeshift headquarters. We used to have a very smart place on the roof of Mornington Crescent tube station, but they found us. Pity, it was nice there.'

Rose thanked her and wearily headed off toward the conduit with her bag slung over her shoulder. Robert watched her go, then turned to Spice.

'Tell me,' he said, sitting down with his legs dangling over the side of the building. 'Zalian is very reluctant to explain the trouble you're in. Is it like this all the time?'

'Of course not,' said Spice, laying down the gun and joining him at the edge. 'There was never any trouble here. There's always been something binding us together . . . a feeling of continuity with the past, I suppose. Nathaniel likes that. He wants to keep things as they've always been. Says he hates the thought of a society which dumps people on the scrapheap if they don't fit in. He lives in a fucking dreamworld, but I guess we still need dreamers. There aren't many left down below any more.'

She lay down along the narrow cement ledge, casually resting her head on one of her slim, muscular arms in what looked to Robert like an extremely dangerous position.

'See, below, if you're unemployed they think you must be a layabout. Nathaniel says it's easier to call someone work-shy than it is to blame the system that failed them.'

There was more than mere admiration for Zalian in her voice. She waved a hand back at the group of people who sat around on the other side of the roof smoking and talking quietly. 'Assuming that any of us could even find jobs below, I don't think we'd want to spend our lives improving the sales of Coca-Cola, or trying to convince the Chinese to buy Chicken McNuggets. There's got to be more to life than always fighting to grab your share.'

'Well then, why don't you do something which helps the community?' asked Robert. He shivered a little, zipping his jumpsuit to the top of his chest.

'We do enough for the community as it is, but not through their system. It's too slow, too bogged down with red tape, hampered by lack of money. Who wants to do the community any favours? People on the ground would rather work for a record company than an old folks' home. That's human nature, isn't it?' Spice rose up on one arm to light a cigarette, her face softening in the flare of the match.

'So how *do* you spend your time?' asked Robert. 'I don't understand what it is that you do up here.'

Spice gave him a crooked smile. 'No, you don't, do you?' she said, the smile turning into a grin. It made her look completely different, friendlier, her cropped blonde hair untidily framing her pale round face. 'That's the beauty of the Roofworld. The same thing has been going on up here for sixty years and nobody on the ground has ever noticed. Be interesting to see if there's anything left by the end of the week.' Her voice was light and unconcerned.

'You don't sound very upset about the possibility of losing it.'

'What's the point? They say the Roofworld used to be brilliantly organized. Now the runs are falling into disrepair and every day the operation gets more slipshod. A lot of the new buildings are installing roof cameras. It's only a matter of time before the system breaks down and we're discovered. Technology will finally catch up with us. Then we'll end up in jail. At least this way it looks like we're gonna go out with a bang.' She looked out across the deserted office buildings, the night breeze lightly ruffling her hair.

'But I'll stay on up here whatever happens. I think I'd still rather fall from a roof than die at home, in front of the video. I've been here for six years and I've watched the Roofworld slowly fall apart. The ones who could have rebuilt the system have been seduced away. Nathaniel's a good man. He really did his best for us. But now he's lost the battle.' She finished her cigarette and flicked it over the side. Robert leaned forward to watch the tiny red spark spiral down to the street as Spice looked away into the grey-black clouds scudding above the skyline.

Rose was astounded. Inside the 'conduit' was a complex of rooms, including a portable shower, toilets, an operations room fitted with lightweight computers, a mess with an adjoining kitchen and a storeroom piled high with climbing gear and weaponry. The shower water was heated by a flexible plastic tank which was wrapped around some of the hot water pipes belonging to the Exchange below and was operated by a simple foot-pump. In minutes she was clean and refreshed. Rose stepped with surprise into a heavy white towel held at arm's length by Zalian.

'It's OK, I have my eyes shut,' he said, opening one and peering over. Rose grabbed the towel and tied it tightly around her breasts.

'Let me dry your back, at least.' Amusement played in his pale eyes. 'What do you think of our temporary headquarters?'

'It's surprising what you can do with an unfurnished property,' said Rose, accepting the back-rub. 'What are the computers for?'

'We run them from the lines going into the Exchange,' he said, sidestepping the question. 'The kitchen has a gas pipe running from the same system. Lee fixed it. You'll be pleased to know that he made it back, by the way. In one piece, too.'

'I'm glad,' said Rose, 'What about Simon?'

'No sign yet. But he's pretty good at looking after himself. Here.' Zalian held up a pile of neatly folded clothes.

'You want to step outside while I dress?' she said, pushing him toward the door.

'No, but I will.'

She pushed the door firmly shut. Zalian's changes in mood made her uneasy. It was as if he was reacting to each new situation on a purely emotional level, running on empty, with no hope approaching on the horizon. No wonder the morale of his troops was so low, she thought. They could never know what he was about to do next.

After she had pulled on the black jumpsuit and zipped it up, Rose walked into the deserted operations room. She stifled a yawn, idly looking over at the computers as she passed them.

Despite the shower, her joints still felt stiff and sore. One of the computer screens glowed softly green in the dim light. It was displaying a list of corporation giants, NatWest, Pepsi, IBM and several others, each with a disk index number. Her interest increasing, she leaned over the console and keyed in the number corresponding to 'NatWest'. The screen scrolled down an endless list of names, dates and financial amounts. She was still staring at the screen, puzzled, when the door opened behind her.

'Rose? You OK?' Cold night air flooded into the

room from where Robert stood. 'Do your arms hurt? Mine are bloody near hanging off.'

'Yeah, mine are too. Apart from that, I'm fine. Coming right out.'

'Quite a set-up he has here.' Robert looked around, impressed. 'Wonder what he needs the computers for.'

'I was just wondering the same thing.'

'Well, let's ask him.'

'You won't get a straight answer.' Rose stepped beneath Robert's arm and out through the door leading onto the roof. 'He's waiting for you to give him the second notebook, Robert.'

'I'll trade him, information for information. There's got to be full trust on both sides if we're to help each other.'

'Fighting words, kiddo,' said Rose, slapping Robert on the back. 'Let's go and see if it works in practice.'

CHAPTER THIRTY

New Age

Zalian had gathered his people together and was mapping out a plan of the night's activities, addressing the remaining members of his depleted order. Most were standing or sitting in a ragged circle on the broad aluminium strips which covered the roof. A few hung back by the conduit, with their hands in the pockets of their black overall suits. All of them looked dejected and cold.

'Rose and Robert here have brought us some new information which, we hope, will help us find the location we need.' Even in the gloom, Zalian's pale iridescent eyes were uncomfortable to catch directly. Robert wondered if these young men and women were under the power of a fanatic, even one so seemingly benign.

'It's almost certain that Chymes will try to locate and attack us tonight. They may even be on their way here right now. None of us can afford to fall from constant guard.

'What I propose is this; that we divide into three groups. Lee will lead the first, Damien can take the second and Spice the third. You'll each cover a specific city sector, using the walkie-talkies to stay in touch. If any of you make visual contact with Chymes or his followers, radio in your position immediately and give a full report, then wait until we can get back-up over to you.

'Don't go in alone, even if you outnumber them. I don't want any stupid heroics. We must work together to capture Chymes himself, or any accomplices who are likely to share his confidence and have access to information.'

'Which group are you gonna go with?' asked a skinny Asian boy at the front of the gathering.

'I'll be here, studying the new information with these two. They aren't as used to roof climbing as you and I need them to help me. I'll radio each group as soon as we have a lead.'

'Wait a minute,' Lee had stood up at the back. The stocky oriental boy was kitting himself with a nylon backpack as he spoke. 'What happens if you still don't find out anything? We don't even know how many of them are out there! They could be setting traps all over the city, just waiting for us to fall into them.'

'That's a risk we'll have to take. He's got twelve of our finest people awaiting execution. We've no choice but to try and to discover their location. If we fail, they also die.'

Although it was clearly intended as fighting talk from Zalian, a murmur of dissent ran through the group. Nobody seemed to think it proper that he should exempt himself from his rightful place on the front line. In earlier, more peaceful times, the doctor's unequivocal manner had helped to maintain discipline, energizing and encouraging them to enjoy their alternative life above the city. Under the leadership of Zalian, each day in the Roofworld had taken on different aspects of an extraordinary adventure. He had given them a sense of community and purpose. He had been their teacher, their guide, their friend and adviser. But now the utopia he had helped to create lay in ruins about them and it was becoming all too clear that he could no longer be counted on to lead them to victory. His faith had been shaken. Too many once-trusted friends had defected to the other side.

'Lee's going to kit you out with every weapon we can find. I know none of you have been trained to fight, but then nobody thought it would ever come to this. I want to say one thing.' The group simmered back into silence as Zalian walked forward into their midst. 'If you believe in the life we have been trying to create up here, you must see that the system continues for another generation. You must do everything within your power to ensure that – somehow – the Roofworld endures.'

Most of the people around him were looking down at their feet, embarrassed. Zalian then addressed himself to individual members of the group.

In order to break up the dismal silence that followed his pep talk, the loyal Lee clapped his hands and began pulling people to their feet. 'Right, Mack, Little Joe, and those of you who have done any weapon-training, this way. Come on, let's move out.'

Slowly, people started to rise and follow. Spice, taking Lee's lead, began to organize her party. Damien, a spiky-haired boy who moved with an awkward limp, was the unenthusiastic leader of the third group. He too began pulling people to their feet and dividing up the supply of makeshift weaponry. Robert and Rose dutifully followed Zalian back into the operations room inside the conduit.

The doctor flicked on an anglepoise lamp and sat down as Rose handed him the dog-eared notebook.

'Let's divide up the pages,' he said. 'If there's anything at all in here that might lead us to the New Age headquarters or the execution sites, we have to find it.'

'Hold it,' said Robert, raising his hand. 'Am I missing something here? What execution sites? What the hell is the New Age anyway?'

'If you're planning to see this thing through you might as well know,' said Zalian, pinching the top of his long nose with a grimy thumb and forefinger. 'The last thing we ever wanted up here was any trouble'. He sat back and looked from one face to the other, realizing that he would have to elucidate before Robert and Rose could be of any use to him. An explanation was obviously in order.

Rose decided to take the initiative. 'You could start by telling us how you entered the Roofworld,' she said.

'I mean, you didn't just answer an ad in *The Guardian*, did you?'

'If you're asking me why I left the ground, let's just say that life had become – unbearable for me,' Zalian replied, clearly ill-at-ease. 'It began with a patient of mine, an old man . . . one day, as he surfaced from an operation anaesthetic, he started to tell me about a place he knew of, one which had existed above the city for decades. He kept talking of this . . . other way of life.' He shrugged and rose, hiking a pack of Pepsis from beside his packing-crate desk and pulling a can free.

'Naturally, at the time I assumed him to be hallucinating, describing a dream, but still the idea intrigued me. Some time later I heard the story again, from a completely different source, so I decided to do a little investigating.

'The whole thing sounded too good to be true – and in a sense it was. To cut a long story short, I was about to abandon my search for this fabled "secret life" when I accidentally stumbled on the headquarters of the Roofworld.' He popped open the can, then slid the rest of the pack across to Rose. 'The place was a total shambles. The previous leader had given up and returned to life below and only a few people had remained behind here. Still, it seemed important – to me at least – to try and rebuild what was left.'

He ran his hand through the long blonde hair which curled across the nape of his neck, smiling now at the memory. 'I declared my intentions and quickly found that there were others who were willing to help me resurrect the Roofworld. They showed me all manner of books relating to customs and rituals which had been practised up here over fifty years earlier. I threw out the arcane and the obscure and kept the laws which seemed to embody something good and useful. I reinstated the Roofworld's ideals and adapted them for a new generation. . . .'

'So what went wrong?' asked Robert.

'I guess I was too successful. More and more people were growing dissatisfied with life on the ground and wanted to join us. Security started to slip. Tongues loosened a little too much. People we rejected as unsuitable knew enough about our operation to blow the whistle. For the first time since its creation the Roofworld was in danger of exposure.'

Zalian looked to the door. 'Wait, let's talk outside. I want to watch everyone prepare. The way things are going at the moment, it may be the last time we're all together.' Zalian stretched his long legs and stood. Once outside, he began to walk slowly along the roof, following the edge of the parapet as if continually challenging the laws of gravity. As he spoke, Robert and Rose were forced to fall in step with him in order to hear. Everywhere, people were packing bags and checking line equipment.

'Then what happened?' asked Robert.

'Other gangs started to appear on the rooftops,' said Zalian. 'They cared nothing for the ordered, idealistic society we had recreated. It soon became obvious to me that someone with enough strength could use the network for harmful purposes. When the inevitable occurred, it was far worse than anyone could have imagined. The group that appeared was literally forged in evil. Its rules and codes became sick parodies of our own.' The wind began to pick up around them, ruffling Robert's hair and tumbling litter across the rooftop.

'The original Roofworld followed the noble ideals of the Greek gods,' Zalian continued, 'and we retained their passive and peaceful symbol – the moon. Our new rivals call themselves the Bringers Of The New Age and are a reverse of all we represent. Their first leader was fried alive above Piccadilly by the usurper they call Chymes. He is a man who has obliterated most of his enemies in a matter of days. Now it seems that only a handful of us are still left in his way. And once we are gone, no one on the ground will be safe.'

'Why?' asked Rose.

'When you look down on something from a height,' said Zalian, 'it seems easier to understand how it works. You learn how to milk the system. You discover its weaknesses. We have broken laws, but we have never murdered and we have never injured those below. Still, we have made the ground system work for us. Our enemies are different. They will steal and kill from the sky when they take control. Then the old rules will be gone forever and the streets will be awash with blood. The slaughter that has occurred so far will have simply become a way of life.'

Zalian looked at his watch and moved off once more, this time toward the centre of the roof upon which they stood. 'They've taken our leaders, our best men and women. They are torturing them for their knowledge and they will kill them when it is the right time to do so. Just as ours is an old society rooted in good, Chymes seems to honour something much more ancient and evil. Sunrise signifies the death of night, their sacrificial ritual denoting the end of the moon.'

'You think they'll attack you, then murder your people at sunrise?' asked Rose.

'It seems likely. But when? Tomorrow? The next day?' They had reached a large arrangement of aluminium ducts. Along one side was a workman's cabin with its door open. Inside, two young women sat rewinding hundreds of yards of nylon cable. Zalian stood silently watching them. 'Our supplies are almost exhausted,' he said. 'They have destroyed nearly all of our depots.'

'You can't give up hope,' said Rose. 'Remember, you can often see the moon during the day.'

Zalian gave a bitter laugh. 'The Bringers Of The New Age will be the new lords of the Roofworld,' he admitted. 'They are tribal, violent, devoid of conscience, bred from the sterile wasteland of what this city has become. To join with them is to enter the realm of darkness.'

'If they outnumber you and they're so strong,' asked Robert, 'how can they be beaten?'

'We should have acted days ago,' said Zalian, appearing not to hear him. 'Instead we waited. I underestimated them. I underestimated *him*.'

'What was Sarah Endsleigh's connection in all this?' asked Robert.

'It was I who asked her up here in the first place,' said Zalian. 'I was Sarah's lover.' Zalian leaned back against the wall of the workman's cabin and rubbed his hand across his forehead. He seemed oblivious to the bitterness of the wind which had begun to pick up across the rooftop. 'It was all my fault. We knew nothing about the new leader of the New Age except his name – Chymes. He sounded like a character from a comic book.'

'Then why did so many kids take him seriously?'

'The man *acts* like a comic book character, carrying out psychotic stunts, filling their heads with crazy ideas and images of blood cults and revenge. He must have every maladjusted thug, every screwed-up junkie, every twisted loner in the city under his control. And now he's killing our family.'

'You were saying about Sarah,' Rose gently reminded.

'I asked for volunteers to infiltrate the New Age,' said Zalian, his voice low. 'Sarah wanted to go. I couldn't stop her. She passed back information she obtained from two members, one they called the Toad and another one called Samuel. But she was discovered. And while Chymes decided her fate, he sent her down to street level with two of his men . . .'

' . . . To dissuade her mother from talking. That was the morning I saw her,' Rose exclaimed.

'One of the men she travelled with was also on our side,' said Zalian, 'but for his own protection we had to keep Sarah unaware of him. Charlotte was a stubborn woman. She'd managed to bully the secrets of the Roofworld out of her daughter. Now she refused to give up her notes. I doubt that she realized the danger she was putting herself and Sarah in by doing so.'

'I knew there was something odd going on that day,' said Rose. 'I'm so bloody unobservant. If only I'd realized that Sarah was there as a prisoner.'

'If you'd known, you may never have made it this far.'

'I very nearly didn't make it through this afternoon,' muttered Robert, shoving his hands deep in his pockets.

'Of course, Chymes didn't believe Sarah when she returned empty-handed. So he sent someone to search the old woman's apartment. Unfortunately, the burglar he chose was a junkie, a crazy boy. He broke into several other flats before searching the right one. He was caught in the act by Charlotte and he murdered her.' Zalian fell silent and stood staring off into the bitter night sky.

'I'm freezing,' Robert complained. 'Can we go inside and start work on the book?'

'What do you think we can gain by studying it?' asked Rose.

'We don't know what *motivates* the New Age,' explained Zalian. 'We need to understand their doctrines, their way of thinking. Why do they perform ritual killings? Do they believe in the supernatural? The power of Satan? A lot of people here seemed to think so. They were afraid of facing Chymes for fear of being – I don't know – destroyed by something diabolical. 'Chymes is a clever man. He rules by using our most basic terror, the fear of primitive evil. If you can make people believe in that, you can control them for life.'

He turned on his heel suddenly, facing away from them. 'Sarah knew what drove Chymes on. I can only pray that she passed the information across to her mother. Once we understand his motives, we can find a way to beating him. I suspect that without Chymes spear-heading this grand New Age, the rest of his men will fall into disarray.'

'And what if your theory is wrong?' asked Robert.

'Then we fail and the last barrier between them and the ground will have fallen. Madness will have triumphed over reason.'

'How much time do you think we've got?' asked Rose.

'Judging by their previous attacks, about three hours.'

Robert beat the others back to the conduit.

CHAPTER THIRTY-ONE

Beneath The Bridge

'That's not the point, Ian. You promised that we'd be able to spend at least part of the Christmas break together. I thought we'd be able to get out of this damned city for a few days.'

'But that was before all hell broke loose. And now that I'm getting somewhere with the investigation, I have to stay in town and see it through. Surely you of all people must appreciate that.'

Janice Longbright had been expecting to stay the night with him, but Hargreave knew that tonight, and every night for the foreseeable future, he had to return to work after seeing her back to her comfortable Belsize Park flat. 'It's not as if I'm angling for promotion, quite the reverse. If I don't put in the hours and there's another murder . . .'

'I know, Ian. And I understand, really. I'd feel the same way. I suppose I'm just being selfish. Why did it have to happen at *Christmas* of all times. . . .' Janice stood in the gap of the doorway, the hall light glossing the tidy, old-fashioned style of her hair. She seemed to be wearing a shade of lipstick that nobody manufactured any more. He leaned forward and kissed her lightly on the mouth. 'I'll see you first thing tomorrow.'

'Maybe I'll put in some overtime myself,' she mused. 'At least that way we could have lunch together. I might even let you shoulder me into the Xerox room with a sprig of mistletoe.'

'You'd need a whole branch to cope with what I have in mind,' said Hargreave, buttoning up his collar and glancing up at the sky. 'They reckon we're going to get snow before the end of the week. I've got Butterworth leading a team of men on the roof areas around Soho, but they've come up with sod all so far. We have to act now, before any remaining tracks get covered.'

'Where are you going? Back to work?'

'I've a meeting with Stan Cutts. Maybe he's going to come clean and give me a lead. I'll call you later, let you know how I got on.'

Earlier that evening, he had received a telemessage from the journalist asking to meet him beneath Hungerford Bridge. It seemed an odd request, but Hargreave was going to make sure that he was there on time, in case Cutts had come up with a decent suspect, or even better had decided to reveal the source of his information.

As he walked along the broad, dimly-lit pavement of Northumberland Avenue towards the embankment and the bridge, he began to grow suspicious. Why would Cutts send him a note rather than simply make a call? He had never done so before. He rounded the corner of the avenue, passing the smart white exterior of the Playhouse, and found himself facing one of London's saddest and most disturbing sights. Here, beneath the dripping ironwork of the railway bridge were the derelicts of the city, the vagrants who had been turned away from the overcrowded hostels of Camden and Soho and Stepney and Bow, who slept in sodden cardboard boxes on the pavement and who fought desperate, bitter battles among themselves for a cigarette or a swig of wine.

It seemed bizarre that they should be camped here, next to a theatre that nightly discharged smartly dressed playgoers who stood looking on and sipping white wine while they waited for the intermission bell to recall them. Even on a night as bitterly cold as this there were hundreds of the down-and-outs, bundles of flesh and rags who blended against the stained brickwork until they seemed to have become part of the bridge's structure.

Hargreave shifted uneasily at the base of the bridge, checking his watch every few minutes. Opposite, the darkened windows of the soon-to-be demolished shops at the bottom of Villiers Street stared blankly back. In a couple of years, new glass and concrete office blocks would stand here, ready to house the new executives who would insist on removing the despairing eyesore beneath the bridge. Then where would they sleep? These days, even the churches locked their doors at night. He checked his watch again, then dug into his overcoat for his cigarettes. Cutts was over twenty minutes late.

Behind him there was a scuffling sound as two vagrants fought for space among the huddled sleepers. He looked up at the grey steel railings of the bridge above.

There were people on the bridge.

The more his eyes adjusted to the dark, the more individual figures he could count. There were four of them – no, five. They were carrying something – it appeared to be a large sack – and tethering it to the handrail with a length of rope. Suddenly the sack was tossed over the side of the bridge, the rope pulled taut and the bulky object swung like a pendulum across the road at the bridge's base.

Hargreave followed the path of the pendulum in time to see the sack crash through the window of the nearest shop with a deafening bang. Before the vagrants had time to stagger to their feet amid coughs and cries, Hargreave sprinted across the road and climbed through the demolished window of the shop. At the end of the now-taut rope was the body of a man, the end of the cord fastened in a noose around his neck. Stan Cutts was lying in a pile of souvenir dolls and teddy bears with his hands tied behind his back, his legs twisted at grotesque angles beneath him. His eyes were wide and still.

Hargreave rose and looked back at the railway bridge. Even now he could hear fast footsteps clanging across the bridge's narrow pedestrian walkway. He knew all too well that the only way onto it from here was to go back up the street and through the terminal. Opening the frequency on his walkie-talkie, he requested a car and a team of men to begin a search, starting from the darkened far side of the bridge. He crouched over the body and began a systematic search of Stan's pockets, first going through his overcoat, then turning the body over to check inside his jacket. Behind him the vagrants stood silently watching, unable to comprehend the cause of this disturbance to their troubled sleep.

Hargreave quickly pocketed several scraps of paper, a couple of ticket stubs and a wallet, leaving some small change and a bunch of keys. As he leaned over the broken body of the reporter, he grimaced. There was a strange, but vaguely recognizable smell in the air. He rubbed his thumb and forefinger across the shoulder of Cutt's overcoat and sniffed his fingers. Faint traces of yellow powder brushed the ridges of his thumb. . . .

A few feet away from him a heavy, triangular piece of glass fell from the top of the shattered window with a crash, making him start. He checked the body once again and this time noticed the painful blisters which surrounded the dead reporter's mouth. He bent forward and examined them more closely. They appeared to be consistent with acid burns. The same smell lingered here, but with a more stinging chemical acridity. He knew the compound, remembered smelling it in chemistry classes. Sulphur. The body had been sprayed or brushed with a large quantity of sulphur powder. And by the look of it he reckoned that Stan Cutts had been forced to swallow sulphuric acid. He rose unsteadily to his feet, his head sinking to his hands. It was all beginning to fit with the theory that he had first started to consider when he freewheeled the computer.

Of course it would be sulphur. It was the basic material most closely associated with the devil. Brimstone.

Friday 19 December

CHAPTER THIRTY-TWO

Search Parties

By 10.30 that evening Zalian's group, including Robert and Rose, had gathered on the roof of the Stock Exchange once more. The previous night's search had proven fruitless. Chymes and his men had failed to launch any kind of attack and an uneasy silence had settled over the roofscape. Much to Rose's annoyance Zalian had jealously guarded his precious notebooks, laboriously copying sections of them into his desktop computer. He now had a wealth of facts and figures at his fingertips, but had so far been unable to draw any firm conclusions from them. The clues to Chymes' grand plan remained elusive, hidden in an over-abundance of information.

Rose and Robert had finally climbed down from the roof in a state of exhaustion at just after 5.00 a.m. that morning. Both of them slept through the day that followed, while all around them the residents of the city continued their traditional Christmas rituals of shopping and getting drunk. Now they were back on the roof once more and this time Rose felt sure that something would occur. Spice's team, nine in all, lined up to receive weaponpacks from Lee, who handed each one a small nylon satchel containing a marine flare, spare line cartridges, a knife and something which looked like a miniature crossbow.

'I wasn't going to have them issued until I'd really perfected them,' he told Spice, passing her one of the crude prototype devices. 'It's the reload. I can't get it to work automatically and the whole thing's really too light for the ammunition.'

'Which is what?' asked Spice, balancing the aluminium crossbow in the palm of her hand.

'It's a modified dart.' He withdrew one from the bag and held it up. 'You can't carry more than six of them around and they're only good for close range.'

'Are the tips poisoned?' asked a girl standing behind Spice.

'Unfortunately, no,' said Lee. 'Zalian wouldn't let me use poison, but I've managed to coat the tips in a mix which will sting in a wound like a son of a bitch. I've no covers for them, so be careful you don't stick yourself.'

'We've got to have something for long distance, Lee. Haven't you got anything in there we can use?' Spice accepted a cluster of darts and carefully pocketed them. 'I mean, they've got all of the razor-coin guns now.'

When Chymes' men had first begun their kidnapping raids, they had stolen Lee's complete supply of coin-guns, which at best had been merely capable of stunning someone, and had adapted them into murder weapons.

'I don't have anything for long distance,' admitted Lee. 'I wasn't expecting a war.'

'OK, finish kitting my team and I'll figure out which area we're going to cover.' Spice walked off, restrapping her belt over her small, muscular frame. In the operations room she talked briefly with Zalian, who had decided that the groups should start the search for Chymes by splitting the central part of London into three sections, beginning at the top of each section and fanning out to meet with each other in the centre.

Damien, the young punk leading the third group, was the first to leave, his team using existing runs to take off across the tops of the city's financial institutions. Then Spice was over the side, her two-way micro-transmitter crackling as she led her group away towards the lights of the West End.

Lee handed out the last of the weapons to his team of eight, who stubbed out their cigarettes, joking nervously to one another, and took off over the empty streets, the rusting steel pillars of the cable stations creaking and groaning beneath their collective weight. Then the roof was suddenly silent and empty, as the combined body heat of Zalian's troops evaporated into the escalating iciness of the night.

Spice aimed her line-gun and slowly squeezed the trigger. There was a nylon hiss and a glitter of steel, a clinking sound as she connected with her target. Quickly, she ratcheted the line in and attached it to the metal bar on the wall of the building at her feet. They had travelled to the north of Oxford Circus via one of the oldest permanent runs in the city, but were now forced to leave it at Portland Place because several of the stations from here were almost completely rusted through. Spice ushered her men forward onto the line and, clipping themselves in place one by one, they silently crossed the deserted street.

Although the front of it was lit by dim sodium streetlamps, the top of the opposite building was in darkness. Spice was the last to cross, nimbly hopping over the broad ledge around the roof and unclipping the line after her so that no one could follow them.

In front of her, somebody clicked on a pocket torch and ran it over the roof to the far side. 'No sign that anyone's been here.'

'Do you think they could be holding Sarah and the others somewhere beyond the station areas?' asked Spice.

'Seems unlikely,' replied the boy with the torch. 'They would have to have used one of the permanent runs at least part of the way.' These runs formed a one way system over the city and were strung from the tops of steel posts which were bolted into the roofs themselves. In order to safeguard them and keep them hidden, most of the stations were constructed on buildings with little or no roof access. Their careful placement and extra height meant that a person travelling on them moved mainly through gravitational force, without having to exert any physical effort. Assuming that Chymes' men kept their prisoners bound in some fashion, it seemed to Spice that it would be impossible for them to travel in any other way than via these gravitational fast lanes.

'This is the end of the North Seven Run, isn't it?' Spice walked over to the boy, whose name was Tom, her boots crunching on the gravelled roof. He pulled a crumpled map from his bag and shone the torch over it. 'It's the North Seven all right, but it ain't the end. There's another three stations, but they're marked on 'ere as unsafe.'

'Where do they go?' Spice traced her finger up a blue line on the map. Several of the others came over to look.

'The last one is Adam, see?' A grubby finger jabbed the map. 'Looks like it's actually in the park, on the north side of Park Crescent.'

'Surprising. The crescent is brightly lit at night. You'd think the line would show from the ground.'

'Depends on how high it is.'

'Parkland. Wonder what it's attached to.' Spice thought for a moment. 'I'm going to go up there to take a look. You hang on here. If the line's impassable, I'll head right back, but either way I shouldn't be gone more than a few minutes.'

'Says here that it's unsafe.'

'Zalian always writes "unsafe" when he's not sure about the condition of a run. I'm the lightest. Anyway, we have to check out all the possibilities. Start working out our next route, will you?'

Spice swung herself out and onto the pale concrete ledge once more, looking back down behind her to where Broadcasting House cut into the road like the prow of an ocean liner. She smiled. 'They insisted that nothing should ever obscure the view north up this street, did you know that?'

'Who did?' asked Tom.

'The original architects. A couple of hundred years ago this was the grandest street in London.' She hoisted herself up to the height of the cable overhead and clipped on her line-belt with practised ease. 'Still looks nice at night, don't it?'

'Go easy, eh?' said Tom. He had always rather fancied Spice, but she seemed to show no interest in men. 'You want to take the walkie-talkie?'

'No, you'd better hang on to it. See you.' She lifted her boots from the ledge and was carried away in a rush of air between the shadowed buildings which housed so many doctors and lawyers and architects, as she headed up toward the southern tip of Regent's Park.

Tom turned to the others. 'Come on, then, let's get our route sorted out. Anyone got any bright ideas as to where to look next?'

'What about the top of the Capital building? It'd give them a good vantage point,' suggested a heavy-set girl with cropped black hair. She and the others were using the break to have a smoke and to stretch tired muscles.

'No, it's too high. We can't get up there from this side. You'd have to take one of the top two north runs for that.'

'How long should we wait for Spice?'

'As long as it takes.'

'What if she doesn't come back?'

'She'll come back.'

Tom sat down with the map, folding and refolding it nervously in his fingers. Dividing up the roof territory and searching it in sections wasn't his idea of a good plan, but in the absence of any other suggestions from Zalian there was little else he could do but go along with it. But if Chymes believed in dividing to conquer, they seemed to be playing right into his hands. He rose and walked over the the edge of the roof, to stare off into the patch of inky blackness above the park.

It was seven minutes to midnight. On the rooftop of Harrods, Damien's group were starting to fight among themselves. The young punk was too new to command the respect of his team, but had been entrusted with leadership because he had somehow won the favour of Dr Zalian. Ever since he had arrived in the Roofworld, Zalian had taken him under his wing and had made a point of providing him with special training. Some of the others, four women and five men, had been angered by this. Now they were annoyed by Zalian's refusal to join them in the search and were quick to show Damien their resentment.

The boy had proven extraordinarily agile at crossing the city, but had no idea how to maintain discipline within his group, which had raggedly and noisily travelled west as far as Knightsbridge. They were now waiting on the roof of the department store while Damien consulted the map, trying to work out where the boundaries of their search area lay. 'We start here and work down to the river,' he said uncertainly, looking up at the sour-faced girl standing next to him.

'How can we, if we're all supposed to meet up at Central One?' She turned aside and spat on the brickwork. Behind her, somebody lit a joint and coughed.

'Hey, put that out! We've got to stay straight in case we run into any of Chymes' men.' Damien reached over and tried to snatch the joint away, but moved too slowly.

'I dunno what you're so worried about. We won't find any over this far,' said Tony, the tall, acned teenager who had lit the joint. 'This isn't anywhere near

New Age territory.' He pulled hard on the joint, insolently jetting the smoke at Damien.

'You know so much about it, Tony, you want to take charge?' Damien's fear showed through, making the others uncomfortable and rebellious. 'We've got to go down to the river. There's no connecting run from here to Notting Hill.'

Tony snatched the map up and held it close to Damien's face. 'We wanna fan out wide and go east, not north,' he shouted in a hard cockney accent. 'Harrods is the start of East Four and we can take it as far as Scott Station above the Albert Hall. Has anybody thought of looking there?' He threw the map back and made as if to set off.

'You can't go anywhere until I say so,' shouted Damien. 'Suppose we split up and one of us runs into an ambush?'

'Be a fucking sight better than all of us copping it,' said Tony, clambering up onto a steel ventilator shaft and hooking his line to the cable overhead. Damien could see that any show of strength on his part would only lead to an outright mutiny. Reluctantly, he turned to face the others. 'OK, folks,' he called, 'looks like we're heading to Scott Station.'

'Can we have a five-minute break first?' somebody called from the back. 'I'm knackered. We only just got here.' Above, Tony hesitated, waiting for a decision from Damien, who was surprised to see that by backing down he had won a small if grudging victory.

'Yeah, all right, but five minutes only. We've got a lot of ground to cover.' Damien unclipped his walkie-talkie and set it down on the shaft as Tony climbed down and joined him. Leading the others, they walked to the centre of the roof and sat.

The front of the department store remained lit with thousands of dazzling white lightbulbs, its windows filled with scenes from Christmas fairytales. Although there was a permanent run attached to the roof of the store, it was rarely used due to the risk of being spotted from the roadway below. The Harrods building was one which too many people raised their eyes to. Its roof could also be clearly spotted by revellers from the garden nightclub situated on top of a department store several blocks away. Zalian had instructed teams to alight there for no longer than was absolutely necessary.

'How long have you been up here?' asked Tony, lighting his dormant joint once more. This time Damien removed any complaint from his reply.

'Just over a year,' he said. 'I was a fitter's mate. Got made redundant. It was all cash-in-hand work and I couldn't find anything else that paid a living wage. I came up here like a shot.'

'Same with me,' said Tony, passing the joint to a girl who sat behind him oiling her line-gun. 'Except I've been here three years now. D'you go back down much?'

'You must be joking,' said Damien. 'I never had anything down there worth missing. Except the movies. I go down a couple of times a week for the films.'

'Cinema skylights, funny how they're never locked. Like the ones in swimming pools and turkish baths. Guess they figure there's nothing worth nicking in places like that. Me, I never bother going down to street level any more.' Tony took a long pull on the joint and held his breath down. 'I used to go out with this girl from the East Four krewe, but they all went over to Chymes. She tried to get me to come. Fuck that, I told her. Don't know now, though. It's not like it was. Zalian's useless, no guts. We get stoned all the time. Hardly surprising, with a junkie in charge.'

As soon as he said this he realized that he had caused any budding friendliness between Damien and himself to be stillborn. Damien, after all, was still the leader and they had all received lectures from Zalian about the group's declining adherence to the rules. The fact that Zalian had been such a disciplinarian partly explained why people had begun to drift across to the other side, where sworn allegiance and exotic ceremony counted more than mere hard work and army-style pack drill.

'We'd better get going.' Tony hauled himself to his feet and swung his equipment bag to his shoulder. The joint did not seem to have affected his coordination. Damien rose without speaking and followed closely behind.

Tony stepped around a ventilation housing and looked over towards the edge of the building, flicking his roach away. There, floodlit from the bulbs below, stood Chymes himself, dressed from head to foot in glistening armourlike black leather, his cape lifting around his raised arms.

Suddenly there was a harsh, tearing sound in the air. Wheeling around, Tony was just in time to catch Damien, who fell forward into his arms with a sudden shout of pain. Protruding from his chest was a short steel shaft, buried deep in the flesh. Surprised by the sudden weight of Damien's body he toppled over, as Chymes' men appeared from the cable overhead and dropped onto the rest of the search party with knives in their hands.

No one even had time to unseal their weapons. Damien had forgotten to order a loading drill before they set off. As his friends fell beneath the fists and knives of Chymes' skinheads, Tony heaved himself out from beneath Damien's body and crawled toward the roof edge, where his walkie-talkie still lay. He realized that it would only be a matter of moments now before one of the others spotted him. Jumping up, he saw that Chymes had vanished from his vantage point. He pulled his newly acquired dart-gun free and ran for the radio set.

With a shock he realized that the low brick stack

ahead would conceal him from the others. Behind him was the scuffle of boots on concrete and the unmistakable sound of someone dying. Thumbing the signal switch, he summoned Zalian.

'Come in, for Chrissake, come in,' he hissed, holding down the 'Send' tab. 'Come in, is there anybody out there? Come in!'

The line was dead. The sound of a bootfall behind made him turn and look up. Chymes himself was staring down at him. 'Cut off? Perhaps you haven't paid your bill recently,' he said, reaching down and ripping the walkie-talkie from Tony's grasp with a jerk of his gloved hand. He tossed it carelessly behind him. For a second, the lights from below illuminated the inside of his hood. His dark eyes reflected a madness more chilling than anything Tony had ever seen before.

'Oh!' was all he had time to say before his reflexes began to work once more and his finger squeezed the trigger of his gun, springing a coated dart into Chymes' thigh. Grunting in sudden agony, the tall cloaked figure clutched his leg as Tony leapt for the walkie-talkie. Seizing it, he opened the line and shouted into the microphone, praying that someone was listening at the other end. 'It's Chymes, he's here. . . .'

Chymes whirled, his cloak flaring, as he grabbed Tony by his neck and lifted him bodily from the ground. He swung the boy over the edge of the roof with ease, letting his feet kick in space. His hood had fallen back, revealing the flowing mane of greasy black hair, the stygian eyes.

'How much better it would have been for you to join us,' said Chymes, with mocking sadness in his voice. 'Unfortunately, membership is temporarily closed, until we have finished putting our house in order. *Destruction brings about the death of material, but the spirit renews like before, the life.*'

The boy looked back, choking in horror and bewilderment.

'That means getting rid of people like you, sonny. It's time for you to hit the road.' He started to release his grip on Tony's neck. The boy let out a strangled scream. Smiling, Chymes leaned into the boy's face. 'Next time,' he whispered, 'listen to your boss. Don't fuck with eagles unless you can fly.'

He released his hand and Tony was suddenly clutching at empty air. Screaming, the boy plunged feet-first down the front of the glittering building. As he fell his thrashing arms and legs destroyed hundreds of bulbs, in a series of electrical explosions which had the theatricality of an extravagant Christmas display filled with sparkling fire and light.

CHAPTER THIRTY-THREE

Roofworld

The operations room was a bizarre amalgam of old and new. Ancient tin station lamps threw pools of light onto portable plastic cases filled with micro-circuitry. Coils of rope and sheets of tin vied for floor space with boxes of technical components, most of them for use with computers. Zalian switched on his radio transmitter, explaining the basic layout and operation of the equipment to Robert as he went along. Rose was able to seat herself in a corner of the room beside one of the lamps, where she could be left in peace with Charlotte's notebooks. Perhaps she could decipher them alone. She could certainly do no worse than Zalian, who seemed to take every opportunity to sidetrack away from the problem at hand.

The leader of the Roofworld flicked a strand of blonde hair from his eyes and booted up the portable computer which stood balanced precariously on the corner of one of the packing cases. As sets of trading hieroglyphics began to unscroll, he pointed the key sections out to Robert.

'OK, you asked me how we manage to get along up here, so I'm going to explain our financing system to you.' Zalian punched the computer keyboard as he accessed one of his coded files. Curiosity getting the better of her, Rose lowered the notebook and came over to watch.

'I think you're going to tell me that you're actually a

bunch of crooks,' Robert said, examining the green screen suspiciously. 'Where else do you get the money for all the equipment?'

'I prefer to think of us as social humanitarians,' said Zalian loftily, 'taking from the rich and giving to those in need. Us.'

Robert looked across at Rose, who shrugged reasonably.

'I'll tell you one thing. When we do take from the rich, we make damned sure that they never notice. We only steal from the major multinational corporations. And how, you may ask, do we manage to get away with that?'

Robert tapped the glowing screen with his fingernail. 'I think I know the answer to that one. You select companies that can stand a few losses.'

'Exactly. I choose companies which I consider to be too large for their own, or anyone else's good, like the ones listed here . . . Coca-Cola, Sony, Barclays . . . they all allow an annual budget for corporate pilfering. If you like, we are simply tapping that.'

Zalian looked at the screen with pride, keying the net profits and losses of one corporation after another, proud to be able to show somebody his secret system.

'Some of the targets I pick are chosen simply because they piss me off,' he added, 'like McDonald's and British Associated Tobacco. And companies with heavy Sun City connections. It's just a matter of relocating a few assets . . .'

'Stealing, you mean.'

' . . . By reworking their computer records from up here. Previous Roofworld leaders before me have been doing it for years in one form or another, except that before computers came along they'd go down into the big department stores and simply steal merchandise, fencing it and redistributing most of the retail value to their own people.'

As he spoke, Zalian inserted another program into the computer. 'Now of course, with the creation of central databanks, we are much more traceable, so we have to make tax-deductible charity donations through officially registered companies. And the way we asset strip the multis is much more sophisticated than swiping a few consumer durables through a skylight.'

'I'm impressed,' admitted Robert.

'You're supposed to be. Lee is one of our best hackers. And right now, he's the only one we've got left. He figures that he can get into just about any system once he's had a look at their overall accounts set-up.'

'But how does he get to see that?' asked Robert, turning to Rose once more and raising his eyebrows.

'That's the easy part,' said Zalian. 'We use the Old Boy Network.'

'The Old Boy Network? What's that?'

'When long-termers have had enough up here they often want to return to the ground. After a few years' service, most roofers eventually start to crave a more peaceful, ordered life. But many still have the spark, even though they're no longer involved with the Roofworld. It's like a drug to them. Years later, they still want to be a part of it. Maybe because they believe in what the Roofworld does. Maybe they just want to re-experience the rush of adrenalin that taking a few risks can give you. We fix up our Old Boys and Girls with jobs at the multis, as janitors, secretaries, clerks, at every level. Most of the larger buildings in the West End have an ex-roofer for a night watchperson. They help prevent us from being discovered and they gather all kinds of information.'

'Isn't that dangerous for them?' asked Rose.

'We don't ask them to do anything which would jeopardize their jobs. They just keep their eyes and ears open and report back to us. In return, we pay them a supplementary wage. A pension, if you like.'

'And all this goes through the files of your own company?'

'Companies. We change them every few years to prevent the Inland Revenue from getting suspicious. You'll appreciate the irony of our most recent business. Valiant Security Lock and Co.'

'You're kidding me,' said Rose. 'They're the people who installed the alarm system in our apartment building. But those guys came in through the front door, not the roof.'

'Old Boys.'

'And that's how you were able to keep a watch on the place.'

'See how easy it is once you're organized?' said Zalian, tilting back in his chair and crossing his long denim-clad legs, pleased with himself. 'You know, we even had them search Charlotte's apartment, looking for the damned notebook. They found nothing and then we realized that our own security system, once it was up and working, kept us from getting back into your building.' Zalian thought for a moment. 'Bit of a cock-up, that. I'll have to make sure we've got someone who knows how to hotwire the system next time.'

'Let me know in advance and I'll arrange to leave a door open,' said Rose with heavy sarcasm.

'We have other companies, too . . . Albion Tiling, Imperial Pipe and Gutter . . . they provide the necessary financial structures through which we can launder money before relocating it. In fact, we just registered our own charity for combating teen drug abuse. I figured it might do something for the ones who come up here and don't stay.' Zalian closed the program and inserted another hard disk into the computer. 'All we're doing is beating the system at its own game for as long as we can possibly get away with it. I always figured that we'd slip up somewhere, that someone would catch on to what we were doing, but nobody's been fast enough up to now.'

'I don't understand,' said Rose. 'If you're got all this money coming in, why are the runs falling into disrepair?'

'It's not through lack of money. We no longer have the right people to help maintain the system. Many of our key teams were enticed over to the other side, to help herald the birth of the New Age. Right now there are more people up here than ever before, but they're not joining up with *us*. Most of them have become willing disciples of Chymes. Let's face it, it's a more attractive package. They're given free drugs, money, sex, whatever he feels like offering them and all that's asked in return is their loyalty. How can we compete?'

'Don't they bother to keep the runs in working order?'

'There are so many crossing the city that nobody's really worried if a few become unusable. But soon it will be too late to return the network to its former standard.' Zalian rubbed at his eyes with the palm of his hand. He looked tired. 'Our plans for saving the system were curtailed when all the trouble started. After it's over – though I very much doubt that we'll still be here – I suppose we could start to rebuild.'

'It must have taken someone very special to come up with all this,' said Robert, watching as Zalian scrolled the screen. Hundreds of familar multinational brand-names unrolled before his eyes, each with its own file code.

'The system more or less evolved by itself through the work of many people. A chain of knowledge, passed down from one generation to the next, and all for what? To provide an escape, a way out of the life below. But now I'm starting to believe that the Roofworld's time is really over. Who needs it any more?'

Robert was wary of this turn in the conversation.

Zalian appeared more tired and haggard by the minute, as if he had already been defeated.

'Before Jay died he said something odd.'

'What do you mean?' The doctor raised his broad skull from the transmitter and stared at him, obviously miles away in his thoughts.

'He said that most of you would be dead by dawn on Sunday. Why Sunday?'

Before Zalian could answer Rose cut in, tapping the book with a tapered brown finger. 'Chymes is more than just a crazy mystic, that much is obvious. Perhaps Sunday has some kind of special significance to him.'

'That's right,' said Zalian. 'Our own operations reach a peak at the time of the full moon. It's one of the few traditions which have remained unbroken.'

'I don't get the connection,' said Robert.

'Diana the Huntress was latterly goddess of the moon. And Apollo corresponded to the sun,' Rose explained. 'If we assume that the New Age represents an inversion of all that is good in Doctor Zalian's society, perhaps we should be looking to the opposite of these gods.'

'I've already thought of that,' said Zalian. 'The Greek deities have no real alter egos. Their opposite numbers in Roman mythology also fail to correspond.'

'Then maybe Chymes' set-up has nothing to do with mythology at all,' said Robert. 'Perhaps it's the very opposite of mythology. . . .'

'It looks more like it's based on a load of Satanic gobbledegook,' Rose pointed out. 'Look here. . . .' She pointed to midway down a page in the notes.

'There are several passages here about the release of power through sexual sacrifice.' Zalian leaned against Rose's shoulder, reading the page with her.

'No wonder they won over so many of your men, Zalian.' said Robert.

'We also have "ritual intercourse for the assurance

of victory" and the "runic power of symbols", although it doesn't say of what kind of symbol. How many of your people are actually missing, presumably awaiting execution? Twelve you said, didn't you?'

'Twelve including Sarah, that's right.'

Robert watched Rose calmly take control of the proceedings. She seemed to fit in up here somehow, acting in a cocky and self-assured manner that matched her personality. He had a feeling that he preferred her as she had been before. At least he had known how to react then.

'The number twelve could have some significance. Something to do with the zodiac?' he suggested.

'One victim for each horoscopic sign?' said Rose, brightening up. 'You mean some kind of black magic ritual based around the creation of a human zodiac.'

'Wait a minute,' said Robert, holding up his hands. 'What are we saying here? It seems unlikely that before Chymes' men carry out a kidnap they stop to ask when the victim was born. "Sorry, can't sacrifice you, we need an Aries." We're better off accepting that the guy is a nut and that his band of merry men are simply cranks and junkies.' Robert rose from his packing-crate stool and stretched. 'This place is starting to get to me. I'm going to clear my head for a minute.'

Outside, the lights of far-off buildings on the other side of the Thames glittered and winked in the cold, moisture-laden air. With the passing of the night's traffic, the sounds from the streets had ceased completely and an eerie deadening silence had fallen.

Robert breathed in deeply, filling his lungs with surprisingly fresh air. His eyes were sore and gritty, yet he felt far from tired. In the harsh morning light he knew that all of this would once again seem remote and fantastic. Maybe there wasn't anybody trying to kill him at all. It could be that he was becoming just as crazy as the others. . . .

'Robert.'

He felt a hand on his shoulder and turned. Rose stood at his side, looking out over the deserted city streets. He could feel the warmth of her palm through the material of his jumpsuit. He wanted to press back against her, but something inside refused to let him, the subconscious knowledge that he would never make love with her, that he was not the kind of man she desired.

'Come back in.'

'You seem to be doing fine by yourselves,' he said morosely. 'I don't trust Zalian. He's had plenty of time to study the book, yet he's found out nothing.'

'I think it's safe to assume that he's one of the good guys,' said Rose. 'The blonde hair, the white teeth. He's too cute to be bad.'

'All the notebook says about him is that he's a reformed alcoholic. That's terrific leadership material. And how come he gets to stay behind in all this?'

'I don't know. We'll ask him if you're that concerned. I'm sure there's a reason.'

But it was too late. Robert's frustration broke through into anger. 'You go and ask ol' Blue Eyes. I've had enough of his bullshit for a while.'

He stormed off across the windswept roof, leaving Rose standing alone, upset and growing equally as exasperated. Robert's behaviour had nothing to do with his distrust of Zalian, she could see that – it was sexual jealousy, pure and simple. He resented her showing friendliness to another man, just as he probably resented her agility and intelligence. It made him feel weak and threatened. Well, he could go to hell for all she cared. She spun around on the heel of her sneaker and stalked back toward the conduit and the operations room. The first report was crackling in from what sounded like Lee's group.

'Nothing so far, Nat. We've come down through Mayfair and we're heading towards the Mall, over.'

'Remember to avoid your map references centre-ten through thirty, Lee,' said Zalian into the microphone. He turned at the sound of the door opening and beckoned Rose over.

'We have to be very careful in parts of the West End,' he explained. 'They have high-resolution roof cameras all around the royal buildings, on top of the embassies and along Downing Street. They're putting more technology up here every day. Most of the surveillance is to help control traffic flow, but there's an increasing amount of equipment appearing that's designed to advance-alert suspected criminal and terrorist activity. We keep having to come up with new ways of getting around it.'

The transmitter crackled back to life. 'Wilco, base. It would help if we knew what we were looking for, over.'

'We'll call you as soon as we have something. At the moment all I can tell you is to keep an eye out for any tracks Chymes and his men may have left and to radio them in before marking them on your map. Call me if you find anything at all out of the ordinary and we'll do the same. Over and out.' Zalian signed off and tipped his chair back. He ran his hands through his hair and closed his eyes, seemingly exhausted.

'There doesn't seem to be much here about the New Age at all,' said Rose, taking her seat once more and flicking through the last five or six pages of Charlotte's notebook.

'Which book are you looking in?'

'The second one.'

'Give me the other one.' Rose tossed the notebook across to Zalian. Outside, the wind began to moan dismally around the corners of the building. 'There are drawings of a number of horoscope symbols here, rams and moons and goats. And some more about you.'

'Let me see.' Zalian took it from her and read several pages before setting the book aside. 'Not a very flattering portrait,' he said finally. 'According to this I'm a "misguided idealist". She had a bloody nerve writing that, considering she never even got to meet me. Charlotte presumably took down the notes from conversations she had with her daughter, but they seem to be in no kind of order. Let's try something else.'

'What do Satanists believe in?' asked Rose. 'Isn't it something to do with the elemental spirits? Fire, water, earth and air? Maybe they're holed up in a place you could freely associate with a particular element.'

'Like a fire station, or the river?' asked Zalian, looking back with a dubious frown. 'Or even the airport?'

'It's worth a try. Make a list of all possible places in the immediate area which you could associate with an elemental sign and have your teams check them out.'

'Do you know how long that would take?' said Zalian. 'There are so many possible hiding places that we wouldn't even begin to scratch the surface looking for them. It's hardly a wonder that they call London the most elusive city in the world. Its character changes from one street to the next. There's no rhyme or reason, no pattern to the place. You could take six people at random from the centre of town, ask them to write down all the places they visit regularly and find that their circles of movement don't overlap at more than one or two points. Each of them would see a different city.' Zalian shook his head and returned to the book.

Only the increasing rush of chill wind could be heard outside, sweeping over the roof, buzzing in the station cables. Within the conduit, the lightbulbs overhead swayed slightly, twisting yellow light between the shadows of the tiny operations room. Rose rubbed her eyes and stared at the book. 'Maybe we should give Dennis Wheatley a call. Or is he dead? Perhaps we could have a seance and get through to him.'

'This is serious, Rose,' said Zalian, throwing down his pen. 'If you're tired, take a nap. I'll listen out for the radio.' He looked down at the blank notepad in front of him, then over at the young woman who sat hunched by the lamp, tilting pages up to the flickering light. As he pushed himself back from the desk he turned to her, reaching out his hand to touch her shoulder. 'All this must seem very odd to you,' he said, a slight smile crossing his face. 'You're handling it as if you've been in the Roofworld for years. Very impressive.'

'I'm dead resilient, me,' said Rose, gently pulling free and rising from her seat. 'Madness, danger, sudden violence, I can cope. It's just like being at home with the TV on.'

'But this is real life,' said Zalian. 'You can't switch channels. And I get just as scared as any of the others, except that I'm not supposed to admit it. Do you want something to keep you awake?'

'Like what?'

'I've been lacing strong black coffee with a little something to keep me on edge.'

'I'd kill for some plain hot caffeine.'

'OK. I'll be back in a minute. Then you come with me.'

Zalian vanished and returned a full five minutes later with a grin on his face, beckoning Rose out onto the roof and around to the rear of the conduit.

Amazingly, there in the shadows was a full-sized hot drinks vending machine, lit up and hotwired to the circuits of the floor below. It provided an extra touch of the bizarre in an already surreal landscape.

'It was a bastard getting it up here,' said Zalian. 'We painted it grey to look like part of the ventilation system, but I'm not sure if the effect comes off.' He handed Rose a scalding plastic cup. 'Cheers.' If he had noticed that Robert was missing, he failed to mention it. Rose gave him a cool, appraising look. She had no doubt that Zalian could be a real charmer. Physically he was imposing. What bothered her, though, was his seeming lack of concern over Sarah. Was he being careful to hide his true feelings about her? Didn't he say that he had been her lover? She sipped her coffee thoughtfully, watching him.

'Stars,' said Zalian dreamily, crumpling his now-empty cup and pointing into the crystalline darkness above them. 'Don't often see those in town.'

'Why not?' Rose tilted her head back. She felt as if the icy void of the space above was reaching down to envelop her.

'The city throws off too much light. It reflects back from the clouds.' Silence fell between them. In the distance, a barge mournfully sounded its horn.

'How does that song go, "Up on the roof"?' Rose hummed a few bars. ' "When this old world starts getting me down and people just get too much for me to take . . ." '

' "I climb right up to the top of the stairs and all my cares just drift right off into space," ' completed Zalian. 'I guess that's pretty much been our anthem. People up here always end up singing it when they're drunk.' He laughed with the memory. 'Lee and Spice tried to get a jukebox onto the top of Mornington Crescent tube station once. They almost managed it.'

'What happened?'

'Oh, they brought it across the rooftops via Camden Lock and one of the runs broke. It fell into the canal, made a hell of a noise. I thought we were going to wake up the whole neighbourhood. It took Lee's collection of rare Presley 45's to a watery grave.'

They fell silent once more. Far below them, the light from miniature rows of streetlamps fluttered in the damp night air.

'That was another thing,' he said suddenly. 'We used to throw parties in department stores. Back in the so-called good old days, we'd take over an entire floor and have a feast. Marks and Spencer on a Saturday night, Harrods for special occasions. Invitation only. Selfridges was good, too.' He turned and looked out at the city spread below, a rumpled blanket of lights and building blocks, like some complex and expensive toy cast aside by a spoiled child.

'I often wondered if we were the only ones,' he said softly. 'Perhaps there are people like us in New York, swinging between the skyscrapers and dining at Bloomingdales. Or in Paris, throwing parties on top of the Arc-de-Triomphe and connecting runs from the Eiffel Tower.'

'I'm sure there are others out there. There must be.'

Rose shivered and Zalian put his arms around her, pulling her closer. In the next moment he had reached down and was kissing her, pressing himself against her body with a strength which made Rose raise her hands in defence. She pulled free and looked into his eyes. What she perceived was a tension, a flash of torment which turned in on itself behind a sapphire-cold gaze. He inclined his head to kiss her again, blonde hair falling lazily into his eyes. Sliding his hand around her back, he pressed her breasts against his broad, warm chest.

'Wait, wait, Nathaniel, I can't do this.' Rose pulled free and stood apart. 'Sarah could be dead or wounded and you don't seem to . . .'

'Fuck Sarah.' He stepped forward and reached his hands towards her once more. Rose moved slowly back. My God, she thought, there's something wrong here. Stay calm and stall him. She twisted her head to one side. Where the hell had Robert gone?

'We should be out there searching with the others,' she said, trying to sound as casual as possible.

'They can move faster than you. Besides, we can do more good here.'

'Can we? We've done nothing so far. There haven't

even been any messages on the . . .' She stopped suddenly. Breaking away, she ran back to the entrance of the conduit.

'Rose, wait!' called Zalian, running after her.

'For Christ's sake, come in, somebody! There are only four of us left, the rest are all dead. Come in . . .' An anguished voice crackled out from the radio as Rose switched it back into life. You turned it off, she thought incredulously, you son of a bitch, you deliberately turned it off. Snatching up the handset, she opened the line for transmission. 'Where are you? Which group are you in?'

'Finally! What the hell's going on back there? We've had a massacre here at West Forty. We need help, bad. Chymes was waiting for us. There are bodies everywhere, Tony's been killed and I can hear a siren. The police will be up here any minute . . .' The voice trailed off in sobs. Rose's voice cut through.

'Listen, how many of you are there?'

'Two of us unhurt, two badly wounded. The rest are all dead.'

'You're going to have to carry the wounded ones. Leave the others, there's nothing you can do, but you must hide or dispose of their bags and line-guns. Check their pockets for I.D. before you leave. You've got to delay the police in identifying the bodies, or it's the end for all of you. Just keep your wits and work as quickly as you can. Think you can do that?'

'We don't take orders from you. Where's Zalian?'

'Nathaniel, talk to them!'

Zalian came to the microphone.

'It's O.K. Do as she says.'

'All right,' replied the voice, steadier now. 'We have a secret stash-place around here somewhere. We can hide the equipment there.'

'OK, do it and hurry. Then get as far away as possible. Try to make it back here. If you get stuck, call me and I'll get someone over to help bring you in.'

When Rose had replaced the handset she turned back to Zalian. 'What the hell did you think you were doing?' she shouted. 'Whose side are you on, for God's sake? Your own people are out there dying and you don't give a damn!'

Zalian looked shattered. He slumped down onto a packing box with his head in his hands. When he spoke, his voice had lost all authority. He sounded like a child. 'You don't understand,' he said. 'There's nothing any of us can do now. It's too late.'

'Wait a minute,' said Rose, ducking through the door and running back outside. She suddenly knew why Zalian had left the conduit by himself earlier on and began to search the roof. She found the crumpled twist of silver foil and spent needle lying in a thin trickle of blood behind the vending machine.

'Malpractice', the notes had said, 'Missing drugs case: Doctor suspended.' She should have realized at the time. It was the only thing that could explain his sudden shifting moods. Unable to face up to his responsibilities, Zalian had begun to take heroin again. She gathered up the evidence and ran back to the conduit, hurling it onto the floor in front of him.

'You bloody idiot,' she cried. 'You're going to tell me what the hell is going on before anyone else gets killed.' She dropped down to his level and gripped his shoulders with both hands. 'What did you think you could gain by turning off the radio?'

Zalian refused to answer at first. He seemed to be staring out past her into the night sky beyond the conduit door, his eyes glazed with the effects of the drug. 'Chymes can't be beaten,' he said at last, his voice barely audible. 'Those who haven't already defected will die by his hand. I couldn't bear to listen to their agony.'

'But you have to find a way of helping them, Nathaniel!' Rose shouted. 'You can't just hide yourself away and pretend that it's not happening. We're the only ones who have a chance of defeating him. We can't just give up. What about Sarah?'

'Sarah has joined with her true master.' His face grew hard. 'They deceived and betrayed me and now they will bring in the New Age together.'

CHAPTER THIRTY-FOUR

Lair

Painfully, Robert hauled himself up onto the overlapping tiles of the roof. This wasn't turning out to be as easy as it looked. When he had stormed away from Rose he had been planning to head back to his flat. Then, realizing that he would never be able to forgive himself for failing to witness the events of the night, his idea had been to catch up with one of the other groups, but without Rose's help his progress had proven agonizingly slow. Stopping every few minutes to consult the complex and confusing station map, or to rest his searing muscles, he realized that by now the other groups must all be far away.

Robert gazed down at his surroundings. He seemed to be on the outskirts of the original City of London. He had left behind the towering cranes and monstrous glass office blocks of the capital's proliferating financial institutions and had entered a much older area of narrow unrenovated buildings and filthy untrodden rooftops. Lying back against the sloping clay tiles he looked up at the stars, allowing his heartbeat gradually to return to normal.

After a few minutes he sat up, wiping the cooling sweat from his eyes. He found himself on top of a comparatively low building, just three storeys high. It had been easier to keep travelling at a downward angle in order to save his aching back, which seemed to suffer more when there was climbing to be done. He leaned over the side and tried to read a street sign which was caught in the misty light above a lamp post. It looked like Whittington, or Whittaker, Avenue, He could clearly make out the EC3 part, at least.

This roof was too steep. He was exhausted. If he stayed here he would probably fall asleep and slide straight off the edge. The next building along was taller, but appeared to have a flat roof. Robert hauled himself to his feet and fished around in his bag for his battery-powered climber. Removing the disc from its pouch, he noticed that his hands were beginning to be covered in stinging callouses.

The bar attachments for hooking lines were less frequently to be found in this area. He had been going in the wrong direction. It was time to turn back toward the centre of the city.

He examined the attachments which came with the climber and found a small collapsible grappling hook, neatly folded flat like a miniature camera tripod. Studying his line-gun, he discovered that it was also designed to launch the grappling hook from a set of grooves cut into the top of the barrel. Carefully he aimed at the top of the wall and squeezed the trigger.

The hook shot far above his target and clattered faintly on the roof beyond. It took him some minutes before he managed to haul the line back in without snagging it. Second time around, the hook caught behind a rubbed brickwork ledge and held fast. Carefully he freed the cord from the gun and rejoined it to his climbing disc. He could see that it was much darker across there than on any of the other roofs so far. He had not had cause to use the disc until now and remembered what had happened when Rose had used hers for the first time. Suppose he slipped and hurt himself, couldn't move, how would they find him? He decided to radio in his position before attempting the crossing. Switching on his handset, he thumbed the pre-set frequency.

'Hello, Rose, Zalian? Come in.' The burst of static made him jump.

'Identify yourself.'

'Rose, it's me, Robert.' He suddenly remembered how he had left and felt sheepish. 'Look, I'm sorry about . . .'

'Skip it, we've got bigger things to worry about. Damien's team has been all but wiped out by Chymes and his men. Where are you?'

'I'm somewhere in EC3.'

'Where's that?'

'That's just it, I'm not sure. I was hoping you could give me some bearings, some landmark I could aim toward.'

'That's great. All we need is for you to get yourself lost. Hang on, we're looking it up. What's the name of the street?'

'Whittington Avenue, I think.' Behind him, the wind lifted an old newspaper and let it fall with a slap. 'Pretty creepy place.'

'Robert? We've another call coming in. It may be important. Can you call me back in a couple of minutes?'

'I guess so.'

Reluctantly, Robert signed off and slipped the hand-set back into his pocket. He picked up the steel climber disc which he had left hanging against the wall and clipped it to his belt. Then, very gently, he squeezed the disc's spring-button and allowed the line to haul him up over the bricks, pushing his feet out as he rose, rather like abseiling in reverse, letting the nylon cord be drawn in until he reached the top. Dragging himself over the peak of the wall was a strain, but he managed it, collapsing at last on the other side in the centre of a long, rolled strip of tarmac. As his breathing slowed the wind began to pick up, skittering an empty drink can along the guttering.

Finally, Robert roused himself and took a look along the gently angled rooftop.

'Oh, *shit* . . .' His mouth fell open. Slowly rising to his feet, he continued to stare ahead. Then he began to move back to the building's edge, fear churning in the pit of his stomach.

CHAPTER THIRTY-FIVE

Late Night Shopping

Martin Butterworth stared morosely into the glittering Christmas window display and wished that he was at home in bed. His breath fogged the glass as he looked in on a mythical world. Three bright young things were taking tea on a summer lawn. They were seated on gaily striped furniture and nestled in a dell of artificial flowers. The two girls were slim and tall and very white. They were clad in deceptively simple striped dresses (deceptive because such simplicity carried an extraordinarily high price tag) and were serving sandwiches from a silver salver to a young man with a psychopathic fixed grin and a missing left foot. The banner above the scene read **'ENTER A DIFFERENT WORLD AT HARRODS'**. Butterworth wished that he could. He looked down at his shoes, lifting one foot to find the sole sticky with blood.

Hargreave tapped him hard on the shoulder. 'There's no point you looking in there, lad,' he said. 'Not on the salary we pay you. You'll have to wait until the January sale.'

The young detective constable turned reluctantly from the carefree world depicted in the window and back to the gruesome mire on the ground in front of it. The body of the boy had all but disintegrated upon hitting the mercifully deserted pavement. Most of the remains had now been removed and the area cordoned off with yellow plastic ribbon. Above them, strings of shattered lightbulbs buzzed and crackled.

'Good selection of household items,' noted Hargreave, cupping his hand and peering into the window. 'Poncey Knightsbridge prices, though.' He pointed to an adjacent kitchen display. 'Mind you, we could do with that mop bucket right now.'

Behind him, two pale young officers dragged a leaking bin liner over to a police van which had been disguised as a British Gas emergency vehicle. Hargreave had gone to great trouble to keep the mopping-up operation under wraps. He had been working back at the main computer room when the call had come through and had left the building at a run. But he was being careful. Supposedly there was a press blackout still in force, but he had no real hopes of holding it beyond tomorrow morning. It was his bad luck that just as he was really beginning to get somewhere with the investigation there had to be another ostentatiously gory death in the centre of the city.

He punched Butterworth painfully on the arm and beckoned him away. 'We seem to be getting warmer, don't we?' he said cheerfully. 'The body's scarcely cold.'

'It's going to be hard getting an identification,' Butterworth ventured, 'the state it was in.'

'That's true,' agreed Hargreave, thoughtfully massaging his stubbled chin. 'A person takes on a subtly different appearance when his face has been turned inside out.' He looked at Butterworth with ghoulish glee, deliberately inviting his hatred. It was the only way to keep the boy from taking the horrors of the night home with him. 'They're growing careless. It's getting to be like *Friday the Thirteenth* around here. But can we wait until then to catch the murderers? Or can we find out what's going on and put a stop to it before commuters come out of the tube stations to find bodies raining down on them like some kind of biblical plague?'

He stared back at the officers as they swung the doors of the disguised police van shut. 'It's getting to be like a bloody Magritte painting around here, except that the victims aren't wearing bowler hats. . . .'

'Sir?'

Hargreave thrust his hand into his overcoat and scratched around, thinking. 'For something this big, I could get a fleet of men up here like *that*.' He snapped his fingers in Butterworth's startled face. His tone told the boy that this course of action had already been discounted. 'But of course, I can't, because the tabloids would have a bloody field day and we'd all be accused of total incompetence. Imagine it, coppers blundering about the rooftops, dropping down lift shafts in the dark. Have you heard our lads when they're all out together? The noise is unbelievable. They're like a herd of bloody elephants. So instead we have discreet teams of two and three operating in broad daylight, by which time the trail of the night before has gone stone cold.'

Butterworth watched the inspector light a fresh cigarette from the stub of his old one. He knew that he had failed to come up with any revelatory evidence of his own since he had been assigned to the case, but still dared to hope that he would not be sent out with the other search teams as a penance. In fact, he managed a confident smile for nearly four seconds, until Hargreave suddenly clapped him on the shoulder, nearly dislocating it. 'So now, my little freckled friend, it's down to you.'

'What do you mean, sir?'

'You're being given a chance to prove your mettle in the field. Tomorrow night. Up there.' Hargreave kept his bright eyes fixed on the boy's appalled face as he pointed roofward. Butterworth experienced a sloshing feeling in the pit of his stomach. He wished that there was a toilet nearby.

'It's alright, lad, you won't be alone. I'm sending Bimsley up as well. He's not quite as gormless as you, but his feet are too big and he tends to trip over them, so you'll have to look out for him.'

Upon hearing his name, Constable Bimsley grinned and waved from the window of the waiting van. It was a long-established fact that Bimsley was considered by many to be clinically insane and that he would do anything for a chance of promotion, no matter how dangerous the task. In his spare time he made parachute jumps and was known to the rest of the force as "Mad Dog" Bimsley. Butterworth looked over at the van and his heart sank into the pavement.

'You can stop doing your impersonation of a basset hound now, lad, it won't be that difficult. I just want you to have a nose around in a particular area that I have in mind and if you meet anyone up there I want you to act like you're in the know. Naturally, you'll have a micro-transmitter on you. All you'll have to do is leave the line open and we'll come up and get you before things get too hot. Now off you go and get a good night's sleep.' Hargreave charily lifted his Oxford toecaps over a patch of drying blood, then watched as Butterworth moved uncertainly toward the waiting vehicle.

During his trip to the computer room earlier, he had run a check on the city's rooftop traffic surveillance and security cameras. Most of the new ones had been programmed to log the movement of anything larger than a cat. The system set in motion a videotape recording of any activity which could be attributed to a form of human interference and noted it on the night's file disks. Cameras at three separate locations had logged activity in the past few hours and had listed the times of occurrences on the printed readout. All of them were within Hargreave's newly defined triangle of operations. Unfortunately, the only way to discover exactly what the cameras had logged would be to play back the tapes themselves and so far he had been unable to gain access to the room housing the monitoring equipment. Hopefully though, he would be able to do this in the next hour.

He looked at his watch and sighed. Janice would be in bed asleep by now, her long legs tucked beneath her in a perfect fifties calendar repose. . . . He yawned as he made his way back to the van, his breath condensing heavily in the air. The weekend was going to be damned cold. He would go and see Janice tomorrow and discuss his mad theory with her. Even if she thought he was wrong, she wouldn't laugh at him.

Most of Hargreave's past successes had been made possible by his justly famous powers of intuition and right now that power was working overtime. Butterworth and Bimsley would set in from one point of the triangle. Two men would cover the other. He and a squad of armed marksmen would be waiting at the apex. With a handful of vehicles stationed on the ground within the triangle, he would be able to have his men up on the rooftops within moments of a sighting. He wanted to feel sure that he could flush his murderers into a trap in the next forty-eight hours, but confidence did not come easily. There were still too many variables to consider.

In the morning he would go to the library, check out his idea and see if it held water. Until then he could not afford to relax his vigil. In the brilliant windows at his back, china-skinned women in silver wolf jackets smiled vacuously on into the night like latter-day goddesses.

CHAPTER THIRTY-SIX

Into Darkness

For almost half an hour the radio remained dead. Finally, Lee managed to call in his position from Hengler Station, situated on the cramped, chaotic roof of the London Palladium theatre. The station had been named after the first person to use the site for the purpose of public entertainment, mainly as a circus. If Charles Hengler could have viewed the building from its rooftops tonight, he would have been forgiven for thinking that its acrobatic traditions lived on.

Having transmitted his position back, Lee and his team finally prepared to leave. So far they had seen nothing, heard nothing, found nothing. They decided to strike south and search the area leading down to the river. For Lee it was a matter of honour to make sure that Jay's death was avenged and so he was determined that his team should be the first to reach Chymes.

Even with the temperature steadily dropping, he was pleased to hear no complaints from his crew. Lee ran a tight ship. He knew that if they could just manage to maintain discipline, Chymes and his thugs could be beaten. What disturbed him more was Zalian's continuing failure to locate the headquarters of the enemy. He pondered this as he carefully checked the area for telltale signs of their tracks, then turned and rejoined his team, the last – as always – to leave the roof and slip away across the city.

Spice's progress at the top end of the North Seven run was hampered by the fact that one of the steel station staves supporting the run had partially collapsed, dipping the cable in an alarming parabola over the tops of the enormous oak tress guarding the edge of the park. It appeared that the last two stations were indeed attached to the trunks of trees within the park itself, although why such a run had been constructed in the first place was something of a mystery. The history of the Roofworld had remained a verbal one and few written accounts chronicling the exploits of its founders existed for fear of such documents falling into the wrong hands. Zalian knew more than anyone else about his predecessors, mainly because he had tapped the memories of those in the Old Boy network.

There seemed no point in travelling to the final station. Here the cable dropped even lower, to vanish into a dark tangle of blackened and bare oak branches, the nearest of which stuck out into the light like a cluster of knife-points. Spice balanced lightly in the fork of the tree and untwisted her line from an overhanging offshoot. She glanced at her watch. It was time to return and stop the others from worrying. They wouldn't be much good to anyone if she left them to fend for themselves. Just then, the tree limbs above her banged and clattered with the weight of a body suddenly landing amongst them. She threw herself flat against the trunk of the oak and looked up through the branches.

There above her stood a shaven-headed boy with a spiderweb tattooed across his throat. Within seconds, Spice realized that she was staring into the face of one of Chymes' chief ministers.

Reese looked down at the girl. After leaving his leader to enjoy another sacrificial diversion, he and Dag had travelled north to one of the disused park stations where they knew they could fix up and get stoned in peace.

Now, with the chemicals coursing through his veins, he was feeling a new hunger.

The girl's outfit tipped her off as one of Zalian's remaining troops. She was attractive in a muscular kind of way, small breasted and strong limbed. And she wasn't showing any fear of him. That was interesting. He lowered himself down, dropping with a simian swing from branch to branch.

'Hey, pretty lady, didn't they tell you not to go out on your own at night? How come your big brave leader ain't looking after ya?'

Spice smiled up at him, beckoning him nearer.

'I think I know what you want. You wanna see what a real man feels like.'

He was still a body-length above her when she grabbed his boots and pulled down hard. He tried to kick out at her face, but his grip loosened on the bough overhead and he fell into a nest of branches further down. Struggling for his coin-gun with one hand, he clawed out at Spice with the other, but was not quick enough. She raised the loaded dart-gun and aimed it at the centre of his chest, firing and sending the dart squarely into his sternum, where it quivered and stuck. Reese screamed. The searing tip flared across his chest with fingers of molten fire. He twisted his body in agony and dropped backwards out of the tree to fall nearly thirty feet to the ground.

'That's what a real woman feels like,' she said, pocketing the gun. Then she fastened her belt-line and swung off between the trees.

From his crouching position atop the nearby terrace surrounding the lower end of the park, Dag looked first to the fallen body of his friend, then at the girl moving rapidly away into the brightness of the city streets, her swaying body outlined in the icy atmosphere like a rag doll on a string.

Leaping up at the line above his shaven head he left

the roof at a run, leaping and sweeping over the side of the elegantly facaded building, then down towards the cable junction where he would be able to intercept her. As he dropped, he pulled the coin-gun free of its casing and aimed as carefully as possible at the bouncing figure ahead. Three, four times he fired, but the movement between them forced his shots to fly wide of the mark. His line arced nowhere near as steeply as hers. He needed to move much faster than this if he was to draw alongside. Reaching up with his free hand, he pulled at the line-brake, opening it wide. Slowly his speed increased, but it was still not enough for him to catch up with her. The drugs he had ingested gave him the extra strength it required to rip the line-brake out from its sleeve and toss it into the rushing wind. Instantly his speed doubled and continued to build.

'Watch out, bitch, you're about to die!' he screamed at her, overtaking at last, twisting and firing wildly behind him. He did not manage to catch a glimpse of her face, but he hoped she was scared.

Now he was travelling at three times her speed. He had never moved this fast on a run before. He swung around in time to see Spice's eyes widen in alarm. She must have realized that he would reach the junction point way in advance of her. The tall, bare limbs of the oak roared toward him at a terrifying pace. With a final burst of speed he shot forward like a bullet from a gun and flew straight into the tree, no longer able to control his flight path. Dag released a shriek of horror as the rapier like tip of a bough plunged into his stomach, then passed out through the small of his back in a single swift movement.

Spice, gliding into the station, her feet touching down on the bark of the trunk, looked across at the flailing skinhead skewered onto the branch. 'Poetry in motion,' she murmured, shaking her head in disbelief. 'Still not lovely as a tree.' She shuddered and pushed on once more, back to the comparative safety of Portland Place.

Rose contacted the survivors of Damien's team and wrote down their current position. She then tried to pinpoint Robert's whereabouts using an ancient hardback *A-Z* while warily keeping an eye on Zalian, who still sat hunched over the battered notebook. Robert had been right. It was dangerous to trust him. He steadfastly refused to be drawn into an elaboration of his remark about Sarah, promising only that from now on his actions would not endanger the lives of anyone. If, however, he decided to take matters into his own hands, Rose doubted that there would be much she could do to stop him. She resolved to stay as near as possible to the radio transmitter in case any further messages of assistance came through.

'Something's odd here.'

Zalian turned around and held up a page filled with scribbled horoscopic symbols. 'These goat and moon signs . . .'

'The zodiac stuff. They're just shorthand symbols.'

'But they're not. There's no moon symbol in the zodiac. Nothing that remotely looks like it. And there are others that don't fit in. Look.' He pointed to a row of faint impressions stretching across the page. 'A figure four. The 37female symbol. A circle with a roof on it. A sickle with a cross on top, what the hell are these?'

Rose leaned across and took a closer look.

'Wait, I know this,' she said excitedly. 'They're old alchemical signs. I think they still use them for trading metal. Show me . . .' She took the book from Zalian's hands. 'A four, that's tin. The female symbol is copper. The moon is silver, that's female too. I think the other two are lead and zinc, but I don't know which is which.' She threw open her hands excitedly. 'It explains the list, the one headed by Apollo and Diana.'

'How?'

'Just as the planets correspond to gods, they also correspond to metals. Quicksilver is Mercury. Copper is Venus, tin is Jupiter, lead Saturn and so on.' Rose dropped her head into her hands, thinking. 'The question is, where would one look for these ancient symbols nowadays?'

'I think I know exactly where you'd find them in this city,' Zalian said. 'At the London Metal Exchange. We've used their hedging facilities in the past, without their knowledge naturally.'

'But why would Chymes hide out there? Wait a minute, can you find out where it's located?'

Zalian punched the keyboard in front of him and waited for a moment while an address scrolled up. 'OK, it's somewhere in EC3. . . .' The street name appeared, letter by letter across the screen.

'Oh, no. . . .' Rose grabbed for the radio mike and switched to Robert's frequency. 'Come in, Robert,' she called. 'Robert, you have to get out of there fast. . . .'

'Too late.' The reply was faint and half-swallowed in static. 'I'm standing here behind about fifty of Chymes' men. They seem to be meditating, or something. They haven't seen me yet, which is just as well. The odds are kind of uneven.'

'We'll get help. . . .'

'Are you kidding? I . . .' The line fuzzed and faded into silence.

'Robert!' Rose shouted. 'Robert, come in!' She threw

down the microphone. 'Shit, they've got him and it's all my fault.'

'Why, because you didn't figure out where he was earlier?'

'He wouldn't be up here in the first place if it wasn't for me,' she said angrily, jumping up from the desk. 'We've got to do something.'

'How can we?' reasoned Zalian. 'By the time we get there it'll be too late.'

'You can stay here if you want to. I'm going after him.' She pulled back the door and ran out across the roof, scooping up one of the nylon equipment bags as she went.

'You don't know the way! Believe me, Rose, we can help him better from here!' Zalian shouted after her, but his words fell short as she reached the low pylon of the cable station and hooked herself up. 'You can't go in there by yourself! It's not a safe run, it's one of the damaged ones!'

Zalian arrived at the foot of the station as Rose clipped her belt-line to the main overhead cable. 'Rose, you don't stand a chance by yourself! It's an old, unstable run. . . .' He tried to grab her legs, but she was too quick for him. Slipping from his grasp, she sailed over his head and away into the windy darkness of the roofscape.

CHAPTER THIRTY-SEVEN

Escaping

The radio, they had heard the crackle from the damned radio. Robert released the handset, letting it bounce onto the tarmac. For a moment everyone seemed to be as surprised as he was. The sudden bitter breeze now sideswiping the roof caused a ripple of movement.

Sweat prickled Robert's face. He looked behind him, at the edge of the guttering, at the street far below, at the line still connected across to the building on the other side of the street. He looked back at Chymes' men. They seemed to have no idea how he had suddenly appeared in their midst. Further behind them Robert could see a long low construction similar to the temporary headquarters Zalian had erected at the stock exchange. The men, for there were by far more males than females, certainly seemed in poorer shape than the ones in Zalian's krewe. They had the wasted, dead appearance of habitual drug abusers. Haunted eyes stared out from pale, sweat-slick faces. All seemed to be wearing a new kind of uniform, black with a red slash on the front, some kind of ritual symbol.

Slowly, the ones at the front of the group began to move forward. Robert stepped back to the edge of the roof and looked behind him once more. His belt-line was disconnected from the main cable across the street, which could only be reached from the rooftop he was earlier standing upon. With a jolt, he realized that the grappling hook was still stuck in the wall with the climber disc-line attached.

Two of Chymes' men reached out for him. One grabbed Robert by the wrist, the other clawed at his face. A shout went up, then another. Robert frantically pulled backwards. The jumpsuit was too large for him and his body slipped within it. The man on his left found himself clutching an empty sleeve. He reached out with his other hand, coiled the fingers and punched Robert squarely in the stomach. The force was enough to break him free and drop him to his knees. Half blind with pain, Robert grabbed for the anchored disc-line and rolled back over the edge toward the roof he had climbed from, just as the outstretched hands of his attackers reached down for him.

He fell fast, the nylon singeing his palms as it slithered through, too quickly for him to be able to break his fall. He hit the angled roof on his back, hard and flat. As he lay there for a few moments, pain billowing in his stomach, he began to slide on the steeply raked tiles. Chymes' men had run to the edge and were looking down at him, shouting and swearing. Already one of them was halfway down the line and another was coming over the top. Robert tried to turn over and gain a foothold, but the force of his momentum rolled him over once, then again, slamming hard on the tiles until he reached the very edge of the roof in a shower of broken slate. For a second he thought he would keep from overbalancing and threw out his arms, then he was over the guttering and hanging in empty air. Above him, skittering and sliding, came his pursuers, how many he could not tell.

His fingers were curled around the gutter in an agonizing grip, arms wrenching from their sockets. The line which had brought him here led across the street and was attached to the wall roughly two feet away on his right. Throwing his boots against the brickwork he released his fingers and launched off into space, hands thrown high. He caught the line with his forearms, shouting with pain as it slipped under his elbows, then beneath his armpits. Hunched over it in this fashion he dropped one hand and grappled desperately with his line-belt, to try and hook it up to the main cable.

Behind him, one of Chymes' minions, unable to halt his slide on the roof, shot over the edge and fell into the street screaming. Another was hanging on to the gutter, replacing Robert in the position he had just vacated. He was joined by a third, a tall skinhead who tried to rise from the roof, but overbalanced, landing hard with his knees on the guttering. There was a metallic bang and the entire length of gutter and drainpipe broke free of the wall, creaking and groaning as it carried its human cargo down to the pavement.

Robert had succeeded in hooking himself up and took off along the cable. He was just over halfway across when he looked back to see someone hunched over the line, sawing at it with a small knife. There was no chance of reaching the other side in time. He threw up his hands and grabbed the line overhead. As it broke with a sharp crack he suddenly found himself dropping like a stone, swinging down toward the wall of the building opposite. Releasing his hands and folding his arms across his face, he hit the large sashed window feet first, his body following through to the floor in a fusillade of glass shards.

Seconds later an alarm bell began to clatter. Robert lifted himself painfully. He was sitting on the floor of a darkened office, its window blown in and scattered across the surrounding executive furniture. A venetian blind had partly broken his landing. He rose stiffly and surveyed the damage to his body. A few small cuts from the broken window, a bad gash on his leg, torn muscles, burned hands. He limped out of the office towards the signposted fire escape at the end of the corridor and when he reached it followed the spiral down to the ground floor.

He was lucky to be alive. Painfully he shoved against the bar inside the steel door and released himself into an alleyway. Above, the alarm bell rang out into the deserted street, unheeded. Keeping to the edge of the building he limped along in the shadows, aware that the shouting and scuffling above him meant that he was still within firing range. To cross the street toward the main road he would have to pass into the light. There was nothing for it but to run. Breathing deep, he broke free of his cover and sprinted across the pavement towards the glowing red traffic signals. The first missile hit the kerb beside him, ricocheting up and ringing off the stem of a lamp-post. He could feel the blood starting to flow freely from his torn leg as he pumped the muscles in it.

There was a sudden hail of razor-coins all around, one hitting him on the shoulder with its flat surface, others bouncing onto the roadway. Above stood a dozen shadowy figures with raised guns trained on his retreating back.

Robert had to look twice at the sight ahead of him. Standing there patiently waiting for the traffic lights to change was a black cab with its yellow "For Hire" light glowing. Finding a free cab at Christmas was a little akin to stumbling across a herd of wildebeest in the underground. He raised his arms and shouted just as another volley rang off the paving stones behind.

Red changed to amber, then green. The cab started to move off. Robert ran behind, frantically signalling. The driver glanced in the rear-view mirror, saw the stumbling figure and slowed. Catching up, Robert pulled open the door and threw himself onto the back seat, panting.

'Where you wanna go, mate?' The driver turned and

looked at him, suddenly unsure that he should have stopped.

'Anywhere you like,' said Robert, closing his eyes in blessed relief as the cab moved off.

Rose was managing just fine. She had crossed Moorgate and was heading into the small roads bordered by Threadneedle Street and the London Wall when the mishap occurred. The run she had been travelling on was clearly marked on the map she had dug from her nylon travelbag. It zigzagged from the old Smithfield market to the Bank, then up towards Finsbury Circus, passing virtually overhead the London Metal Exchange. By now, travelling on the run had become almost second nature, simply a matter of hooking on and off whenever she reached a break in the line.

She was thinking about Zalian as she shoved out over Gresham Street and failed to notice that at this point the gradient of the run was almost non-existent. Consequently, she had reached the exact mid-point of the cable when she came to a halt. Rose raised her hands and tried to slide the metal sleeve along the line, but it would not budge. Perhaps the sudden coldness of the night had contracted the metal sufficiently to seize it. Grunting and slowly twisting in the breeze she gripped the sleeve with one hand, the line with the other and pulled as hard as she could, but failed to move even an inch. Ahead of her, the weatherbeaten cable station creaked ominously with the movement of the wire, light falls of rust pattering from it to the rooftop below.

The realization dawned that she had left the roof without collecting one of the walkie-talkies. Suspended from the overhead cable by the line extending from her waist, she hung like a stalled nativity angel above the deserted road.

Twisting her shoulder down as far as it would go, Rose pulled at the nylon sack on her back until she had managed to open it. Several items had cascaded on the ground before she managed to locate and remove the small emergency kit. Its contents were a disappointment – bandages, salve, matches – nothing to cope with the present situation. The weather-worn struts of the pylon supporting her clattered suddenly and the line dropped a foot. Involuntarily she released a shout of surprise. Zalian had warned her about the condition of the run. Who knew how much weight and movement it could stand before collapsing?

She was half-heartedly attempting to wipe medicinal lubrication onto the cable running beneath the sleeve of her line-belt when she heard Chymes' men pounding across the rooftops ahead of her. Looking up she saw them, running in directionless confusion across the flat broad roof opposite, less than fifty yards away. Her heart missed several beats as she realized that they must have seen her. Although their guns were drawn, they seemed to be more concerned with firing at a running man in the roadway below. She looked back down at the figure and quickly recognized the loping gait and above all the protruding ears. She was about to call out his name, but succeeded in stopping herself just in time. If he turned around now, his pursuers would surely trap him in a razor-sharp hail of metal. She was forced to watch, agonized, as her one hope of rescue retreated into the distance.

Moments later there was a muffled retort followed by a hiss and another line was fired across hers. It struck a point on the opposite wall and locked. Where the two cables crossed there was a sudden vibration as someone dropped onto the bisecting line.

'Didn't anyone ever tell you not to hang about in the street at night?' She turned to find Simon swinging from the cord with a demented grin on his face, the rags of his clothes fluttering in the wind like those of an ancient phantom pirate.

'Sweet Jesus, I thought I was going to die up here,' she gasped. 'I'm stuck.'

'Thought you must be. You looked like a Christmas-tree fairy from a distance, just dangling there.' Simon's lanky body swung to face hers. Grabbing her around the waist with one arm he lifted her up and unclipped her belt-line with his free hand. 'Keep still,' he muttered through gritted teeth. 'I don't want to drop you.' He clipped the freed cable into his own steel sleeve and lowered her, letting the weight increase on the line until he was sure it was safe. As he did so, the line from which Rose had been suspended gave way as the station pylon behind them buckled and fell from its position on the roof.

'Another thirty seconds and I'd have crossed the great divide,' said Rose, peering down into the roadway with alarm as the metal clanged on concrete far below.

'You've progressed a long way since I last saw you. Been taking night classes?' Simon burst into a fierce grin as he released the brake on his sleeve. 'Apart from travelling on a condemned route you're lucky to be still in one piece. Chymes' men are crawling all over the area. There seems to be some kind of gathering taking place. I think he's getting ready to make his move.'

Rose clung to the chain around Simon's bony hips and together they swooped off on the new cable to the comparative safety of a darkened sidestreet. 'Thanks for the rescue,' she called into his back. 'Where were you heading?'

'To headquarters,' he shouted. 'There are massacres taking place all over the bloody city. Chymes is starting to cull the pack. What does Zalian think he's playing at? Why hasn't he come up with anything?'

'He's getting back into drugs. He's convinced himself that Sarah has deserted him to be with Chymes.'

'Bullshit. It was because she was crazy about Zalian that she agreed to go and spy on Chymes in the first place. It was just too bad that she was found out. He should be out there with his own men instead of sitting around pining for his bloody girlfriend.'

The cable rasped and rolled as they crested the concrete peaks of the city's financial institutions, skimming over the streets like nocturnal dragonflies.

'I don't want to interfere,' shouted Rose, 'but it seems that unless we can get Zalian to snap out of it, someone is going to have to take charge from him.' She clutched tightly to Simon as they lifted and fell over a creaking station pylon.

'It should be either Lee or Spice,' Simon called back. 'If anybody understands the Roofworld half as well as Zalian, it's them. Although there's one other person who seems to know the territory just as well as Nathaniel.'

'Who's that?'

'Chymes.'

'Don't *you* think of joining him!' cried Rose. 'We hardly have anyone left as it is.'

Far behind them, the broiling mass of Chymes' disciples had recovered from the intrusion of the outsider at their pre-battle meeting and now awaited the signal from their leader which would herald the start of their final attack.

CHAPTER THIRTY-EIGHT

Imperator Rex

Chymes liked to hold his meetings in the darkest hour before the dawn. His men appeared ill-at-ease in their black tunics. Some wore silken sashes and badges. A few wore black masks, also made of silk. Their dress suggested a uniformity and discipline which they did not, however, possess. They fidgeted on the pale concrete of the vast open roof and complained as they waited for their master to arrive and deliver his speech. The darkness of their surroundings was lifted only by the twin orbs of light perching high in wrought-iron holders which glowed with a pale green fire on either side of the speech platform.

At either end of the great upturned billiard table that was Battersea Power Station a pair of vast fluted chimneys stood, each one rising over three hundred feet into the air. In the blackness of the bitter night they soared like colossal guardians, champions of a forgotten machine age. The white vapour which had long since ceased to pour from them was smoke-washed from sulphurous origins, making this the perfect place for Chymes to impress his creed upon the Order Of The New Age.

Presently the Imperator himself appeared, resplendent in a robe of dull gold leaf. It glittered and rustled with a faint metallic sound as he took his place on the stand. Gradually the talking died away and all eyes turned to the single standing figure on the platform.

'In the name of the Lord Of The Universe, in the name of Isis,' he began, the sonorous boom of his voice reaching to the very back of the gathering, 'I stand here before the members of this order as we prepare for our ultimate triumph.' His baleful eyes roamed across the assembly as if challenging every person present to defy his attention.

'I have talked before of the aims of our order. I have mentioned the need to remove all obstacles which stand in the path of our success. The old Roofworld which so many of you chose to leave has outlived its time. Who of us now shares Doctor Zalian's vision of peaceful equality, an order offering sanctuary from the cold harsh world below? We all know what happens to the weak creatures in the flock, my friends. They are devoured by the strong, absorbed by those who prefer the liberation of power.

'Remember this: the world you left behind on the ground has gone forever. Faith, compassion, tolerance, conscience – these are qualities which have become as outmoded in the modern city as the pencil is by the computer.' He glanced from one blank face to the next as he continued his speech. 'No longer is there any need for those below to care about the weak, the poor, the sick, because for the first time in the long history of this city, there is nobody left to care.

'Zalian calls *our* order corrupt, but when did he last look at the society which exists below and at what it has become? It is now a society of jackals, not a chain as strong as its weakest link, but a chain made entirely of strong links, because the weak ones have all been cast aside. Where once we took care of our people in the name of the Empire, now each of us stands alone. On that point, Doctor Zalian and I agree.' An angry murmur passed through the gathering. Chymes raised his hand for silence. His polished steel fingers shone a ghostly green in the light of the twin lamps.

'But Zalian thinks that it is man's greed which has caused this change. He is wrong. I shall tell you why the society below our feet is no longer fit to govern itself. It is because the purity of our national spirit has been made impure and has been tainted with adulterations. Foreigners now rule our land. And it is time for us to purge the impurities from the rotting carcass. We must cleanse and transform. We must *correct*.

'Some of you think that our rituals and our symbols have been mere empty gestures, You are wrong. Each has been a point along a path of spiritual discipline which will allow us to supercede the most barbaric and corrupt social orders. Hidden within the Fire Of The Sages is the substance which will transform us into the emissaries of the New Age. By taking control of the Roofworld, our metamorphosis will be complete. Only then can we turn our attention to the purification of the ground. Tomorrow night the final rituals will take place. The twelve key members of Zalian's order will be sacrificed. The doctor and his Roofworld will be destroyed. And the New Age will have begun.'

Chymes took a pace back and surveyed his audience. It was clear that his passionate vision of a ruthless and pure new society was not shared by many. In reality, few had grasped any understanding of his motives and even fewer realized that Chymes' final conquest would be accomplished by some kind of supernatural intervention that he had yet fully to explain. All his disciples really understood was that Chymes rewarded their loyalty and that in the struggle for the control of their domain they had wisely joined up with the strongest side. They had seen the shape of the opposition and for them victory was now a foregone conclusion. Chymes strode away across the roof. They may not have seen the full picture now, but eventually his people would be made to understand. The old order on the ground would fall, slowly at first, dividing and transforming from within. And then, finally, there would occur the resurrection of a collective national psyche, and a single flawless shining light of reason.

And Imperator Chymes would stand as its creator.

They would thank him one day, all of them.

Saturday 20 December

CHAPTER THIRTY-NINE

Illumination

DAILY MAIL December 20 Saturday

It's a farce!

Police bungle 'rooftop rambo' cover-up

LONDON'S MANIAC SNIPER has struck again. There are now five people dead, including a reporter, yet police officials continue to deny the existence of a crazed gunman lurking on London's rooftops.

All five victims were gunned down in cold blood earlier this week as they went about their business in the city. So far no date has been set for a public inquest.

But now the police may have to admit that there has been an official cover-up. In a statement made early yesterday evening, Detective Chief Inspector Ian Hargreave, the outspoken, controversial officer responsible for last year's 'Leicester Square Vampire' fiasco told press officials that there was no need to alert the public to the possible danger of a killer on the loose.

Gang warfare

'We have every reason to believe that these killings were the result of powerplay between gangland rivals,' said a visibly distraught Hargreave. 'The reporter who died had close associations with one of these gangs and his death was a reprisal for revealing secret information.'

But senior Yard officials are far from satisfied with the

progress of the investigation. Now an enquiry may be set up to find out:

WHY the press were denied information access
WHY it is taking so long to identify the bodies
HOW the victims were secretly smuggled away
WHO is the real suspect behind the slaughter

So far there have been over two hundred separate sightings of the sniper reported to overworked police by the general public.

This morning London Transport reported a reduction in the number of people travelling into the West End for their Christmas shopping. 'I'm buying my grand-children's presents locally,' said Mrs Elizabeth Spragg of Shepherd's Bush. 'You never know who could be up there watching and waiting with a sawn-off shotgun.'

SEE: Rooftop Rambo's Private Arsenal; Is He Using Weapons Like These? Centre spread

'What a load of inaccurate, scaremongering rubbish,' said Janice Longbright, screwing the newspaper into a ball and aiming it at the wastebasket. 'If they could see the state of the victims they wouldn't wonder why it's taken so long to identify them. Where are you going now?'

'To the library, to test out a theory,' said Hargreave, pulling on his overcoat. The dark rings beneath his eyes attested to the fact that he had been working at the office for most of the night. He had managed to conduct a number of interviews with relatives of the deceased, but in each case the story was the same. None of the victims had been seen by their families for the past two years. All had been officially reported missing, their files remaining open and unresolved for want of further information.

Hargreave rooted in his jacket for another cigarette, but found only an empty packet. He sighed irritably.

It was typical that Janice did not smoke. She smiled sympathetically at him, her auburn hair tumbling around a broad face glowing with a ruddy, wholesome sheen. She looked as if she was about to leap up and play a game of badminton. Endless cups of vile black coffee had helped to give him the nervous energy he needed for the day ahead and he had a feeling that he would need to call upon every reserve before the day was through. 'As long as you're here, why don't you come along with me? I'd like your opinion on something. You might be able to tell me whether I'm going completely mad.'

They left police headquarters together, breath frosting in unison as they walked arm in arm, no longer caring who saw.

'They're taking the investigation away from me if I haven't come up with the goods by the time of their bloody press conference.'

'When's that?'

'Three o'clock this afternoon.'

'Do you think you'll have anything to show by then?'

'I'll let you decide,' said Hargreave with a wry smile. 'It took me a long time to get any kind of an angle on this whole business. That's because I've been approaching the case from a different perspective. All along I've felt less concerned with the actual physical characteristics of the crimes and more bothered by the underlying motives for committing them.'

Briskly they marched up the steps of the public library and through the double doors into a damp, white-tiled corridor.

'When I came to enter the details of the first victim in the computer, I named the file *Icarus*. Right from the start, there seemed to be something ancient and mythical about the murders. It was as if each slaying was being carried out according to some grand masterplan. The silt, the sulphur, the connection with wildfowl, there were ritual elements that no modern explanation could account for.'

Hargreave led Janice down a flight of narrow wooden steps into the basement of the library, where most of the reference books had been transferred onto hard disk. The cool, dimly lit room was deserted. He seated himself at a formica-topped table and switched on the nearest computer console. Immediately the monitor glowed into life and began to run an autocheck through its system.

'It was Cleopatra's Needle that put me on the right track. I began to check into the customs of the ancient Egyptians. Remember we talked about Anubis? Well, Anubis has a Greek equivalent in Hermes and from Hermes we get a series of writings, or *Hermetica*, which place a Greek philosophy in an Egyptian setting. These writings are works of revelation which deal particularly with theology and the occult and they gave rise to all manner of bizarre secret societies, including this one. . . .' Hargreave consulted the index menu on the console and typed in the code he required. He directed Janice's attention to the screen.

HERMETIC ORDER OF THE GOLDEN DAWN

SECRET CHIEFS OF THE ISIS-URANIA TEMPLE

FOUNDED LONDON 1888 BY WILLIAM WYNN WESTCOTT,
LONDON CORONER WITH KEEN INTEREST IN OCCULT SCIENCES
/INITIATES REQUIRED TO STUDY THROUGH GRADES OF NEOPHYTE,
ZELATOR, THEORICUS, PRACTICUS, PHILOSOPHUS.
/MEETINGS HELD AT MONTHLY INTERVALS, WITH SPECIAL

ASSEMBLIES AT THE TIMES OF THE EQUINOXES.
/STUDY SUBJECTS INCLUDED:
ASTROLOGICAL SYMBOLS
ZODIAC AND SEVEN PLANETS
CIPHERS
HEBREW ALPHABET
TWELVE HOUSES OF HEAVEN
TAROT
ALCHEMICAL AND TALISMANIC SYMBOLS
ORDER OF THE ELEMENTS

SEE ALSO/
*Freemasons
*Rosicrucians
*Alchemists

'I don't see any present-day relevance here,' said Janice, tipping forward in her chair. 'Surely this sort of mumbo-jumbo went out of vogue at the end of the Victorian era.'

'It did, you're absolutely right,' said Hargreave excitedly. 'But it's currently enjoying a major revival. Suppose another such society now exists in a different form, one which fits the fashionable theories of the present day? Watch.' He moved the cursor beneath the final word on the monitor and pressed 'Return'. The screen cleared, then filled with copy. 'I followed every lead, the history of every secret organization imaginable, but I kept coming back to the practice of alchemy. It's been around for at least a couple of thousand years in one form or another. The art of transformation, both physical and spiritual. The idea is that you transform an impure, unrefined substance into a perfect, pure form via certain key rituals and ceremonies which purge out the undesirable elements.

'This pure form can be a tangible object, like a chunk of gold, or it can simply be an elevated state of mind –

a psychic plane.' He traced a finger to the middle of the screen.

ALCHEMY

PROCESS OF GRADUAL TRANSFORMATION MATCHED TO ASTROLOGICAL CONFIGURATIONS
/SYSTEM OF TURNING LEAD INTO GOLD HAS PARALLELS WITH CLEANSING OF THE HUMAN SPIRIT
/PURIFICATION IS SAID TO PRODUCE LATENT SUPERNATURAL ABILITIES

POSS DERIV/ *AL KIMIA* (Arabic)
/ *CHEM* (Egyptian)
/ *CHYMIA* (Greek)

FIRST RECOGNIZED ALCHEMIST/ *CHYMES*

'Now I request more information on the Egyptian derivation of the word meaning "alchemy" and look what I get.' Hargreave tapped the keys once more. Janice rested her arm on his shoulder and watched as the screen cleared itself and began to scroll down new information.

CHEM = BLACK/ 'LAND OF THE BLACK SOIL'
BELIEVED TO BE REFERENCE TO COLOUR OF SILT ON BANKS OF NILE RIVER

'The first process in alchemy requires the death of a substance via its "blackening".'

'The boy who died in Piccadilly Circus. . . .'

' . . . With a shovelful of Egyptian mud in his mouth. Suddenly everything else begins to fit.' Hargreave's fingers flew across the keyboard. 'Each alchemical process is associated with a certain symbol, just as each metal represented in alchemy has an association with a particular planet. So we get . . .'

ALCHEMICAL RITUALS

THE BODY MAY BE PURIFIED BY THE *RAVEN* AND
THE *SWAN*
REPRESENTING THE DIVISION OF THE SOUL INTO
EVIL (BLACK)
AND GOOD (WHITE)
/THE IRIDESCENT FEATHERS OF THE *PEACOCK*
OFFER PROOF THAT
THE PROCESS OF TRANSFORMATION IS
UNDERWAY
/OTHER BIRDS ASSOCIATED WITH ALCHEMICAL
PROCESS INCLUDE
PELICAN (NOURISHMENT THROUGH BLOOD)
AND *EAGLE* (VICTORIOUS
SYMBOL OF COMPLETED RITUAL)

'Our killer has reinterpreted an ancient text. The steps to alchemical purification are being taken in the form of ritual slaughter.' Hargreave sat back and lit a cigarette. 'He thinks it's going to grant him supernatural powers.' He switched the computer into Print Mode and began to reproduce the relevant sections of the file onto paper.

'All right,' said Janice, 'so we know why it's happening. Somebody still has to find out where these people are operating and bring them in before anyone else gets killed.'

Hargreave rose and separated the paper which was spewing from the back of the printer, tearing it into single sheets. Carefully he folded them into his overcoat pocket. 'We only have until tomorrow – at dawn,' he said.

'How do you know that?'

'It ties in astrologically, doesn't it? Look at the date.'

Janice twisted her wristwatch around and read it. 'I don't get it.'

'No, but somebody else will if we don't wrap this up in the next twenty-four hours.'

'What's our next move?'

'We've got to get more men up there and start sweeping the roof areas I've marked out. But before that I'm going to have to find a way of stalling the press conference for a few hours.'

'Why stall them?' said Janice. 'We could just feed them a little misinformation. Let's be honest, Ian, you couldn't lose any more face than you've lost at the moment.'

'You know I don't approve of dishonest working methods.'

'And *I* know that your ass is on the line.'

'You have a point there. Can I leave it to you to come up with a reasonably plausible theory?'

Janice's face broke into a grin. She gave him a broad, salacious wink. 'I'm sure I'll be able to think of something,' she said.

CHAPTER FOURTY

Into Focus

This time, the dream was different. The face was there, of course, and so was the implicit feeling of danger, but now there was something else as well. The empty grey eyes were smiling benignly, the lips moving in a half-heard singsong litany that faded and fuzzed beyond the edge of sleep. Robert could feel himself moving closer to the figure in the hopes that, finally, it would impart some knowledge to him, some kind of revelation. The face belonged to someone who knew much more than he, a higher intellect, a sharper consciousness. The face beckoned, the voice dipping and swaying until its sound surrounded and penetrated his soul. He moved closer and closer still.

And suddenly it came into focus – the face, the knowledge, the revelation, as if someone had moved a camera lens to its correct setting.

In his dreams he beheld the visage of a man who was everything that he was not, a man devoid of conscience and emotion, a man capable of endless cruelty in the name of righteousness. It was the new face of Universal Man, it was the face of the future. . . .

Robert awoke with a start. He lay naked on top of the bed, the pores of his body glistening with sweat. Sitting up suddenly, he cocked his head to one side and listened. Someone was trying to get into the apartment. He looked across the darkened room with the curtains tugged shut, at the luminous hands of the bedside alarm clock. After his narrow escape Robert had returned to the world below, to his apartment and to disturbing, dream-filled sleep – despite Zalian's earlier warning that it would be dangerous to do so. Now it was nearly mid-day. Silently he slipped off the counterpane and pulled on the old black jeans which lay in a bundle beside the bed.

Straining to hear, he was aware of the outer hall door clicking, as if someone had managed to open it, then close it again very gently. Robert crept to the bedroom door and peered through the narrow crack at the hall-way beyond. An indistinct figure stood motionlessly in the unlit corridor, listening. Satisfied that there was no sound forthcoming, it tiptoed to the first doorway in the hall and let itself into the room beyond.

Robert smiled to himself, aware that the 'intruder' had mistakenly entered the toilet. Some intruder. It was bound to be Rose performing her 'renegade plumber' routine. Stepping into the hall, he clicked on the over-head light. 'OK, Rose, flush, rinse and come out with your hands up. I could tell it was you from the moment . . .' A face peered around the door frame. It wasn't Rose. It was a wild-eyed skinhead with yellow teeth and the word 'DEATH' tattooed on his forehead and he was carrying a cricket bat in one hand. It took Robert a second or two to collect his thoughts before he darted back into the bedroom and locked the door from the inside. He was an idiot to have come back to his apartment to sleep. He should have known that they might come looking for him. He only hoped that he could warn Rose before she was harmed.

With a triumphant bellow the skinhead hurled him-self at the door with such force that the top half of it immediately split away from its hinge. There was a moment of silence, then his cricket bat burst through one of the wooden panels in a cascade of splinters. Robert yelped as he grabbed his leather jacket and belt-line from the floor and ran for the window, fumbling with the stiff burglar bolt before finally managing to throw it open.

Outside, on the narrow steel fire escape which his landlord had been forced to install by the council for the safety of his tenants, Robert stopped for a moment and listened as Chymes' scullion continued to try and smash his way into the bedroom.

Robert looked down. Whereas his old instinct would have been to head quickly for the ground, now his first reaction was to continue upwards. But if he did that, he would quickly be caught by someone who was far more adept at travelling above the streets than he. Half-way towards the floor above he paused and returned until he stood just above the bedroom window. There was another crash and he could tell that the skinhead was in the room. Heavy footsteps fell, aiming for the far wall. Robert stood poised above the open window frame. Suddenly the shaven head appeared looking out into the street and Robert brought the open half of the window down on it as hard as he possibly could. The bottom of the frame hit the nape of the skinhead's neck and, continuing down, slammed his head on the concrete ledge.

Robert held on tight to the top of the frame, pressing down with all his might. Reaching around, he placed his bare foot on the lower lip of the window and bounced up and down on it experimentally. The skin-head gurgled and howled as his bruised windpipe was repeatedly closed. Behind the glass his limbs thrashed about, unable to seize upon the cricket bat which had fallen to the carpet. Eventually he smashed through the pane above with his coiled fist. At the sound of the breaking glass, people in the street below began to look up and point.

After one last mighty shove of his foot Robert moved his leg away just before the skinhead managed to seize it in his bloody fingers. He glanced down at the would-be attacker who now lay sprawled across the window ledge gasping for air, then ran for the roof, praying that this time he would not be followed. If Rose had also returned to her apartment the previous night, she could be in great danger.

Rose was still in bed when he rang her number from a battered, frosty telephone booth in Camden Town. He had run there from the apartment in his bare feet, figuring that it was best to put a little distance between himself and the skinhead, just in case Chymes had any more of his men hanging around the area.

'You're not making any sense, Robert,' she said sleepily. 'Call me later. I'm hanging up now.'

'Put this phone down, Rose, and I swear that if I don't kill you somebody else will.'

'Then speak more slowly.'

'I'm saying that you have to get out of there and right now. They came for me and it's a safe bet that they'll be coming for you too.'

'OK, OK . . .' She sounded as if she was about to fall back to sleep at any second. 'Just another half hour, then I'll get up . . .' The voice began to tail off.

'*NOW*, you have to get up *RIGHT NOW!*' There followed a moment's silence. When Rose next spoke, she sounded much more alert. 'All right, Robert, Jesus. I'm up, OK? I'll meet you. Just tell me where.'

'Fine,' said Robert, relieved. 'Is there a back way out of your place?'

'Yeah.'

'You'd better use it. And can you bring me a sweater or something? I didn't have time to find my shirt or my shoes. And bring money. I can't go back to my apartment. Meet me at Chequers Coffee Shop in Chalk Farm. If you're still tired we can check into a hotel for a while.'

'Sounds sleazy. I'll be there in twenty minutes.' The line went dead.

Robert was sure that people were mistaking him for a tramp as he paced about in front of the coffee shop. The buckles of his line-belt were cold on his bare chest. He pulled the leather jacket a little tighter as he saw Rose alight from the bus and run towards him. She was wearing the black jumpsuit that Zalian had given her, with a heavy black scarf around her neck. For someone who had been in bed twenty minutes earlier and had spent the previous night on a roof, she looked appallingly attractive.

'God, Robert, you look awful!' Her hand flew in front of her mouth as she released a snort of laughter. Robert made a sour face. 'I always look like this after I've been attacked by a cricket-bat-wielding maniac,' he muttered. 'It's not safe on the ground. We have to go back up and stay there until this is over.'

'After all the fuss I made about being allowed back down,' said Rose, tutting. 'I could have slept at headquarters.' Robert had the distinct impression that she would have been happy to stay up there for as long as Zalian wanted her to remain.

'Maybe you're right,' he admitted. 'I guess I'd rather fall off a building than be bludgeoned to death in my sleep. Where's the nearest roof station from here?'

'I've been thinking,' said Rose as they walked into the freezing wind which swept along the desolate pavements of Euston Road. 'If you were Chymes and you wanted to mock Zalian by creating an order which was the reverse of his, what would you choose as your foundation?'

'Well, Zalian's borrows its lofty ideals from the Greek gods. A heaven filled with mythical deities.'

'. . . While Chymes' men were found on the roof of

the London Metal Exchange. Sounds a little more down to earth, doesn't it?'

'You're using that tone of voice you seem to reserve for announcing weird theories.'

'This isn't weird, it's logical. Think of an ancient art which stems from the very earth itself.'

'I don't know. . . .' Robert threw up his hands, unable to think. 'Black magic. Witchcraft.'

'Oh, come on. The thought of bank managers and postmistresses dancing around naked in the forest is so unappetizing. I was thinking more along the lines of alchemy. You know, base metals and stuff. I vaguely remember reading a book on it, full of symbols, like Charlotte's notes.'

'I thought alchemy was all pointed hats and pots full of boiling lead,' sneered Robert. 'Be a bit out of date now, wouldn't it?'

'Not at all. There are still alchemical societies – hermetic orders – operating in England today.'

'But what would Chymes stand to gain from such an arcane practice?'

'A supernatural advantage, perhaps.' Rose thought for a minute. 'Power over the weak, that's what it always comes down to, isn't it? There are still people who see the world operating on a vast plan which can be mastered providing you possess the right knowledge.'

'If we're going to have a fight about religion, it can wait until another time.'

'Ah yes, religion,' said Rose, narrowing her eyes menacingly. 'White missionaries training uneducated blacks to mouth hymns they don't understand in order to save them from their own heathen deities. A perfect example of "Your God isn't good enough, have mine instead." '

'Look,' began Robert, exasperated, 'religious worship has helped a lot of people to come to terms with themselves . . .'

'And it's started an awful lot of wars. Perhaps Zalian's is just the latest in a long line of religious battles.'

'Go back to what you were saying about the symbols in the notebooks. . . .'

'OK. Has it ever occurred to you that the most enduring symbols are all interconnected?'

'How do you mean?' asked Robert.

'You know, the sun is always regarded as male and it's equated with gold, and the right hand side of things and fire . . .'

'Right, and the moon is always female and left and silver . . .'

'And is associated with water.' She gave him a quick smile. 'All part of the grand plan.'

'Let me get this straight. You're suggesting we apply this to Chymes and Zalian. . . .'

'I'm just wondering what you get left with if you pair them off against each other. Two sides of the same coin?'

'The ideas that run around in your head never cease to astound me,' said Robert as they reached their point of ascent. 'I'm surprised you get to sleep at night. Maybe you should be running the Roofworld instead of Zalian.'

'Maybe I should at that,' said Rose, half to herself.

CHAPTER FOURTY-ONE

Police Manœuvres

'He *says* we just have to take a look around,' said Butterworth over his shoulder. 'What he means is, he'll have our gonads if we fail to come up with something.'

'I don't give a stuff,' said PC 'Mad Dog' Bimsley. 'He's your boss, not mine. Are we at the top yet?'

'One more floor. Pick your feet up.'

The fire escape opened onto an acre of flat tarmac. Butterworth looked at his watch. It was almost ten o'clock. Around them the lights of Piccadilly shone in dazzling morse, like a landing strip for a millionaire's private aircraft. The roof of the Ritz was, unsurprisingly, much nicer than any of the other roofs in the area, swept clean by the winds rustling through the bare tops of the trees in Green Park.

The press conference earlier that day had been a joke, with Hargreave not even present on the platform and only Janice Longbright preventing the investigating officers from being crucified by the journos. Whether they bought her cock-and-bull story about a lone gunman now being held for questioning would remain to be seen. The boss really seemed to be going out on a limb with this one.

Butterworth wiped the sweat from his forehead and left a sooty black smear in its place. In the past two hours, he and Bimsley had climbed the fire escapes of half a dozen buildings, to no avail. Butterworth looked back at the hulking police constable, who seemed to be enjoying himself immensely, despite his apparent inability to walk in a straight line without falling over. In a way it was hardly surprising, because the man was so enormous. He reminded Butterworth of nothing so much as an upended navy-blue interior-sprung sofa. Grasping the railing of the fire escape, his hand closed over it and pulled his body up like a creature rising from the depths in some terrible fifties monster movie. Butterworth failed to feel protected, however, as Bimsley's vast bulk seemed to be offset by the smallness of his brain. His monosyllabic sentences and stumbling footsteps conjured an image of a driverless juggernaut searching for a place to crash.

Butterworth walked out across the tarmac and looked down into St James's Street, where idling hacks had once collected customers from Lock's the hatters and Lobb the bootmakers, where Wren and Pope and Byron and Walpole had lodged, where the half-mad caricaturist Gillray had hurled himself to his death and where now only taxis passed before sterile car showrooms and empty airline offices. He sighed, wishing for a London that was no more, wishing he could return to being a student instead of being forced to follow in his father's famous fingerprints. Perhaps he would crack this case with a feat of extraordinary deductive expertise and, having provided proof of his inherited abilities, retire at once.

Behind him, 'Mad Dog' Bimsley slipped on a dead sparrow and fell over. What would Father have done? Butterworth gave the matter careful thought, attempting to spin lines of reason between the outcropping facts. Time for a recap. Why did all the murders occur from above? Because the murderers hid out on the rooftops. Murderers plural, because no single person could have managed to inflict such horrendous wounds, let alone hoist the bodies into such bizarre positions. What else was it that Hargreave told him? To watch for a gang, an internecine war, a vendetta against rivals. But could anyone really exist up here? How would they move around without being spotted, for God's sake? Butterworth scratched his chin, turning slowly on the roof, wondering what on earth to do next. It was no good. He simply didn't have his father's aptitude for this sort of work. He'd give it up and go back to pottery. Ceramics weren't life-threatening.

He was pondering this problem when he noticed the gossamer-thin cable snaking out from the uppermost cornerstone of the Ritz to a building at the end of Jermyn Street. It certainly wasn't a communication line or an electrical cable because it was simply tethered to the wall. Puzzled, he turned around to face Piccadilly. After a break across the roof, the cord reconnected at the far end of the Ritz, where it ran across the road to Stratton Street. Butterworth's eyes widened. 'Come on, Bimsley,' he said. 'I think we're onto something.'

Bimsley was sitting on the tarmac rubbing his knee-caps. Slowly he unfolded himself and rose to his awe-some height. 'It's all right for you,' he grumbled. 'You've got a jumper. I'm perishing. Is that police issue?'

'No,' admitted Butterworth. 'My gran knitted it for me.'

'If I'd known it was going to be this cold,' said Bimsley, rubbing his ears, 'I'd have brought a balaclava.'

Still grumbling, he tripped at the top of the fire escape and would have hurled them both to certain doom had Butterworth not grabbed hold of the railing in front of him. After this, the young detective constable moved back until he was a good six feet away from Bimsley, just in case the latter's ungainly pace sent him cartwhee-ling off into space. As they left the roof of the Ritz, Butterworth revealed his thoughts to the constable in a manner policemen usually reserve for explaining the zebra-crossing code to mixed infants.

The boy – for despite his size, he was a boy – grew excited at the thought of closing in for a kill and lost control of his limbs to an alarming degree, so that by the time they had succeeded in climbing to the roof of the gallery on the corner of Albemarle Street, Butterworth had decided to stay so far out of Bimsley's reach while he charged the roof in search of the enemy that their conversation had to be conducted as a shouting match.

Methodically they searched the roof among the conduits and geometric outcrops of brick for a continuation to the cable that had been sighted from the Ritz and quickly they found it. That was not all they found. For, slithering along the line at great speed to arrive on the roof in a tumble, like parachutists coming in to land, came all manner of people. Butterworth's heart went into freefall as the extraordinary army plunged down and landed all around him. He turned about to locate Bimsley, who was standing immediately behind him looking as if he was about to catch a basketball in his mouth. Both of them remained rooted to the spot as the black-jumpsuited swarm passed by on either side.

Spice, Simon and the rest of Zalian's team entirely failed to acknowledge the presence of the two policemen as they raced across to the far side of the roof, shouting to one another. Several of them appeared to be wounded. Droplets of blood were scattering onto the tarmac as they ran.

Bimsley threw a couple of desultory punches at the passing figures, but mercifully failed to connect. Moments later amidst a chattering of steel and a hiss of cable the band had launched off and away in the direction of St James's Square, leaving Bimsley and Butterworth standing alone and bewildered on the gallery roof.

‘What the hell was *that* all about?’ said Butterworth, amazed. ‘They didn’t even stop. Why on earth did you try to hit them?’

‘I’m allowed to,’ said Bimsley indignantly, ‘I’m a policeman. We could have arrested them for trespassing.’

‘Did you see how fast they were moving? As if the devil was after them. We’re going to need reinforcements.’ Butterworth scratched his head and stared off at the retreating figures who were even now barely discernible as they passed against the granite fascia of the Ritz. He unclipped his micro-transmitter and flipped it onto an open line, but before he could make a report there was a sudden clattering noise behind him and within seconds the roof was full of people again.

They were skinheads by the look of them, scrambling and sprinting between the conduits in pursuit of the first group. They wore a different style of uniform, black with a red slash across the chest. One of them kneed Butterworth in the groin as he passed, only to be grabbed around the shoulders by Bimsley, who lifted him high in the air, turned him upside down and dropped him on his head. By the time Butterworth had managed to undouble himself and rise from the gravel, they too had gone over the side and away toward the lights of Piccadilly.

‘I got one!’ shouted Bimsley, pleased with himself, hoisting the dazed boy into the air. Still clutching his crotch, Butterworth raised his head in time to see the skinhead twist his arm into his suit and flick out a blade. He wriggled in the policeman’s tight grasp and suddenly slashed the knife in an arc at the surprised Bimsley, who hastily dropped his catch and jumped back. Bimsley looked down to find his uniform gaping open in a slit. A button fell to the ground. He released a bellow of rage and threw himself towards the boy, who brandished the knife first in one hand, then the other, bouncing lightly forward on the balls of his feet like an extra from *West Side Story*.

'Put it down, boy,' called Butterworth ineffectually as Bimsley bodyslammed the skinhead with such force that the knife was sent skittering across the gravel. The young detective ran after it, but as he bent to retrieve the weapon there was another sound from behind, as two more skinheads dropped to the roof. The odds were changing too fast. Bimsley rolled away from his quarry to face the newcomers, which allowed the boy to leap to his feet and sprint for the side of the building.

'Come on,' he shouted at his partners as they reached for their coin-guns, 'leave them. We've got to get back to Chymes.' Momentarily unsure, the skinheads finally dropped their hands from their suits and ran to join their friend. Seconds later, Bimsley was behind them and closing fast. Butterworth's throbbing groin prevented him from bolting after his attacker. He watched as all three reached the edge of the roof and jumped clear to the next across the alleyway at the side of the gallery. Bimsley was lumbering close behind, almost within grabbing distance of the last man, then he too was at the edge, but was surely moving too slowly to make the leap.

Butterworth watched in horror as Bimsley threw the vast mass of his body into the air and vanished with a surprised shout over the side of the building. By the time he had caught up to the edge, Chymes' men had vanished into the night. Filled with dread, Butterworth peered down to the floor below.

His partner was hanging by his forearms from the ledge formed by a keel moulding above a window, a couple of feet down from the parapet of the roof. Butterworth gave a small scream. 'Don't move!' he shouted. 'I'm coming over to get you!' He turned around and ran back, drew a deep breath, then dashed for the chasm between the buildings. Landing heavily, but in one piece on the far side, he reached down to Bimsley, then thought better of it. How could he ever lift the man up? He had to weigh two hundred and fifty pounds at least.

'I'm slipping,' Bimsley pointed out. To confirm his point, one arm slid from the window ledge and he dangled awkwardly out over the street. Butterworth searched around desperately, as if expecting to find a lifebelt posted somewhere.

'Aaaah!'

He stuck his head over the side in time to see Bimsley's other arm vanish from the ledge. He was now hanging by his hands. There was nothing for it but to try and pull him up. Butterworth knelt down and wedged his knees behind the parapet, then reached over as far as he dared to go. 'Give me your hand,' he called. The boy responded and grabbed out with a meaty fist. Butterworth felt as if he had suddenly hooked a marlin and was half pulled over the edge himself.

'Christ,' he grunted, straining with all his might to keep from toppling, 'you weigh more than my *car*.' The pain in his arm was agonizing, but after what seemed an eternity Bimsley managed to hoist one tree trunk of a leg onto the ledge. Half-righting himself, he reached out and grabbed Butterworth's other hand. At this particular moment the young detective had not been braced to take on an additional hundred pounds, with the unfortunate result that he was jerked sharply off his feet and sailed cleanly over the parapet with a shocked squeak.

The circus life had never held much appeal for Butterworth. The antics of acrobats had always bored him. He was beginning to wish he had paid them more attention now, as he hung from Bimsleys' hands a hundred feet above the pavement. The policeman's knees were hooked to the ledge above. Butterworth felt himself slipping as Bimsley's palms began to sweat. He tried to swing his feet at the window beside him, but the movement caused Bimsley's hold on the ledge to grow more tenuous.

'Stop fidgeting about,' shouted Bimsley. 'I've got a good mind to let you go. Any judge would sympathize.' His grip on the ledge slipped another couple of inches as his jacket turned inside out and fell over his face. Butterworth looked down. He regretted that he hadn't really lived enough to have his life flash before his eyes. His arms felt as if they had been torn from their sockets. Another few seconds and it would all be over.

'I can't hold on any longer,' grunted Bimsley, muffled by his jacket.

'You have to. I can't get near the window to break it.' Butterworth kicked out his legs and the pair of them slipped further, trapeze artistes breaking apart.

'I don't want to die, at least not holding onto a complete wanker like you,' was the last thing that PC 'Mad Dog' Bimsley managed to say before his foothold on the ledge broke and the two of them fell bellowing into space.

They hit the curved canvas entrance canopy of the art gallery with such force that they completely demolished it, rods and guy wires lashing and springing in all directions. Bimsley's fall was broken to some extent by the tensioned canopy before he tore through it and landed jarringly on the pavement. Butterworth's fall was broken by landing directly on top of Bimsley's stomach. As miles of canvas poured down on top of them, Bimsley realized that the fact they were both still alive would allow him the privilege of beating his partner senseless, just as soon as he recovered from the unconsciousness he now felt rapidly approaching. The material floated down over them in a shroud of purple stripes like a collapsing parachute and Butterworth's clouding thoughts adopted the nature of a serious change in his career plans.

CHAPTER FOURTY-TWO

Unmasked

White eyes rolled up into dead flesh. Lee turned aside, sickened. The roof was awash with the girl's blood. Her naked body, torn open and abused, had been thrown aside like an abattoir carcass that had slipped its hook. Lee and his krewe had reached the dirt-encrusted gables of Soho's Brewer Street as they covered the final sector of the night's search area. The body they discovered there had wounds so horrific that Lee had prevented the others from passing near it. Morale within the group was already at an all-time low. This was the last thing any of them needed to see.

He wondered if Zalian was aware of the extravagance of his enemy's obscenities. The body glowed a luminous white in the bitter chill night, glued to the brickwork in coagulated gore. Lee tore his eyes away to where the other members of the search party stood, disturbed and restless. There was a bad presence here. They could all feel it. 'OK, gang, let's move out.' He turned from the body and clapped his hands together. 'Nathaniel's waiting for us.' As the group behind him prepared to leave the roof, Lee turned to take a final look at the dead girl.

'If you want her, you can have her. But you have to really *want* her.'

The voice sent nails of fear scratching under his skin. Slowly he raised his eyes from the corpse.

Rising between the turrets of chimneys, the hooded

figure of Chymes addressed him. Lee lowered his hand slowly, until the tips of his fingers rested on the handle of his dart-gun.

Chymes walked slowly forward with broad, measured steps. In his gloved steel hand he held a silver harpoon locked into a crossbow. 'You wouldn't get that thing halfway out of your pocket before I hit you, boy.'

Chymes' step never faltered as he drew nearer. The harpoon glinted in the moonlight. Lee looked back at his krewe. Three of them had their guns raised, but no one dared to fire. Who could tell how many men he had covering him from the nearby rooftops?

'Where is Zalian?' The vast black cloak cracked and flapped around Chymes' leather-clad legs.

'You'll never find him.' Lee was surprised to find himself shaking.

'I don't think you realize your position. If you tell me the truth I may only blind you. Let's try it again: where is Zalian?' Chymes raised the harpoon until the tip of it was level with Lee's eyes.

'Tell him, Lee!' called Little Jo, the youngest of his team. 'If you don't, I will.'

'Take her advice, Lee. This battle need not concern you. Your surrender is a foregone conclusion. This is now between myself and your master.'

'He's not my master. We are all equal.'

'How very democratic. But hopelessly weak. Where is he?'

'You'll have to kill me before I tell you.' Lee stood his ground, icy droplets of sweat running between his shoulderblades. Chymes' finger slowly tightened on the trigger of the harpoon.

'He's on top of the Stock Exchange!' screamed Little Jo in near hysteria. Chymes' face remained hidden within the hood, but Lee could sense his smile of triumph. He slowly lowered the glittering harpoon. On cue, a dozen of his men rose from the mortared stacks of the roof behind. Their heads were shaved, their faces blank and sickly. Realizing the hopelessness of a victory when faced with Chymes himself, Lee had earlier instructed his krewe to take flight in such a confrontation and now as a single body they did so, leaping for the overhead cables of the run. Two were felled immediately, one by razor-coin and the other by Chymes' crossbow, before they had a chance to reach the lines.

Knives drawn, Chymes' men ran forward and attacked in a hand-to-hand assault, sending their opponents sprawling to the ground in their blood frenzy. One of them lifted Jo, the girl who had cried out, above his head and was about to throw her screaming into the street below when he was floored with a mighty kick in the stomach from Mack, Jo's seven-foot friend and protector.

Lee hurled himself at Chymes, reaching him before he had a chance to reload the crossbow. The hooded man did not flinch a muscle beneath the thud of Lee's fist. It was as if his body had been constructed from a resilient metal alloy rather than flesh and blood. Lee realized that such an attack could only result in his own death and pulled away with a yell, slipping free as Chymes reached out to grab him. But he moved too slowly. The leather glove connected instantly, seizing Lee by the throat and raising him from the ground. Pain burst into searing light before Lee's eyes as his windpipe was slowly crushed. Chymes raised his head and laughed, low, slow and mirthless. 'Keep struggling,' he whispered. 'It's *much* better if you struggle.'

Lee swung his leg high and kicked Chymes squarely in the chest. Thrown back, his hood fell to his shoulders. Lee cried out as he recognized the face of the man who had once been in his own krewe.

Chymes released his grip in order to pull back the hood, but it was too late. The damage had been done.

Lee ran for the edge of the roof and had managed to throw a line over the cable before Chymes succeeded in recovering his balance. As he sped away down the line with the remaining members of his team he saw the bodies of his two friends lying dead in the street below, gashes of blood filtering from the sidewalks, a police car screaming to a stop in front of a corpse and through them all he saw the face of Chymes, the face of the man he and Zalian had once trusted as a brother. The man whom they thought would one day lead the Roofworld on to even greater glories.

CHAPTER FOURTY-THREE

Turning Point

'They'll be on their way here right now, Simon,' said a voice at the back. 'There isn't time. Let it drop.' The knife caught the light of the bare overhead bulb as it pressed against Zalian's throat. Nobody moved. The thickening silence was broken by someone coughing.

'He's going to level with us, or we'll all stay here and wait for Chymes together.'

'His men outnumber us by five to one,' said Lee. 'They know that we're on the roof of the Exchange. It'll be a slaughter.' He stepped forward into the shifting light thrown by the overhead bulb and grabbed Simon by the arm, lowering his voice as he spoke. 'We're wasting valuable time. Come on, let him go.'

'Not until he tells me why he won't lift a finger to save himself – or us.' Simon pressed the knife against flesh and pulled Zalian's head further back. Lee took an elaborate step away, aware of what Simon could do when he was antagonized. He had returned to the roof with his krewe to find the young punk standing over the doctor while he sat hunched at the computer console, half-asleep. On a nearby chair lay the doctor's drug paraphernalia, a piece of silver foil containing brown powder, a spoon, spent matches and a needle. It was clear that Zalian was in the grip of severe narcosis.

The remaining members of the Roofworld had grouped outside and were crowding around the door of the conduit. Some of those present were wounded and there were others who had yet to return from the night's search. All could feel the tension that was building inside the little room, a hostility that threatened to tear the exhausted gathering apart.

'What do you expect him to do, Simon?' said Lee tiredly. 'Every time we run into Chymes we lose more men.'

'That's because we have no overall strategy, no plan. We've got no leader, Lee, look at him.' He pointed at Zalian, who sat silently staring at a patch on the floor between his feet. 'Rose says he turned off the transmitter last night. It's alright for us to fight Chymes for him, but he doesn't have the balls to face the man himself.'

A feeling of dread began to descend on Robert. After arriving in the middle of the fight between Simon and Zalian, he was now anxious to get the hell off the roof before Chymes and his crazies turned up in full force.

'We still don't know the location of the execution sites,' Lee pointed out. 'Fighting between ourselves isn't going to solve anything.'

'Then make him tell us,' said Simon angrily. 'What's the big deal with Chymes that you can't face up to him, Nathaniel?'

'Before this conversation gets too heated, let me tell you about a couple of things we've found out,' said Rose, pushing through the group and picking the notebook from the desk. 'Put the knife away, Simon, you're not going to solve anything with that.'

The punk glowered defiantly at Zalian, then looked back at Rose. Finally he let the knife fall to his side.

'You told us Chymes stands for everything that's opposite to your world and we've taken our cue from that,' she said, explaining her alchemical theory to the assembled gathering. 'This afternoon I checked it out with the British Museum library. Chymes – the original Chymes – was supposedly the inventor of alchemy. And the doctor here is Jewish, aren't you, doctor? "Nathaniel"? Sounds pretty Jewish to me.' Rose's gaze met a host of puzzled faces. She moved back to Zalian. 'I looked it up. The word "alchemy" comes from the Middle East. To antagonize you, Chymes chose to base his "opposite society" on a science with Arabic origins. I guess he planned for the two of you to be natural enemies, right from the start.'

'Well I'm sure that's very fucking interesting, Rose,' said Simon. 'But what practical help is it?' He turned his knife over, but was reluctant to return it to his belt.

'I'll tell you. We located him once before – last night on top of the London Metal Exchange – and we can do it again. If we know where he gets his strength we'll be able to figure out his weaknesses.'

'It's no use,' Zalian pleaded. 'He seems to know my every thought. He can't be beaten. It's like he's my mirror image, a twisted black mirror. Everything I do, he undoes. Every move I make, he's ahead. How can you defeat someone who doesn't behave in a human fashion?'

'You don't turn off the radio transmitter,' said Simon. 'You don't pump smack into your veins and curl up in a ball and pretend he's just going to go away.'

'No, I . . .'

'That's how we defeat him,' said Rose. 'If you're his equal, you must know him just as well.'

'No, I'm not his equal. He has night sight.'

'What do you mean?'

'He can see in the dark. Don't ask me how or why, but he can.'

'It's true,' said Simon. 'I've seen him run across a roof and jump the gap between two buildings in pitch black. It's like he has some kind of supernatural gift.'

'Wait a minute,' said Spice, 'what is this, the fucking Twilight Zone? Let's get real for a minute.' She reached forward and grabbed Zalian by the shoulders. 'Doc, you have to snap out of it, or we're all dead.' She turned to Simon. 'Is there anything we can do to bring him around?'

'I'm not incapable of answering for myself.' Slowly, Zalian raised his head and brushed the hair out of his eyes to look at her.

'Then tell us everything you know about what he's likely to do next. If you guys are so alike, surely you can figure out what his movements will be. So he can see in the dark, big deal.' Spice pulled him around to face the desk. 'We got this far. Come on, Doc, don't fade out on us now.'

Everyone in the group seemed to agree with her and began talking at once. Zalian rose slowly and held out his hand for silence. 'You don't understand,' he said, slurring his words slightly, 'Chymes stole Sarah away from me. He seduced her and won her over to his side and slept with her to deepen his victory. He destroyed her faith in me. Maybe not completely, but enough to stop her from trusting me with her notes. Instead, she gave them to her mother. She deliberately betrayed me and he's gloating over the fact that I know it.'

'All the more reason for us to beat the shit out of him,' said Simon enthusiastically.

Robert glanced nervously at his watch. Twenty past one. It felt much later than that. He was sure that Chymes and his men would arrive any second and wished they could all move somewhere safer to settle their differences.

'Wait a minute, this is all wrong,' said Lee, stepping forward. 'Sarah was nuts about you. She'd never have betrayed you, *never*. She couldn't stop talking about how much she loved you, for Christ's sake.'

Robert had had enough. He pulled free of the crowd and moved to the back of the conduit. He stepped out onto the freezing roof, where two members of Spice's crew kept watch for invaders. Lighting a cigarette he drew a deep breath, pulling the warm smoke deep into his lungs. Out here it seemed as if nothing could disturb the arctic calm of the night. He looked up into the sky. The moon was half obscured by fleeting cloud. They were all mad, he decided, surviving on a lunatic Lewis Carroll logic to which it was all too easy to succumb. Even so, their only hope of defeating Chymes was to restore their leader to his full strength. Robert considered the problem for a few minutes, then headed back into the arguing crowd in the doorway.

'She loved you enough to join up with the New Age,' Lee was saying. 'I was the last one to hear from her. She even said that she'd find a way to get a message to you if she was taken. Those aren't the words of a cheating woman, Nathaniel.' There was a moment of silence while Lee's words sank in.

'I agree with Lee,' said Spice finally. 'I don't think that Sarah could have betrayed you. If you ever manage to figure out where the hell she is before we all die, you can ask her yourself. Meanwhile I suggest that we do something about fighting back, or we elect ourselves a new leader.' The silent gaze of the group fell upon Zalian. The doctor searched the grimy, earnest faces surrounding him.

'What's it going to be?' asked Simon, exasperated. 'Stay here and get killed, or are we gonna go to war?'

Zalian mumbled something under his breath.

'I didn't hear you,' said Simon, craning forward. 'What was that?'

'Let's go to war.'

'All *right!*' Lee clapped his hands together and suddenly the group began to cheer up. Spice ushered everyone from the door of the conduit and moved to the equipment shed in order to start refilling the depleted supply bags.

'Let's get organized before Chymes gets here,' said Lee, swinging a pack onto his shoulders. 'We'll head further in towards the West End and regroup. If they attack us here, we're finished.' He looked across at Rose, who was staring at him with wide eyes.

'What's the matter?'

'It just occurred to me,' she said slowly, half to herself. 'Sarah promised that she'd try to get a message to you, even if she was captured? I think I know where the message is. I've known all along. God, I get worse. What a bimbo!' And with that she ran off.

'Wait!' called Zalian. 'Don't let her go off alone.'

'That's right,' said Simon. 'She tends to get stuck.'

'I'll meet up with you in a little while,' Rose shouted back. 'Where are you headed?'

Spice stopped loading her bag and looked over to Lee. 'What about Euston station? We've got a storage locker there.'

'Good thinking,' agreed Lee. 'Rose, when you're through just come to the station forecourt and we'll show you the way to the roof. Stay in radio contact. You sure you don't want anyone with you?'

'No, I'll be all right.'

'Where are you going?' called Robert, irritated by the fact that she seemed to have no intention of asking him along. Rose ran over to him. 'Back to my apartment,' she said. 'On the day Sarah came to plead with her mother, she was accompanied by two of Chymes' men. But one of them was actually working for Zalian, remember? While he was waiting for Sarah to come down, he scratched something on my front door. I told you about it when we first met, I just didn't think anything of it at the time.' And with that, she vanished over the side of the fire escape before Robert had a chance to reach her.

'Come on, let's move out,' said Lee, kicking shut the door of the conduit. 'Chymes and his charm school rejects will be here any minute.'

'What about taking to the streets below?' suggested

Robert, instantly realizing that he should have known better than to ask. Around him, everyone jeered.

'He'll never force us back down there,' said a small red-haired girl who looked about eleven years old, 'even if he takes the exchange.'

Grouped together, they looked rather pitiful and exhausted, like a gang of undernourished chimney-sweeps. After a brief respite Lee, Spice and Tony were goading them into action once more, leading the way from the roof.

Suddenly, one of the watchmen raised the alarm. The doctor ran unsteadily to the edge of the roof and lifted a small pair of field glasses to his eyes, searching in the direction of the guard's pointing finger.

'Somebody's going to have to keep an eye on him,' said Lee. 'We don't want him dropping off into the street.'

'They're coming,' Zalian shouted back. 'Forty, fifty of them, about half a mile off. Damn. What's the time?'

Robert glanced down at his watch. 'Just after two.' He noticed that the date-square had clicked over to the twenty-first. The twenty-first of December . . . didn't it have some significance in the calendar? He turned to Zalian excitedly. 'Today, it's the day of the winter solstice. The turning point of the sun!'

'Well, if Chymes is an alchemist, he's bound to make this his time of triumph. It means we only have until sunrise to pinpoint the sacrificial sites.' Zalian attached his belt-line under Lee's watchful eye and launched himself away from the roof of the Exchange. As he did so he called to Robert, who had already harnessed himself up and clipped onto the line just behind. 'I hope Rose knows what she's doing. We should never have let her go alone.'

Robert could not answer. The raw, arctic air rushing into his face prevented him from catching his breath. The muscles in his arms and legs seemed on the point of seizing up. He was sure that he would be able to sleep right through the Christmas celebrations after this, if he managed to stay in one piece until then.

Spice and the others occasionally had to help Robert and Zalian in their clumsy progress across the rooftops but at least, for the first time, the whole group was travelling together. Below, the city would be at its most silent in these, the approaching dead hours of the night. Far behind them, the massed forces of Chymes' New Age had landed on the roof of the Exchange and were systematically destroying Zalian's secret hideout in the conduit.

The group passed over Jockey's Fields and Bedford Row, across Theobald's Road, via the new office blocks which had replaced those so badly destroyed in the second world war, and on to Bloomsbury Square, the first and noblest of its kind, where once the Gordon rioters were hanged and where now a giant car park had been built. Here they paused to catch their breath, suiting up against the glacial night as a light snow began to fall.

'That's all we needed,' said Simon. 'If this gets any heavier it'll be almost impossible to see the line-bolts. We'd better stick to the established runs.' He looked nervously back at Zalian. Above them, large white flakes drifted lazily down from a laden sky, slowly obliterating the moon. The significance of this was not lost on the doctor.

'The snow will reduce our travelling speed,' he called to Simon, 'but it'll reduce theirs as well. Who has the notebook?'

'I thought you took it.' Robert searched his bag.

'No matter,' Zalian shrugged. 'I don't think it can help us any more.'

What he really meant, thought Robert, was that now he had regained some of his former strength, he would no longer need to rely on the book as an excuse for his procrastination. 'We could have done with the moonlight on our side. Chymes' night sight will enable him to gain on us.'

'I guess we're really on our own now,' said Spice. The group's earlier mood of euphoria had dissipated somewhat. With muscles torn and minds taut with the effort of just trying to stay alert, they looked up into the unfurling clouds and waited for the approaching blizzard to encircle them.

CHAPTER FOURTY-FOUR

Homing In

Kneeling down on the curving brass-plated step of the porch, she shone the torch at the base of the front door. At first glance she thought that one of the tenants had obliterated the markings. Then she saw them; a series of small scratches in the green paintwork. Rose remembered the morning Sarah had visited the house. She had dashed out into the rain to buy orange juice at the corner supermart and on her return had found one of the ugly skinheads accompanying the girl digging his penknife into the kickboard of the door. At the time it seemed the kind of simple-minded, thoughtless act she had grown inured to living in London. Now though, the lacerations beneath her torchlight took on an entirely different meaning. There seemed to be several letters – an 'M' or an 'H', it was hard to tell, a space, then a 'T', an 'E' and an 'L':

Presuming that the space indicated a missing letter, the word could be 'HOTEL' or 'MOTEL'. Rose sat down on the step and withdrew her walkie-talkie, hoping that the crackling radio static would not disturb her sleeping neighbours.

She had used one of the fixed runs to return to Hampstead, figuring that it was better to keep the muscles in her arms supple than to relax in the back of a cab and risk seizing a tendon. Travelling across the rooftops held no terror for her now. On the contrary, it was being on the ground that seemed odd. The buildings and trees seemed to rear up around her and the sky was all but obliterated. With a feeling of regret she had left the run at the top of a whitewashed shopping complex just beyond Hampstead tube station and had walked through the empty back streets to the house. Here the increasingly heavy snowfall had begun to settle and coat the desolate roads.

'That's right, like "HOTEL", without the "O". Any ideas?' Rose clicked the 'Receive' switch over.

'Could be anywhere, couldn't it?' Robert's voice buzzed over the microspeaker. 'The Hilton, the Ritz, Claridge's . . .'

'No, I don't think so.' This sounded like Zalian's voice cutting in. 'We've already covered most of the big hotels. Rose, can't you tell at all whether that first letter is an "M" or an "H"?'

Rose clicked the torch back on and leaned close to the scratchmarks. 'It's hard to say. It looks like both.'

'If the word is "HOTEL", why leave out the "O"?'

'It's the only curved letter in the word. Maybe it was too difficult to scratch out. Sorry, guys, I think I've reached a dead end.'

'You tried. We're at Hardwick Station, on top of Euston. We don't think Chymes knows where we are at the moment, but it won't be long before his scouts locate us.'

'I'll come and join you there in a few minutes after I've had another look at this door. Over and out.'

She replaced the radio in her bag and snapped off the

torch. There was a footfall behind her, the sound of a nailed boot on concrete. She was just beginning to think that she had imagined it when a tattooed hand shot out and sealed over her mouth.

'Keep very still, or I'll twist your fuckin' head off.' Rose caught a glimpse of shaved head, a grazed, bloody cheek, the glimmer of a switchblade.

As the hand was removed from her face, the blade of the knife forced her back against the door. The front of Reese's jacket was soaked in blood from the dart that Spice had fired at him in the park. He lurched closer, pressing the blade dangerously hard in Rose's chest. 'We met before, you and I. Remember?'

'No, no, I . . .' Rose's breath came in short gasps.

'There were three of us.'

'You were here with Sarah, you were the other one!' Rose's eyes widened in fear.

'That's right. We're tidying up the loose ends tonight. Chymes wants to meet the girl who's been causing him all this trouble.' He glanced down and saw the scratches on the door.

'That traitorous bastard was writing something, wasn't he?'

'You should know,' coughed Rose. 'He was standing right next to you at the time. You were too thick to notice what he was up to.'

Reese pushed his free hand into his pocket and withdrew a pair of handcuffs. 'Well, now you'll get a chance to find out where the message leads.' He pulled Rose's hands together and snapped the handcuffs over her wrists. 'Sorry there aren't two of us to help take you back, but my mate's hanging in the park with a tree sticking out of his stomach at the moment.' He stared down at her body. 'You're a pretty one.'

His rancid odour assaulted her nostrils as he leaned closer. Suddenly he ran his tongue over her face. 'You're going to see the sun rise over the city, lady.' He grinned, displaying an array of fragmented yellow teeth. 'Only the city won't be able to see you.' He lowered the knife and dug into his pocket, producing a length of rope.

'Help me!' Rose suddenly screamed at the top of her lungs, leaping to her feet and jabbing her foot squarely into Reese's testicles. 'Help, rape!'

A light went on in one of the windows above, then another.

'You cow,' groaned Reese, grabbing Rose by the hair and hauling her out of the porch into the snow. Slipping and stumbling on the wet pavement, she screamed as Reese pulled her away down a side road towards the heathland at the bottom of the hill. Although lights had been lit in the houses around her, nobody ventured out into the street. Twice she slid over, falling hard on her side, to be lifted back up and dragged off once more. As Reese drew her deeper into the dimly lit slopes of the park, she knew that her chances of escape had all but vanished.

Robert leaned back against the curving glass canopy of the station and let the snow settle on his burning face. 'I guess I'm really out of condition,' he panted, rubbing his shoulders. He looked across at Spice, who had travelled the same distance, but was not even breathing heavily. 'I'm surprised you haven't grown arms like a gorilla.'

'It's rough at first,' said Spice. 'You get used to tearing ligaments and spraining joints, but after a while your body tones up and adapts. That's our one advantage over Chymes' men. Most of us have been up here much longer than they have. Their physical strength is no match for ours.'

'But they have the advantage of numbers.'

Spice lit two cigarettes and passed him one. 'If you thought it was tough getting here,' she said, quickly changing the subject, 'you should try the Wren run some time.'

'St Paul's, right?'

'It's short, but it's the steepest of all. It was the first run to be built, before anyone had cracked the physics of run construction. They chose St Paul's because it used to be the site of a Roman temple dedicated to Diana.'

'The moon crops up yet again,' said Robert. 'What's our next move?' He blew a jet of blue smoke into the frosty white air.

'We go to the back of the station, where the tracks start, and collect the rest of our supplies.'

'In the fifties this was one of our main bases,' said Zalian, walking over to them. 'Up until 1963, when British Rail saw fit to destroy the famous Euston portico and the adjoining hotel. Come on, let's keep moving before the cold sets in.'

From the back of the station, tracks from eighteen platforms fanned out in a criss crossing network of tangled steel.

'Can't we be seen by people on the concourse below?' asked Robert, stepping warily along an uncomfortably narrow concrete post running between two vast sheets of sooty glass.

'No, the roof looks opaque from down there,' said Zalian. 'Anyway . . .'

'Yeah, I know. Nobody ever looks up.'

Ahead, Lee and Tony stepped onto a wide concrete square with a large metal electrical box in the centre of it. 'Jay relocated the wiring in here and refitted it to hold emergency supplies,' said Lee, wiping snow from the lid and producing a key for the padlock on its side. Throwing the box open, he pulled out an assortment of cables, knives, bandages, flareguns and – incredibly – a six-pack of beer and what looked like sandwiches.

'Spice's secret stash-place,' Tony grinned, helping Lee to unload the box.

'I *thought* it was secret,' said Spice indignantly, catching a beer. 'Don't worry, I've got others you don't know about.' Robert remembered her hiding place on the Planetarium roof.

'You seem to have thought of everything,' he said, popping the top of a freezing can.

'Not everything,' replied Zalian. 'Otherwise we wouldn't be in this mess in the first place.'

Simon began passing foodpacks back along the line. Everyone was now beginning to feel the cold.

'Do you think there's any mileage in this "message" business?'

'Even if there is,' said Spice through a mouthful of stale ham sandwich, 'it's much too vague to do anything about.'

'Come on, somebody must have an idea.' A depressing silence fell across the krewe, as snow settled silently over the vast glass roof.

'I've got one.' Robert was standing at the end of the platform with his back to the others, looking out across the western side of the city.

'Let's hear it.'

'No, you have to *see* it.' He ran lightly back and grabbed Spice's hand. 'Come and look.' He positioned her exactly where he had been standing, then threw his arm out at the cityscape. 'What do you see, Spice? Think of the letters.' There was a momentary silence as Spice scanned the horizon.

'Oh, my God . . .'

'What is it?' Simon, Tony, Lee and the others crowded alongside. There in the middle distance stood a tall circular tower. Written around the top in enormous yellow neon letters, the word 'TELECOM' could be deciphered through the falling snow. After the final letter, there was a single gap before the word repeated itself on the other side of the column.

Sunday 21 December

CHAPTER FOURTY-FIVE

Night Duty

At a quarter to three on a Sunday morning, the softly lit side-foyer of London's University College Hospital was peaceful and deserted. Seated side by side on the scuffed leather couch, surrounded by empty acres of muted pastel carpet, Hargreave and Butterworth waited for the return of the doctor. 'What was I supposed to tell him?' hissed Hargreave angrily. 'Your father rings me in the middle of the night wanting to know why you're in hospital, what was I supposed to say?' He shifted irritably on the seat. 'Now, I have the deepest respect for him as you know, one of the finest commissioners this country ever produced, a man honoured by royalty. I could hardly say that his son just fell off the top of a building, destroyed public property and put his colleague in the hospital with half a dozen broken ribs. You're a great disappointment to me, Butterworth, really you are.' Hargreave rose from the couch and paced the faded patterns of the carpet.

'I'm sorry, sir,' began Butterworth. 'The doctor asked me who my next of kin was.'

'You didn't have to tell him, boy. Having your father on my back is the last thing I need right now. I'm hanging on to this investigation by the skin of my teeth. I've done everything I can to buy more time. Do you realize what's happening somewhere above our heads even as we stand here?' Hargreave's voice became taut and strangled.

'Hordes of nutcases are trying to wipe each other out. We're heading for some kind of massacre before dawn. It's a very important moment in the alchemist's calendar, the turning point of the sun. They're all going to get supernatural powers before breakfast! Of course, they have to perform a bit of genocide in order to complete the transaction, but that's black magic for you. Naturally, nobody can tell me where this transformation is going to take place. Meanwhile . . .' He thrust his head forward until his face filled Butterworth's startled vision. '*Meanwhile*, eight of the force's finest, not counting Bimsley you understand, have been admitted to this hospital in the last hour nursing a variety of bizarre injuries. Right now there are two young ladies in Casualty telling the doctor that they were walking home from a Christmas party when a policeman fell on them from out of the sky. The report of the incident reads like a bloody Monty Python script.'

Hargreave passed a hand over his forehead, exasperated. 'The monitor tapes show footage of at least ten figures, none of them police, attacking each other with guns and crossbows. You yourself have undergone physical contact with these people, but are you any the wiser for it? Are you, be buggered!' Hargreave's face was pulsing a deep crimson, largely with the effort of remaining *sotto voce* in the cavernous hospital hall.

Butterworth sat forward, wincing with the movement. The bandage around his shoulder covered a blue-black mass of contusions. 'One of them mentioned a name, sir. An unusual name.'

'Which was?' Hargreave jumped forward, thrusting his huge red face beneath Butterworth's startled eyes.

'I've forgotten it.'

'Well, I dare say it'll come back to you when you return to the scene,' said Hargreave, suddenly grabbing Butterworth's bruised arm and hoisting him protesting to his feet.

'The doctor has my X-rays. Shouldn't we wait to see how I am?'

'I can tell you better than X-rays.' Hargreave poked Butterworth viciously in the ribs with his forefinger. 'Nothing wrong there.'

'I don't feel well.'

'Of course you don't feel well. You've lost face. You're ashamed of being a dim witted little tit who couldn't organize a bunk-up in a brothel. That's understandable. You have let your commanding officer down. Which is why I'm giving you another chance, to make amends.'

Butterworth's heart sank to the bottom of his cracked ribs.

'I've got every man we can spare up there in the field. There's no one left to team you with. Anyway, you'll be better off working on your own. There's less risk of you killing anyone.'

'But sir, I can't go back up there by myself. If they see me I'm done for!'

'Then I'll tell your father you died like a man in the course of your duty,' said Hargreave maliciously. 'You might even be decorated posthumously.'

The police van squealed through the empty streets as Hargreave wrestled the wheel around one sharp bend after another. He's gone mad, thought Butterworth, breaking into a cold sweat at the thought of returning to the heights above Piccadilly. The long hours, the unsolved crimes, the sleepless nights, they've finally gotten to him. He watched the shop fronts retreating in the rear window of the van, wondering if this was the last time he would ever set eyes on them.

'If we don't act tonight, we'll have the deaths of God knows how many more on our conscience. Besides which, I am *not* going to let the police be made fools of again,' Hargreave was saying as he mounted two wheels on the pavement and nearly took out a Belisha beacon. 'Remember to use your radio if you get into difficulties. I'll be close by. Don't try to tackle anyone by yourself, understand?' The vehicle tilted around the one way system at the base of Tottenham Court Road and slewed diagonally across the lanes to one side. Hargreave suddenly stamped onto the footbrake, catapulting Butterworth into the front seat. 'We are employed by Her Majesty's government to serve and protect,' said Hargreave through suitably clenched teeth, 'and that, for once, is exactly what you're going to do.'

As the detective constable righted himself and checked his body for missing organs, Hargreave slid back the door and pointed up at the roof of the Centrepoint tower. He had stopped the van by the ugly stone fountains that squirted feebly before the half-deserted office block. 'That's where they've been sighted. Up there. I've no more men available in this area. It's up to you now.'

Butterworth squinted upward, but failed to locate the top of the building through the falling snow.

'There's a night guard expecting you. Try to prevent yourself from dying. It'll save me having to explain to your old man.' And with that Hargreave slammed the van door shut and took off, skidding on the slick snow which had failed to settle on the tarmac of the empty traffic lanes.

My God, thought Butterworth, pulling his jacket tightly over his chest as he climbed the steps to the main entrance of the office block, he doesn't care if I get torn limb from limb, just so long as he wraps this business up tonight. He's only interested in saving his tarnished reputation. Funny how he doesn't volunteer to join me up there. He looked at his watch. Ten past three on a wintry Sunday morning. Supposing these rooftop maniacs really did develop supernatural abilities . . . that would really be something. Perhaps they would show him how he could get them as well. No prizes for guessing the first person he'd use them on.

As Butterworth nodded through glass at the night guard and was admitted into the shadowed gloom of the entrance hall, his mind turned to thoughts of roaring log fires, throat-tingling brandies and goose feather eiderdowns. As he rose toward the roof in the elevator he thought of sultry tropical women with tawny limbs and languid smiles. And as he stepped out onto the snow-blasted roof of the West End's tallest building, he thought about the possibility of being thrown to his death in the fountain a million and one floors below.

CHAPTER FOURTY-SIX

Dream State

She was no longer alone, of that much she was sure.

Each dawn had brought with it the certainty of death, each day a stay of execution. Her twisted limbs no longer flinched in frozen pain. Starved and thirsty, her mind had freed itself from the pinching shackles of reality to float within an endless waking dream. Yet she was conscious of movement all around her. There were others here now, many others trapped and crying, some passively trussed with heads lolling to their chests in mute acceptance of their impending termination.

Each evening he would come, his boots ringing on the steel rim above her head, his cloak cracking like an ocean sail. Silently he would peer into her face, searching her dark eyes for a spark of life, tenderly touching her frozen cheek before passing to the next crippled figure that lay wedged behind the humming neon letters.

At night, the harsh yellow light penetrated the nest-filled corners of the vast steel structure. Sleep-deprived birds, their feathers beating clouds of soot, pecked at her filthy clothes to tear away loose threads and bear them back to the riveted gables of the tower. Then, in the darkest hour of her night, they had brought the coloured girl, the one whose tear-streaked face she had seen before in what seemed to be another age. She fought to reanimate the workings of her once active mind, to recall the face and understand its importance in the inexorable design of fate which had brought her to this windswept place of death.

'Sarah!'

For the briefest moment the image sharpened and there she was, looking into the smiling West Indian face, in the same house as her mother.

'Sarah, wake up!'

And then just as suddenly the rest of the memory flooded back, the pleading, the abduction, the anger of a man filled with the bitterness of betrayal and now the sacrifice, high atop the Telecom Tower. The voice was calling to her again. Why wouldn't it let her sleep? The West Indian girl, tied to the sign not ten feet away, was speaking urgently.

'Sarah, listen to me. It's going to be dawn soon. They're going to kill us. Can you hear me? We've got to get down from here!'

Stupid girl, didn't she know? There was no escape from a man like Chymes. If indeed he was a man. Slowly she allowed the deadening snow to seal away the pleading voice and return her to the safety of her dreams.

CHAPTER FOURTY-SEVEN

Flight to The Tower

'How many of them can you see?'

'Six from this side, maybe seven, I'm not sure. It's hard to tell in this weather.' Zalian lowered the infra-red binoculars and passed them over to Lee. 'They're between the letters. You can just make out their arms and legs. Bloody good camouflage job.'

'If they've been there since they were captured, they're probably all suffering from exposure,' said Lee, refocusing the glasses. 'It's going to be difficult getting them down and moving them to safety.' In the distance, the yellow letters of the TELECOM sign flickered hazily through the obliterating snowfall.

'We have medical supplies,' Spice pointed out. 'I'd like to know how Chymes is planning to perform the executions.' She held out her hand for the binoculars.

'You'd think the tower would be crawling with guards,' said Lee, handing them across. 'I suppose there might be some around the other side.'

'There are hardly any footholds on the whole of the central structure. It's a perfect hiding place.'

'Maybe Chymes' men are stationed elsewhere. It would have to be somewhere with a vantage point to the tower. What have we got in the surrounding neighbourhood?' Spice unfolded her roofmap and spread it out on the glass canopy as the others gathered around, huddling inwards. With the temperature plunging, it made sense for them to stay as close as possible to each other. 'There's Fitzroy Square nearby, but they're all low-elevation buildings. You're better off in Cleveland Street or Charlotte Street, on one of the taller glass office blocks. Ad agencies, sixties construction, mostly flat roofs.'

'That's where they must be, but I don't get it.' Spice stood straight and shook the settling snow from her hair. 'A run from the tallest building in the area would still be too steep for them to reach the tower by, particularly without the use of our technology. No, they can't be travelling into the tower via a run.'

'Perhaps they've strung level lines from the tops of the offices in Charlotte Street. That would take them halfway up the building,' offered Robert, pointing at the map with a numb forefinger.

'It's a sheer curved glass wall, Robert. There's nowhere for the run to go. There's nothing to attach a line to until you get near the top. There's one other possibility. Is there a crane in the area?'

'Yes, there is. Look, you can see the top of it from here.' A short distance from the Telecom Tower a tubular steel crane rose above the office blocks, its arm extending in a gravity-defying arc towards a darkly luminous ceiling of cloud.

'Look through the glasses,' said Zalian, returning from the far edge of the canopy. 'There's a line running from the tip of the crane to the tower. That's how they're passing back and forth. All they have to do is release the line at the appointed hour of execution and the tower becomes impregnable.' He took the binoculars from Spice and threw them back to Lee. 'We could try to storm the crane, but Chymes will be waiting for us. No, we'll have to do something they'd never expect us to attempt.'

'Couldn't we try to gain access to the crane's control room?' asked Spice.

'Forget it,' replied Zalian. 'That's what he'd want us

to do. Concentrate on the tower. We can't enter it from within, he'll have seen to that. Look at the outside. Including the roof, it has nine platforms, nine possible vantage points. Most of them are maintenance decks for the satellite dishes. Chymes will have men stationed on every level. But he'll keep them back in the shadows, near the inner core of the building, where you can't see them. He prefers a sneak attack to a frontal one. There isn't a way we can land a single one of you on that structure without him seeing you coming.'

'So what do you suggest, Doctor Zalian?' asked Spice defiantly. 'We're going to freeze to death if we wait around up here much longer. And it's going to be light soon.'

'There is a way,' said Zalian quietly. 'But if this wind keeps up it'll be highly dangerous.' Naturally, this acted as a cue for everyone to start talking at once. He held up his hand for silence. 'Lee, do we have enough haulers to go around? How strong are they?'

'Hauler?'

Simon leaned across and explained to a puzzled Robert. 'It's a small motor which attaches to your line-belt. It allows you to travel along a line with an upward gradient. It's only good for short distances, though.'

'There are plenty over at the Capital building,' Lee replied. 'Only the motors ain't so strong. Jay was still figuring out how to improve them. In these conditions they'd take maybe a fifteen-degree angle, certainly no more.'

'Suppose I can get you that on a long run.'

'Which run?' Lee's black eyes glittered with interest.

'A new one. I'd have to lay it first.'

'For Christ's sake, there isn't time to build a run!' shouted Spice.

'Yes there is.' Zalian turned to her. 'One stop. From the Centrepoint skyscraper direct to the Telecom Tower.'

'You're crazy!' Spice shook her head in disgust. 'Besides, the Capital Building is nearer.'

'Yes, it's too near, too convenient,' said Zalian. 'Chymes will already have thought of that. We'd be walking straight into a trap, I assure you.'

'Centrepoint to the tower . . . that's a hell of a distance, Zalian,' said Robert. 'What are you going to do, fly?'

'See?' Zalian pointed Robert out to the others. 'Someone around here acts like he has some sense.'

'The microlite? You must be joking,' said Simon vehemently. 'It's still in pieces, hasn't been serviced for months.'

'I'll have to take that chance.' Zalian was already heading to the back of the station roof with Lee at his side. 'What's the longest line we have?'

'Three hundred metres at the most. We'll have to cut several together to cover the distance.' Lee had to break into a trot to keep pace with Zalian. Behind him, the others followed on.

'Is there a way of splicing the lines smoothly?'

'That's not the problem. The main risk is that without an anchor somewhere along the line, the wind will play hell with it, and anyone travelling along it. Plus, after the weight of the first couple of riders, it'll start to stretch. Over that kind of length the tensile strength will change.'

'That's OK. We can keep altering the tension from the Centrepoint end.'

'Wait, Nathaniel.' Lee caught Zalian's arm as he prepared to launch off from the side of the station roof. 'I don't know if the microlite will take the weight of so much line. It would have trouble in these conditions without the problem of an extra load.'

Zalian smiled bitterly. 'It's all we have, Lee. You got any better ideas?'

'Hey, slow down!' called Robert. 'What do you want us to do?'

'Half of you come with me. We'll need help carrying the components of the microlite. It'll make more sense reassembling it at line base. The rest go with Spice to collect the lines, then meet me on top of Centrepoint.'

Butterworth briskly paced the perimeter of the Centrepoint building in a desperate effort to stay warm. By the time his entire right leg had fallen asleep he realized that he was fighting a losing battle. There had been no sign of Hargreave's suspects beyond a cluster of damp footprints in the snow and, by the fresh fall that had now all but covered them, these must have been made some time ago. He checked all around the building to see if he could find any cables similar to the ones he had found on the Piccadilly art gallery, but without any luck. Contained by a moat of tarmac, Centrepoint was far too high and isolated a building to string a line from or to.

After another fifteen minutes spent circling the parapet, Butterworth had run out of people and things to hate and was forced to consider hating people who until this moment he had only mildly disliked. Just as he was planning a suitable fate for his father's new wife, the doorway to the roof opened and half a dozen people poured through it, stopping in complete surprise when they saw him.

Before he had even a chance to think of evasive action someone grabbed him from behind, placed a knee in his back and forced him to the ground. His attacker revealed herself to be a young woman of no more than five feet five inches, a fact which Butterworth fervently prayed would never reach Hargreave's ears.

'Don't move a muscle and you won't get hurt,' said Spice, shifting her knees onto Butterworth's arms. 'Tell us where Chymes is.'

'Don't – know – who – what – Ow!' was all the young detective constable managed to say before being dragged to his feet by his captors and shaken like a duster.

'Is – Chymes – at – the – tower?' said someone very loudly, mouthing the words as if dealing with an imbecile. Butterworth could only stare, fascinated by this extraordinary behaviour.

'It's no use, he's probably strung out on drugs,' the man who had mouthed at him said to his friend. 'Most of Chymes' men are.'

'Come on, this isn't the sort of guy Chymes would enlist,' said Simon, rattling his chains at the terrified policeman. 'Look at him, he's scared of his own shadow.'

'Who – are – you?' asked Spice. She too appeared to have picked up the strange habit of speaking loudly and slowly.

'P-P-Police,' Butterworth managed to stammer.

'In an orange windcheater?' scoffed Simon, plucking distastefully at his nylon jacket. 'Sartorial standards seem to have taken a nose-dive in the force.'

'What are you doing up here?' asked Spice, narrowing her considerably attractive eyes at him. 'Are you alone?'

'If I don't report in in the next five minutes, the whole building will be surrounded,' ventured Butterworth, looking around hopefully. When everybody started sniggering he began to suspect that his bluff had failed.

'What are we going to do with you?' Spice ran a playful hand across his jacket.

'I was sent up here to find out what's going on,' Butterworth volunteered, even though no one had actually asked him to explain his presence. Once they had allowed him up from the floor he decided to reach for his radio, but was surprised to find that it was no longer in his jacket.

'I have an idea,' Spice dangled the radio tantalizingly

before him and whispered into his ear. 'Come with me.' She pulled the policeman to one side, then beckoned one of the other girls from the group. Minutes later, Butterworth found himself sitting in a warm ventilation shaft at the back of the roof listening to an attractive, but extremely strong, young lady who had promised to explain what was going on slowly and in great detail, in terms she felt sure that even he would understand. It took him a few minutes to realize that he had been handcuffed to one of the inlet pipes.

'That gets PC Plod out of the way for the time being,' muttered Spice. 'Let's get these cables spliced together.' She and the rest of the group ran back to the shelter of the stairwell, where they had collected the longest lines they could find. Spice took a small hard-fuel burner from her backpack and set to work as the others warmed their hands in preparation for the task ahead.

'Calling Doctor Zalian.' The crackle of the transmitter was muffled by the nylon zipbag from which it issued. 'This is Chymes with a message for the good doctor and his few remaining disciples.'

'Shit!' Spice quickly tore open the bag and turned up the volume on the receiver. 'Be quiet, everyone.'

'Doctor, I hope you are receiving me loud and clear.' The group gathered around, listening intently. 'I wish to make it known that I bear you and your people no grudge for your recent actions and to prove the point I am now prepared to accept you within our ranks. It is not too late for you to join us for the rebirth. Besides, what other choice do you have? We can take you whenever we wish. We already have your new friend, the little black girl. Remember the phoenix rising from the ashes, Doctor Zalian. You must make your decision before first light. Either you become part of the New Age, or you will be destroyed by it.'

'OK, anybody want to change sides?' asked Spice. 'I

thought not.' She reached down and turned the receiver off.

'That'll never fly.'

Robert looked at the snow-dusted tangle of nylon and steel on the rooftop ahead of him. Dragged from its hiding place it looked singularly unimpressive, like a giant broken umbrella.

'Shut up, Robert,' said Lee. 'There's a lot to carry, even with six of us. You'll have to take some of the wing rods.' He passed a number of slotted aluminium tubes across, then crouched down by the engine, which seemed to be no larger than that of a golf cart. 'If we can get this back to Centrepoint in the next half hour, it shouldn't take us much more than that to assemble it.'

'Have we got gas?' Zalian knuckled the side of the tank.

'There are still some spare tanks in the storage room back at Cubitt Station. That was the last run we made.'

'Where's that?' asked Robert.

'King's Cross, but it'll take too long to fetch them. You'll have to go with what there is, Nathaniel.'

Lee and Robert passed back the pieces of the microlite until they reached the enormous nylon sails. 'What about these?' Robert lifted one of the pale sheets. 'Surely they're too big to carry.'

'They unzip. Watch.' Lee tore the sections apart with ease and began to roll them as if packing a parachute. 'All right, as soon as you've got as much as you can take, head out. We'll see you back there.' Lee stopped one of the men. 'Centrepoint is too high to scale in this kind of weather. When you reach it, run a line to one of the lower floors and then take the stairs from the inside.' He turned to Robert. 'The night guard is one of ours.' He shrugged almost apologetically. 'Actually, he's Spice's father.'

The journey to Centrepoint was a laborious one. Weighed down with equipment, the group travelled slowly. To make matters worse the wind was picking up, driving the snow in billowing seams over the tops of the buildings. Robert could feel his strength beginning to ebb in the battering zero-degree wind-chill. Although the black jumpsuit he wore seemed to be well insulated from the cold, snow steadily sifted into the collar and his ears felt as if they could be snapped off. When they finally reached the vast concrete office block, entering through an open window on the seventh floor, a wall of dry tingling warmth enveloped them.

'Don't get too used to this heat,' said Zalian. 'We're going back out in a moment.' There was a collective groan. Doggedly they made for the fire escape stairs and began climbing.

'I wonder if I might have a word with you.' Simon beckoned Robert as soon as he saw him approaching across the roof. 'There's bad news.' Simon's bony eggshell face looked apologetic. 'They have Rose.'

'What do you mean? How do you know?'

'Chymes called through on our radio receiver a short while ago. One of his thugs picked her up at the house.'

'Dammit, I should have gone with her. Is she all right? What else did he say?'

'Oh, nothing much. We're all about to die horribly, the dawn of a new era, the usual ranting drivel.'

'So why did he bother to call?'

'He doesn't know where we are. I think he was hoping that we'd give the game away, rise to his bait and transmit back to him so that he could trace the communication. Needless to say, we didn't give him the satisfaction.'

'Good. That means that while we're still running around loose out here, he can't be certain of victory. And he doesn't realize that we know the location of the sacrificial site.'

'We still have to get there,' said Zalian, 'so quit talking and lend a hand with these struts.' He and the others had laid out the components of the microlite and were fastening the wing rods together with spanners. Robert looked at his watch. 'We'd better get a move on. I reckon we've got less than two hours until sun-up.'

It took a while to complete the assembly, but once they had fixed the last bolt into place and stepped back, the damned thing looked as if it just might fly. The nylon wings arched in an arrow above the engine like a motorized hang-glider. At its base were three tiny wheels, supported on a triangle of aluminium tubes. Lee had removed the seat to make the contraption lighter, which meant that Zalian would have to support himself on a network of tensioned wires, something for which he had acquired quite a skill in the past few years.

Reunited, the group followed en masse as Lee wheeled the microlite to the edge of the roof. One end of the line had been attached to a steel mast at the corner of the building. Lee's main concern was that Zalian would be able to keep the cable playing out smoothly from the back of the craft once he was in flight. It would take just one snag to rip the microlite out of the snowswept sky and hurl it down into the streets below.

'The only place you'll be able to land is on the roof,' Lee warned. 'If they've got people posted up there, the deal's off. You'll have to release the line and turn back.'

'I don't think so.' Zalian pointed to the tank. 'Judging by the amount of gas left in this thing I'll have to put down anyway.'

Spice appeared at Zalian's side with a giant-sized plastic Safeway shopping bag. She shrugged apologetically. 'I couldn't find anything else to put the line in,' she said. 'When you get to the tower, attach the line to the base of the radio mast on the roof. As soon as you've done that, we'll begin tensioning it from this end.'

'As you play the line out from the anchor-point, you'll have to keep the microlite at a fairly constant speed,' said Lee. 'Does anyone have any other advice?'

'We think it's unlikely,' added Simon, 'but in case they hear the engine as you land we're sending a team to the crane to create a bit of a diversion. They'll try to make it look as if we're attempting to take control of the structure.'

'I doubt that they'll hear the microlite coming,' said Zalian, tightening his jacket. 'The roof is way above the spot where the hostages are being held. My biggest problem will be finding a way down to them.'

'There has to be a door on the roof to allow service access to the radio mast,' said Lee, wrapping the microlite's starter cord around his knuckles and pulling. 'You'll find it.' After half a dozen yanks, the engine had still not turned over. On the seventh it sputtered fitfully into life. 'It's all right,' Lee assured Zalian. 'It won't die on you once it's up and running. Leastways, it never has before.'

'Thanks, Lee,' said Zalian, holding him with a jaundiced eye. 'You're a great comfort.'

Everyone moved back from the edge of the roof as the microlite began to bounce and turn on the snowcrusted tarmac. Spice helped Zalian fold himself inside the tiny craft, then lifted the bag containing the spliced line onto his lap so that it was wedged beneath the steering controls.

'If we ever needed a little luck,' he said with a grim smile, 'I guess the time is now.'

As the frail vehicle wobbled toward the edge of the roof, Robert could barely bring himself to watch the take-off. Zalian gripped the pilot arm thrusting up between his knees and hunched over it. He seemed oddly out of proportion to the aircraft, like the driver of a miniature train. The microlite was five feet from the edge, then three feet, then it had dropped alarmingly over the side, to rise again a few seconds later into the sky.

Zalian steered diagonally across the path of Tottenham Court Road rising toward the north, but was obviously finding it hard to keep the vehicle's direction constant in the buffeting wind. As he grew smaller in the sky, the cable poured from the back of the apparatus to form a vast bow above the roadway.

'He'll have to pick up the slack quickly before it snags,' shouted Spice. 'The line is almost as low as the trees.' As she watched, the vehicle tilted and rose on a sudden air current, pulling the cable out of danger. It took just a few more seconds for Zalian and his matchstick craft to vanish in the deepening silver snow-mists which swirled above the buildings.

CHAPTER FOURTY-EIGHT

Aurora

At the moment it was still dark, but in another few minutes there would be no mistaking the softly flushed gleam of pink which would start to take hold in a corner of the sky. Zalian sighted the Telecom Tower clearly below him. He was coming in above it and now began to descend in a steep banking manœuvre that caused the cable behind him to whip and pull against the craft. Beneath the sound of the rushing wind he could hear the engine of the microlite beginning to sputter and stall. The weight of the played-out nylon line threatened to drag the craft down just a few hundred yards short of his destination.

In desperation he jammed the engine's throttle wide for one final burst of power. As the craft jerked forward, there appeared dead ahead the box like struts of the tower's radio mast, wreathed in pale spirals of snow. Zalian pulled hard on the steering arm to avoid hitting them, but as he did so a fierce sidewind hit the hammering nylon wings of the craft and completely overturned them.

As the sails blew inside out, the rods holding them in place cracked together, causing the vehicle to whip over and drop from the sky like a crippled insect. Zalian and the microlite fell gently in the buffeting wind, hitting the side of the radio mast as the bag containing the end of the line tumbled down to the roof of the tower. Zalian was vaguely aware that his arm was bleeding badly as he pulled himself upright between the mast staves, then dropped carefully to the floor. He was just in time to grap the tail of the cable as it snaked away over the low balcony at the edge of the roof. He pulled it as taut as his burning right arm would allow, then secured it at the base of the mast, sealing the end of the line in place with a small steel grip. Staggering to his feet, he looked around.

Up here, on a circular steel-and-concrete platform roughly thirty feet in circumference, he could feel the wind like a malevolent creature trying to lift him under the arms and hurl him over the brink of the tower. No more than a quarter of a mile away stood the vast arm of the construction crane. He could just make out a number of shadowy figures clinging between its struts and wondered if they had seen his craft falling from the sky.

Zalian crossed to the edge of the roof and peered down. Now he could clearly see the bodies lashed behind the enormous neon letters of the sign below, could even recognize some of their faces. Still there seemed to be no guard, no member of the New Age keeping watch, yet Chymes and his men had to be here. Where the hell were they? He turned around. At the centre of the mast base was a steel door leading to the platform below. Zalian forced his freezing limbs into motion, seized the icy bar handle of the hatch and pulled. Nothing happened. The door was bolted from the inside. Zalian swore as behind him faint slivers of vermeil struck the edges of low snowclouds and the dead colours of the night began to wash away with the arrival of the dawn.

'If I tighten the line any more I risk tearing open one of the spliced sections,' argued Lee, releasing the ratchet and letting it fall to the roof. 'It's better if I go first and test it. There's a chance that the belt-lines won't ride over the splices. Give me a full five minutes before you follow on.' He hooked himself to the now taut cable and climbed over the parapet. Launching out over the sputtering fountains below, he dipped alarmingly above the stores at the corner of Oxford Street and for a moment it seemed that he would plunge into them, but then he soared upward in a smooth arc, gathering momentum with each passing second.

As he crossed high above Goodge Street and Charlotte Street, he prayed that the snow would obliterate his arrival on the roof of the tower. The tiny motor of the hauler whined and strained as he sped along the cable. The fulcrum of the vast crane passed by on his left. He could clearly see Chymes' men standing on the struts along the arm and realized with a jolt that they had spotted him. Then he was being lifted up, his speed beginning to slow as he snicked over the last of the spliced cables to arrive at the base of the radio mast where Zalian stood with arms outstretched, ready to break his fall. Even so, the landing was hard and he slammed into the steel box struts, jarring his shoulder and elbow.

A few minutes later Spice arrived in the same way, having been unable to wait any longer to find out if the line was safe.

For Robert, it was the most terrifying journey he had yet made. The run was higher than the tallest point of the Skelter Run. The blinding snow whipped his face, making it impossible for him to see. Suddenly he heard the hauler scream in protest, then cut out completely as it hit one of the cable splices and came to a stop. He reached his arms above his head, thumping the side of the motor with an ice-numbed hand. The outer case was scorching hot. A sudden gust threw him sideways, swinging him on the line. The force of it shifted his weight just enough to pull the hauler to one side of the splice and the motor began to hum again, free of further obstacles.

As Spice and Lee pulled him to a stop at the radio mast, he felt like falling to the roof's floor and thanking God for allowing him to arrive at the tower in one piece, until he remembered why they had come here in the first place.

'We'll have to go over the side,' agreed Lee. 'I can't see any other way of getting down to them.'

'If we do, they'll fire at us from the crane.'

'Simon, the access door is barred. Do we have a choice?'

Simon looked back into Lee's dark eyes. 'I guess not,' he admitted.

As the others arrived, Zalian and Lee fixed grappling hooks to the lip of the roof and prepared to lower themselves over. 'As soon as you land, go to the bodies and cut as many of them loose as quickly as you can,' shouted Zalian. 'It'll be daylight in a matter of minutes. Either Chymes and his men will appear to carry out the executions themselves, or they have a way of performing them by remote control.'

As Sunday dawned, anyone passing in the vicinity of the Telecom Tower who chanced to look skyward would have seen an extraordinary sight, as Zalian and his followers abseiled down the sheer face of the structure to the glowing letters encircling its peak and their enemies stationed atop the Fitzroy Square construction crane began to open fire. Lee gripped the rope below Nathaniel, braced in case his leader's remaining good arm should fail him.

'It's safer to leave the lines connected,' cried Spice, skidding on the snow-slick platform just a few feet above the captive figures. 'We may end up having to use them again.'

The group had spread out along the circular steel ramp, one above each of the prisoners, as a hail of razor-coins spattered the wall which extended down below their feet.

'Their ammunition should be falling short,' Zalian shouted. 'We're well beyond their range.'

'They must have modified some of the guns.'

'Over here. It's Sarah.' It was Simon who called out, crouching above the letter 'M' and pointing downwards. The girl was unconscious, wrapped in layers of transparent sheeting, presumably to prevent her from freezing to death. A mass of spiky dyed hair stuck out above the plastic, giving her the appearance of a badly packaged supermarket chicken. She had been tied to the letter with what appeared to be thin steel cable. Few of the others seemed to be aware of what was happening. Despite their insulation, several of them looked as if they were suffering from severe exposure.

Further around the tower Robert discovered Rose, dazed and battered but still conscious. She kicked at the lettering, wriggling as much as the cable connecting her to the wall would allow. 'Robert, is that you?' She twisted her head around, trying hard to see. 'I was sure that you'd never get here in time,' she called. 'It's almost light.'

'How's he going to do it?' asked Robert. He dropped onto his knees and bent forward as he carefully studied the cable which surrounded her. 'How is he going to carry out the sacrifice?'

'I was hoping you were going to tell me. It must be something to do with the wiring that connects the neon letters of the sign. He was here earlier on, checking it. I could see him from the corner of my eye.'

'I think you're right.' He turned and called to Zalian. 'Be careful how you cut them loose. It looks like Chymes has wired them up to the lettering.'

Lee climbed over the side of the platform and joined him. He stared at the cable and nodded sagely. 'Yeah, that's what he's done, all right. There must be a time-switch somewhere that turns off the current to the letters as soon as it's daylight. Only now it looks like it'll bypass straight into the cables circling their bodies.'

'Then what are we waiting for?' asked Spice, producing a knife and climbing over to the first of the letters. 'Let's cut them loose and get out of here.'

'Make sure you sever the cable on the right side of the connection,' warned Lee.

Robert was unable to shake off the disturbing feeling that somehow they had walked into a trap. There was not a sound up here save the moaning of the wind and the quiet crying of several of Chymes' captives. As Zalian and the others grunted and hacked at the electrical lines, he looked around. For a second he had the impression of a figure, a glimpse of spinning gold somewhere overhead, then it was gone. Another feeble hail of coins hit the wall below them. No one seemed to be coming over from the crane. He broke through the cord which was knotted over Rose's chest with a snap and caught her as she suddenly fell free of the wall, hauling her as gently as he could to the platform above.

Rose climbed out from a cocoon of clear plastic and rubbed the circulation back into her arms and legs. 'I think I just lost ten pounds wrapped in that stuff,' she said.

'I guess he wanted to keep you alive and oven fresh for the dawn fireworks.'

'You should have heard him earlier, striding around spouting mumbo-jumbo. He thinks he's going to transform himself into some kind of god by absorbing the energy from our bodies. Mentally, the guy is definitely three coupons short of a toaster.' Rose reached out her arms, 'Quick, give me a hug.'

Robert was about to move forward and hold her when he sensed the presence of a figure moving behind him. Whirling, he saw Chymes standing directly overhead, leaning on the platform railing, dressed in his cloak of beaten gold. He cradled a crossbow in the crook of his arm. So that was why no one had come over from the crane. Chymes and his men had been stationed here all the time.

'If you'd told me you were coming for a visit, Nathaniel, I'd have arranged something special in the way of a welcome.' His voice was hoarse with barely controlled anger. Zalian slowly rose from his perch atop one of the letters and raised the knife he had been using to cut Sarah free.

'My men are in the roof restaurant just below us. I'm sure they would like to renew their acquaintance with you.' He reached down and tapped on the glass with the end of the crossbow. A shaved head appeared at the bottom of the steamed-up window, then another. Chymes took a step forward. 'So this is all that's left of your force, is it? What a sorry little group. Tell me something, Nathaniel. How is it that you remaining few have managed to stay so incorruptible? So holier-than-thou, so *right*. What do you think it is that makes you so special?'

To Robert it seemed that Zalian and Chymes were suddenly the only two people occupying the windswept platform. Spice, Lee, Simon and the others stayed back, motionless. Chymes' aim with a crossbow was legendary.

With a careless gesture he tossed back his hood to reveal his face. Dead grey eyes stared down above an aquiline nose and thin, expressionless lips. His cheeks were lined with the painted symbols of war he had earlier fashioned from the crusted gore of his victims. Robert started, his heartbeat quickening. It was the face which had haunted his dreams for so long, the face of Westcott and Mathers and Crowley and Ayton and all the founders of the Golden Dawn, the face of the Rosicrucians and the Kabbalah, the astrologers and Freemasons, the tatwas and the Tarot. Here encapsulated in one man, he suddenly understood, was a universal history of magic which ran through the ages like an ever-flowing river, whose presence existed as a revelation and a warning in the dreams of those who bore the same spirit.

'... And so here we are, Nathaniel, on a tower soaring from earth to air, with fire growing on the horizon and water falling from the heavens. The four elements, balancing perfectly to create a golden purity, that alone would be transformation enough. But it takes blood to elevate such a ritual into the realm of true Satanic power.' Chymes leaned further forward over the rail. Suddenly he began to smile. 'Why don't you join me? The thought of ruling the Roofworld together isn't *that* unbelievable. We're more alike than you think. You've even developed the same stigmata, I see.'

He stepped closer to Zalian, whose now useless arm continued to drip from a blackened gash. Chymes reached forward and slowly removed his black leather glove, revealing the glistening steel hand which took the place of flesh and blood.

'I've changed, Nathaniel,' he hissed obscenely. 'At first I wanted everything you had. I wanted your woman, your life, your power. And now that you have nothing, I see our situations reversed. We are two sides of the same coin, don't you see? You share my abhorrence of the world below. You loathe its greed and cruelty just as much as I. The natural equilibrium that existed for so long on the ground has now been destroyed. Look at them!' The steel hand drove out and downwards as he pointed an accusing finger at the streets far below. 'The slums are being renovated as stockbroker apartments. The pharmaceutical salesmen are offloading their banned products onto the third world. The oil companies whose by-products create skin-bonding incendiaries are advertising their share offers on television. How the devil must be laughing!'

For a moment the wind around the tower died and an eerie silence settled with the snow, until Chymes began to speak with renewed vigour. 'We can only be rid of this poisonous hypocrisy through the transformative power of sacrifice. Why not be part of a new, purer race?' He took a step further forward to the edge of the rail. 'The whole of the city is sitting below us, ours for the asking. Think of it as the ultimate aggressive take-over bid. All you have to do is nod your head and we can end the bloodshed right here. There can only be one single united Roofworld and I have the power to make it whole again. You must give me your decision *now*, Doctor.'

Robert watched the two men on the platform ahead of him, knowing that Zalian would sooner be killed than accept the proposition being presented to him. Finally the doctor spoke up. 'What is the point of ruling with fear, Chymes? Don't you see that balance can never be restored as long as one individual exerts power over another? All you're doing is simply trading evils. No, we cannot join you.'

'Then you and your people die.'

Chymes levelled the crossbow at Zalian until the blade of the loaded spear was aimed between his eyes. Before anyone had a chance to react, the wall of the tower was suddenly lit with dazzling crimson splashes. The other team had begun their planned distracting assault on the crane and were firing marine flares up at the control cabin. Dull explosive thuds shook the air around them.

Zalian suddenly sprang forward at Chymes and kicked out at the crossbow which released its charge, the poisoned spear clattering harmlessly over the side of the railing. As the two men fell upon each other, tumbling precariously over the steel struts of the platform, the rest of Chymes' skinhead brigade appeared from below and attacked Zalian's men, who promptly brandished the knives they had been using moments before to free the hostages. Robert pulled Rose to one side as Reese flew at her, switchblade in hand. She threw a kick at him as he hurtled past, swinging on the steel railing and returning to head-butt Robert, who was sent sprawling across the ringing metal floor.

Simon was stabbed in the shoulder by one of the descending skinheads. He rounded on his attacker with a roar and pushed him over into the sprawl of cables which surrounded the neon lettering at his feet. Lee was able to shake someone twice his size from his back and spin, knife held high, to slash his surprised assailant in the throat before he fell away over the railing, plunging several hundred feet into the unblemished silvery streets below.

The others stumbled over the cocooned bodies on the ramp, locked in combat. The snow swirled heavier now, masking friend from foe, obliterating the far side of the platform.

All but three of the prisoners had been released, but one of those three Robert knew to be Sarah Endsleigh, still strapped in a maze of wiring beneath the letter 'T'. Above them, the first rays of watery sunlight pierced the snow-clad roof of their world. There was no more time left. Robert darted between the struggling figures, ramming his adversaries aside, and reached the unconscious girl just as the enormous yellow letters began, one by one, to flicker into darkness. He threw himself flat on the platform, reaching down for the cable above Sarah with the point of his knife.

Dawn was breaking, but the pale morning was eclipsed by the light of the flares as they threw carmine shadows across the snowclouds which rolled overhead. The letter 'O' of the word 'TELECOM' buzzed and fluttered out, followed by the 'C', then the 'E'.

Robert had sawn halfway through the cable surrounding Sarah's waist when a blinding pain flew across the back of his head and he fell forward across the giant steel and plastic letter, his legs swinging freely out into space.

Reese massaged his fist, lookind down at the two inert bodies. He grinned, clipping an arrow into place on his crossbow, then taking careful aim at the centre of Robert's back he slowly squeezed the trigger.

Butterworth's size-10 police-issue boot hit Reese squarely on the backside and he fell forward, discharging the crossbow at empty air and somersaulting past Robert into the raging sky. The young detective constable dropped to his knees and reached down to Sarah, slipping the electric cable over her head and catching her under the arms. As he hauled her up to safety he heard a crackling sound issuing from the neon letters below. With an acrid bang the ends of the cable became live, dancing and slapping the wall in a spray of sparks.

'You should have chosen to join me, Nathaniel.' Chymes towered over his past mentor, forcing him to his knees. His metal hand reached down and tore away the black sweater covering Zalian's throat. He started to squeeze, digits like steel pistons slowly biting into warm flesh. 'Instead I will tear out your heart and we will keep it to remind us of the sacrifice you made for our ascension to power.'

Nathaniel began to choke and gasp, his legs buckling and splaying behind him as the vice like fingers pinched over his larynx. The cloaked figure before his eyes started to blur and fade. He felt himself being lifted high by the icy steel grip around his throat.

Further around the platform, the sulphurous golden light of the remaining letters died and a relay switch diverted the current into Chymes' two remaining prisoners, killing them instantly. The momentary distraction of the overloaded electric cable caused Chymes to remove his attention from Zalian. The grey pupils of his eyes rolled up into his head and, as his sacrificial victims convulsed and expired, he emitted a low bellow of pleasure.

Suddenly the air about them became filled with a powerful static charge. Chymes' body began to shudder, the gleaming cloak filling with a bizarre, unnatural light. His fingers gradually uncoiled, releasing his gasping prey. Robert raised his aching head to see cords of snow dropping like spirals of DNA onto the shimmering phosphorescent figure, wrapping it in a glowing web. The forces of nature seemed to be bending themselves about him, like iron filings in a magnetic field. Unable to make sense of the vision before his eyes, he let his head fall back once more.

'The final transformation has begun, Zalian. I can feel its power within me!' Chymes' voice boomed out from the centre of the roaring vortex, low-pitched and distorted:

' "*In the name of the Brotherhood of the New Life,*
Of the Shrine of the Golden Eagle,
And of the Kabbalah – Denudata,
Delivered in truth by the Mage of Abra-Melin,
I am reborn!" '

He threw his arms wide, his hands piercing the walls of the tornado of light. With a final agonized effort Zalian lashed out at the storm centre, grabbing at the golden cloak and catching the side of Chymes' head with his fist. The punch combined with the weight of his body to pull the Imperator over. He slammed down to the platform as Zalian pulled himself upright.

Chymes swung his leg up and kicked hard, catching Zalian in the stomach and sending him backwards, but the blow lacked power. Whatever energy he had gained from his sacrifice had yet to manifest itself in physical strength. As the Lord of the New Age attempted to stand, Zalian returned with a double-fisted punch that sent him reeling to the edge of the ramp.

For a second, it seemed as if Chymes would regain

his balance, then he slowly fell backwards onto the lettering behind him. 'You'll die a hundred times over for this,' he bellowed, clawing to the top of the letter. As he began to slip, he instinctively reached out for the electrical cable which was now throbbing with diverted current. There was a blue flash as his steel hand made contact with the bare wire and the fingers welded themselves over the flex in a molten seizure. Chymes' body thrashed and banged against the wall of the tower, his teeth grinding together in a silent scream as the steel hand refused to release him from the pulsing cable.

Fingers knotted over his throat, Zalian fell to his knees with a cry. It seemed as if he too could feel the searing pain. He was about to reach out his hand in a gesture of help when Spice pushed him aside. 'There's nothing you can do for him, Nathaniel. Come away.' She hauled the horrified doctor to the back of the platform as the static faded from the air and the storm resumed its natural pattern once more.

Deprived of their leader, the skinheads seemed suddenly confused. Several of them came to the front of the ramp and stared over at Chymes' blackened body with mouths agape. Nathaniel's remaining men used this opportunity to mount their strongest attack yet on the now disoriented group.

Further around the tower, Robert was rubbing the back of his head and trying to raise his body from the flat top of the 'T' across which he had fallen. Each time he moved, the world around him dipped and spun crazily. Back on the platform there seemed to be screams and shouts as blurred figures lunged at each other. Had Chymes really vanished in a blaze of celestial fire? What on earth was going on? He chuckled dizzily to himself. It was hardly on earth. . . . Robert managed to hoist himself into a sitting position. Snow settled on his nylon suit and melted as he forced his paralysed mind to remember where he was. Moments later, just as the memories of recent events were neatly and obligingly slotting into place, he did a stupid thing. He sat back and fell straight over the edge of the 'T' like a diver dropping from the side of a boat.

The battle had ended. The remaining members of the New Age were skulking away like wounded animals, adrift without their leader. There had been many casualties, but mercifully few fatalities. Zalian sat on the platform with his head leaning against the railing, watching Sarah's gradual return to consciousness. As she opened her eyes and made sense of the scene before her, he reached over and slipped his arms through hers.

'All – I ever wanted,' he said, 'was you – by my side in the Roofworld.' She slowly raised her face to his. He smiled and pulled her tightly to him, lightly kissing her forehead. One look at her eyes told him all he needed to know. Gently, Sarah returned the kiss.

There was something pressing against her ribs. Puzzled, she looked down. Protruding from just below Zalian's heart was the shaft of a steel arrow, buried deep and angled upwards. By the time her eyes returned to his, the doctor was dead.

'Can somebody give me a hand?' Rose pleaded from her position atop the letter 'T'. Robert's sneakers had become wedged in the metal struts supporting the bottom of the letter. Rose was holding him upright by hanging onto his ears, the only part of his anatomy that she had been able to grab as he dangled upside down from the side of the windswept tower. Robert was releasing pained yells at three-second intervals. As Lee and Spice reached her side, Rose leaned over to him and grinned. 'There's a reason why God gives us these physical attributes,' she said. 'It's a good job your mother didn't decide to pin them back when you were a kid.'

'They'll stick out more than ever now,' he howled miserably. 'I'll look like bloody Dumbo.' Finally the three of them managed to haul him back up to the safety of the platform.

'Rose! Look!' Simon was pointing from the railing to the spot where Chymes had been electrocuted. 'He's gone!'

The steel hand of the Imperator still hung fused to the cable, but the corpse had disappeared. Ahead, barely discernible through the blizzard, a large golden eagle circled and swooped before fading into the ashen dawn.

As Robert slumped to the steel deck nursing his wrenched and swollen ears, Detective Constable Butterworth appeared and gazed sternly down. He proceeded to give out measured stares from one face to the next, then produced a notepad from his jacket pocket. 'You are all under arrest,' he began. 'Anything you say will . . .' It was as far as he got before being grabbed on all sides and wrestled to the floor.

Wednesday 24 December

CHAPTER FOURTY-NINE

Butterworth Reports

Outside Hargreave's office, the snow sparkled on the windowsills in a thick three-day-old glaze. Inside, despite the central heating, Hargreave felt every bit as cold as the tramps freezing in the alleyways behind the station. . . . 'Wait, wait a minute. Let me refresh your memory as to the facts in this case. As a result of the mysterious activities performed by this person on the night of Saturday the twentieth of December, we were left on Sunday morning with seven – count them Butterworth – *seven* corpses, all discovered at the base of the Post Office Tower, another four bodies in the surrounding area, the wreckage of a single seater 'plane and, let me see, about sixty office windows smashed by *arrows*, for God's sake. We had reports of bombs going off, fire in the sky, screams in the night and assorted UFO sightings. We have a statement from a young girl who swears she was attacked by a golden eagle on her way to work on Sunday morning. In addition, somebody seems to have vandalized the British Telecom sign at the top of the tower. And this, this *joke* is the best report you can turn in?'

Hargreave threw the thin folder to the desk with a bang and knocked over his tea in the process. Butterworth suppressed a smile as he offered his boss a Kleenex.

'It wouldn't hold water as a bloody high school essay and you know it.' Hargreave uprighted himself, clutching the dripping tissue. He narrowed his eyes thoughtfully. 'You're up to something, lad. I'm not daft. I wasn't born yesterday. Who gave you that black eye?'

'I told you, sir. It was the result of landing on PC Bimsley.' Butterworth touched his face gingerly and smiled.

'Bimsley, bollocks,' Hargreave snorted, turning his blotting pad upside down and leaning on it. 'Tell me again. Never mind the report, just put it in plain English.' He rubbed a hand across his face in a familiar gesture of exhaustion. 'I know it's difficult, but think of me as your friend rather than superior officer. Come on lad, be *honest*.'

Butterworth cleared his throat and began. 'Well sir, as I understand it, there was a gentleman named Mr Chymes, a one-time mental patient whose file I believe you are in receipt of. My informant tells me that this Mr Chymes had developed a penchant for climbing tall buildings, that he was in the habit of kidnapping passersby at random and that he subsequently took to murdering them on the tops of his favourite London landmarks.' Butterworth stepped back, pleased with his recital.

'Your informant?' asked Hargreave wearily, 'I believe you have managed to mislay him?'

'Went missing shortly after releasing this information to me, sir, just as it . . .'

' . . . Says in the report, I know.' Hargreave dropped the sopping blotter into his wastepaper bin. 'And you believe this "informant". Ergo, *I* am supposed to believe your cock-and-bull story. So there were no "gang wars", no ritual killings, just the workings of a deranged maniac who conveniently managed to pick out a number of people already on our Missing Persons files and murder them, moving all over the city from victim to victim, alone and unaided.' He sighed deeply and sat back in his chair. 'Considering the various recorded times of the deaths he must have been moving at twice the speed of Concorde to have managed them all.'

Hargreave closed the file which lay in front of him. He looked like a man whose spirit had finally been broken. Butterworth almost felt sorry for him. Almost.

'Do you understand how close I came – how close *we* came – to solving the case of the century?' he asked. 'Do you know what it would have meant to this department? Or what it would mean to me personally, to be able to clear my name at last, after that sodding vampire business last year? Well, Butterworth, if you ever do decide to come clean, make sure I'm the first to know, eh?'

'There is one more thing, sir,' said Butterworth. 'I tendered my resignation this morning. Not cut out for this sort of thing, I'm afraid.'

Hargreave's eyes grew narrower still. 'I'll have you,' he said. 'Don't think you'll get away with whatever it is that you're up to because there'll be an official investigation into this whole business.' He rose from his seat and grew red in the face. 'In fact, if I didn't know better I'd say that you collaborated with this nutcase. Nearly a hundred reports of strange disturbances on the night of December the twentieth. That's how many people we have who are prepared to swear in court that they saw everything from dancing goblins to bloody Superman in the sky!'

He thought for a moment, then dropped back into his chair. 'Unfortunately,' he said quietly, 'I cannot follow up the statements of these fascinating witnesses as I am being relieved from work for the time being, pending a full investigation.' He stared morosely at the tea pooling along the edge of his desk. 'You might be interested to know that it is your father who has seen fit to have me suspended from duty,' said Hargreave with a grimace. 'He seemed to think that I was unfairly singling you out for the rough stuff. *Somebody*,' he added suspiciously, 'seems to have tipped him off.'

Butterworth performed an inward leap of joy.

'Go on, then,' the Detective Inspector groaned. 'Get the hell out of here.'

'How did it go?' she asked, sliding her arm around his waist.

'Not in here,' hissed Butterworth from the side of his mouth. 'Wait until we get outside.' Reluctantly, the girl removed her arm. As they walked to the car, she gave him a provocative smile. 'So,' she said. 'How long do I have to wait before you come and join me?'

Butterworth considered the question for a moment. 'Well, they may make me work out my notice and Hargreave will probably want me to appear for the investigation, then of course I shall have to get rid of my apartment, and find someone to take the tropical fish and I'll have to sell the stereo, but hopefully things should be sorted out within a month.'

The girl reached up on tiptoe and kissed him. 'I'll be around to haunt you until you're ready to leave the ground. You know where to find me.' She pointed the forefinger of her right hand up at the sky and began to walk away, swinging her hips with knowing sexuality.

'The sooner you get through down here,' she called, fishing into the pocket of her jeans, 'the sooner we can pick up from where we left off in the Centrepoint building.' She tossed him the key to the handcuffs she had been persuaded to unlock when last they met. Her laugh continued after her figure had vanished beyond the corner of the police station.

Butterworth climbed into the car with a happy grin on his freckled face. He was pleased that he had finally figured out what to do with his life. Hargreave would never discover the truth about the Roofworld. After, all, hadn't he failed to solve the Leicester Square Vampire case?

In the computer room, Hargreave lit a cigarette and began to scroll through the screen pages of the *Icarus* file one last time. All the facts had been at his fingertips. His research had given him every answer except one. He ran the cursor down to the final page of his notes.

NAME OF SUSPECT/W.W. CHYMES

PHYSICAL CHARACTERISTICS
6FT 2INS CAUCASIAN BLACK HAIR GREY EYES
LEFT HAND MISSING ORIGIN OF DISABILITY UNKNOWN
LONDON DIRECTORY LISTING
26 LILLIE GARDENS WEST HAMPSTEAD
CURRENT STATUS REGISTERED MISSING
WANTED FOR QUESTIONING IN RELATION TO THE FOLLOWING CHARGES
FRAUD 6/2/83
ARSON 9/5/84
AGGRAVATED ASSAULT 26/3/86
MURDER 11/9/87
OTHER KNOWN ALIASES INCLUDE
J. BOEHME, 35, PRITCHARD AVENUE, EDINBURGH
R. BACHMAN, 14, NETTLEFIELD TERRACE, ISLINGTON, LONDON
G. HERBERT, DELACOURT SQUARE, NORWICH
S. PARTRIDGE, 35, WESTERDALE ROAD, GREENWICH, LONDON
(more follows)

Hargreave drew heavily on his cigarette and examined the screen. To the questions 'Who', 'Where', 'When' and 'How' he could find satisfactory replies.

But the reason '*Why*' still eluded him. He had traced his rogue alchemist from alias to alias and the computer had authenticated every address. He had assembled a profile of each person on the list and noted their similarities. All those named were in their mid-thirties, all had successful careers and were registered members of the same national societies and he suspected that all were probably Freemasons. It was, however, impossible to bring any of them in for questioning, for the simple reason that all had died not long after the turn of the present century. He had run a double-check through the computer and, sure enough, the name of Chymes recurred in different aliases back down through the years.

It didn't make sense. By his calculations, Chymes would now have to be approximately one hundred and twenty years old. So what had he been dealing with here? Some supernatural being who kept appearing through the ages like a vengeful wraith?

Hargreave enjoyed a good conspiracy theory and naturally had his own. He imagined the existence of a centuries-old society whose leaders had taken turns to adopt the mantle of the ancient alchemist known as Chymes. But to what end? Perhaps he should investigate the matter further, starting at the address last listed by the computer. . . . But then another thought struck him. If the press ever got hold of this one, they would drag his tarnished reputation through the shit once and for all. He hesitated.

No, it was too great a risk to take.

Reluctantly he lowered a nicotine-stained index finger to the keyboard and pressed the 'Erase' tab, watching the strings of characters strip from the screen as he sealed the contents of the file disk, probably forever. A feeling of empty depression immediately began to descend. There was only one way of curing it. He decided to complete something he had started some while ago. Turning off the console, he rose from the desk to go and find Janice.

As he gently clicked the office door shut, the fathomless secrets which had unfurled across the computer screen with a dying luminosity were banished into an equally mysterious maze of micro-circuitry.

Sergeant Longbright was not the kind of woman to forsake her duty for any length of time. However, there was a sexual edge to her cold-showers-and-no-nonsense appeal that Margaret Thatcher would have envied. Even now, a few hours before Christmas Day, she was down in the morgue with Finch arguing over some incorrect paperwork.

Hargreave liked that. 'Hullo,' he called, cheerily waving across an array of waxy, opened bodies. 'I thought I might buy you a seasonal drink.'

'That's very nice of you,' said Finch, wiping his bone-saw clean and replacing it. 'I'll have a pint of bitter.'

'Not you, you bloody grave-robber, I meant Janice.' He looked around the room. 'Not very Christmassy in here, is it? Couldn't you stand one of the corpses in a corner, maybe paint its nose red and cover it in tinsel?'

The sergeant looked up from her report folder and gave him a broad, white smile. Even her teeth were sexy.

'We've got some mistletoe over by the body drawers,' Finch pointed out, 'although I wouldn't expect much passion from this lot. Most of them have had their insides removed. Anyway,' he said morosely, 'it's all right for you, up there with your computers while I'm down here, elbow-deep in someone's stomach doing your dirty work.'

'The least you can do is buy him a drink, Ian,' said Janice. 'After all the help he gave you.'

All the help in the world isn't going to prevent me from being sacrificed in the coming investigation, thought Hargreave, casting his eyes over the lanky forensic scientist who, as usual, smelled as if he had doused himself with a gallon of cheap aftershave. 'Oh, all right,' he said grudgingly. 'You can come too. But only if you wash your hands first.'

While Finch was cleaning up, Hargreave leaned across a biopsy sink and kissed Janice lightly on the cheek. 'I was wondering,' he said, 'if you might consider something as oldfashioned as becoming engaged to me.'

'I might,' conceded the comely sergeant. 'So long as you promise me one thing.'

'You name it.'

'Please don't consider proposing to me in here as well.'

'It's a deal.' He grinned and hugged Janice self-consciously, as if half-expecting the other residents of the room to sit up and applaud. It wasn't going to be such a lousy Christmas after all.

FIFTY

Back To Earth

The group had gathered inside a small, covered station on the roof of Greater London House, overlooking a mist-veiled section of the Thames. Earlier the shelter had been ransacked and battered by Chymes' men, but at least it provided refuge from the wind. The other remaining members of the Roofworld were nursing their wounds atop special quarters set up on the roof of the Capital building on the road leading north out of the city.

'At least Nathaniel is at rest now,' said Sarah. 'Lee and I buried him in a quiet part of Highgate cemetery.' She walked to the door and watched as a small police cruiser moved upriver through the sluggish grey water. 'It looks as if it's about to snow again. On Christmas Eve, too.'

'Let's go back to the Exchange,' said Spice, rising to her feet. 'It's warmer there. I'm bloody starving.'

After a minute Lee joined Sarah at the doorway. 'Whatever we saw – or think we saw – on the tower,' he said, 'the fact remains that Chymes' body disappeared as the dawn arrived.'

'Maybe his men took it,' suggested Simon.

'No – I have a feeling that there was a lot more at stake in this war than any of us realized. We can't afford to let down our guard – ever again.' He smiled. 'Guardians of the City of London. It's a dirty job, but someone's got to do it, right?' He dug around in one of the remaining undamaged packing boxes and pulled out an unbroken bottle of wine. Plastic cups were produced and passed around.

'Rose tells me you're going back down tonight, Robert.'

'That's right,' said Robert with some embarrassment. 'I've got work to do on the ground. Sarah has kindly granted me the rights to her mother's book.' He glanced across at Rose. 'I understand that your detective constable is coming up here to join the Roofworld.'

'I knew that we could persuade him as soon as I saw him again,' said Rose.

'What do you mean? The only time you've seen him was when he saved my life on the top of the tower.'

'No, I met him before that. He was the constable who came to interview me after Charlotte Endsleigh's death.'

Robert's jaw dropped in surprise.

'Rose recognized him at once,' said Spice. 'Luckily, he didn't take much persuading. We'd only left him alone at Centrepoint for a few minutes before he decided to come galloping to the rescue.'

'He came on the run from Centrepoint by himself?' asked Robert, incredulous.

'No, he stole someone's scooter from the car park. But the thought was there.'

'He starts up here next month,' said Lee. 'Which means that the connection between Charlotte and the Roofworld looks as if it will remain a secret. He does of course bring with him a working knowledge of police operations in the city, which is something we should be able to find a use for. The Roofworld can be as it was before. The tabloids will find something new to scandalize readers by next week. We'll stay hidden from view.' He poured some wine into his cup and raised it. 'Here's to the new project.'

'What new project?' asked Robert.

'The first run to cross the river,' said Spice. 'We're moving into south London. Maybe we'll start up in other cities after that. Lee and I quite fancy New York. We could probably get a run fixed between the towers of the World Trade Center.'

'Of course, the logistics would take a little longer to work out, wind factors and so forth. We might have to make a large cash withdrawal from McDonald's to pay for the equipment. . . .'

The plastic cups were raised in a toast as heavy, obliterating snow began to carpet the streets of the city once more.

'From the moment I came up here I had the feeling that I might stay on,' said Rose. The padded blue jumpsuit was buttoned to her chin, tiny bronze locks of hair curling over the raised collar. She held Robert close, her hands thrust deep into his pockets. Together they perched in the corner of the fire escape built at the rear of the National Gallery, their breath appearing in a single cloud. Carol singers filled the square ahead, shuffling about in the icy winter air as they prepared for the next service, due to begin at dusk.

'Zalian seduced you, didn't he?' asked Robert. 'Oh, I don't mean sexually, so much as he filled you with the whole idea of life up here. I knew from the start that it wouldn't suit me. I like the ground comforts too much. You may find that you do, too.'

'I don't think so.'

'It's going to take a lot of rebuilding.'

'I've got Lee, Sarah and the others to help teach me. I'll let you know how I get on.'

'I could always come and visit.' Robert stepped back to the edge of the fire escape, zipping up his jacket as he did so. 'Although I'm not sure that I'll ever have such a good head for heights again.'

'You didn't do so badly,' Rose called as he started

down the trellised steps. 'Promise you'll stay in touch. I want to know how your script turns out. Where are you headed?'

'Home, via Leicester Square. I've still got these.' Robert dug into his pocket and removed a handful of torn bills. 'I have to give the guy in the video arcade the other half of his money. He kept his half of the bargain, now it's my turn.' Neither of them were aware of the fate that had befallen the young informant.

Rose rested her elbows on the fire escape railing and started to laugh. 'You think you have problems,' she called. 'I've just inherited the Roofworld mascot. A stupid-looking dog. It's about a hundred years old and has to be carried most of the time, but his master was killed.'

'I'll keep an eye out for a girl and a dog charging across the rooftops of Regent Street. What's it called?'

'Just Dog.'

''Figures. Look after yourself. You're too valuable to wind up falling off a building.' Robert watched her face, lingering for a moment at the turn of the steps. 'You know,' he began, 'if you and I had met under different circumstances . . .'

'Get out of here,' said Rose. 'I'm not your type. Never was.'

He quickly continued down the escape, clattering on the steel rungs. Rose stayed, leaning against the ladder rail until his figure was lost within the snow-crusted configurations of metal.

The dream no longer came to him through troubled sleep, as if it had been exorcized by his final confrontation with Chymes, part of a memory of terror and darkness which had risen from the distant past into the light of another age. Robert slept well. He had nothing to fear. Now, as the early morning light from a raw blue sky flooded his office, he stared from the window, thinking about the girl with green eyes who worked in the library. He had seen her several times now and found it hard to stop imagining her during the day.

Staring idly across at the buildings opposite, he noted with surprise that one of the gargoyles had a red paper heart tied around its neck. He looked down at his desk calender and chuckled. 14 February. Only one person could have put the heart there. For the rest of the day he searched the rooftops, to no avail. Their distant contours remained devoid of movement, standing black and stark against the cold winter sunlight.

He often looked to the rooftops after that and frequently spent his summer evenings among the warm spires of stone on the roof of his own apartment building, watching the traffic circulate far below like multi-hued corpuscles in the bloodstreams of the city.

At the beginning of May, he delivered the first draft of *The Newgate Legacy* script to Paul Ashcroft. The agent greeted him warmly and accepted the manuscript with ill-disguised eagerness. 'I'm *so* glad you were able to find Sarah,' he cried. 'It would have been such a loss if the book had gone to waste.'

'Do you mind if I ask you something?' Robert accepted an enormous tumbler of whisky and sat down opposite the old man. 'How much did you know of Sarah's whereabouts?'

'Well,' said the old man with an irritating twinkle in his eye, 'after your efforts I suppose we should at least be honest with one another. You see, I rather knew *where* she was, but I'm afraid that I'm far too old to go gallivanting about . . . these days.' He smiled knowingly at Robert as he swallowed his whisky.

I fell right into that one, thought Robert as he walked home through the shadowed streets. Duped from the start by the Old Boy Network. He shook his head in wonder, trying to imagine how many other secret societies stretched across the city, forming an invisible web of favour and reciprocation, grievance and revenge, linking the respected businessman to the reviled criminal. Two sides of the same coin, darkness and light. He was just crossing the road by the old Scala Cinema in King's Cross when he saw what seemed to be the figure of a woman, silently watching him from a granite perch high above the traffic.

At once, he knew it was her.

Regretfulness stirred uneasily within him. For a moment he wanted to join her above the city, but for him there were too many ties to be broken. He had friends now, obligations which were necessary to keep. But that did not stop him from envying her her freedom to come and go as she pleased, her flaunting of the codes which governed his life. She was there for just a moment, motionless, silhouetted against a sky of spectacular crimson streaks.

One day we'll meet on equal terms, he thought, and then we'll see. When he looked again, she had vanished into the extravagantly carved turrets of sun-heated stone which stood like mad sentinels high above the city streets.

A Selection of Arrow Books

☐	No Enemy But Time	Evelyn Anthony	£2.95
☐	The Lilac Bus	Maeve Binchy	£2.99
☐	Rates of Exchange	Malcolm Bradbury	£3.50
☐	Prime Time	Joan Collins	£3.50
☐	Rosemary Conley's Complete Hip and Thigh Diet	Rosemary Conley	£2.99
☐	Staying Off the Beaten Track	Elizabeth Gundrey	£6.99
☐	Duncton Wood	William Horwood	£4.50
☐	Duncton Quest	William Horwood	£4.50
☐	A World Apart	Marie Joseph	£3.50
☐	Erin's Child	Sheelagh Kelly	£3.99
☐	Colours Aloft	Alexander Kent	£2.99
☐	Gondar	Nicholas Luard	£4.50
☐	The Ladies of Missalonghi	Colleen McCullough	£2.50
☐	The Veiled One	Ruth Rendell	£3.50
☐	Sarum	Edward Rutherfurd	£4.99
☐	Communion	Whitley Strieber	£3.99

Prices and other details are liable to change

ARROW BOOKS, BOOKSERVICE BY POST, PO BOX 29, DOUGLAS, ISLE OF MAN, BRITISH ISLES

NAME...

ADDRESS...

....

....

Please enclose a cheque or postal order made out to Arrow Books Ltd. for the amount due and allow the following for postage and packing.

U.K. CUSTOMERS: Please allow 22p per book to a maximum of £3.00.

B.F.P.O. & EIRE: Please allow 22p per book to a maximum of £3.00.

OVERSEAS CUSTOMERS: Please allow 22p per book.

Whilst every effort is made to keep prices low it is sometimes necessary to increase cover prices at short notice. Arrow Books reserve the right to show new retail prices on covers which may differ from those previously advertised in the text or elsewhere.

A Selection of Legend Titles

☐	Eon	Greg Bear	£3.50
☐	Forge of God	Greg Bear	£3.99
☐	Falcons of Narabedla	Marion Zimmer Bradley	£2.50
☐	The Influence	Ramsey Campbell	£3.50
☐	Wyrms	Orson Scott Card	£3.50
☐	Speaker for the Dead	Orson Scott Card	£2.95
☐	Seventh Son	Orson Scott Card	£3.50
☐	Wolf in Shadow	David Gemmell	£3.50
☐	Last Sword of Power	David Gemmell	£3.50
☐	This is the Way the World Ends	James Morrow	£4.99
☐	Unquenchable Fire	Rachel Pollack	£3.99
☐	Golden Sunlands	Christopher Rowley	£3.50
☐	The Misplaced Legion	Harry Turtledove	£2.99
☐	An Emperor for the Legion	Harry Turtledove	£2.99

Prices and other details are liable to change

ARROW BOOKS, BOOKSERVICE BY POST, PO BOX 29, DOUGLAS, ISLE OF MAN, BRITISH ISLES

NAME..

ADDRESS...

....

....

Please enclose a cheque or postal order made out to Arrow Books Ltd. for the amount due and allow the following for postage and packing.

U.K. CUSTOMERS: Please allow 22p per book to a maximum of £3.00.

B.F.P.O. & EIRE: Please allow 22p per book to a maximum of £3.00.

OVERSEAS CUSTOMERS: Please allow 22p per book.

Whilst every effort is made to keep prices low it is sometimes necessary to increase cover prices at short notice. Arrow Books reserve the right to show new retail prices on covers which may differ from those previously advertised in the text or elsewhere.

Bestselling SF/Horror

☐	Forge of God	Greg Bear	£3.99
☐	Eon	Greg Bear	£3.50
☐	The Hungry Moon	Ramsey Campbell	£3.50
☐	The Influence	Ramsey Campbell	£3.50
☐	Seventh Son	Orson Scott Card	£3.50
☐	Bones of the Moon	Jonathan Carroll	£2.50
☐	Nighthunter: The Hexing & The Labyrinth	Robert Faulcon	£3.50
☐	Pin	Andrew Neiderman	£1.50
☐	The Island	Guy N. Smith	£2.50
☐	Malleus Maleficarum	Montague Summers	£4.50

Prices and other details are liable to change

ARROW BOOKS, BOOKSERVICE BY POST, PO BOX 29, DOUGLAS, ISLE OF MAN, BRITISH ISLES

NAME...

ADDRESS...

....

....

Please enclose a cheque or postal order made out to Arrow Books Ltd. for the amount due and allow the following for postage and packing.

U.K. CUSTOMERS: Please allow 22p per book to a maximum of £3.00.

B.F.P.O. & EIRE: Please allow 22p per book to a maximum of £3.00.

OVERSEAS CUSTOMERS: Please allow 22p per book.

Whilst every effort is made to keep prices low it is sometimes necessary to increase cover prices at short notice. Arrow Books reserve the right to show new retail prices on covers which may differ from those previously advertised in the text or elsewhere.